Uprising

Book 2 of Jason's Tale
From *After the Fall* Series

A Novel

David Nees

Copyright © 2019 David E. Nees

All rights reserved.

Uprising, Part 2 of *Jason's Tale* in the *After the Fall* series, is a work of fiction and should be construed as nothing but. All characters, locales, and incidents portrayed in the novel are products of the author's imagination or have been used fictitiously. Any resemblance to any person, living or dead, is entirely coincidental.

To keep up with my new releases, please visit my website at www.davidnees.com. Scroll down to the bottom of the landing page to the section titled, "Follow the Adventure".

You can also click "Follow" under my picture on the Amazon book page and Amazon will let you know when I release a new work.

ISBN: 9781794606425

Manufactured in the United States

For Carla

You give me the support, love, and space
to allow these stories to come to life.

Grateful thanks for to my beta readers, Eric and Ed. Your insightful and detailed comments are always so helpful to making my work more polished and professional. I appreciate your generosity of time.

And thank you, Catherine, for your careful proofreading. So many words, so many opportunities to make mistakes, but you catch them.

Again, my cover is the work of Onur Aksoy, a gifted cover artist. You can find his other work at https://www.onegraphica.com/

Uprising

Part 2 of *Jason's Tale*
From the *After the Fall* series

*"Shall I tell you what the real evil is? To cringe to the things that are called evils, to surrender to them our freedom,
in defiance of which we ought to face any suffering."*
—Seneca, Roman stoic philosopher, 4 BC - 65 AD

*"The only thing necessary for the triumph of evil
is for good men to do nothing."*
—Edmond Burke, Irish statesman and Member of Parliament,
1729 - 1797

Chapter 1

The man made his way hurriedly through the shadowy streets. There were no lights to relieve the darkness; the soft glow of oil lamps illuminated only a few windows. The crescent moon and stars gave little light. Even so, he worked to keep to the shadows as he hurried along. The town was quiet, as it was most nights. He could hear an occasional pedestrian hurrying along somewhere in the dark.

The man moved close to the buildings seeking more darkness when he heard footsteps. He didn't want to be seen; no one did. It was after curfew and, if caught out, he would be arrested, with an uncertain fate in store for him. Others had been so detained and had reported aggressive interrogation, often accompanied by beatings with fists and clubs.

The questions were always the same: "What are you doing out? Where are you coming from? Who did you meet with?" The authorities had suspicions that there was a subversive element in Hillsboro. A group of people who, although law-abiding, did not approve of the dictatorial power of those in charge, who objected to the restrictive rules and were getting themselves organized.

The man sensed he was being followed. He quickened his pace. He was taking a circuitous route to his assigned apartment. If he was not certain that he was alone, he would not return home but would instead keep moving on the streets, even if he had to walk all night, in order to protect his family. He was endangering them, but he rationalized his nocturnal outings by telling himself that he was working to create a better social order for his family. If someone were caught and was thought to be doing anything subversive, not only did they disappear, but their family might vanish as well. The disappearances did not have to be publicized. Everyone who interacted with a targeted family would know its fate. The word always got out. Don't stand out; don't oppose the existing rules and authorities.

A sense of panic began to grow, creating a tight knot in his stomach. His body tingled with fear, the hair on his neck bristled. He began to run. When he had gone a half block, he stopped abruptly. Did he hear footsteps suddenly stopping? Or was his mind playing tricks on him? Summoning his courage, he spun around. There were only shadows behind him. Nothing moved. He turned back, taking a deep breath and started walking again. He decided the clandestine meetings were beginning to unnerve him.

After turning a corner three blocks from his home, he thought he saw two shadowy shapes ahead in a doorway. He turned around to go back and found two large men standing at the corner. With a shock, he realized his instincts were correct. He had been followed. His knees began to buckle. He turned again and saw the shadows disengage from the doorway and start in his direction. He lurched across the street in a desperate attempt to flee. It was futile. The men moved quickly and surrounded him and he sank to the ground under their blows. Not a word was spoken. They dragged him, weakly struggling, to a waiting van. They threw him in the back and drove off down the dark streets.

Hillsboro, like the rest of the country, was still suffering from the after-effects of the electromagnetic pulse attack. Now, two years later, stability had still not been restored, and Hillsboro had not returned to normal.

The town was not completely under control. In spite of the best efforts of the civil authorities and their militia to impose martial law, there were still small numbers of outlaws operating within the city. They snuck in from outside or were residents who did not want to conform to the strict martial law imposed.

The EMP attack had destroyed electrical power, communications, and transportation throughout the U.S., leaving the country in a state of anarchy. The possibility of any rapid restoration was near zero. Many people had died that first year, mostly the old and sick. More waves of deaths had followed as antibiotics had run out in communities and sickness had spread from lack of clean water and proper sanitation.

There had been a massive exodus from the large cities as disease and starvation reigned. Many smaller towns, like Hillsboro, had tried to resist the influx of refugees. Those that couldn't had soon been overwhelmed, and the anarchy that engulfed the big cities erupted, making life nearly intolerable. Towns that had been fortunate enough to be able to build barriers and resist the flow of people looking for any help they could find had avoided such a fate.

There were tense and often ugly standoffs between those lucky to be inside of a defended town and those outside. The refugees were all desperate. Some were heartbreaking: families with starving children, struggling to find scraps to eat and shelter from the weather. Some had become outlaws, desperados embracing violence or driven to it in order to gather the resources needed to survive.

No relief agencies were coming to the rescue. FEMA was not functioning. There was no group that would arrive to bring some level of order and distribute food and shelter. People were on their own. They would get no help from the federal government. And, having grown up in modern society, they were not prepared to survive without its structures of support.

Hillsboro had walled itself in. During the first year, the city's government had directed citizens to work on dismantling houses and buildings in a perimeter around the central core of the city. Kids had been put to work extracting and saving the nails, scavenging the wiring from the buildings, and collecting anything that could be useful. The main rubble had then been used to construct a wall of sorts. It rose in a jagged fashion, six to ten feet high. It was primitive, ugly and porous, reminiscent of the barricades of the French Revolution. A cleared space grew outside of the walls, marked with concrete slabs that had been foundations and open basements now flooded with stagnant water.

Chapter 2

Jason Richards sat on the porch of his farmhouse in the valley. He had left Hillsboro about six months after the power went out. He had seen the growing corruption, the establishment of martial law, and the abandonment of democracy. Not wanting to stay and tangle further with the increasingly corrupt authorities who had taken over, he had set out to live in the mountains, to survive alone until the crisis passed.

Loneliness had proven to be his biggest adversary, and it wasn't until he'd found Anne and her family that his life began to turn around. He had gotten himself adopted into the struggling family and had helped them to thrive in the post-attack world. Along the way, he and Anne had fallen in love.

They had fought for their lives, defending their farm from bandits. The whole valley had fought a deadly battle with a gang run by a man called Big Jacks. Two members of the valley had been killed but they had decimated the gang and Jason had executed Big Jacks.

Life was now a rich delight for him. He had a new son, now a year old; his step daughters had developed into strong, confident young women; the oldest, Catherine, had a suitor, Lieutenant Kevin Cameron who was with the army platoon stationed in Hillsboro. Lieutenant Cameron had played a part in helping Jason get the farming in the valley restarted. With their supply of non-hybrid seeds, they could not only feed themselves but supply food to the city and still be able to set aside seed for the next year's planting.

The valley had gotten the restored grist mill in Clifton Forge working so they could grind their grain in large quantities. If they could establish a barter economy with Hillsboro, life could begin to get back to some level of normalcy, even if it was more like the eighteenth or nineteenth century than the twenty-first.

Billy Turner hiked up the driveway of Jason and Anne's farm, the gravel crunching under his feet. He saw Jason sitting on the porch watching him. Jason smiled and motioned for him to come up and join him. "What brings you down here?" Jason asked as Billy sat down.

"I'd like to take some of what I've grown...what you've grown in the fields I loaned you, use the grain to make some moonshine and sell it in town."

"Billy, we talked about this before. I leased your fields for a cut of what we get for selling the produce and grains. I wouldn't do it to supply you for making moonshine. I told you that up front."

"I know, but it looks like a good harvest from the winter planting. I figure we could get two crops this year. We'll have a surplus. Seems to me I can use some of that to make liquor."

"Last year, when your dad passed away, you told me you didn't like moonshine."

"Don't like drinkin' it, but I don't mind makin' it, especially now if I got somewhere to sell it. It's what I know best. Reminds me of doing it with my pa."

"I know it's been lonely for you since your dad died after the battle." He gave Billy a gentle look. "But you'd rather moonshine than farm?"

Billy stared at the porch floor, uncomfortable. "That, or hunting," he said. "I like being in the woods either way."

"But you also know farming. Your family's farmed this valley for generations. Isn't that what your daddy would want you to do?"

"My family made moonshine in this valley for generations too. And my daddy was a moonshiner." Billy's voice took on a note of pride.

"You know my answer. Making moonshine in this valley will only bring trouble."

"What kind of trouble?" Billy asked, now looking back at Jason.

"Gangs, outlaws. It will draw attention to us and can bring the wrong kind of people. Remember, if we're trading it, we're telling everyone about our valley."

Billy wasn't so sure and a doubtful expression crept over his face.

Jason continued. "Look at what we went through to get where we are. I don't want anything to endanger what we've achieved, no matter how slight the risk."

"Trading food with the outside world's a risk," Billy replied.

"Yeah, but that's one worth taking. We need things the town provides and they need what we provide. It's a natural connection."

"So's selling moonshine to city folk."

"Maybe, but moonshine's like waving meat in front of a hungry bear. And moonshine is easy to steal." Jason sighed. "It'll attract attention, the wrong attention. I don't want my labor going to that."

"Well then, from the fields I'm working. They're my fields now that my pa's passed."

Jason paused, leaned forward with his elbows on his knees. "They are your fields now. The Turner farm is yours, no question about that." He looked directly at Billy. "But I can't let you start up the still. The risk to the valley is too great. Maybe after another year, if things settle down, but not now."

Billy started to protest, but Jason went on, talking over him. "I know it doesn't seem fair...and maybe it isn't, but it's the wise path, the cautious path to take right now. Maybe later, but not now, Billy."

"It *ain't* fair. It's what I want to do and you won't let me do it."

"I'll support you in whatever you want to do, even moonshining, if it's not in this valley."

"You know it ain't safe to do it outside of the valley. You never know who's going to raid you if you're down in the flatland."

"That's why I don't want it here. It could bring trouble for us."

Billy stood up, frustrated. "I'm not sure I want to stay. I ain't saying I'm giving up my farm, but it seems like there ain't much for me here. Catherine and Sarah don't want me around and there's no one else...and I don't think I like farming all that much."

Billy saw Jason shrug as he started off the porch. "What you do is up to you as long as it isn't moonshining here. I'll help any way I can."

Billy didn't look back as he headed down the drive towards the road.

Anne came out on the porch as Billy walked away. "What did he want?"

"He wants to make moonshine. I told him no. Then he said he might leave the valley."

"To go where?"

"Maybe Hillsboro." Jason turned to his mate. "That worries me. Hillsboro was headed in a bad direction when I left and it doesn't seem to have gotten any better."

"You think he'd get into trouble there? Why are we going to trade with them if they're so bad?"

"I'm trying to head off a possible conflict. If we set up mutually beneficial trading, the town will see us as an asset."

"And that will get them to change?"

Jason shook his head. "Probably not, but it could get them to not act against us. That may be the best we can do." He sighed. "Anyway, trading will be good for both parties. I just hope the town sees it that way."

He got up and leaned over to kiss Anne. "I'd like us to be able to live in peace."

Chapter 3

Joe Stansky waited for the two men in his new office suite. His days of operating out of the back of his strip club were a thing of the past. He had taken over the bank building in the first year after the attack. He housed his gang on the same downtown block, along with much of the resources he had gathered.

Joe stood about five feet, ten inches tall and had a thick, powerful body. The good life had put extra pounds on him but they didn't hide his strength. He was still an imposing figure. He had eyes that looked out from under heavy lids; piercing and penetrating. They were eyes that stared hard at you, measuring and evaluating. They sharpened what was otherwise a puffy, big boned face. A life of crime and graft had honed his perceptions well and he could quickly spot phonies. He had a ruthless desire to succeed aided by a willingness to do whatever was necessary to accomplish his goals. As the *de facto* leader in Hillsboro, he was not a man to be trifled with.

Joe had not understood what the electromagnetic pulse was when it occurred. But he was not stupid and he was used to functioning in chaotic environments. After the EMP attack, Joe's first action had been to find out what the hell had happened, and then he had sat down to figure out what to do about it. Joe did not have a victim's mentality. He would work this event to his advantage, and would spend no time lamenting the change. This was a chance to redefine himself. If society was going to be altered, Joe decided he would alter his status in the new order. He would run the town. Action was needed.

Tonight he was angry. The town was still not fully under control in spite of his efforts. Refugees presented a constant unwelcome pressure, along with the danger of the outlaws among them who infiltrated and stole weapons and food. They were desperate. Joe didn't like dealing with desperate people; they were unpredictable. But now he faced a different problem, one he didn't need...and wouldn't tolerate.

Frank Mason arrived first. He was the political leader of the town, head of the Safety Committee and the presumptive mayor. It was night, but the entrance was lit by a single floodlight. Precious fuel was used to keep the entrance lit, allowing Joe's armed guards to check everyone entering the building. Frank made his way up four flights of stairs into a private suite. The room was dimly lit by oil lamps that still struck Frank as starkly out of place in such a modern office. There was not enough electricity to light the offices of even someone as important as Joe. The rich aroma of a Diamond Crown cigar permeated the air. Joe sat behind an imposing desk and motioned for Frank to take a chair on the other side.

"What's up, Joe?" Frank asked as he sat down.

"Something to drink?" Joe responded.

"If you're pouring some good stuff, not the crap they're making here."

Joe got up and went to the cabinet on the side wall, took out a bottle of Maker's Mark, and poured Frank a couple of fingers. "No ice, but it's supposed to be better this way." Ironically, ice was only available in the winter months. He handed the glass to Frank. "Let's wait for Charlie."

Just then Charlie came through the door. "Sorry I'm late, the car I'm using...had trouble getting it running. These old cars work but they're a pain to keep running sometimes...bad gas, I think."

Charlie Cook, the chief of police, was the other public face of leadership and authority in Hillsboro. He was older than Frank and Joe. He had white hair and a soft, friendly face that gave him a grandfatherly look. The look seemed to work in Frank's estimation. He was once a tough cop, but now had grown relaxed and easygoing; taking on more the role of a PR person than a serious law enforcement officer.

"You want a drink?" Joe asked.

"Yeah, thanks," Charlie replied. He inhaled the aroma from Joe's cigar, grimaced and took out one of his precious cigarettes. Joe motioned for him to sit next to Frank.

After some silence as the men savored the bourbon, Frank asked again, "So what's up? Why the meeting?"

Joe leaned back in his chair and looked hard at the two men. "I allowed you two to run things here in town. But you let me down—"

"What do you mean?" Charlie asked.

"Don't interrupt me. I'm not happy with what's going on. You understand what that means?" Joe leaned forward, giving both men a long, dangerous look.

"What's the problem?" Frank asked. "The city isn't completely under control, but we're better off than most of the others. These are hard times. You know that."

"I know I don't like what I see developing."

"What are you talking about?" Frank asked.

"Two nights ago my men picked up someone for a curfew violation—"

"I didn't see anyone brought into the jail," Charlie said.

"I told you, don't interrupt me." Joe locked his gaze on Charlie and stared at him until Charlie finally lowered his eyes. "The guy was an engineer. He told an interesting tale about a group of people, some of the technical people, who are not happy with things in Hillsboro."

"A lot of people aren't happy with things. It changes day to day," Frank said. "But you're not suggesting there's anything more going on, are you?"

"Something more than just small groups causing trouble is going on and I'm not gonna let it become a revolt," Joe said.

"You said he *was* an engineer. What's happened to him?" Charlie asked.

"That's not a question you want to ask, Charlie," Joe said, again staring the hapless chief of police down.

He jammed his cigar out in the ashtray and stood up. "I let you two pretend to run the town. I collected the resources. I stole the goods from the other towns. I made sure everyone was fed. And both of you enjoyed the benefits." He began to pace back and forth. "And now you don't even know something is going on behind our backs." He stopped and leaned over the desk. He stared at the two men. "What the hell good are you?"

Frank swallowed hard. "Charlie and I present the face of civic authority to the public. You operate in the background, that's how we work it. The people are taken care of and everyone's happy."

Frank had been a politician since well before the attack. He was a natural. He was adroit at maneuvering with power brokers and finding the winning side on any issue. He had consolidated his power after the attack by working with Joe and Charlie, and now he was the single public persona of power and authority in Hillsboro.

Joe turned on him, his voice low and threatening. "Then why is there a revolt being planned? One neither of you dumb fucks know about?"

Frank didn't answer. Charlie had nothing to say. It seemed best to wait out Joe's anger.

"I provide what this city needs—uses. I'm the one." Joe thumped his chest. "Do I get any thanks? No, I get some smart-ass technicians plotting to replace me." He was shouting now. "Me. I'm the reason they're fed, I'm the reason no gangs have overrun the town. Now they're objecting to me running things? I'll show 'em what happens if they step out of line—I'll take them out. I'm not putting up with it." He sat down and, for the moment, seemed to Frank to be over his rant.

Frank tentatively ventured back to the subject. "Will letting them know the local gangster is the real power in our town help? No insult intended."

Joe gave him a nasty look but didn't say anything, so Frank went on. "The main Army force has moved on. There's only a platoon left behind. We've got Captain Roper in our pocket, sending good reports to Colonel Stillman and keeping that lieutenant out of our hair. We're getting stronger and we're in better shape than all the other towns around to weather the next tide of refugees. Isn't that the game? To keep the citizens safe and fed and they'll support us when things return to normal?"

Joe raised an eyebrow. "You think things are gonna return to normal any time soon?" Frank didn't respond. "And if everyone's so happy, again, why the fuck am I uncovering a revolt? I'm not going to let this go on. You know what happens to disloyal people? They get whacked." He looked from Frank to Charlie. "Don't forget it."

"It's time to take the gloves off," he continued. "I'm going to root out this revolt and bury it. Everyone's got to know who's boss and who's in charge...and that ain't you two."

"So what do you want to do? You want to be mayor? I don't think that's a good idea," Frank said.

"Worried about your role? Maybe about your cut? Or do you just want to protect your title? We got people thinking they can change things. They get comfortable and start thinking they know better how to run things." He thumped his chest again. "I run things in this town."

"Joe, don't go overboard," Charlie pleaded. "Let me dig into this and find out how deep it goes. I can talk with people; find out more of what's happening. We don't need to get everyone all riled up."

"You won't get to the bottom of it. You didn't even know this was going on, and you still wouldn't have if your men had picked up this guy. He'd give you some bullshit excuse for being out and you'd slap his wrist. I'm keeping everyone safe and fed and this is what happens? I'll make them sorry they ever thought to cross me."

"Joe." Frank leaned forward with his most persuasive voice. "Not everyone is against you. This may be only a small group. A group we can root out and shut down. Let's not attack the whole population and get everyone upset. Remember, most of the people are happy to be kept safe and fed. They'll go along with us...with you. And if we...you, don't alienate them."

"So you want me to keep being nice and stay in the background, that what you're suggesting?"

"For now, don't change things. Let Charlie and me get to the bottom of this."

Frank watched Joe digest what he had said. His comments were self-serving, but he knew Joe would see he had a point. He understood his role was to sell stability to the citizens, and that ability gave him a certain amount of power and leverage.

"And another thing," Joe said. "Everyone's now talking about this group of farmers in the valley that wiped out Big Jacks and his gang. They're building them up like they're some kind of heroes. That guy, Jason. People are making him into a celebrity. That don't help. I'm telling you, it makes these people in town think they don't have to follow the rules."

"Just give us some time to check the problem out," Frank said again.

"I'll be nice for now, but we're going to let the public know that I'm in charge. I'm not going to argue about it. You're both here because I made my decision. I'm going to be the Director of Resources."

Charlie shook his head, looking down at the floor. "I don't think that's a good idea."

"I don't care what you think. You just need to do your job...and that means following my orders. I want you two to get this publicized."

Frank sighed. He knew this was the new card he was going to have to play. But Charlie didn't get it. There was a time to protest and a time to just play the cards the way they fell. That was what he was going to do.

He sighed and held up his glass. "How about a refill?"

The next morning Charlie and his wife, Mary, were sitting at the kitchen table enjoying some coffee with breakfast. There was a limited supply, which made the brew all the more to be savored.

"I didn't hear you come in last night. What kept you out so late?" Mary said.

"A meeting downtown, with Frank and some others. The planning work never stops. Sometimes it seems we talk more than we do things."

"Well, you and I need to talk as well. I haven't had a word with you for two days," she said.

"Is something wrong?"

"I don't know. Do you remember Donna Bishop?"

Charlie looked blankly at her.

"She works at the same food center where I volunteer. She's married to Jim, the engineer who worked on the wiring for your headquarters, you know, to get the electricity going."

Charlie nodded.

"Well, I talked with Donna yesterday, and she said Jim hadn't come home the night before from a meeting he went to. She wanted to know if your men had picked him up, you know, maybe he'd been out after curfew?"

Charlie stared back at his wife. A knot was slowly forming in his stomach.

"I told her I didn't know but I would check with you. She asked if you could help find him. She's worried. They have a five-year-old son." She paused, then added, "It's not like anyone gets lost nowadays."

Charlie just kept looking at Mary.

"Charlie? Is something wrong?" Mary looked at her husband. "Answer me."

"Nothing's wrong. I haven't heard anything and we didn't pick anyone up that night."

He could feel her eyes on him. They had been married for twenty-five years and she could read him like a book. "Well, let me know if you find anything out," she said. "You know, when a family loses one of the adults, it's especially hard on them in these times."

"I'll do that," Charlie said, getting up. He went back into the bedroom and got his hat. At the front door, he kissed Mary. "Maybe you can let Donna know I'll do what I can. But you know I can't work magic."

"I will, but I know you, Charlie Cook. Something's not right. I can see it in your face. I hope you'll tell me about it."

"Things are fine. It's just that the job has stress and some of that stress doesn't go away, even when things begin to get better. I gotta go." He kissed her again and headed quickly out of the door.

Chapter 4

One morning, as Jason was leaving to inspect his fields, he stepped out on the front porch and stopped in his tracks. There, standing in the yard, were six men. They were dressed in a mix of mismatched clothing. Two wore full buckskin breeches, while the other four wore patched jeans or wool pants; all but one had on deerskin tunics either alone or over ragged cloth shirts, with the last wearing an oversized sweatshirt. They all wore tattered caps, some woolen and some baseball. They had long hair and most had beards. The men were armed with rifles, either slung over their shoulders or resting with the butts on the ground.

"Who are you? What do you want?" he asked the group.

One man took a step forward. He was tall and lanky with a sinewy strength showing in his movements. He had light brown hair and bright, sharp hazel eyes. "We from up north, near Linville Falls. You Jason?"

Jason nodded, watching the man.

"We come to talk. Heard you was gonna trade with Hillsboro," the man said.

"That's right. You want to come up and sit down?"

"We be fine here," the man replied.

Jason nodded, thought about the reply, and carefully sat down on the porch steps. Strangers always presented a tense moment. The men in the yard sat or squatted on the ground and cradled their rifles in their laps.

Suddenly the front door opened behind him. "Jason, what is going on?" Anne exclaimed, starting to come out. Jason got back up. He wasn't sure what effect a woman would have on these men.

"Excuse me," he said to the men in the yard and turned to go into the house. The strangers didn't move, but he was aware of some of them tensing up and shifting their rifles.

As Jason stepped inside the door, Anne looked at him. "Who are those men? Are they dangerous?" she asked.

"I don't think so. They know who I am and they want to talk. Something about our trading with Hillsboro."

"Should we get our rifles?" Anne asked, not with alarm. She had been through enough with Jason to know what to do.

"You and Sarah go up to the shooting positions on the second floor...quietly. If anything goes wrong, you can cover me. I think I'll be fine, but—"

"I know. We always err on the side of caution. Be careful out there." She kissed him and headed for the stairs.

Jason went back out to the porch and sat down again on the steps. The men in the yard still looked tense. "My wife is understandably nervous about strangers. We've had our share of bandits coming around."

The leader nodded. "We ain't bandits. If we was, we wouldn't be a-talkin'." He had a very old-fashioned, Appalachian Mountain accent.

Jason cracked a slight smile in agreement. "So what do you want to talk about?"

"Talk about trading with Hillsboro."

Jason stared at the man. "You know my name, what's yours?"

The man stared back at Jason, looking him solidly in the eye, never wavering, his face opaque, unreadable. "We'uns Jessup and Early clans. I'm Clayton Jessup."

"You've come a ways. How did you hear about me...and how did you find me?"

"We heard about the gang you whupped at the bridge. We know this valley, some of us related to Turners...you go back couple of generations."

Jason was surprised. "You heard about the fight clear up there?"

"Word gets out," Clayton replied.

"So you live in Linville Falls?"

"In the area. We don't live in a town. Ain't safe there. Where we live, ain't no roads or towns."

"Well, I'm glad to meet you, Clayton. So what do you want to know about the trading?"

"We wanna join in. We got skins, meat, and herbs. We lookin' to trade for ammunition, boots, some soap, tobacco."

"You aren't trading up north?"

"Only small villages near us up north and they all empty. Johnson City be the biggest town. It's run by a crazy man. We don't go near it."

"You live in the woods. Why don't you farm?"

"Can't farm much where we live, but we grow a bit, we get along."

"How many of you are there?" Jason wondered out loud.

Clayton didn't answer, just stared at Jason with an unfathomable look. "We enough," he finally said.

"Didn't mean to pry. If it was up to me, I'd be glad to have you come along with us. But I have to ask the others. We've formed a group to work together."

"We ain't interested in no group. We just want to trade. Looks like you got that set up, from what we hear."

"You've come a ways. I guess you want an answer now."

"We can wait a day. If you can get an answer, we come back tomorrow."

"I can do that," Jason said.

"We be back tomorrow morning," Clayton said, getting up. The others rose with him, and the group turned and headed off into the woods, melting away in the trees.

Jason watched them go. Just then Anne and Sarah came out.

"That was very strange," Anne said.

"Very strange," Jason replied. "It was like talking to colonial frontiersmen."

"Or Indians," Anne said.

"And what do you know about talking to colonial frontiersmen?" Catherine asked with a mischievous look in her eyes as she joined the family.

"Just guessing. But these families go way back. They have a long history here in the mountains. It seems like they just shifted gears a couple of hundred years and carried on."

"What did they want?" Catherine asked. Jason filled her in although there wasn't much to say.

"What was that he said about Johnson City? Did he say whoever was in charge was crazy?" Anne asked.

"Yeah, that's what he said. It doesn't surprise me. I'll bet there's a lot of communities out there with crazy people running them. They probably run the gamut from religious zealots to paranoid schizophrenics."

"What does *gamut* mean?" Sarah asked.

Jason looked at the sixteen-year-old. "Young lady, we have got to get you back to school. I don't want you to grow up ignorant."

Sarah smiled her most beguiling smile. "You mean I can't get by on my looks?"

Catherine gave a derisive snort.

Anne shook her head and looked at Jason, her face serious. "So you better get around to the neighbors to let them know about our visitors."

"You're right. I'll take the pickup. Don't want to use the fuel, but this is important. I suggest staying out of the woods today."

Chapter 5

Charlie had been troubled all through the day. The possibility that Jim, the engineer who had wired up the station, could be the man that Joe had kidnapped was eating at him. He couldn't make himself believe that it was a coincidence.

He brought it up again at dinner. Charlie and Mary didn't have to go to the food centers. They enjoyed the perks of Charlie's position and had their own rations, even if they had to do the cooking on a wood stove.

"Did you talk with Donna today?" he asked.

"No, I was going to mention it to you. She didn't show up for her shift for the last two days. I asked around and no one had seen her. I know where she lives, so I took the liberty of walking over there to see if she or her son were sick and might need some help. No one was at the apartment. There was a padlock bolted to the door from the outside, like the apartment was vacant." Charlie felt his stomach tighten again and put down his fork.

"I knocked on some doors up and down the hall and finally found someone home. I asked her if she knew what had happened to Donna. It was weird, Charlie. She seemed scared. Asked me who I was and why I wanted to know. She kept looking up and down the corridor. I told her I knew Donna from working with her in the kitchens. I didn't mention you since she seemed so nervous. She said she didn't know anything and I shouldn't ask around if I knew what was good for me. Then she closed her door in my face. Can you believe it? Why was she so scared?"

Charlie didn't answer.

"Charlie, what's happening? Why would Jim not come home and where did Donna and her son go? People don't just move away nowadays. There's no place to go and no support outside of town."

She was looking right at him, and he knew his face had given him away. "Did something bad happen to them?" She kept staring at him. "Charlie, I know you. Something's not right, I can see it."

"It just pains me when I hear of anything going wrong, that's all."

"But they just disappeared. How could that happen?"

"I don't know, but I'll try to find out, like I said two days ago. But you have to leave these things to me. Don't start becoming an amateur detective. You've never done that before and now's not the time to start."

She threw her napkin down on the table and got up to take the plates away, "I wasn't trying to play detective, I just wanted to find out if Donna was all right when she didn't show up. Now you've got me even more worried."

"There is nothing to worry about," Charlie said. He shoved his chair back from the table. "I told you I'll check into this. Just don't go around asking questions. Leave things to me."

His wife of twenty-five years just looked at him but didn't say anything.

Lieutenant Cameron snorted and handed a bulletin to Sergeant Rodney Gibbs sitting at a desk across from him. "Get a load of this crap."

It was a mimeographed sheet that passed for a newspaper. In it Frank Mason, as Director of Safety and Civil Order, was extolling the virtues of Joe Stansky and announcing him as Director of Resources for Hillsboro.

He reached for his cup of coffee, leaned back in his chair and took a few sips while waiting. A sour smile grew slowly on Gibbs's deep brown face.

"What do you think of it?" Cameron asked.

"Sounds like Stansky's coming out of the shadows. We pretty much have known he controls the resources in town."

"Yeah, but Director of Resources? What the hell is that?"

"It's what he *is*. If he controls the resources, he gets to be the director." Gibbs handed the bulletin back.

"That kind of concentration of power isn't healthy," Cameron said, scowling.

"We should just concentrate on this upcoming farmer's market. If Stansky wants to award himself titles he can do it. Frank Mason doesn't seem to mind, after all."

Charlie paced back and forth in Frank's office. "Joe's getting too powerful. You know it. Now that we've made him Director of Resources, how are we going to control him?"

"How did we *ever* control him?" Frank's tone was dry, without emotion, but Charlie noticed that he appeared to slump a little behind his desk. "From the start he had a jump on me...on both of us. He started commandeering resources faster than we did. If we didn't want to have ourselves a little civil war, with everything smashed and no order established and the refugees overwhelming us, we had to work with him. Charlie, all we've been able to do is keep Joe from doing stupid things, things that would upset everyone. It hasn't been so bad. We keep a smooth face on things for the public, and we all get along. Things go well for Hillsboro."

"So we just go along with whatever he does?"

"I didn't say that. We've done a pretty good job of civilizing him. Things could have been a lot worse for Hillsboro...and for us. You can't really complain, can you?"

"No. But now he's kidnapped this engineer and who knows what he's done to him. You heard him when I asked about it. He told me not to ask questions like that. But that's what I'm supposed to do—ask those kinds of questions. I'm a cop."

Frank leaned back in his chair, watching Charlie pace back and forth.

"How many others have disappeared?" Charlie continued. "We have no idea. And to make things worse, Mary knows the guy's wife. Now she's disappeared along with their son. Mary went to their apartment when the woman didn't show up at the kitchens—she helps out there—and the door was padlocked...from the outside, like it was vacant. Something's happened to the man's family, I can feel it."

"Jesus, Charlie, don't go off the deep end here. There's got to be a good explanation for this—"

"I wish there were, but I can't figure one out. You know people just don't move away. It isn't like that anymore."

Frank went on as if Charlie had not spoken. "And tell Mary to leave this alone. She shouldn't be playing detective."

Frank rubbed his eyes and looked up at Charlie. "For Christ's sake, stop pacing and sit down." Charlie settled himself in one of the chairs in front of Frank's desk. "You got to realize who's holding the cards here...and it isn't us. You have to work with what we've been dealt, which means we can't oppose Joe directly. You know that. And sometimes we may *not* want to know everything that's going on. You understand what I'm saying?"

"Deniability?"

"Something like that. Think about it."

Chapter 6

The shop where the wires and cables were made had been an old, empty warehouse. Now cast iron wood stoves filled the center of the shop, heating rows of iron pots. The stove's chimneys had been hastily improvised; the smoke hung heavy in the air, even with the windows open. In one corner of the building people were taking generators apart on long tables, while others were joining lengths of existing wiring.

The EMP had damaged many wires and cables—the longer the cable, the worse the effect had been. Copper windings had been fused making them useless. One end of the cavernous building was mostly taken up by a growing collection of bins filled with scavenged copper. The main project of the center was to make entirely new wires by drawing heated copper through dies. It was a project that had been put together with little specific expertise. Lots of mistakes occurred—the wire still often broke during the drawing process—but progress was being made.

A growing quantity of spools of fresh-made wire joined the spools of patchwork, and nearer the main door were spools of crude cables that had been made by winding the new wire together. These wires and cables were waiting on a mill to harness waterpower in order to run the repaired generators. When this source of power came on line, they would be the key to distributing the resulting electricity throughout Hillsboro.

When Charlie arrived, he found the foreman wrestling with a dislodged chimney, trying to get it reconnected so the stove could be lit. He was sweating and cursing as Charlie approached. "Does a Jim Bishop work down here?" he asked.

The foreman, an older man, looked over at Charlie with an irritated expression on his face. "Who wants to know?"

"Me, I'm the Chief of Police and I've got some work for him to finish, down at police headquarters."

"I haven't seen Jim for a couple of days," the foreman said.

"But he works here?"

"Yeah. He helped set this up. Don't know where he is, but we carry on. Maybe he was put on some other project." He paused for a moment. "But he liked working here. Said this was the project that would make the biggest difference to the city."

"Anyone here know him...personally? Not just from working here."

The foreman gave Charlie a serious look. "Is he in some kind of trouble?"

"No, but I need to find him."

"If it's about something at your headquarters, I can send someone out to help."

"No, I need to talk with Jim. Who around here knows him?"

The foreman pointed to a man across the shop floor who was directing several workers as they took apart a large generator, the kind used for emergency backup power. "You can try Stan. He and Jim often talked. Don't know how close they were, though."

"Thanks." Charlie walked over to Stan and introduced himself. "What were you before the attack?" he asked.

"I was a mechanical engineer. Now I'm a jack of all trades. See this baby? We got it from the First National Bank. If we can strip out the fused copper windings, wind in new ones and re-wire it to by-pass the semi-conductors, we might have industrial level generating power. Of course it won't start by itself and won't be self-regulating. Those circuits won't be recovered. But we can get it to make raw electrical power...a lot of it."

"What kind of voltage will it put out?" Charlie asked.

"Damned if I know with no regulating circuits. Jim covered that end of it. He said he could create some chokes that could get us usable power."

"Speaking of Jim, you know where he is? He hasn't been home or at work for a couple of days."

Stan paused, "Is he in some kind of trouble?"

"Everyone keeps asking that. No, he's not."

"Well, you're a cop, so why else would you be looking for him?"

Charlie ignored the question. "Help me out. Who did he hang out with? Who did he know? I'm trying to find him and no, he's not in any kind of trouble."

"He had some friends over at the water mill project. I think he knew people working on many of the restart projects. Jim was interested in all aspects of getting the city back on its feet."

"You got any names?" Charlie asked.

Stan's face went blank. "No, I don't have any names to give you. I didn't know those people. I only know about them because Jim mentioned he met some guys over there. He didn't elaborate." He paused. "Sorry. I can't help you." The man turned back to the generator and the other two men who were staring nervously at him.

The water project was near the edge of town, close to the river where it cut through the southwest part of the town. A crumbling water mill was being rebuilt. In its day it had been powered by water drawn from the river.

A channel had been cut to divert the river water to a millpond from where it could be fed in a controlled manner to the water wheel.

The remains of the old channel had been staked out but it would need to be cleared in order to bring a flow of water from the river to the pond. Workers had begun to take out trees that had grown in the hundred-year-old ditch. It was slow, backbreaking work with only hand tools available.

The mill's workings were either missing or rotted beyond repair. The search was on for another mill, which could be taken apart and relocated to the site. When the structure was rebuilt, and when water flowed in the newly-dug canal, Hillsboro would have a working, steady source of power operating securely within the town itself.

"I don't know anything about him," said Bob Jackson, the head of the project. Charlie grimaced. His legs were starting to complain from all the hiking around.

"Some people at the electrical project said he knew people over here...met with them at times."

"Never met with me, and none of the others as far as I know," Bob replied.

"That's not what I was told."

The man shrugged. "You were told wrong."

"I'm going to ask around...since you don't seem to know anything," Charlie said.

"Suit yourself. You're the chief of police. Guess you can do what you want." The man's reply held a hint of sarcasm, or anger, Charlie couldn't tell for sure.

He was just as unsuccessful with the other men. It was another long walk back to headquarters. He knew in his gut that some of the people he had spoken to were hiding things from him. Maybe the reason was just simple paranoia, but maybe it was something more. Charlie couldn't tell.

Chapter 7

Leo Stupek's full name was Leonard, but no one had used that name for years. He had severely beaten the last person who had.

He was looking through a one-way glass window that had been taken from the police headquarters. He was watching Donna Bishop. The woman had a black hood over her head and was tied to a chair in the middle of the basement room. A Coleman gas lamp in the corner provided illumination. Her clothes were torn. Her shoes had been taken, leaving her feet bare against the cold floor.

On impulse, Leo raised his forefinger and tapped twice on the glass. She turned her head blindly towards the sound. Leo let her wait, knowing it was increasing her anxiety. This was a critical moment, when he would confront her and begin the process of breaking her down.

He had two purposes. First, he wanted any information she held, though he did not expect much. Second, he wanted her for himself. She was a good-looking, thirtyish woman who now had no future. Leo would give her a future, one of his choosing. She might object, but she had a five-year-old son, and Leo would use him to control her.

He opened the door. The hooded woman turned her head at the sound and stiffened. Visibly summoning her courage, she asked, "Who's there?"

Leo didn't answer. He just looked at her, taking in the moment, this moment of control. Finally he stepped up to her and pulled the hood up, revealing her face. Startled, she cried out and stared up at him.

He watched her take him in. He knew his thick, six-foot body was intimidating. He knew his deep-set dark eyes looked like they could see right into her. And he knew the gaslight falling across his face was making the effect more dramatic.

"Who are you? Why am I here?" she asked.

Leo let the silence stretch for a moment before he said, "You're here because I want you here."

"What's happened to my son? You didn't hurt him, did you?" Panic began to rise in her voice.

"Your son is fine. I may show him to you later, if you behave."

"Please let me see him," the woman begged.

"Later, like I said...if you behave."

"What do you want?" she asked.

"Your cooperation, to start with."

She looked at him, a mixture of confusion and anger showing in her eyes.

"Your husband was involved in some bad things," he said. "They were bad for Hillsboro...and for you and your son. We had to stop that. Now your life has changed. Things will never be the same, but if you convince me you'll cooperate, I can help you and protect your son. The choice is yours."

"What's happened to Jim? What have you done with him?" Donna Bishop yelled, glaring at Leo.

"All will be explained in due time. For now, you have to cooperate with me. You have your son to think about now...only your son." And with that he pulled the hood back down over her face and turned and walked to the door.

"No, wait!" she shouted. "Tell me what's going on!"

Leo didn't answer but left the room, closing the door behind him. He watched through the glass as the hooded woman began to jerk against her bonds, sobbing.

Six hours later Leo went back into the room, carrying a gray metal folding chair and a folded woolen blanket. Her head jerked up at the sound of the door opening. Leo set the chair up facing her and sat down, the folded blanket on his lap.

"Who's there?" she asked again.

He pulled the hood up. She was now shivering violently. She had been tied to the chair in the cold basement for a total of ten hours. Fatigue and cold had overtaken her.

"What do you want?" she asked weakly. "Why are you treating me this way?"

"Do you want to see your son?" Leo asked in a quiet, but cold voice.

"Yes," she whispered.

"Do you want to get warm?" he asked.

"Yes."

"I can take care of both of those things for you."

"Why are you doing this? I haven't done anything wrong."

"Your husband did. He plotted to attack our city. To try to destroy the order we've established."

"I don't understand. He would never do that. We work hard. We follow the rules. You don't have any right to do this."

"I have every right. Your husband crossed the line. That had to be stopped. He put you in this position. He endangered his family."

"You have to let me go, let my son go. We haven't done anything wrong. If Jim was involved in anything, we never knew about it. Please believe me. Whatever you think Jim did, we weren't involved."

"You were. He involved you."

"No!" she shouted.

"It's something you'll have to accept. Your life has changed now."

"What do you mean?"

"You must think about your son now. Jim caused this, and he's gone. Now there is only your son to think about. You want to save him, don't you?"

She nodded.

"Good," Leo said. He stood up, shook the blanket out and draped it over Donna's shoulders. "You belong to me now. I control the fate of your son and I control your fate. Do you understand?"

She shook her head. He could see her incomprehension, and the growing terror behind it.

"You will. The first thing is to accept your new role and learn to do what I say. If you obey me, you'll get to see your son. He'll be well taken care of, and you'll have a relationship with him. Don't obey me, and you won't see your son and he *won't* be so well taken care of."

He watched as her body began to shudder violently, and then she sagged against the bindings and began to cry.

The next day Leo was in Joe's office in the bank building. He preferred the comfortable back room of the old bar and strip club. It was familiar territory and always full of men he could count on. It was their turf. This place felt foreign to him.

But a lot had changed since the attack, including his boss's profile. Joe was now the Director of Resources, whatever the hell that meant. All Leo knew was that his boss controlled the town. And Leo's job was to make sure Joe had the muscle to keep control.

"What'd you find out from that engineer?" Joe asked when Leo sat down.

"There's some kind of resistance going on. We got a couple of names, but he died before we could get more out of him. We're looking for them now."

"You haven't rounded them up?"

"They've gone underground. I guess they figured they'd be exposed after Jim disappeared. We'll find them."

"So what's this resistance?"

"A small group of technicians, who want more freedom, more say in how things run. Just what you guessed."

"Ungrateful bastards." Joe spat the words out, his face in a scowl.

"One interesting thing is that they seem to be taking inspiration from this guy Jason, the farmer who defeated Big Jacks' gang."

"How did he get involved?"

"He's not, but he's their model. Something about freedom and creating a more equitable society as things rebuild."

Joe looked thoughtful. "That guy could become a problem, even from a distance. But these technicians, we can't let them hold us hostage."

"We'll find 'em. We'll eliminate the trouble makers and the rest will fall in line."

Joe was silent a moment. When he spoke again, his face had cleared. "The local thugs are bothersome enough, but they're almost useful."

Leo knew Joe wasn't talking about his own men. There were independent criminals in town, not controlled by Joe. Some were homegrown; others had filtered in through the porous barriers. They preyed on everyone, stealing clothes, ration cards, whatever they needed. Most of them were armed with knives, but a few had guns. Leo looked at him.

"How so?"

"They make people want the protection we provide. It's useful to have them around mugging people, making them want more security."

Leo smiled. Joe had an interesting take on things.

Joe leaned forward "Get this under control. It's every city for itself now. We have more weapons, than the other towns. We're going to get them under my control." He pointed his finger at Leo. "You know the bosses in Charlotte always had our back. We paid for that by giving them a cut on what we made. So where are they now? We haven't heard from them and we're not sending them anything. We're cut off, on our own. We need to organize the region. Who knows what's happening outside our area? We got to be ready when outside authorities show up."

Leo felt a grin creep over his face. He nodded. If this was the way the world was going to work now, Joe seemed to be ready for it.

Chapter 8

In the two weeks that led up to the trek to Hillsboro, the farms in the valley were a bustle of activity. The grain harvest was in, both the winter wheat and the early barley plantings. Almost everyone worked together on the threshing and winnowing, with the farmers moving from one farm to another by turns. Then they loaded the grain onto farm wagons drawn by pickup trucks and took it to Clifton Forge. They scoured the valley and every inch of Clifton Forge for sacks with which to bag the newly ground flour and corn meal.

Everyone put in long hours. Lieutenant Cameron was there to help, along with six others from his platoon who had volunteered to come to the valley with him, including Sergeant Gibbs and Specialist Tommy Wilkes. They spent a whole week there, working from dawn to dusk and then sleeping in tents in Anne and Jason's front yard. Catherine was overjoyed to have her fiancé there to work beside her. Sarah did her share as well, while keeping up a flirtatious relationship with Tommy Wilkes under the watchful eye of her mother. Sarah had met him when the army had shown up the year before, just before her baby brother was born.

The soldiers would also provide extra security for the trip to Hillsboro, and along with the familiar Humvee, they had also brought a big troop truck to help transport everyone. It had taken them only a day's drive to reach the valley, but the slower pace dictated by the heavy farm wagons would mean a return journey of a day and a half. In addition to the milled grains, the wagons would be carrying loads of beets, spring onions, and the cucumbers and peppers that had gotten an early start in the cold frames.

The Jessup and Early clans showed up at the farm three days before departure. This time they came in greater numbers, twenty-four rugged looking men and women in all. They had carried their goods on their backs, through the woods and over the ridges from the north. They brought skins, fur pelts, smoked game meat, and wild food and herbs from the forest— fiddleheads, cattail tubers, wood sorrel, spring beauty, and ramps; along with scallions and sassafras roots and wintergreen. The forest would provide many more offerings as the summer advanced.

The air was full of enthusiasm, the activity hectic. The Jessups and Earlys set up camp all around Anne and Jason's farm, their tents and tarpaulins spread out in a haphazard fashion through the apple orchard along the edge of the woods, in noticeable contrast to the neat row of military tents in front of the house. They pitched in to help load the wagons. The valley residents were buzzing about the possibilities this trip would bring, and those who were going were excited at the chance to mingle with the people in town after two years of isolation. Anne needed to stay close to the house to tend baby Adam, so she made most of her contribution by cooking for the workers outside. In the final forty-eight hours, some of the other women joined her to allow the rest to work non-stop.

The day of the trip to Hillsboro dawned clear and cool, but with the promise of more warmth. It was late May, and the weather in the mountain valley could not have been better. The fields and the forest were fresh and green; the air was crisp and filled with the fertile odors of spring. It was a day of promise, lifting the spirits of the valley residents as they walked down to Anne and Jason's farm to gather for the trip to town.

The convoy vehicles had been assembled in the yard. The two large farm wagons with towering sides, the largest wagons in the valley, sat side by side, hitched to the pickup trucks that would tow them. A third pickup was parked at the edge of the front yard next to the huge troop truck. People milled about in the front yard and on the porch, talking excitedly, or busied themselves finding places for their personal bags. With the large contingent of Jessups and Earlys, buckskins outnumbered valley clothing by more than two to one. Most of the clans would ride in the troop truck, but three had chosen to climb into pickup beds and settle themselves among their packs of trade goods.

"I feel like we're going on a special holiday with this trip. I know it's all about business, but it almost feels like a vacation," Anne remarked to Jason as they walked through the yard, checking the loads. There was little to worry about. The packing teams had placed each sack carefully and had painstakingly tied tarps across the loads to protect the precious cargo during the bumpy ride.

"I imagine this is the way people felt on market day, even in the Middle Ages," Jason replied, smiling. He was looking forward to this first trade as a start to a better life for everyone. The disturbing news he had received from Cameron couldn't dampen his spirits.

"I talked to Kevin," he said. "We can take Adam to the hospital to get him checked by the nurses. Kevin seems to think there may be some baby vaccines left."

"That would be good. Childhood diseases are going to be coming back in a big way if someone doesn't start making vaccines again soon."

"Modern medicine is one thing we're going to miss more and more. It worries me as well."

Catherine had already joined her beau, Kevin, as he directed the loading. Sarah had come out of the farmhouse and quickly made a beeline for Tommy Wilkes. She made no secret of considering him her boyfriend, and Jason knew that Tommy enthusiastically supported the idea. Both girls were happy to have their suitors around, and. the trip to Hillsboro would give them some time together without the exhausting work of the last two weeks.

The farm convoy set out late in the morning. Catherine got to ride in the Humvee with Kevin, Tommy, and Sergeant Rodney Gibbs. Sergeant Gibbs offered her the front passenger seat, next to Kevin who was driving. He and Tommy sat in the back to keep a watchful eye out during the trip. Sarah, much to her frustration, had to ride with Jason and her mother in the truck towing the leading wagon.

A half hour after they passed out of the mouth of the valley and into the more open land along the Pickering River, they saw a faded, rusty pickup truck, its worn paint now barely visible after decades in the sun, with a trailer hitched to it on the side of the highway next to a lonely mailbox.

Five grinning people were standing next to it waiting for them. They were from the two farms out here that owed a debt to the people of the valley for stopping Big Jacks's gang. If not for his sudden defeat, Big Jacks would have moved up the river and destroyed them. The convoy stopped, greetings were happily exchanged, the soldiers were introduced, and then the convoy pulled away with its new addition and a trailer-load of milled grain and spring potatoes.

That night they camped in the empty parking lot of a deserted gas station off the highway. Gibbs set up lookouts for the night, one on the roof of the gas station and another at a vantage point behind the lot. The soldiers would stand watches by twos, changing every three hours. Jason was surprised to see some of the clansmen collecting their weapons and some of their packs and gathering in a cluster away from the rest of the group. He noticed Cameron and Gibbs standing and watching this development intently. Then Clayton separated from the men and walked back to Jason. Cameron came over to join them, and Clayton told both of the men that they would be setting up outpost watches of their own.

"Better to see the enemy before he gets to the camp," Clayton said by way of explanation. "You hear us call out or fire, you know someone is coming. You get ready."

"You better let us know when you're coming back in, so we don't shoot you," Jason said.

"We be coming in when it's morning. You see us." With that, Clayton and the men melted into the surrounding fields.

The night passed quietly. In the morning, after some tea and dried meat, the convoy set out. They would arrive in Hillsboro by noon.

Chapter 9

Hillsboro was making a holiday of the trading day. The meeting area had been set up in a downtown parking lot, and a limited group of people had been invited to enjoy the spectacle. The city leaders had arranged a barbecue to provide a festive meal for everyone. They had had to divert several work parties for over a week to hunt down the wild pigs, but it would be worth it for the public relations effect. The city didn't want the effect limited to the people who could fit into the available space set up for the trade, so all the food centers in town were offering barbecue for the citizens in honor of the special day, setting up outdoor seating on the streets or in adjacent parking lots and parks. Games had been arranged for the children, both on the fringe of the meeting area and at all the centers, and with the food being free—no ration cards needed to be punched—a large attendance was guaranteed.

Unbeknownst to the officials, the town was abuzz not solely because of the festivities and about the prospect of a free meal. Much of the excitement was about the visiting farmers themselves. These were the people who had defeated Big Jacks's gang two summers ago. A few survivors from the gang had drifted to Hillsboro and had managed to talk their way in by agreeing to join the city militia.

Encouraged by their new comrades, the ex-gang members had told and retold the tale of the epic battle, including Big Jacks's execution. They had added embellishments about the ferocity of the valley defenders to make their defeat seem less embarrassing, and with each retelling the story had grown, becoming legendary in scope. Jason's reputation as a warrior and leader grew with each retelling.

The arriving farmers would be met at the checkpoint on the road into the city and then escorted to the area set up for trading. Both the city and the farmers would set out their goods for inspection. After inspecting the goods and eating, the two groups would then retire to an empty store to negotiate and complete their trading.

The convoy came through the outer fringes of old Hillsboro. The houses stood with windows broken, doors standing open, the grass overgrown and gone wild, the shrubs growing into their natural shapes. It was a depressing sight. Everyone in the vehicles stopped talking as they looked out on the devastated scene. The mood changed from a joyful, holiday spirit to one of somber contemplation. The houses gave mute witness of so much lost; not only lives, but society as everyone had known it.

When they got close to the city proper, the homes stopped at a ragged line, with only a few partial shells remaining beyond. They passed into the cleared area, a broad band in which the buildings had all been torn down. Even the trees had been cut down, leaving only the rows of foundations and basements partially filled with stagnant water. They were like grave markers on a battlefield. At the far edge of the clearing there rose up a long, irregular rubble wall built of dirt, cinder blocks, the bodies of ruined automobiles, chunks of concrete, wooden planks, and sheets of corrugated metal, with sharp shards of steel and glass sticking out along the top. The wall swept across all the streets except the one they were on. Up ahead where the road passed through the wall, a moveable barricade had been set up.

As they neared the wall, the remaining bushes had been burned away, leaving only the bare, blackened ground. The opening was manned by a cluster of ten militiamen. The convoy pulled up to the checkpoint and stopped in a line. The militiamen were all holding rifles. From his pickup second in line, Jason watched Cameron get out of the Humvee and walk forward to the barricade.

The conversation lasted longer than Jason expected.

"How long does it take to get the gate opened?" Anne wondered out loud.

Finally Kevin walked back. He did not get back into his Humvee but came up to Jason's window. "The guards say you have to leave all your weapons here. You can't enter the city armed."

"What?" Jason said. Kevin had a pained look on his face. "Did you know about this beforehand?"

"No. This didn't come up."

"I don't like it. You can't override them?"

"They don't answer to me."

Just then Tom Walsh walked up along with Clayton Jessup. "What's going on?" Tom asked.

"The guards just told Kevin we have to leave our weapons outside the city...we can't go in armed."

"What the hell?" Tom exclaimed.

"Ain't doin' that," Clayton said. His voice was quiet and firm.

"Anyone else you can talk with?" Jason asked. "I assume you can go in with your weapons."

"Yeah. I'm in the army. We're not governed by any rule like that. But regular citizens in town can't be armed. The city had to do that to re-establish order and it's still in effect. I'm sorry I didn't think it would apply to all of you."

"You go in and find someone in charge and get them out here," Jason said.

"Better be quick," Tom added. "We don't want our new friends from up north to get impatient and decide to leave. We all might just have to give them a ride back to the valley."

"We wait...for now," Clayton said.

Kevin turned and walked back to the gate. As he passed the Humvee Jason saw him gesture to the others to stay inside. At the barricade his firm voice carried back to the vehicles. "I'm going through to talk with someone in authority to get your orders changed. These people are to not be bothered while I'm gone. Am I clear?" The man he had spoken to nodded and the lieutenant stormed past him.

It took Kevin only minutes of fast walking to reach the barter site, but there was nobody there worth talking to, only civilians, a few minor officials and a sprinkling of watchful militia around the perimeter. He set off for City Hall, cursing the time it was taking. He hadn't taken the Humvee because he had wanted to leave Gibbs and the others to make sure nothing crazy happened while he was gone.

He had not gone a block and a half before he saw Frank and Joe walking towards him. The two men were accompanied by three guards carrying M16s. The guards looked more like Joe's personal gang than militia, Kevin thought. "Mason, I need a word with you," Kevin shouted. The men stopped as he approached.

"The farmers are at the checkpoint. They've been told they can't bring weapons into town. They're all armed. You have to be armed out in the countryside, especially when you're hauling valuable goods."

Both men looked at Kevin. Finally Frank said, "And so, what's the problem?"

Kevin stepped closer to Frank. One of Joe's bodyguards started forward, but Joe stopped him with a gesture. Kevin said, "The problem is they need to be allowed to take their weapons with them into town, so I need you to talk to the guards."

"I can't do that," Frank replied.

"You're the head of the Safety Committee around here," Kevin said. Then he turned to Joe "Or maybe you run the committee. One of you can authorize what I'm asking. Don't give me the 'I can't' routine."

Joe didn't say anything. Frank shook his head.

"You better come to the checkpoint and tell them yourself. If some agreement isn't reached, you may not have a trading session," Kevin continued.

"Let's see what's going on," Frank said. They walked quickly back to the trading area, where Frank commandeered an old Pontiac with militia markings.

Jason had gotten out of the pickup and was fighting the urge to pace. It wouldn't help the others for him to look nervous. He walked up to the lead Humvee where Catherine was talking to Rodney Gibbs.

"Do you think there will be any trouble getting us in?" she asked.

"I don't know, Catherine," the sergeant replied. The two of them were leaning against the grill of the Humvee. About half the people in the convoy had disembarked and were milling uncertainly around the troop truck behind the two wagons. "The town has a lot of rules and restrictions. I should've seen this coming."

"Probably should have," Jason said. They looked around at him. "I don't mean to sound critical, but this is a big screw up."

"You're not wrong. Let's see what the lieutenant can accomplish," Rodney said.

There was the sound of a vehicle's tires crunching over debris. After a moment, Kevin came into view, followed by five men. Three carried automatic rifles. The other two wore suits and ties. The militia guards parted to let the group through.

Jason went to meet the men. "Did you work anything out?" he asked Kevin.

"Jason, this is Frank Mason. He's the chairman of the Safety Committee. That's the main authority in town. And this is Joe Stansky. He's recently been appointed the Director of Resources."

The man named Mason stuck his hand out. After a distinct pause, Stansky extended his hand as well. Jason shook hands with the two men. He looked them over. "Where's the mayor?" he asked.

Frank Mason smiled at him. "The mayor died of a heart attack last year, and the town council decided to select a smaller group to run the city for the duration of the crisis. The Safety Committee essentially sets the rules for civil order and establishes a militia for general defense."

Jason stared at the man. He seemed familiar...and then it came to him. "I ran into you two years ago. Before I left the area. Your goons roughed me up one day. As I remember, you told me to stay out of Hillsboro unless I turned all my supplies and weapons over to you."

Frank's face remained impassive as he stared back at Jason. "I'm sorry, I don't remember. A lot was going on two years ago and we were struggling to not have complete anarchy break out." Then he smiled suddenly. "You're Jason Richards, the guy who fought off the gang...what was that guy's name?"

"Big Jacks," Joe Stansky said in a flat voice. Jason could feel the big man's gaze measuring him.

"Yeah! That was quite a feat. And now you've got the farms organized. Congratulations on doing such a good job. We're happy to welcome you to Hillsboro."

"It's not much of a welcome when you want us to disarm just to come into town," Jason replied.

"I told them that you regularly carry weapons. It's a normal thing to do outside of the city," Kevin said.

A flicker of irritation crossed Frank's face. He still smiled at Jason, but when he answered his voice carried a harder edge. "Outside of the city we don't have a problem with you carrying weapons, but inside of the city we do. And you come under the city's rules when you come to town."

"Well, that won't work for us. First of all, we can't leave our weapons behind unsecured. They might disappear." Jason paused and forced himself to smile back at Frank. "Second, how do we know we'll be safe in town, being unarmed?"

He glanced around at the others. The farmers had come up in a group behind him. Sergeant Gibbs and Specialist Wilkes stood off to his left, while the two clans were gathered behind the farmers—all of the hill men had their rifles with them, though most were slung over their shoulders. They all watched attentively while giving Jason space to talk with the officials.

"We can arrange to store the weapons safely," Frank said. "You can even inventory them to make sure you get them all back. And I can assure you, you will be safe in town. No citizen will try to harm you or your people."

"It's not the citizens I'm worried about, but your militia. Remember, I've seen it in action, how they were abusing citizens. I'm not willing to let myself or my people get on the receiving end of that."

"That was two years ago," Frank said. "That's all changed. They were a bit rough around the edges back then. Things weren't under control. Now they're well trained and everyone knows the rules and follows them." He spread his hands earnestly. "I control the militia and we want to do business with you. You and your group will be just fine."

Jason looked calmly at Frank while his mind raced. He wasn't convinced by Frank's assurances. He could feel the eyes of the entire convoy on his back. Turning to Kevin, he was about to ask him what he thought when Tom stepped forward to stand beside him.

"Tell this SOB we don't disarm," Tom said in a growl. "We lost people defending ourselves and we're not going to lie down and be told what to do. He wants to trade, he lets us in like we are."

Just then Clayton Jessup came up to Jason and Tom. In a clear voice he announced, "I don't give up my rifle for no one. 'Specially city folk."

"Who's that?" Frank asked Kevin.

"That's Mr. Jessup. He represents some woodsmen from further up north. They've come to trade with the town as well." Kevin kept his gaze focused on Frank, and added, in a slower, more emphatic tone, "It would be nice to show him some respect and to welcome him to Hillsboro."

Jason saw Joe Stansky's eyes narrow. Frank ignored the suggestion. "Well, they can come in, but they have to abide by our rules." He paused for a moment, visibly controlling his irritation with the lieutenant, then continued. "Look, I can't give you special treatment. You'll be safe and your weapons secure, but I can't go around making exceptions. I start doing that and I'll have trouble in town." He folded his arms over his chest and stared at Jason.

Tom's face turned red. "You want food? You want something to eat? Then you let us in and treat us with respect. I don't care what rules you set for the people in town, but you don't dictate what we do." He was shouting now.

Claire Nolan's voice rang out from behind. "I lost my husband fighting for our lives! We didn't get any help from you and we don't want any. You asked for this trade, now let us in or we go home."

"My pa died defending us." Billy Turner yelled.

As the shouting increased, Jason turned and saw that the clansmen were spreading out and unslinging their rifles from their shoulders. Joe's bodyguards tensed and brought their weapons up, as did the guards at the barricade.

"Order!" Frank shouted.

The soldiers standing behind Cameron were bringing their rifles to the ready position and looking at their lieutenant. "Oh my God," Jason thought, "Anne and the baby. We can't start shooting." He raised his hands in the air. "Quiet!" he shouted at the angry farmers. "Quiet down!"

Chapter 10

Just then there were a series of siren whoops that none of them had heard in years and an old Cadillac sedan with "POLICE" written on the sides pulled into view and skidded to a stop right behind the barricade. The sound caused everyone to pause. Three police officers got out of the car. Jason recognized the white-haired man who got out on the driver's side as Charlie Cook, the chief of police.

Chief Cook adjusted his jacket and stepped through the gap with his two officers. They were all in their police uniforms, official-looking in spite of their visibly worn condition.

"What's going on here? We got some kind of disturbance?" the police chief said in a crisp, authoritative tone.

Kevin turned to him. The lieutenant's face remained calm, but Jason saw a hint of relief in it. "Charlie, these are the farmers we invited to town to trade. Now Frank tells me they can't come into town with their weapons."

Chief Cook looked thoughtful at what was obviously not news to him. He turned to Frank. Frank raised an eyebrow as if to say, *what are you going to do about this?* "Lieutenant, we do have an ordinance about weapons," Cook said after a moment.

"I know, but that's for the town people. It shouldn't have to apply to this group."

"I told you, we can't make an exception," Frank jumped in.

"I think it would be useful to hear Charlie's view," Kevin said sharply.

"Well, it wouldn't look right," Charlie said after some time, his voice now more tentative. He didn't look at Frank. Frank was already visibly angered by Kevin's openly expressed disagreement with his authority.

"Who's speaking for the farmers?" Chief Cook asked.

Everyone turned to Jason. "I am," he responded.

"So you're not willing to abide by the town's rules in order to come in and trade?"

"We're not willing to give up our weapons, if that's what you mean. We'll abide by all other rules you've got set up. Maybe you can fill us in so we don't get blindsided like this again."

"Their weapons are important to them. Outside of the city they're necessary for survival, both for hunting and for defense," Kevin offered.

"Lieutenant, you're part of the military authority here in Hillsboro, but we set the rules for our citizens and how we operate in town," Charlie said. "How about you take control of the weapons and your men assume responsibility for the safety of the group? I'll be responsible for our citizens...for them not harming anyone."

Kevin turned to Jason for his response.

"Let me talk to everyone," Jason said. He walked back with Kevin to the space between the Humvee and the lead pickup, with the group following and gathering around him.

"What does he mean when he says you'll take control of the weapons?" Tom asked the lieutenant.

"He doesn't know. It just sounds good to Charlie. But he *is* the chief of police and that should count for something. What I can do is tag them for everyone, with their owner's names, and secure them in our compound. You know Sergeant Gibbs and Specialist Wilkes. They're men we can trust. They can be directly in charge of the arms."

"You trust this man?" Clayton asked Jason.

"With my life. And I trust the two men he just mentioned."

"I don't trust that guy doin' all the talking," Clayton said.

"I don't trust him either," Jason replied. "How'd he get so important?"

"He's a politician. Makes for a good opportunist," Kevin replied.

"Who's the big guy?" Clayton asked.

"Joe Stansky. He seems to control the resources in town, which makes him pretty powerful. I think he started corralling supplies well before we arrived. I'm guessing he's been the guy with the real power for some time."

"I worry about us getting ripped off when we're in town," Tom said. "Why don't they just trade with us right here?"

Clayton nodded in agreement. "Save a lot of fuss," he said.

"They want to make a big show of this for the citizens," Kevin said. They're making it like a holiday celebration. There's going to be a barbecue and extra food. Anytime you get extra food, you'll have a big crowd."

"You can't get the whole town together in one spot. Hell, it'll be unmanageable and we'll never get our business done," Jason said.

"Only certain people, mostly VIPs, the city bosses, and the inspectors get into the main event, where we'll be doing the trading," Kevin replied. "They're also putting out free food at other locations around town to celebrate the event."

"So we've got some leverage here," Tom said. "They need this to happen."

"Not on this point, it seems," Kevin replied. "I think Frank and company are fearful of the people seeing you walk around armed and obviously free to act as you please. There's not much freedom here in Hillsboro." After a pause he added, "Peace and stability, but not much freedom."

Jason thought for a moment as everyone digested what Kevin had said. "We don't want to give up our weapons, but we also want to complete this trading. We have what they need and they have things we need. It'd be a shame to not make all this work, even if it's not off to the best start."

He looked at Kevin. "I don't want to stand on principle. I want to be practical. Putting our weapons in your hands...if that would make this happen—and if you can make sure you keep some military presence with us, since I don't trust this guy Frank or the police chief—I could accept that." Jason turned to the others.

"I'll go along with it," Tom said. The other farmers nodded in agreement.

"And your people?" Jason asked, turning to Clayton Jessup.

"Goes against my grain." Clayton looked at Kevin. "I don't know you, but Jason says you okay. His reputation is good with us, so I'm agreed."

"Settled." Jason said. "Let's mark our weapons and get things going."

Chapter 11

After the weapons were collected the convoy made its way through Hillsboro to a parking lot filled with a couple hundred cheering people. A large section was cordoned off with barrels and orange tape. The convoy pulled into the empty area and parked.

The farmers quickly unloaded a few of the sacks of flour and meal for samples, with the bulk remaining in the wagons. The city had provided stacks of folding tables on the edge of the lot, along with chairs, and the farmers set them up in two rows and laid out samples of their milled grain and mounds of garden vegetables. The baked goods had been carefully wrapped to maintain their freshness, and when the bundles were unrolled, the bread still smelled as if it had just come out of the oven. The enchanting aroma set people's mouths watering. The clans laid out their skins and produce on mats placed on the ground. Tom and Clayton followed the town's inspectors around as they examined the goods, accompanied by a clump of well-dressed townspeople who didn't seem to be doing anything but gawking.

The farmers had a list of items they wanted in exchange, and the Jessup's and Early's had another. The lists were similar, containing antibiotics, pain pills, diarrhea medicine, boots, and ammunition. In addition, the farmers had brought some broken equipment that needed welding—plows and discs and a hitch—and drums to fill with diesel and gasoline. The plan was that, after inspecting the goods, the city officials would list what they had of the requested items and the two groups would begin to negotiate a trade.

The atmosphere was turning festive in spite of a strong militia presence. The smoke from the long row of grills on the downtown end of the parking lot wafted over the area, stimulating everyone's appetite, including the farmers and clansmen. Soon after the inspectors had finished their rounds, the cooks began serving, calling everyone over. In spite of their misgivings, the farmers, clansmen and townspeople began to relax and enjoy themselves.

"Mmmm, that's good!" Anne slurped at her fingers and offered her pinky to little Adam.

Jason just grinned at her, his mouth stuffed with pork and bread.

He looked around to find Sarah and Catherine. They were among the army group, sitting with their beaus. "Looks like the girls are enjoying themselves. Let's hope this is a sign of the rest of the day going well. We didn't get off to such a good start."

Anne smiled at him in agreement. She pointed to a group of well-dressed people. "It's strange, they're so dressed up."

"They probably see this as a holiday like you do. Maybe we should have put on our Sunday best," he said with a wink.

"Are you kidding? This was a lot of hard work to get here." She laughed.

When Anne and Jason had finished eating, Anne picked up Adam and they went over to Tom. He was seated next to a town official, talking animatedly about life in the valley. Kevin had told them that the negotiations would be done in one of the empty stores that faced the parking lot, but nobody seemed anxious to break the moment.

"Anne and I are going to go to the hospital to see if we can get Adam vaccinated," Jason said. "We should be able to be back in time for the negotiations."

"So if you're late I'll have to do it?" Tom asked.

"I think you'll handle things just fine."

"All right," Tom replied. "You go. They're still checking over our lists back at City Hall or wherever. No one seems to be in a hurry to stop eating. See to your boy."

"We'll be back as soon as we can." He took Anne's arm and they headed out of the parking lot.

At the edge of the trading area they came upon more of the militia. They were positioned behind saw horses set up in the street that formed a barricade blocking off the entrances to the parking lot. Two militia members stopped them as they began to walk down the street.

"You can't go down there. You're restricted to the trading area."

Jason and Anne stopped. Jason looked at the man in surprise. "We're going to the hospital. I know where it is. We need to get our baby checked out while we're here in town."

"Sorry. I can't let you leave the area. Those are my orders."

Jason felt his anger rising. This was another affront and he had no more patience left for it. Anne, seeing Jason's agitation, put her hand on his arm. "Don't argue with him. We have our baby with us. We'll go back and get this worked out with Kevin." She gripped his arm hard.

Jason gritted his teeth and nodded. This was not the time or place to make a scene. Without another word they turned away, back to the parking lot and the festivities.

Kevin looked up when Anne and Jason walked back to where he was sitting with Catherine. "What's up?" he asked.

"We're told we can't go to the hospital. It seems we are all confined to the parking lot," Anne said. Jason said nothing. Kevin could see that he was struggling to control his rage.

Kevin jumped up "Let me get to the bottom of this." He strode off mumbling to himself about how everything was conspiring to make this day a failure.

After a moment of plowing through the crowd of people eating or inspecting the farm goods with great interest and enthusiasm, he found Frank and Charlie standing with Joe and his bodyguards. The bodyguards stiffened as Kevin stepped right past them.

"What the hell is going on?" he yelled in Frank's face, heedless of startled onlookers. "First you want to confiscate their weapons, and now I find people can't leave the area. Are you deliberately trying to sabotage this day? Because you're doing a damn good job of it."

Frank stepped back. "What are you talking about?"

"Jason and his wife just found out they can't leave the area. They want to go to the hospital to get their baby checked. This is outrageous."

"Look, we can't have these people running all around town. Their business is here, and here is where they should stay. They aren't here to sightsee."

"Everything you've done so far has been insulting to these people. Do you get that?"

"I get that they don't seem to want to follow our rules. They've been pretty clear about that. We can work with them, but they have to respect our rules."

"Is that a new rule now?" Kevin said. "We confine visitors to specific areas of town? I seemed to have missed that in the manual."

"You can be as sarcastic as you want, but we don't want them running all over town. Isn't that right, Charlie?"

Charlie was slow to respond. "Well," he said finally to Kevin, "Frank and I talked about it, but I wasn't aware that we made a decision. Apparently Frank thought we did and informed the militia of the fact."

"So you are not in charge?" Kevin asked.

"I'm in charge of the police, and we work alongside of the militia, but Frank is the direct head of that group. You know that."

"Yeah, I know that responsibility gets passed around when it's convenient. Look, I'm not going to argue with either of you. I'm going to transport these people to the hospital myself. If you don't want an embarrassing scene, better tell your militia to not get in my way." He turned on his heel and walked away.

Jason and Anne were standing where Kevin had left them. Catherine had joined them. "I'll take you to the hospital," Kevin announced.

"I'm going with you," Catherine said.

"You stay with Sarah," Anne said.

"She'll be fine. She doesn't need me to babysit her."

Anne gave her daughter a stern look. "You are to stay near her and don't let anything happen. Things are getting weird enough without something happening to my girls."

Catherine looked back at her mother with an angry face, but reluctantly agreed.

"We'll be back before you know it," Kevin said to his fiancée.

After he had dropped Jason, Anne, and the baby off at the hospital, Kevin drove straight to headquarters. He stomped into Captain Roper's office. "Captain, you've got to get over to the trading area—"

"I'm getting ready to head over there now." The captain gave him a pleasant look. "How's it going?"

"Okay, in spite of the city," Kevin said with great emphasis. "Frank and Charlie seem to have done everything they can to screw this up...from the beginning."

"What are you talking about?"

"Right from the start, the city started making up rules I didn't know about and springing them on the farmers. If I hadn't been there, we wouldn't be having the trading day, just a barbecue celebrating nothing."

Roper sighed and sat back. "Tell me about it."

Kevin proceeded to fill him in on the day's events.

"Look, you're the commanding officer here. Maybe you can talk some sense into these bozos. They won't listen to me. They seem obsessed with showing the farmers who's boss. It's as though they resent that these people are not under their control."

"I'll do what I can," Roper said, getting up and grabbing his hat.

The three nurses doted on baby Adam taking turns holding him. Watching them, Jason wondered how many medical staff were still at the hospital. He had seen no one outside and few others inside. There were glimpses of figures lying in beds through half-open doors. The halls had an empty, untidy look. The three women all seemed tired with fatigue showing around their eyes, but there was something else...

"We have some doses of DTP vaccination," one of the nurses said. "Let me find Dr. Morgan, she needs to authorize the shot." She headed down the corridor, while the two older nurses continued to play with Adam.

A few minutes later a woman in a white coat walked up. "I'm Dr. Morgan, Janet Morgan. I remember hearing about you last year." She shook hands with Anne and Jason as they introduced themselves, then she turned to the nurses and took Adam into her arms, looking at him carefully. "Looks like your son is thriving on the farm. Are you able to nurse him?"

"I can nurse him just fine," Anne replied. "Our diet is actually quite varied and healthy, so I have no problem producing milk."

Dr. Morgan turned to the two nurses, "Gwen, you and Cecily go over to the north ward. It's due for a walk," she said. Dr. Morgan returned her attention to Anne. "I'm so glad to hear that. It sounds like you're doing better in the area of food than we are here in town."

"What do you mean?" Jason asked.

The doctor paused and grinned oddly at him over Adam's shoulder. "Tell me, do I look thin to you?"

She did. Come to think of it, so had the nurses.

She laughed softly at his expression. "You don't have to answer. I can tell from your expression. You see we have a limited diet. Mostly soups and stews with anything that the food teams have been able to collect. Everyone stays hungry, but at least no one is starving now. Today is a very special day, with you coming to town. It's like an extra meal for us." Her face clouded, and a concerned look came into her eyes. "Roberta should be back with our plates by now. I hope she didn't have any trouble getting our servings..."

"The people we saw at the meet," Anne said. "So well-dressed, I didn't even think—"

"Nobody's having trouble fitting into their old favorite dress this year," Dr. Morgan said, her smile back. She handed the baby back to Anne. "Though I think people are getting tired of the look." The first nurse returned and spoke briefly with the doctor; she looked irritated and asked a couple of quiet questions, then turned back to them. "We have some of the DTP vaccine, so I'll authorize one for your son. We should have some MMR shots left, but apparently we can't find them. The baby should have that as well."

"Can you explain these?" Jason asked. "I'm new to this parenting."

"Sure. DTP stands for diphtheria, tetanus and pertussis. MMR stands for measles, mumps and rubella."

"If you can give Adam the DTP vaccine, we'll come back for the other one. Do you think you'll find it?" Anne asked.

"We'll make sure we find it," Dr. Morgan said. The nurse flinched at her tone.

"It's not easy to make trips to town," Jason said. "It's expensive in terms of time and fuel."

"I understand. There's no rush, although I wouldn't wait months. Just come back when you can combine the trip with something else you have to do. I'll make sure to keep one dose available for you."

"Thank you so much," Anne said with a smile.

"Great. Now if you'll just follow Laura here, she'll give your baby his inoculation." Anne nodded gratefully, and the embarrassed nurse led her away. Jason would have followed as well, but a look from Dr. Morgan stopped him. The doctor waited until they were alone in the hall.

"What I'm doing here has to remain secret. No one can know. None of my nurses are going to say anything."

"You mean with the vaccinations?" Jason said, surprised. She nodded. "Well, I...don't think we've said anything about that specifically. Just that we wanted to get Adam checked out." He wondered uneasily what Kevin had said. "Are the vaccines that precious?"

"Well, yes...even though we're not seeing many pregnancies, I don't have a free hand with supplies. We've gotten a small increase in births since your story came out last year. As things settle down, people seem to be getting less worried." She grabbed Jason's arm and leaned closer to him, lowering her voice. "There's a lot of fear in town. It's gotten worse over the past year. When I say I don't have a free hand, it's not just paperwork. If anyone in authority knew I gave you the vaccine, I could be jailed, my ration card reduced...or worse."

"What do you mean, 'or worse'?"

The doctor looked around, then walked them further along the corridor, away from one of the patient rooms. She continued in a low voice. "People have disappeared. People who crossed the authorities, or who the authorities think crossed them. Sometimes it's not clear what happened." A look of anger or concern crossed her face. "You must understand, people don't just disappear nowadays. Everyone is pretty much accounted for with the militia in control. All the food is centralized, so we all have to be registered—to have a ration card—in order to eat. And if you don't show up at your food center, you're not eating. The only way you could disappear is if you left town...or if something happened to you."

"You sure they just didn't decide to leave? I did two years ago."

"And leave their families behind?"

Jason had no response. The doctor went on. "And I've heard that sometimes the families disappear as well. Neighbors talk about people coming at night and taking them away. Some people won't talk about it at all."

"Do the authorities know this? Has anyone told them?"

"It is the authorities. At least that's what everyone thinks. No one's talking...because they're afraid. Nobody fully trusts the police, and they certainly don't trust the militia. Look, last year one of our doctors was helping Lieutenant Cameron collect some supplies for your baby's birth. Well, he started to complain about how things were being run. Asking why we couldn't have more freedom of expression, freedom of movement. I heard him. Others heard him as well and now he's gone. We don't know what happened to him...where he went."

She continued after giving Jason a moment to absorb what she had said. "In addition to that, the authorities are also taking the children away. I don't mean secretly. This is official policy."

"Taking the children?" Jason said in shock.

"Separating them from their parents. They're being kept in a separate building downtown. The word is the place is set up like a boarding school. It was started for orphans from the initial chaos after the EMP attack. Now it's used to free parents to work on rebuilding essential systems in the city. But many of us think they're indoctrinating the kids."

He stared at her. "What?"

"Sounds crazy, doesn't it? Listen. The only times parents can see their kids is on weekends, and not always then. But the word is that if the parents have done something wrong, crossed the authorities somehow, they get assigned to work the weekends. And those parents may *never* get to see their kids."

"Doctor..." Jason tried to make his tone very diplomatic. "I just *saw* kids playing back where we parked the convoy. I was looking right at them."

She nodded. "They're kids whose parents are not in trouble with authorities. They're let out for today. For this big happy day City Hall wants to bestow upon us all. But you can be sure there are some kids still being shut up in the school."

"You said indoctrination. You think they're trying to turn the kids against their parents?"

"Or they're using the kids as leverage over the parents. Maybe both. Who knows what those in power are trying to do. But there's a pattern here. A disturbing one when added to how they're controlling the rest of our lives. It's like living in a police state."

"What about the Army? Can't they help? Lieutenant Cameron is an honest officer. I can personally vouch for him."

She shook her head. "The Army is window dressing. Showing everyone we're still in the U. S. of A. so everything's fine. But how many are even in town anymore? A bunch left early this spring. There may be only thirty or fewer left. They're so reduced in number that they can't really do anything. And no one's sure we can trust them."

"They may be few in number, but I'm told they're in contact with the colonel who left this spring. Maybe they could get him back here to clean things up."

The woman shook her head in doubt. She closed her eyes and ran her hands over her face. After a moment she looked up at him and smiled tiredly. "Please keep what I've said to yourself. Don't talk to anyone. You never know who might be an informant and you could get me and my nurses in trouble. I just want someone outside of the city to know things are not good here."

"I'll keep this quiet, but I don't know what I can do about it."

The doctor nodded. "I don't know either. But you're like a hero to many in town...what you did in killing Big Jacks. People see in you the freedom and independence they're missing here."

"I'm no hero. I just did...we all just did what was needed to save our lives, protect our families."

'You've become more than that to people in town."

"I'm not some liberator. My focus is on my family and on the valley."

"Well I want someone outside the city to know, and you're the best person to tell. My nurse has probably been telling your wife a similar tale. There are bribes sometimes used to get people to follow official policies, and, if that's not enough, coercion. Never outright threats, but the way things are said, you get the idea you better go along. And there are informants all around. No one's sure who to trust." She stepped back, "With all that said things *are* getting better. We get regular meals now, as I said. No looting, almost no crime or gangs stealing. And the people in charge are working on projects that will be good for us."

"Like what?"

"Getting the electricity back on. That'll be a big help. And improving sanitation. I'm grateful for all of that. I'm just worried that we're heading down a very bad path."

"Again, I don't know how I can help," Jason said.

Dr. Morgan smiled at him. "I don't know either, but it helps to let someone outside know my concerns."

Chapter 12

They didn't have to wait long before Kevin arrived in the Humvee. "Did you get all the vaccinations done?" he asked as they drove back through town to the trading area.

"No, we have to come back again. They couldn't find one of them," Anne replied.

"Would it be possible to see other parts of the town, maybe the other food centers?" Jason asked. His curiosity was peaked from his conversation with the doctor.

Kevin looked at Jason in the rearview mirror. "We've got time?"

Jason nodded.

They soon drove up to another large parking lot. More people were at this one than had been at the convoy site. A stage of sorts had been erected at one end. It appeared to be made of lengths of metal scaffold tubing joined together with wood planks attached on top. It stood about five feet high with a set of stairs at one end. It looked to be a place regularly used to make announcements or hold meetings. Workers busily tended a row of mismatched grills from which rose the mouth-watering aroma of grilled pork. A gaggle of kids on the sidewalk were being coached through a carnival-like game of tossing softballs into a series of buckets.

They got out of the Humvee.

"Let's look for someone in charge," Kevin said.

People began to approach. At first Kevin got most of the attention with his uniform, along with a lot of uneasy looks, but as the townspeople realized who the visitors were, a crowd began to grow around them. Finally they found the organizer working feverishly to get a kid's three-legged race organized. Upon being introduced to Jason and Anne, he abandoned his efforts and hustled the group up onto the stage. Anne was taken aback. She had thought they would just mingle and watch the activities, but now they were on stage, in front of everyone.

There was a battery powered bullhorn on the stage floor. The man picked it up and put it to his lips, and began squawking a loud, elaborate introduction.

"Oh God," Anne muttered.

"They didn't even do this when we got to the trading area," Jason said in a low voice.

The games stopped and everyone began to converge on the stage to join the excited people already lined up in front. The rotund announcer watched happily. When he judged that the crowd had thickened enough, he introduced Jason as the man who had killed Big Jacks.

The murmuring stopped. And then the crowd exploded.

Jason stepped back almost reflexively as the people cheered loudly. The announcer went over to Anne and whispered to her. She answered and he put the bullhorn back to his mouth, "AND ANNE...RICHARDS!"

Another roar. Anne looked as pale as she held Adam close with a protective hand over his ear. She felt herself flush.

The organizer scanned the crowd while the shouting was going on. Finally, he raised the bullhorn and asked Jason to say a few words.

The cheering dropped off and stopped with remarkable obedience. The man turned and held out the bullhorn to Jason.

Jason took it and stepped forward. For a moment he seemed uncertain about what to say. "Thank you," he said. "Thank you. We...my family and the farmers of our valley, are glad to be in town...glad to do some trading. We're happy to be able to bring food for everybody."

"We're glad you came, too," a man shouted. "We get to eat barbecue, and it don't count off the ration card!" The crowd cheered.

"Tell us about the battle," another shouted.

"How'd you take them out?" Came another shout.

"Well..." Jason looked over at Anne for support and launched into an explanation of the battle. The crowd stood in rapt silence.

"Is it dangerous outside the city?" someone called out.

"No. Well, it's more dangerous than before the EMP attack, but if you're careful and know how to defend yourself, it's not that bad. We're doing well outside of town."

Jason went on talking and answering questions about life outside the city. The organizer then interrupted.

"Let's hear from your wife," he said to the crowd. Cheers of approval went up.

Jason handed her the bullhorn and took Adam from her arms. She pulled the trigger. It squawked loudly and she jumped back. Everyone laughed.

Anne hesitated, then tried it again, her voice sounding funny, amplified through the poor speaker. "Hello," she said. The crowd applauded and cheered.

"I'm not sure what to tell you," she continued.

"Did you have to kill anyone?" someone shouted out.

"In the first attack...yes. And I had to deal with the aftermath of both battles." She went on to describe the attacks directly on their home that occurred before the large battle at the bridge.

"You weren't scared?" another asked.

"Yes. I was scared. I guess we all were. But during the battles we knew we had to keep fighting, keep shooting, keep taking the enemy down." She paused. The crowd went silent. "It was that or be killed, and we weren't going to be killed."

Another cheer erupted, and clapping that did not die down for a while.

"What's it like...outside?"

"It's beautiful. Our valley is the most beautiful place I know. That's one reason I wanted to defend it...why we all did. The air is fresh, the mountains grand, the water is clean...I don't know of a better place to live."

Everyone grew quiet again, and she went on talking about the valley and how she loved living there. The crowd hung on every word. After a couple of minutes the organizer, now quite uncomfortable, surprised her by coming over and taking the bullhorn from her hand.

"Thank you for talking with us. I'm sure you have to be going and we have barbecue to enjoy." He then started herding the group off the stage.

Back in the Humvee, Kevin remarked, "We seemed to make the organizer uncomfortable."

"Maybe we gave the crowd a different view of life outside the city. One they aren't getting from those in charge," Jason said.

"They seemed to have heard all about us," Anne said. "You seem to be a modern-day hero." She looked at Jason. "Do we have time to visit another center?

"Maybe one more," he replied.

They drove over to another center. This time a lot of tables had simply been set up in the street outside the food center itself, but there was a podium on a low stand. After finding the organizer, a professional-looking woman with copper-colored hair that she had teased into a bouffant, they gathered behind the podium. Again the crowd started cheering when Jason and Anne were introduced.

"I heard you can hit a tin can at two hundred yards. Is that true?" Someone in the crowd shouted.

"Probably. It's what I was trained to do in the Army."

"Is your wife a good shot?"

"You'll have to ask her, he replied.

The questions continued. The people were hungry to hear about the outside world. Anne and Jason told them how life outside the wall was possible, maybe filled with more danger, but also filled with more freedom and satisfaction. Jason noticed that the organizer seemed to be getting increasingly antsy, like the first one. The woman was more timid about cutting them off, but she finally thanked and hustled them off the stage.

"We seem to be sounding a bit subversive," Jason remarked as they drove back through town. He didn't sound pleased with the idea. "The organizers definitely got uncomfortable when we talked about personal freedom and life outside the town, did you notice?"

Anne nodded. A silence fell. Both Jason and Anne felt the weight of their experiences return.

Chapter 13

When they got back to the trading area, the people were now relaxing and enjoying the food. No one was looking at the goods anymore. Kevin drove past the barriers and the glaring militia, and pulled the Humvee back into its former place. Anne said she was going to find something more to eat and then nurse Adam. Jason headed for the store where the negotiating was to commence.

It was one of the empty retail spaces that faced the large parking lot. They walked past two guards at the doorway. Inside, Jason noticed the dimness and looked back at the windows. They had been covered with paper to keep the negotiations obscured from curious onlookers.

A long row of folding tables ran across the middle of the room, and three large whiteboards had been nailed to the right-hand wall. There was light coming from the ceiling. Two fluorescent lights were on; a costly extravagance. He stared at them in surprise. Somewhere close by he heard the sound of a generator running.

It appeared that the main negotiations had already begun. Tom Walsh stood in the middle of the row of tables, addressing the town representatives with Clayton Jessup by his side. Jason didn't see Frank Mason, but someone he had been introduced to, Robert Goodman, a man assigned to help Mason, was sitting in a chair beside the platform and seemed to be leading the discussions. There were a half dozen other people sitting at the tables who had been helping to tabulate the goods. Two of them were frantically scribbling in pads, evidently taking notes. Some seemed to be just observing the process. Jason grabbed a seat next to Tom, near the center of the room.

Jason sat quietly, wanting to get a sense of where they were in the negotiations. Tom and Clayton alternated between speaking to the group and walking back and forth between whiteboards with papers in their hands, making sure the counts had been accurately recorded. Periodically the two would sit down, then Robert Goodman or another city representative would take the floor to make a point or correct a count. Occasionally Tom and Clayton would join with a couple of city people for a brief huddle at one of the boards. It was a strange process of, not only checking the tallies, but also hashing out a consensus on how much one thing should compare to another in trade value.

During the talking Jason noticed a man standing along the side wall of the room just behind the tables. He was a large, tough-looking guy in a black leather jacket, with deep-set, humorless eyes. He was slouched against the wall with his arms crossed. Jason could see the bulge of a weapon under his jacket. His disdain for the proceedings showed on his face. *A dangerous man*, he thought.

After a while the negotiations were finished. So many rounds of ammunition for so many bushels of wheat, drums of gas and diesel for so many bushels of flour or corn meal, so many Percocet for so many bushels or baskets of vegetables, so many skins or pelts for ammunition and medicine. The long lists they had worked from had been carefully confirmed over the prior three hours of inventory review along with trade ratios; all diligently recorded by both sides. They were done.

Outside the store, Tom breathed a sigh of relief. "I'm glad that's over."

As they started back to the parking lot, they saw Frank Mason standing on the sidewalk smiling affably at them. He held a small black shopping bag.

"Jason," he called out, "I'd like to talk with you for a few minutes."

They stared at him as the city representatives poured past, looking as tired of talking as they did. When Robert Goodman emerged he saw Frank and walked over to him.

"Can we sit down?" Frank asked. "I've got a bottle of good whiskey to celebrate the trade deal. And I've got some questions for you."

Jason looked around at the others. "Okay, but we need to get back soon to exchange the goods and get packed. We want to leave early tomorrow."

Tom said, "I'll go get the exchange going. You stay and talk if you want." His face and tone did not disguise his disapproval of the idea. Clayton Jessup was already across the street.

Jason followed Frank back into the storefront. The long room was now empty, but the overhead lights were still on; the generator still running. Frank put the bag down on the near end of the row of tables with a slight clink. He set out two glasses and produced a bottle of Jim Beam.

"So what do you want to talk about?" Jason asked, taking a glass of whiskey.

Frank lifted his glass. "First, here's to a successful day. A good trade made for all." He and Jason raised their glasses and sipped.

"It wasn't easy but it worked for both parties."

Frank's face took on a serious look. "The reason I want to talk with you...somewhat in private, is that we'd like to purchase some seed from you."

Jason sat still in his chair and sipped his whiskey thoughtfully. Finally he responded, "We don't have any extra seed to do that. Give us a couple of years of harvests and we can think about that. But not now."

"That's unfortunate. We could use the help right now," Frank said.

"What do you want the seed for?"

"It's to allow us to begin farming. We have open plots of land that we can use to raise crops. And we need to replenish the whiskey supply. This," he pointed to the Jim Beam bottle, "won't last forever."

Jason's voice was sharp. "We definitely don't have enough seed to use for whiskey-making. In any case, I thought you had some seed stock."

"We do, but it's hybrid seed. You know we won't get a second generation out of it."

"But it will allow you to do some of what you want to do for one season. And further, if we gave you some non-hybrid seed, wouldn't we just be putting ourselves out of business?"

"I wouldn't say that," Frank replied.

"So, what would you say?" He wanted to press the point, get it out on the table. "We make our livelihood farming, bringing you food. You'll be developing goods and services we'll need. That seems like a good relationship. Now if you farm, you can just cut us out of the loop. What do we get out of that?"

"Well, I would say that we all have to help one another. These are difficult times. We're not in conflict. We have to work together to secure our future. You don't want gangs taking over and neither do we."

"Our reception here in town didn't seem like we were working together. It seemed more like potential conflict."

Frank waved his hand in dismissal. "That was just a misunderstanding. Now that we know each other better, we won't have issues."

"Does that mean we will be able to bring our weapons into town the next time we come?" Jason asked.

"No. That's an important rule we have to maintain in order to keep the peace. But we can see about lifting the other restrictions."

"Like moving around in town? Coming and going as we please?"

"Maybe...we'll see. But let's get back to what I asked. We need to work together."

Jason made his voice calm, reassuring "I think we need to learn more about one another, get to trust one another better, get comfortable with each other. Then we can talk about sharing seed stock. In the meantime you won't starve. You have some food reserves of your own, and you can trust that we have a strong self-interest in doing business with the town, so there will be shipments coming from the countryside. We'll have time to see if your request will work for us."

Jason finished the last of his whiskey and stood. "Thanks for the drink. It's been a long time since I tasted something like that."

Frank nodded and got up. He held out his hand, and Jason took it.

"I do hope you'll reconsider my request."

Chapter 14

T he work went on until well into dark; unloading the farmer's wagons and then loading in all the supplies they had traded for. Items were checked and rechecked. Finally it was all done, and the farmers and clansmen circled their pickups and wagons to set up camp for the evening. Most of the clansmen spread bedrolls on the asphalt, while many of the farmers slept in the troop truck or in the cabs of the pickups. Anne had brought an old canvas tent, large enough for the whole family, which Jason erected on the pavement using bags to anchor the corners Four soldiers who had been assigned to the convoy were staying the night; they claimed places in the Humvee and in the cab of the troop truck,.

Anne retired early with Adam. Sarah was sulking over not getting to spend any time with her boyfriend Tommy. He and Rodney Gibbs were busy watching over the visitor's weapons and would not rejoin them until the convoy left town. Catherine had told Sarah that she would give up her seat in the Humvee so that Sarah and Tommy could ride back to the valley together, but she was still upset.

"I can't say I blame her," Catherine said to Kevin. They were standing together at the side of the troop truck, looking out at the strangely dark town. She put her arms around him. "If I hadn't gotten to spend time alone with you, I wouldn't be happy either."

"I can't go and pull Wilkes off the guns," her beau said quietly. "Well, I could. I'm not going to."

Catherine nodded. She hadn't been going to ask. "Do you really think there's that much of a risk? At your compound?"

"No," Kevin said. "But I haven't felt completely sure of things since we got here." He nodded toward the Humvee. "I don't think my people need to stand watches here tonight either. But I'm going to have them do it. And I'll join them. If people here think we're doing it to keep an eye on you, that's just fine with me."

They heard someone approaching and turned. Jason emerged out of the dark. "I need to talk to you about something," he said to Kevin.

"I had a disconcerting conversation with the doctor at the hospital. She didn't want me to tell anyone, but I know I can trust you."

"What did she say?" Kevin asked.

"We've all sensed some fear in town since we've arrived...didn't need to have anyone tell us about that. But what I heard may be the cause, and it sounds worse than I thought."

Kevin and Catherine listened intently as Jason related his conversation. When he was done, she turned to Kevin.

"Did you know about this?"

Kevin's eyes were dark and thoughtful. "I know about the school but not the rest. I've seen some evidence of intimidation, the lack of freedom. You'd get that with martial law in place. But I haven't heard of people disappearing. As far as I know, that hasn't been brought to the army's attention. It seems what you have are rumors."

"There's enough smoke from what I've heard to assume a fire somewhere underneath," Jason replied.

"Can you do anything?" Catherine asked Kevin. "You can't let things like that go on. Can you investigate?"

"I don't have that power. Captain Roper does, but we don't really have the resources. Remember, we're on the same side as the civilians, working for stability in Hillsboro...a return to normalcy."

"But at what cost?" Jason asked.

Kevin shrugged. "You have any suggestions?"

"I don't know about Captain Roper, you might talk with him. But from what you tell me, it sounds as if he's not that interested," Jason said.

"You have to be careful, whatever you do," Catherine said. "If a dispute arose between the army and the town, I've counted a lot of militia, all well-armed, and there aren't many of you."

He smiled. "You're right. We're badly outnumbered, if it ever came to a standoff. But Captain Roper says that isn't an issue."

Jason sighed. "I just wanted to make sure you knew about what I heard. I trust you with the information." Suddenly his face turned hard as he looked out at the dark buildings. "But I don't think it's our problem, the valley's problem. This is why I left Hillsboro. These people have let this happen to themselves."

"So whose problem is it?" Catherine asked.

"It's their own. We can't save the city if the people allow crooks like this Joe Stansky to run things. And Frank seems like just another crooked politician."

"It may not be our fight, but it may come back to haunt us if we want to keep doing business in the city," Catherine said.

"Some truth to that," Kevin said.

"Yeah, and now Frank Mason's asking for us to give them some seed." Jason explained the conversation he had with Frank.

"Watch out for him," Kevin said. "You may have called it right. He wants to be independent of the valley. It doesn't sound like a good move for you."

"It could be," Jason said. "If we had a more trusting relationship, we could share more and more with them. We'll still be the ones with the farming expertise, but it could enhance our ability to work together. Of course, that is with more trust than we have right now

"We should talk more about this later, with the others," Catherine said. She didn't want to keep discussing Frank or the town's problems. She turned back to her fiancé and smiled at him. Her eyes pulled Kevin to her; they slipped into their own private world, one where she didn't have to talk, words not being needed

Jason sighed and said goodnight. Without waiting for a reply, he turned and faded into the dark to join his wife.

Chapter 15

Charlie walked down the hallway of the Bishops' apartment building with a pair of bolt cutters in his hand. That morning he had awoken with the conviction that it was time to do some old-fashioned police work. Mary's concern for Donna Bishop and her family had become his. Added to it was an overarching worry that this was evidence of something worse going on, something that could engulf and destroy not only him, but the whole town.

Charlie thought he was essentially a good man, but he knew that he often took the path of least resistance. He enjoyed the perks that his cozy relationship with Joe had brought him, but, when he was honest with himself, he had to admit that they were the result of his compromises throughout his career.

Joe had been easy to compromise with when he was just a local crime figure. There were always going to be crime figures. The trick was to limit how much harm they could do. Charlie had been able to live with that for decades, but now he sensed something worse, something that would take him beyond where he felt he could go.

When he reached the door of the apartment, he put the bolt cutters to the padlock and, with some effort, snapped the hasp, sending the lock clattering to the floor. Behind him another door opened. Charlie turned at the sound. He locked eyes with an elderly woman peeking out and she quickly pulled back, shutting the door. He heard the dead bolt slip back into place. With a shrug, he opened the door and stepped inside.

He found furniture broken apart and strewn about, with couch cushions cut open and chairs overturned. All the dresser drawers had been removed from their chests, their contents spilled on the floor. The destruction looked to Charlie's practiced eye to be, not merely vandalism, but a search of the apartment with no regard for leaving its contents intact. In the kitchen, the cabinet doors were all open—two of them had been ripped off their hinges—with only a few dishes left in the cupboards. There were no clothes in the closets. And the mattresses had been removed from the bedrooms, and were not to be found anywhere else in the apartment.

After his first walk-through of the apartment, without touching anything, Charlie paused to take it all in, trying to get an overall feel of what had occurred, letting his senses absorb the scene. Then he began to slowly poke around in more detail. He didn't know what he was looking for, but, remembering his early days as an investigator, he kept his mind open to help him recognize anything that might be important. He was looking for clues to what Jim and Donna were involved in, who they communicated with, anything that would lead him forward in his search for answers.

He found several papers and signed drawings that told him the son's name. It was Danny. After ten minutes, he found a postcard-sized photograph of the family under a pile of broken items pulled from a dresser drawer.

Charlie picked it up and stared at it. It had been taken in a grassy field, probably a park. He recognized the man from the rewiring job at the police station. Jim Bishop had been energetic, helpful, and willing to do extra work if Charlie had needed it. The woman was very attractive, looking to be in her early thirties. She had blond hair, bright blue eyes and a smile that lit up her whole face. Their son was a happy-looking little kid with sandy colored hair that stuck out from under a New York Yankees baseball cap. Charlie smiled, wondering how that went down, here in North Carolina. He slipped the photograph into his shirt pocket.

He went back to searching through the debris, but turned up nothing else of value. However, he now had a picture of the family. He knew what they looked like and could try to find people who had seen the family, any of them, which would get him another step further. He left the apartment, picking up the broken lock on his way out.

Back at police headquarters, he looked up the one remaining police artist he knew, Philip Cole. From assignment records, made after the EMP attack, Charlie learned that Philip was now working on one of the waste projects. He sighed and headed back out on the streets to find him. In this post-attack age, even the police walked or rode bicycles unless there was a real emergency. Everyone was thinner, and, until such time as they caught a disease, healthier. Charlie couldn't deny the fact that both he and his wife had lost weight and gotten into better shape. The highly processed foods had long since run out, and no one really got to indulge in overeating. Candy and ice cream were things of the past. The most one could hope for was biscuits with honey on them for a rare treat.

He found Cole a half hour later at the burn pits on the east side and told him he had a job for him. "I need you to draw some people from a photograph. I need drawings of the whole family and then ones of each family member. Multiple copies of each, so I can hand them out to my officers."

"How many total?"

"Make me ten of each. And I want detail, Philip. As realistic as you can."

"You'll have to get permission from my supervisor. I'll be a couple of days away from my work crew if I do that for you."

"Show him to me and I'll get you cleared. This is important."

"What's up?" Cole asked.

Charlie shook his head. "Not for you to know. You just do the drawings but don't talk about them."

Cole nodded. "I get it. Just like the old days. Well, it sure beats shoveling shit. It'll be good to get back to drawing."

"Do a good job and I'll see if I can't get you back to drawing and illustrating on a regular basis. Maybe for the town paper or making maps or something. Your talents are wasted handling a shovel out here."

"I agree. But you think I get to make that point? I appreciate you helping to make it for me."

Charlie talked to the supervisor and for the next two days Cole reported to police headquarters to do the drawings. When he was finished, Charlie distributed them to ten of his most trusted officers.

He had reason to believe that Joe Stansky had infiltrated the police department, even before the attack. Police were not immune to bribes and Charlie knew Stansky had successfully co-opted members of his force. Since the attack, Charlie had seen some of his officers meeting with Stansky's men. In addition, Joe always seemed too well informed about police activity for Charlie's comfort. He had thirty-eight officers left in the department, and he estimated that he could rely on the loyalty of only about twenty of them. He pretended that there were no distinctions, but he made sure to quietly acknowledge and support the officers loyal to him and let them know they were important to the department. It didn't hurt that some extra rations and other resources found their way to these men and women. The others certainly seemed to be eating relatively well. As far as he knew, they remained unaware of Charlie's measures to take care of this small group.

When Cole finished his work on the afternoon of the second day, Charlie quietly passed the drawings out to the ten officers. Now he needed to wait. If the family was out there, he would hear about it sooner or later. And he wanted to be the only one who heard. He told the officers not to discuss this assignment with others and to keep the questions low-key. He wasn't sure why, but his instinct was to conduct this inquiry undercover. Not even Frank would know. At least not until Charlie could figure out what was going on.

When the group got back to the valley, everyone pitched in to help unload the goods. The valley residents divided up their shares while the clansmen began to pack up their goods for their trek back home early the next morning. At the end of that long day, everyone gathered back in Anne and Jason's yard to enjoy a last meal together—bowls of soup with venison on the side.

The next morning the Jessups and Earlys shouldered their packs and disappeared into the forest.

Jason stood on the porch and watched them depart. Anne came up and slipped her arm through his.

"What are you thinking? Want to go back into the woods?"

He turned to her. "No way!" he exclaimed. I want to stay here with you and be a boring country farmer and make lots of babies."

Anne smiled. "I don't know how many more babies I have in me, but I'm game to try for more as things settle down."

Jason smiled at her and wrapped his arms around her. Then in a more serious tone he said, "Clayton wasn't sure he wanted to do more trading with Hillsboro. I hope I can convince him to not start outlawing—stealing from cities. He said he might start doing that."

"That wouldn't be good. He could kill innocent people," Anne said. "But he's not like Big Jacks."

"No he isn't, but if law and order ever returns he would probably be put in that category. I'm not sure there will be any differentiating between outlaws. And I'd certainly like to have him on our side if we ever have to defend ourselves again."

"Who would we have to defend against? There aren't any large gangs like Big Jacks left, are there?"

Jason looked towards the woods and said quietly, "I'm worried about Hillsboro."

Chapter 16

Two weeks after putting up the pictures of Donna and her son Les Hammond stepped into Charlie's office, quietly laid a piece of paper on his desk, and left without a word.

Charlie read the handwritten report. Someone had seen Donna Bishop in one of the militia buildings, the one that was partly housing for the men and also doubled as a jail. She had been in the company of Leo Stupek.

Charlie pondered the report. No sign of the husband, but the wife hadn't left town. Where was the kid? He'd be at the school. Charlie smacked his forehead. He knew he should have checked there already.

There were three bicycles left in the bike room, the old ten-speeds no one wanted to use. The good police bikes—multi-geared mountain bikes—were all checked out. Charlie grabbed the red Schwinn and headed over to the school. It was amazing how fast his childhood skills had gotten re-sharpened after the attack.

No one answered the door at the school for a long time, and then the man who answered refused to let him in without the manager's approval.

When the manager came, trailing an assistant, he seemed reluctant to speak to Charlie.

After introducing himself as the Chief of Police, Charlie continued, "I'm looking for a lost boy."

"We don't release student information."

This was more resistance than Charlie had expected. "I just need take a look around."

"What's the name?"

"Can't tell you that. Police confidentiality." If he gave the name it might get back to someone who shouldn't know anything about what he was doing.

"I can't just let you wander around. We have to protect the kids."

Charlie gave him an understanding smile. "If I was a regular citizen, you'd be right, but since I'm the Police Chief it's quite safe. And, by the way..." Still smiling, he looked the man directly in the eye. "You don't want to interfere with police work."

"What are you investigating?" the manager asked.

"That's none of your business," Charlie replied. "This is a minor case, but we don't release information about any ongoing investigations." The man didn't seem to be a real principal, so Charlie figured this was all the explanation he needed or would get.

The manager looked somewhat doubtful but didn't comment. "I'll have my assistant escort you around," he finally said.

Charlie thanked him and set out with the woman. "How old is the boy?" she asked.

"Not sure. Between five and seven."

"We'll start with the class of the five-year-olds."

Within minutes Charlie found Danny Bishop in a long room full of children sitting on the floor. The boy didn't have the Yankees cap, but Charlie recognized him at once. An instinct of caution kept him from calling out to the child. He turned to the woman and asked to see the next couple of rooms.

After the tour, he spoke to the manager again. "The kid isn't here. It was a long shot but thanks for helping." He didn't mean it, but he had decided to stay friendly with the man.

On rare occasions Leo had brought Donna's son over to his apartment. The visits were precious to Donna but she had to keep making up stories about where his father was. After taking the boy back to the orphanage he would return and emphasize that the more confidence he developed in Donna, the more she'd get to see her son.

Donna was beginning to understand what Leo wanted. He hadn't violated her, but she feared that was to come. For now, in the weeks since he had released her from the basement, he had only given her instructions on how to behave, how to dress, how to wait on him. It seemed to Donna that she was being put through an obedience course. One that had an ending that she didn't want to imagine.

Thankfully, Leo's other duties kept him busy enough that she had time alone. But during those periods she was weighed down with worry and sadness about how their lives had come undone. What had Jim been involved in to warrant such harsh treatment? She sensed that she would never be allowed to go free. No one was looking for her. The best she could hope for was to protect her son. What would happen to her was secondary. She began to steel herself to that reality.

By now Joe had amassed a large cache of weapons through his systematic looting of National Guard armories in the region. It included M16 rifles, 9mm automatic pistols, .45s, and M110 sniper rifles with scopes. There were also M60s and two M2 machine guns. He had thousands of rounds of ammunition in multiple calibers. There M224 60mm mortar tubes with a hundred rockets to feed them. There were boxes of A67 grenades, M83 smoke grenades, and M47 riot control grenades. In addition there were Mk 153 rocket launchers with attendant rockets and Mk19 grenade launchers. The weapons made Joe's organization one of the best-armed groups in the state

Leo was sitting in Joe's office when he announced, "We're going to take over Hickory soon. I want to get them under my control."

Leo gave him a sharp look. "What do we gain from that? It could cost a lot of lives."

Joe got up from his desk and went over to the liquor cabinet. He brought the bottle back and refilled Leo's glass. "It gets us more power. And it means I don't have to look over my shoulder and worry about them. We need a regional organization, a collection of cities and towns, and a combined militia. Places like Charlotte, or maybe even Washington, eventually, are going to come around some day and want to put us under their thumb. All this," he waved his hand around the room, "could go away. Or at best we'd just be their lackeys. I'm not gonna be anyone's lackey." Joe sat down and leaned back in his chair.

Leo took a sip of his drink. "Gotta hand it to you. You think big."

"We don't know what's going to happen over the next couple of years. Hell, we may wind up with a bunch of regional powers. I plan to be one. And if a national power shows up, I want as much leverage as I can get. I want to be a force they have to reckon with."

Leo relaxed and listened.

"Taking over Hickory, getting them under our control, will only help Hickory in the end. They can't see the big picture like I can. They think they're just going to maintain, waiting for the government to show up, whatever that means. What will they get? Maybe nothing but more rules. I can see what's coming. That's why I made it this far. I grabbed the supplies right away and everyone had to deal with me. Who thought of that? Not Frank or Charlie. I'll do the same regionally and no one will push us around." The big man lapsed into silence, his sharp eyes looking past Leo, looking, it seemed to Leo, at the future. "This is not about greed, Leo. That's not the focus. Power is the key. And power means resources, lots of resources." He leaned forward over his desk, smiling, "And all that power gives us control over the wealth." Joe's eyes grew bright with enthusiasm. "You see? First the power, then the control, then the spoils."

Later that day, Frank stopped by Joe's office to talk with him.

"These farmers, I think they're going to be trouble," Frank said. He was seated in a chair in front of Joe's desk. "Especially that guy, Jason."

Joe thought about that for a moment. "He's already some kind of bullshit hero to people." Joe had heard the stories the survivors of Big Jacks's gang had brought with them.

"He could be a rallying point for insurrection."

"Not while I'm running things." Joe clenched his fists.

"It's more than that. I tried to run the idea by them of trading us some of their seed. They wouldn't go for it."

"Why'd you do that?"

"It would make us independent of them. We could grow our own crops. Then we could ignore them and not let them into town."

Joe sat up. "What are you talking about? Can't we just find seeds of our own...in a warehouse somewhere?"

"They wouldn't work after one season."

"Where did you hear that?"

Frank explained the problem.

"Damn seed companies," Joe muttered. "How the hell do those farmers do it?"

"They've got some special seeds. Non-hybrid ones that work year after year."

"Then maybe we go get them. We raid the valley and take a bunch of seed. Hell, take it all. We grow our own. We got the militia to protect the crops. Screw 'em. Let them make it on their own."

"That's what I was thinking. The more the valley interacts with the town, the more they may become a symbol to use against you. They already have a big reputation here. Bigger than we thought. We don't want the citizens inspired by some outside characters."

"So we just raid them."

Frank's face reflected a cautious look as he weighed Joe's declaration. "They wouldn't give the seed up without a fight," Frank said slowly.

"So?"

"They're pretty well armed and good at defending themselves. Plus they have the support of the army here in town."

"Screw the army. We've got more men and more firepower than they have. And it won't even come to that. We got Roper covering for us." Joe paused to pull out a cigar. "No, the army won't interfere."

"Well, we don't know where the seeds are kept."

Joe ignored the comment. "Here's what we do. You, Charlie, and Leo go to the valley and talk with them. Use some excuse, like you want to see their operation to make sure they can meet our production needs. Maybe they need more workers, we can supply that. Figure out where the seeds are kept and how they'll be defended. Then we'll know what we're up against."

Frank looked doubtful. "I'm not much for spying. I wouldn't know what to look for."

"You don't have to. Leo can do that. You're his cover." Joe stood up. "Just get this ready to go. I don't want to have that Jason guy around if we can get him out of the picture."

The six met in an abandoned office building, up on the fourth floor where the windows let in the moonlight that was their only illumination. There were no flashlights, they had no candles, and a fire was out of the question. The risk of someone seeing the flicker of light could bring the authorities. So they sat at a table in the soft light of the night.

Steve Warner was the unelected leader of the group. They were a mixed bag of professionals and technicians—a mechanical engineer, a welder, a mechanic, another electrician like himself, and a chemistry teacher from a local high school. They were meeting because Jim Bishop had been captured. No one could know how much Jim had told them. They all felt threatened. Some of the group had already gone into hiding after learning of militia inquiries about them. They had chosen to live in the dangerous under-culture that still existed in Hillsboro, scrambling for food and shelter, always moving to stay ahead of the militia, and watching out for others in the same situation who would rob or kill for food or weapons. It was a precarious existence, but they had concluded that it was better than torture and death at the hands of Stansky's thugs.

"We're not getting anywhere. We've agreed not to become a terrorist group and sabotage the development in town. But we're not getting any reforms," Steve said.

"Not all the other engineers are supporting us," Stan, one of the men who worked in the wire shop, said.

"And as we get power and communications back, people will get more comfortable and not want to upset the status quo," another said.

"We've got to get all of the technical community to go on strike. Maybe the medical staff as well. Demand changes or we don't help rebuild the town," another said.

"We'll be labeled as extortionists or terrorists," Steve replied. "And we'll never get everyone on board. Some people are happy with how things are run and willing to keep helping with the rebuilding."

One of the welders spoke up. "The more important someone is, the less they want to buck the authorities. Seems like they just want to be part of the power structure, no matter how the rest are treated."

"We have to do something dramatic. I don't care if everyone won't follow our lead. If things get too much better, no one will buck the system," one of the mechanics said.

"You want to start a revolution?" Steve asked.

"Maybe. We're running out of time...and options. you know that. When we get the power restored, you think anyone will want to stand up to Stansky? We're helping to solidify his authority."

Steve Warner sighed in frustration. "I know time's not on our side, but I can't support a revolt. We don't know if anyone outside of our small circle will support us," he said.

"Then we better find out pretty soon," Stan replied.

Steve knew the meeting was ending with everyone frustrated. As a group they held some of the keys to normalization for the city, but they couldn't figure out how best to use that leverage.

Chapter 17

ori Sue knew her effect on men.
Before the EMP, she had enjoyed using it. She loved the country
western bars and had frequented them after her shift at the K-Mart
was done. She couldn't remember ever having had to buy a drink. She had
even tended bar sometimes when they had needed extra help. It had been
fun and, being very popular, she sold a lot of drinks.

Now the taps were all dry and the bars were closed. The K-Mart had been
stripped and left empty. Lori Sue had no special skills beyond cashiering,
so, when the Hillsboro authorities had thrown together their emergency
work details with desperate haste, she had been assigned to manual labor.
Young people had been particularly valuable in the frenzied rush to build the
town wall. She had helped to pull houses apart, and her dead Honda Civic
was now part of the wall's base, its rear bumper visible on the inner side.

Lori Sue had lived with her mother before the attack. Her parents had
divorced when she was six. She was often left on her own as her mother
went out to the honky-tonks with a string of boyfriends. When her mother
was home she drank a lot and Lori Sue had to keep their small house in
order. Shortly after the attack, Lori Sue's mother ran off with a man who
had a gun and some food and promised to take care of her. Lori Sue never
saw her again.

The hard work and poor diet meant that the workers on the wall were
constantly being worn down and used up. After a year on the wall, Lori Sue
knew she needed another way of surviving. She had to get out of that job.

It hadn't been simple. Every able-bodied person in Hillsboro got a ration
card every month to use at the food centers. There were occasionally cases
where people had no current work assignment, and could pick up their
ration cards at City Hall, but those cases were rare and extremely brief. If
you could work, you were given work. Your team boss gave you your ration
cards. If you quit working, the cards stopped.

Quitting meant starvation.

Lori Sue had three days left on her ration card when she quit the wall.
She thought about what she could do to survive for two days. On the third
day she washed up, changed clothes, put on what makeup she had left, and
headed downtown to the militia headquarters.

The militia offered possibilities. They had their own separate rations, and they seemed to have a little more of everything. Joe Stansky's gang, headquartered downtown, near the militia also seemed to have extra resources, but they had a reputation for being dangerous. Lori Sue avoided the gang's territory. She would pin her future on working around the militia's block of office buildings.

Lori Sue was quite thin from working on the wall, but she still exuded a sexy cuteness. She had dishwater-blonde hair which now hung naturally, without benefit of styling gels. She had full lips, an upturned nose and green eyes that flashed when she smiled. It was the smile that got them. Once, a hopeful young man who had been buying her drinks had told her he was going to write a country song about her. Lori Sue had appreciated the compliment, but she had never gotten to hear the song. The attack had occurred instead.

That third night, she had begun to loiter outside the main entrance of one of the militia buildings. When the guards had looked at her inquiringly, she had smiled at them.

That had been the beginning.

Exchanging sex for ration cards, and other goods was a whole lot easier than slaving away at the wall. She had never gone back to her work site after that evening. She had immediately moved into an unused apartment in another neighborhood in case anyone official came looking for her.

Now she was twenty-one. Her figure had filled out. She was one of only a few women in the business. With a no-money economy and only the ration cards and work assignments, few saw any advantages in pursuing it.

Fulfilling men's desires worked well for Lori Sue. Along with the ration cards, she traded for clothing, shoes, wine and liquor, and jewelry. She would collect anything she thought could help ensure her survival. There were still gaps between meals sometimes, but nowhere near as often as she had feared. As her clientele grew, she could be selective; she turned down many more men than she accepted. Sometimes she would turn down a man even if it did mean skipping a meal. The militia was a rough bunch; she sometimes thought there wasn't much difference between them and Joe's group of thugs.

As time went on, she was amassing a cache of supplies—storable food and medicine, bandages, and even a weapon. In a drunken, debauched evening with a militia supply clerk, she had secured a 9mm Glock, with fifty rounds of ammunition to go with it. Afterwards the clerk had been terrified that she would let it be known how she came to have the weapon. Lori Sue had assured him that if he looked out for her she would keep their secret safe. This leverage only helped to improve her income. She kept the gun hidden in the heating duct of her apartment. Citizens were not allowed to possess weapons, but Lori Sue was not going to be caught defenseless again by any further catastrophe.

The militia had gotten used to her, and she enjoyed the run of most of the buildings. There was always harassment from the men, which she was adept at deflecting; her style was to never be intimidated and to give back just as much crap as was dished out. It generally resulted in a good laugh all around.

On one of her forays downtown she noticed a new face on the street. The woman was thirtyish, attractive with a refined but sad-looking face. Her blonde hair and blue eyes stood out. She wore an elegant housecoat with seemingly not much on underneath. It looked odd to Lori Sue. The woman didn't look like she belonged with the coarse sort of men found in the militia.

She was walking toward Lori Sue. Lori Sue stared at her, but the woman wouldn't meet her eyes as they passed each other.

She puzzled over the woman. It would not have shocked her to meet another female in the compound; she knew most of the others who worked the militia and politicians, and she didn't believe this woman fit that mold. And yet here she was, dressed oddly, walking alone by the cluster of militia buildings.

With no downtown office economy in existence, why else would she be here? There was simply no reason why anyone would willingly be within blocks and blocks of here unless they were connected with the militia, or with the politicians who ran the city...or worse, with the gang that Stansky had assembled. This was the domain of those who ran the city and those who enforced obedience from everyone else. Joe Stansky had his office and headquarters here, the politicians had their offices here, and the militia was housed here, with Stansky's gang located close by. This woman just didn't fit. She wasn't dressed for any role Lori Sue could imagine, and she had looked too nice, cultured perhaps, for any roles that fit a single woman in this neighborhood.

Lori Sue came to a stop and turned to stare after the receding figure. Could she be the wife of one of the political types? She hadn't met any and as far as she could tell, the militia was shy on wives.

It was still mid-afternoon, too early for showtime. Lori Sue decided to follow the woman.

After two blocks, the woman crossed the street and turned into the entrance of the Hillsboro Inn. Lori Sue grew even more intrigued. She knew the hotel, in its current incarnation. It was used as occasional housing for high-ranking militia and top-level members of Joe's gang. She had been escorted to some of the unused rooms in it, both times by militiamen of medium rank, and always surreptitiously, as if they had not been completely certain of their right to be there. Mostly the place was for bigwigs. Lori Sue quickened her pace and followed the woman through the glass doors into the dim lobby.

The woman headed toward the right-hand wing. Past the unused elevators, she went to the stairwell, picking a tallow candle out of a basket by the door and lighting it from a wall sconce before entering. Lori Sue trailed after her, waiting ten seconds before going through the stairwell door. She didn't take a candle but navigated the dark stairs by touch and memory.

On the fourth floor the woman exited. Lori Sue rushed up the stairs and caught the door just as it was about to close. The woman had stopped two doors down the hall. She sighed as she turned the knob, and Lori Sue saw her whole body slump for a moment. Then she went in.

Lori Sue eased the stairwell door shut and hurried down the stairs. This was Leo Stupak's territory! It wouldn't be good to be caught here.

Later, talking with the men in the former offices that had become the militia dormitories, she learned that the woman's name was Donna. According to some, she was Leo's new woman. He had brought her in after her husband had been arrested. She cautiously mentioned that the woman had gone into the Hillsboro Inn, and one of the men nodded and said he had heard that was where Leo kept the women he collected.

Lori Sue kept up the friendly banter as she gathered information. Information was like other resources; she gathered and stored it for possible future use. She didn't know when, or if, she might need it, but it was better to know more about what was going on than to be in the dark.

Over the next few days Lori Sue shifted her schedule and made a point of being in the area of the militia block where she had first seen Donna. There was a bar set up on the street level in one of the buildings housing the militia, with a window on the street. Only small quantities of alcohol were served, including harsh homemade whiskey, random beers, and even more random bottled liquors, depending on the day. Militiamen got drink allowances with special ration cards, with higher ranking men getting the better choices of alcohol. Lori hung out there, hoping to get a chance to learn more about the woman she saw. She had a new reason now. If this Donna had Leo's ear, she could be helpful to Lori Sue; connections never hurt. She wanted to move up in the hierarchy and not have to whore around with the grunts for survival.

On the third day, Lori Sue was rewarded when she saw the woman emerge from the hotel and come down the street. She was dressed just as oddly as before. She walked past the window where Lori Sue was watching and then surprised her by opening the door and entering. She walked up to the bar and gave the bartender a slip of paper. He immediately told a militia corporal to watch the bar and disappeared into a back room.

"What kinda note did you hand him to make him run like that?" Lori Sue asked as she went over to Donna.

Donna glanced up. Lori Sue smiled her best and friendliest smile, but the woman turned back to the counter.

"I'm just trying to be friendly. It's hard to find a female to talk to. Your name's Donna, right?"

Donna turned back to Lori Sue, her face draped in sadness. "I'm not interested in talking."

"Are you okay? You don't look so good."

Lori Sue was astonished at the long, trembling look Donna gave her. The woman's eyes did not seem to fully focus, and her clenched hands shook on the bar. After a long moment, she seemed to get control of herself. "I'm fine." She turned away again.

Lori Sue took a chance and touched her arm. "Please, don't blow me off. I need to talk with someone. I'm on my own and could use a friend."

Again Donna turned back to stare at her, more sharply this time. "Why do you hang around here?" she said in a harsh whisper. "This is not a good place. Get out."

Lori Sue was taken aback by the sudden change. "I got to survive," she said simply. She leaned forward. "But I could use a friend. We need to help each other out, you know?"

The bartender came back with two cardboard boxes in his arms, one on top of the other, and passed them to Donna. "Here ya go. Don't drop 'em," he said with a smirk on his face.

Donna lowered her eyes and turned to go.

"What're you staring at?" the bartender said to Lori Sue. "Get lost and don't go hitting people up for free drinks."

"Shove it up your ass," Lori Sue said and followed Donna to the door. Outside, she reached up and took the top cardboard box. "Let me help you."

Donna almost stumbled at this intrusion. "What are you doing? What do you want?"

"Like I said, I could use a friend and you look like you could too."

"I can't help you. I don't think I can be friends with you. You don't know what's going on with me. You should get away...far away from here."

"I'm stuck here, like all of us. I'm just trying to survive. I know you're connected to Leo, so I figure you might be able to help me."

Donna went rigid and stared at Lori Sue. Now her eyes flashed with a barely suppressed fury, and she spoke through clenched teeth. "You don't know what you're talking about." Her voice came harsh and low. "He only lets me out to do errands like this. I can't help you and if you know what's good for you, you'll get out of here now. Give me that box and go away!"

Lori Sue put the box back on top of the other one. She watched Donna walk slowly and carefully back to the hotel, growing smaller and smaller. There was a guard standing outside the entrance now. He let Donna in, and then he looked down the street at Lori Sue until she turned and sauntered the other way. There was something more than met the eye here and she needed to puzzle it out.

Chapter 18

I'm going to Hillsboro," Billy said.

He was sitting on Jason's porch. It was evening.

He looked for a reaction from Jason. Jason just watched him.

"I talked to some of the people at the trade, that guy doing the negotiating, Goodman? I told him I can hunt and make liquor. He said he'd find me work if I came to town...seemed happy to have me."

"Big move," Jason said quietly. "You thinking of riding with us when we go back for Adam's other shot? Could be a couple of months. Don't know exactly when."

"Now I've made up my mind, don't think I want to wait that long."

Jason's eyes narrowed. "That's a long way to walk. Take you, what, a week?"

"Less, I think. It looked like pretty easy walking to me."

"Desperate people out there, Billy."

"They'll never see me," Billy said. "I'll be all right."

"So, right away." Jason looked away toward the tree line for a moment before he spoke. Billy could see he was gathering his thoughts. "Your family came here with the very first settlers, Billy," he said contemplatively.

Billy looked at him, wondering where he was going.

"Anne's told me a lot of stories about this valley, and one thing I noticed was that there were Turners in every one." Jason smiled. Then the smile faded and his expression turned serious. "Your dad kept to himself— sometimes with a vengeance. But he came out to fight for this valley. So did you." He turned back to Billy. "I know you and I had some problems, but I think we got past them. Figured you'd want to stay where all the Turners have stayed."

Billy felt the force of Jason's quiet entreaty. He gritted his teeth. He could hear all the things that Jason wasn't saying.

After the battle, Jason and Billy had had a run-in over Billy's spying on Catherine and Sarah. And it hadn't been just with Jason; Catherine had threatened to shoot him over it. In the subsequent year relations had healed, but Billy knew the incident would always be there between them. Certainly it would be for the girls.

"I had kind of hoped you might join the army," Jason said after a moment. There was a note of regret in his voice. "I'll tell you the truth, I'd be happier if you did that."

Billy said nothing. He was nervous about leaving the valley. He'd never been to Hillsboro before. His decision was going to throw him into the unknown.

"You've made up your mind then? No changing it?"

Billy shook his head. "Ain't nothing for me here. I don't like farming...and I might meet someone to be with in town. Ain't no one here in the valley." Billy couldn't fully express his loneliness since his father had died. Billy's relationship with him had been troubled, but the silence of the farm since his death was too deep to bear. With the old man gone, Billy had no one.

"You nervous?"

"Maybe a little. Never been there before."

"You know there's some bad characters in town. You don't want to get mixed up with them."

"Says you. I ain't seen 'em."

"Maybe you haven't looked close enough."

"I can take care of myself." Billy scowled at Jason. He was starting to get defensive.

When Jason spoke again, his tone was gentle. "Just be careful who you take up with. Remember, you want to be on the side of the good guys. You remember the story I told you about the sniper, the young kid that got caught up with Big Jacks?"

Billy nodded.

"Things didn't end well for him. I expect, given the chance, he wasn't such a bad kid, but we'll never know. I don't want things to go bad for you, that's all." Jason sighed. His eyes were sad as they met Billy's. Then the older man nodded to him and slowly got up from the porch chair. Billy stood up with him.

"When are you going?" Jason asked.

"I'll set out tomorrow. Got everything packed. You can work my fields. Ain't givin' 'em to you, but you work 'em, you keep what you grow."

"If things don't work out, you know you're always welcome back. This is your home."

"I know...and...thanks. For all you did...for Pa and me."

"You're welcome. You want to say goodbye to Anne?"

Billy shook his head. "You tell her I said goodbye. I ain't good at such things."

With that he turned to go.

Billy arrived at the entrance checkpoint six days later, just after noon. His backpack, stuffed full when he left, was now considerably lighter. He had gone through most of his food except for his last two pieces of jerky. The pack now held only camp gear, ammunition, his 9mm semi-auto pistol, a rain slicker, and a few clothes. The weather had been good, and he hadn't needed the slicker. At night he had found shelter in abandoned houses or buildings along the roads he walked.

He wore a flannel shirt, partly unbuttoned as the day was heating up, and denim jeans with patches covering his knees. He was glad to have a solid pair of boots and some good socks. He felt good. The days of walking had eased his mind; he was looking forward to a new start in town. He hadn't seen a living soul, hostile or otherwise, during the trek. He had stayed watchful, in case he needed to hide, but he thought that most strangers would have been just as glad not to see him.

His .30-06 rifle was slung over his shoulder, and he had a hunting knife strapped to his belt. The guards at the barrier, only three men this time, had been closely watching him since he had appeared at the edge of the razed area.

When he got near the barrier, they finally challenged him. Billy guessed they had waited until he was within their shooting range, which meant they weren't very good shots. He figured his skills would be in demand. Billy called out, "I'm here to see Mr. Goodman. He wants me to do some work for him."

"What the hell would he want you for? You look like some dumb hillbilly," came the reply.

"Ain't none of your business, but he asked me to come see him."

"Smart ass, ain't you."

Billy just stood there. He figured it wasn't any use to argue with them. "Ask him yourself, if you want."

"We let you in, how you gonna find him?"

"Figure I'll just go to wherever the headquarters are. They'll know."

"Can't bring that rifle into town. You'll have to leave it here."

Billy thought about that for a moment. "It's my hunting rifle. Mr. Goodman wants me to do some hunting for the town."

The men at the barrier appeared taken aback by this information. They spoke inaudibly. Then one turned back to Billy and called out, "Got to leave it with us. If Mr. Goodman wants you to have it, he'll have to let us know. We'll keep it until we hear from him."

Billy shrugged and started to un-shoulder the rifle.

"Hold it!"

He looked at the guards. Their weapons were leveled.

"Keep it over your shoulder till you get here!"

He pushed it back over his shoulder and walked to the gate. He unslung the rifle and handed it to the man, and the other one pulled the barricade slightly aside so that he could walk through.

The man holding the barricade said, "Go down this road until it bends to the right. You go left on Stafford, for three blocks. When you reach Ogden, turn right. Goodman ain't at City Hall. You want to look for the bank building. That's where he'll be."

"Be sure you keep my rifle safe," Billy said. He reached over and released the five-round magazine from the weapon and stuffed it into his coat pocket, giving the man an impertinent look.

The man holding his rifle scowled back at him.

Billy's good mood was a little darkened by the encounter. He followed the directions and found his way to the bank building. It was the tallest building he had seen so far, and the block it was on seemed much more active with people scurrying about going in and out of buildings. The parts of the town he had been walking through were mostly quiet, with few people to be seen. The building was a block away diagonally from another one with militia-marked vehicles parked along it and men standing around outside.

Their headquarters, he thought.

Getting in to see Goodman required leaving his knife and his backpack with the guard inside the bank building. He hoped they wouldn't go through the pack. He figured that they would confiscate the 9mm if they found it. Having it felt reassuring in this new environment.

After a long wait, he met with Goodman who gave him a note assigning him to a room over in the militia block. He also got a note to take back to the barrier guards so he could retrieve his rifle. His main job would be hunting, but Goodman also wanted Billy to help out with a still the town was constructing out near where they were setting up a hydropower project. The work was being done by people who had read about distilling in books from the library, but no one in town had any practical experience. Goodman said he figured Billy might bring some real-world knowledge to improve the process.

"Whiskey bottled before the attack is getting rare," Goodman said. "And the grain is too precious. If we're going to divert some to making whiskey, the product better be worth it."

Billy could understand that.

He spent a few days wandering around Hillsboro, getting shouted at occasionally by the militia. However, his pass indicating he was a hunter, which allowed him to go in and out of the city, kept the harassment to a minimum. Coming from the quiet and isolation of the valley, he found the bustle and activity in town somewhat disorienting. Even without mechanization, the noise level was far above the valley's stillness.

Some aspects of life in the city Billy didn't think were very good. There was no well handy for washing or getting a drink of water. Washing meant hauling water in buckets to store in your apartment. Then you went outside and did a sponge bath, without much privacy. Eating was done communally at the food centers set up around town. The food usually consisted of a stew of wild plants, with whatever the hunters had killed cut up and thrown in.

Your ration card got you in, and your work got your ration card renewed. He asked what happened if you were sick or injured, and was told that allowances were grudgingly made but there was always pressure to weed out malingerers. Those who chronically came up short were threatened with expulsion. The prospect of trying to survive out in the wild and dangerous countryside kept people in line.

Billy had eaten worse than what they served in the food centers, though not often. He felt safer inside the wall than he had felt on his overland journey. But the feeling of freedom he had felt, both in the valley and during his hike to town, faded. He began to wonder what he had let himself in for.

"I haven't found out anything about Donna. Don't know what's become of her, but I'll keep after it." Charlie knew the discomfort in his voice gave him away even as he busied himself with his bowl of food.

"Nothing?" Mary said. She shook her head. "That's so odd! There's not that many people in Hillsboro anymore and no one leaves. Where would they go?"

"I don't know. People probably still leave, for all I know. We don't keep tabs on that." He cleared his throat. "I did find a picture of the family and had an artist make me some drawings. I have some of my men looking out for them. We have to give it more time."

"What about the boy? Did you check the school? He'd be too young to work."

Charlie nodded.

"And?"

He was quiet. He stirred his spoon in the soup bowl.

"Charlie? What did you find?" Mary looked sharply at her husband, her voice betraying her stress.

Charlie sighed. "Look, what I'm about to tell you can't be repeated. I'm investigating this quietly, you understand?"

Mary looked at him. "You're beginning to frighten me."

"Just keep this between us...promise?"

Mary nodded.

"I found the boy still in the school. Right where he's supposed to be." Mary stared at him. "So the family didn't leave town. We can be pretty sure of that. They wouldn't have abandoned him. If they were leaving, they would have just all gone together on a weekend."

Mary put a hand to her mouth. "What happened?"

"I don't know. I can only guess." Charlie's teeth were clenched. There was nothing he could say that wouldn't panic Mary.

"Well, where are Donna and Jim? They wouldn't go off and leave their son."

"I just don't know."

"My God, Charlie, what's going on? How could this happen? They're good people. You know Jim, he did work for you."

"I know. Something's wrong, but I don't know what. That's why I want to keep this quiet while I try to find out."

"Does Frank know about this? Can he help you?"

Charlie looked down at his bowl and paused for a moment. "I don't want to bring anyone else into this until I know what's happening and who's behind it. I have to be careful until I know more."

"Oh Charlie. This scares me. You don't think Frank is involved, do you?" Charlie shrugged. She went on, sounding confused. "I know we have martial law, no real rights as citizens, but the people in power, you and the others, are honest. You're doing what's best for Hillsboro, not harming good people." She paused. "Is that Joe Stansky behind this?" Her tone grew more critical. "You know I've never liked him or how you cater to him. I didn't like him, even when he was just a sleazy bar owner—"

"Please don't start on that again. I told you I don't know. For God's sake, let me find out more. Then I'll know what to do...for us and for them."

Mary got up and came around the table to hug her husband, wrapping her arms around his chest and putting her head next to his. "You're a good man, Charlie Cook. I'm not angry with you. I know you'll do the right thing. Just be careful."

Charlie wondered how good a man he was. He sensed that things were getting bad—and he might be caught on the wrong side. He stood up and turned to hug his wife back. Their kitchen, their house, their comfortable life suddenly seemed very fragile.

Chapter 19

Success on a hunt always meant more work for Billy. The problem was distance—and weight. He would field-dress whatever game he shot and then have to lug it back to town, in his pack or over his shoulder depending on its size. The trip back could be more work than all the rest of a hunt.

Billy liked going hunting more than ever now. It got him out of town and into the quiet of the woods to the south and west of town, Sometimes he was lucky and found game in the overgrown yards of the abandoned neighborhoods beyond the wall which had been re-colonized by wildlife. If he was quiet, he often came across small herds of deer. The other hunters missed this possibility with their noisy trek on the way to the woods.

Even when he did have to go all the way to the forest he wasn't upset. He enjoyed being outside the town. Those times always drove home the stark difference between the quiet countryside, the uninhabited suburbs along with the forests and fields, and the town with its streets and buildings and noise.

Now he didn't have to worry so much about ammunition. Goodman had offered to have the militia give him a different rifle, but Billy liked his .30-06. He was happy to accept a scope for it, an adjustable-power one that he could use in the woods. Billy had only shot with iron sights and it had taken him a box of ammunition to set the scope up, even with some instruction.

This evening he had done very well, and at the moment he was almost regretting it. He had bagged a large deer, and now the heavy carcass was draped over his shoulder as he made his way back into town. He carried more game in his pack. He had not gone far before he had shot the deer. He was thankful for that as it gave him a shorter walk back to drop the carcass off at the main food center. He looked forward to heading back to his room after that to crash for some much-needed rest.

His route took him through a rundown part of town. He was often unsure of exactly where he was, but he knew the general direction to go until he could find some landmarks. He had been trudging along under his load for perhaps fifteen minutes when, turning a corner, he saw four men halfway down the block. They were crowding around a small girl in the middle of the street. It was early evening; the light was fading, but there was still enough that he could see them clearly. There was talking back and forth, and then suddenly one of the men grabbed the girl's arms from behind and put his hand over her mouth, cutting short a scream. Another stepped up to the struggling girl, reached out and tore open her pale blouse. She started kicking and he slapped her face. Billy could hear it half a block away. The man then ripped her bra off, exposing her breasts. The girl was older than Billy had thought.

Billy stopped in his tracks. A rush of emotions surged through his body. A protective instinct kicked in. He set the deer carcass on the ground, slipped off his pack, and unslung his rifle.

"Hey!" he yelled, aiming at the man who had torn off the brassiere. "Stop that. Whaddaya think you're doing?"

The four men turned to look at the lone figure pointing a rifle at them from about sixty yards away.

"Better move on if you know what's good for you. This ain't none of your business," shouted the man in Billy's sights. The others looked less certain.

"You stop and let her go." Billy yelled. He couldn't think of anything more forceful to say.

The men were all focused on him now. The one holding the girl still had her in a tight grip, his hand clamped over her lower face.

The man who had called to him grinned and flashed a knife. "You don't want to get cut up, do you?"

The man holding the girl from behind took his hand from her mouth and pulled a knife of his own, putting it to the girl's throat. "She could get her neck cut if you don't get outta here," he shouted. The girl started to yell, but he jerked the knife up against the bottom of her jaw and hissed something into her ear. Billy thought he saw a dark trickle start from the knife point.

"So what's it gonna be?" the man called, grinning. "You want her to get cut from ear to ear? Better get along and she won't get hurt. We're just gonna have a little fun with her."

"Yeah, she won't act so uppity after we're done," another said.

Billy slowly swung his aim over to the man holding the knife at the girl's throat. The man was shielded by the girl, but he stood a head and a half taller than her.

"Don't leave me with these pigs," shouted the girl.

The man scowled down at her and the knife started to move. Billy had the man's head centered in his scope. Without hesitation, he gently squeezed his hand and the rifle bucked against his shoulder with a sharp explosion of sound and flash. The .30-06 bullet struck the man's forehead. He never heard the sound. The hollow point delivered the maximum amount of kinetic energy to the target. The back of his head exploded, scattering brains over the concrete. He snapped back, his hands losing their grip as signals to the muscles were abruptly shut off. He was flung to the ground.

The other three froze. Billy worked the bolt action in a fluid motion, chambering another round. He shifted the rifle to the man standing nearest the girl. The man saw the barrel swing towards him and jumped to the side, turned, and ran down the street. The other two followed. They were soon around the next corner.

"Holy shit!" the girl exclaimed. She jumped back from the body on the pavement. "You almost killed me!" She looked at her blouse and then bent down and peered at the sidewalk. "That asshole tore my buttons off. You can't find buttons nowadays, and this is still a good shirt...fucker."

She stooped and picked up three buttons and stepped away from the dead man lying in a pool of blood and brains. She trotted up to Billy. Her sky-blue blouse flew around her, and Billy's eyes were caught by the bounce of her breasts, now covered, now uncovered. He stood transfixed.

"You're a hunter," she observed, looking down at the deer carcass. "What're you gonna do with that?" Billy just stared at her. "Oh, my name's Lori Sue, what's yours?"

"Billy. Billy Turner."

"Glad to meetcha." She stuck out her hand. "Very glad to meet you tonight."

"What were they doing?" Billy asked. He didn't really know what to say.

"Whaddaya think? They were getting ready to rape me. They're pissed 'cause I won't give 'em a tumble. Wouldn't even if they had something to trade. Shit, I got standards." The girl looked over her shoulder at the body lying on the sidewalk in a pool of blood and brains. "That bastard in particular. He's probably got the clap. He sure does stink."

She turned back to Billy. "We better get out of here. Someone coulda heard that shot. They might be coming soon." She reached for his backpack. "Let me help you with that."

"No, uh, I got it." Billy put on his backpack and hoisted the deer carcass back over his right shoulder.

"Follow me."

She led Billy through a maze of streets and alleys, off to the right from the direction he had been heading, until they came to a five-story apartment building. It had probably looked seedy even before the EMP attack, and now many of the first-floor windows were broken. The front hall was filled with wind-blown trash, and when the girl pushed the door shut it didn't close properly. A horrible reek hit Billy, and he quickly held his breath. There were piles of feces in the corners.

"It's worse when it's fresh. The stink goes away a bit after it dries out," she said as she led him to the stairs. Billy was about to put the deer carcass down, but she told him no. "Someone'll steal that, sure as you're standing there. That or some dogs'll get it. There's a few dogs left...don't know how they survive. Come on," she said and started climbing the stairs. On the fourth floor she stepped into the hall and went halfway down it, pulled out a set of keys, and unlocked a door. "Come on in. We'll be safe here."

Billy stepped in and set the carcass down against the wall inside the door. He unslung his pack and set it next to the deer, along with his rifle. The door opened directly onto a living room. There was a red corduroy couch with tears in the arms and cushions, and across the room from it a low table and two similarly broken-down stuffed chairs. To the left he could see a small kitchen with pots and pans lying out, unwashed. A short hallway led off to the right.

"It ain't much, but it works," Lori Sue said. Her smile looked a little embarrassed. "No one wants to live in this area of the city, so I can be pretty much alone. There's only two others in the building, older people on the second floor. No one wants the first floor, too easy to get robbed. And I got the keys to the whole building." She held up a set of keys on a large ring that had been lying on the table and smiled at her declaration of victory over landlords and building owners.

"But you can't lock the front door."

"Yeah, that's a pain...but I can open up every other door in the building." She smiled at him.

"I got to take this deer to the central feed station."

"Can we take some meat off it first?" She had an eager look on her face.

"No, I can't do that," he said, surprised. "They expect the whole deer. That was one thing they made a big deal about, taking meat for myself."

Lori Sue knelt and began to rummage through Billy's pack. She pulled out two rabbits. "Looky here. We could keep these. How'll they ever know?"

"I'm supposed to bring all the meat to the center."

"I hear you, but I ain't had a good meal in two days. And don't almost getting raped qualify me for a good meal?"

Billy didn't have an answer. "Look," he said awkwardly, "I gotta go drop this deer off."

"Okay. But leave your pack here. I'll keep it safe." Billy shook his head. "Well, leave one of the rabbits at least and I'll cook you a meal you won't forget when you get back." She stuffed one of the rabbits back in.

Billy hesitated. "Not sure I should do that."

"No one will know. And it looks like you could use a meal yourself. Come on. We'll have a good meal when you get back, and I can repay you for saving me." She stepped up close to him. His eyes kept shifting from her face to her now-and-again exposed breasts. She reached up and put her hands to the sides of his face. "You'll be happy you returned, believe me," she said, her voice now husky. "I want to thank you properly. You saved my life."

Billy swallowed hard and nodded. "You know how to skin that?"

"No, but I'll get a fire ready. I'm sure you can do it when you get back. Hurry, I'm hungry." He pulled his pack back on and picked up the deer carcass while she darted to the kitchen to set the rabbit on the counter. When she got back he could see the hunger in her face.

"The sooner you get back, the sooner we get to eat," she said as she pushed him out the door.

Billy returned in a half hour. Lori Sue had thrown on a gray sweatshirt, and when Billy knocked she grabbed the rabbit and led him up to the roof of the building. The little fire she had built out of scraps of wood was crackling merrily on a piece of sheet metal she had taken off the side of an air conditioning unit. "We can cook up here. Anyone who smells it won't know where it's coming from." She held up her key ring. "And no one can get to the roof but me. See, I've got the keys."

Lori Sue had torn off a piece of an old TV antenna to use as a skewer for the rabbit. Billy expertly skinned the rabbit and impaled it on the metal shaft. They sat back against the air conditioning unit, with one of them turning the spit every minute.

"How long you been in town?" she asked.

"How'd you know I'm not from here?"

"You're too country."

Billy looked hurt at the comment.

"I didn't mean that in a bad way," Lori Sue hastened to add. "It's just that you have a...a woodsy way about you."

"What's that supposed to mean?"

"I don't know. Shit, don't give me a hard time. It's just that you know how to shoot and clean a deer, catch a rabbit and skin it...how the hell do you catch one anyway?"

Billy smiled. "A rabbit? You set a snare."

"What, like a drum?"

"It's a loop of wire. You set it out where the rabbits usually run, and when they go through the loop they snag it and the loop closes and catches them."

"You hang 'em?"

"Like in the air? Not quite, but sometimes they get their necks broke or choke to death."

Lori Sue felt a moment's sadness. Then she inhaled the aroma of the rabbit wafting over her. "That's gonna taste real good." She snuggled up close to Billy.

They ate in silence, concentrating on tearing the rabbit apart. Lori Sue ate ravenously, happy that Billy was letting her eat more than her share. She could have put away two or three rabbits by herself.

When they were done, Lori asked, "Where you staying?"

"In the building where most of the militia are. I got my own little room there."

"Not tonight," she announced, standing up and wiping her face with her sleeve. She took his hand and led him back to her apartment.

She told him to take a bowlful of water from the buckets in the kitchen if he wanted to wash up. She went into the bedroom, stripped down to her panties, and took out a precious vial of perfume. She put a little behind her ears, between her breasts, and on her belly. She only had to wait a moment before Billy was standing in the doorway. His eyes went wide and he started to pull back, but she went up to him and kissed him hard on the lips.

She could feel him tense up, but she persisted until he relaxed and began to respond. "You ain't been around girls much, have you?" He started to protest, but she shushed him and led him to the bed. "It's okay. Has to be a first time for everyone. Besides, I like it."

She helped Billy out of his shirt and sat him down on the edge of the bed, kneeling to unlace his boots and pull them off. His pants followed, but she was wise enough to leave his underpants on for the moment. She sat down next to him and they began to kiss, with Billy awkwardly exploring her body. His eyes were opened in wonder one moment and closed the next as they kissed. His hands explored her curves and forbidden places.

When she was ready she slipped off his underpants and her own. He wasn't sure what to do, so she guided his hand to that most mysterious place. Billy was panting now. Lori Sue pulled him onto her.

It was over in a few short minutes. Billy lay back, breathing deeply, seemingly somewhere else. Lori Sue gently kissed him back to the moment. "You sure were in a hurry. We have to try that again."

"Can we?"

"Of course, stupid. As much as you can handle." She smiled at him. Billy was young. He smelled nice—woodsy, not dirty or unhealthy like so many of the men in town. And he could provide food, he was gentle, he was a bit innocent and yet energetic. Yes, she wanted more.

It turned out Billy could handle quite a lot; the night proved energetic for both of them.

Chapter 20

Charlie needed more information. He wrestled with the question of who to talk to for a whole day. Who could help him shed some light on what was going on without tipping off Frank Mason, or, worse, Joe Stansky? Finally he decided he had to go back to the water mill and talk to Bob Jackson, the superintendent, about Jim. He got on his bicycle and began to make his way through the streets out towards the river.

The head of the water project gave him a baleful look when he entered the mill. That palpable distrust was the one reason that Charlie felt he could talk with him...that and a hunch that the man might have some information

"Look," Charlie told him. "I know Jim's missing. His son's over at the school. His wife dropped out of sight, and then she was recently spotted in the militia block. Now, I know something is wrong. I didn't have anything to do with all of that, but I'm trying to find out what's going on so I can help his family."

"You're telling me you don't know what's going on? That's a laugh. You been in a coma for the past year?"

"What do you mean?"

The man shook his head. "I shouldn't be talking to you. You're part of the problem, along with Mason and Stansky."

Charlie thought about that for a moment. "I know it looks that way. But I haven't told anyone about my investigation. I don't want anyone but me to know about it until I know what's going on."

"Then what're you gonna do? Report to the authorities?"

"If there's a problem, if something is wrong in the city—"

The man snorted and gave Charlie a disdainful look. "There's plenty wrong in the city."

"Okay," Charlie said, "I admit it. We have martial law, we're still only a couple of steps from starving, there's limited freedom, and everyone is under strict control. I know that, but think about the times we're living in."

"Easy for you to say. You get all the perks. You get to make up the rules. I don't think I've ever seen you at a food center...got your own eating arrangements? I'll bet you're eating better than the rest of us."

Charlie felt his expression betray him.

"I thought so," Jackson said in a sharper voice. "Now why don't you go back to your special arrangements and leave me alone."

Charlie sucked in his breath. ""No," he said quietly. He met the other's gaze. "Because something's wrong, something beyond martial law issues and it's my job to find out what it is." His voice was rising. "And you're going to help me. Maybe I've had special privileges but I've helped keep order. Now if there's something else going on, something worse, I'm not a part of it, but I'm going to get to the bottom of it." He was almost shouting now.

"Shhh. Everyone can hear you. Let's go outside." The superintendent grabbed Charlie's arm and led him out a side door. The man let go of his arm and they walked along the side of the building.

When Jackson spoke again, his voice had lost its contemptuous edge. "Maybe you *are* concerned...or maybe this is just an act. But you know something's going on. Something that got Jim killed."

Charlie nodded, waiting.

The man took a deep breath. "I may be doing a stupid thing, but if you come down here in one week I'll take you to meet some people. You come after dark. You come alone, and you'll get blindfolded. You won't see who you're talking to. You agree?"

Charlie nodded.

"If we see anyone following you, no one will be here. Got it?"

Charlie again nodded. His gut twisted. A week from now he was going to know more than he probably wanted to know.

When Jackson told the others, the table erupted with voices of concern and dissent.

"Have you gone nuts?" one of them shouted. "This could get us all killed."

"It may help us," he replied. "We're not getting anywhere and we need some help. Chief Cook won't know who he's talking to. We'll watch him with lookouts. If we see he's being followed, we arrange a signal and we all just disappear. No one will know we were there. If he's alone, we can talk to him and maybe get him on our side."

"He's not on our side. He's part of the problem," another said.

"Look, I'm the one at risk. If he's going to use a meeting against us but doesn't know who anyone is, he'll only know who I am and they'll come for me. I'm the one putting his life on the line."

Some nodded at his point.

"They'll get to us through you," someone said.

"No, they won't. Because I'll make them shoot me. I'm not going down without a fight." Jackson knew the fate that would await him if they captured him. He was tired of living in fear. He glared at the others. "I'm not going to let them torture me. May as well take a few out, 'cause I'll be killed one way or the other."

His sincerity was obvious. It swayed the group, and they agreed to the meeting.

Chapter 21

The old pickup truck rocked and bumped its way carefully along the country road. Leo was driving. Frank was squeezed in next to him, with Charlie on the other side. Behind them, the four militia guards bounced around in the back, holding their M16s close. At the abandoned town of Clifton Forge, Leo turned left to follow the Pickering River. Twenty minutes down the road, he saw the girders of the bridge. He pulled up and stopped the truck about ten feet short of the turn onto the bridge. He got out. "Stay in the truck," he said over his shoulder to the guards.

He walked towards the bridge, examining it. It was a truss bridge, with the iron beams rising on each side, crossing over the top and laced with a triangular pattern of supports bolted to them. The murmuring river below was perhaps three car lengths wide; the bridge itself was about five car lengths from end to end and single lane. The valley's farm wagons must have been a tight fit. He heard the others climbing out of the cab.

"So this is the site of the famous battle?" Frank said.

Leo walked onto the edge of the bridge and looked across it. There were only a few signs left to suggest a battle had occurred. On the roadside beyond the bridge one could see a few bones half-embedded in the earth that you might not have recognized for human if not for the skull barely visible in the grass. The bloodstains were long gone, the full skeletons had been torn apart by animals, and any personal items had been scavenged.

"The gang really drove into a trap," Leo said.

"How's that?" Frank asked.

"See the ridges on either side of the road?" Leo pointed beyond the bridge. The land rose up cliff-like with rocks studding the face. A creek draining the valley had cut a narrow gorge through the low ridge to join the river. To make a road, the builders had widened this cut just enough to put the road through.

"If the farmers were up there on the ridge tops, the gang was in a shooting gallery. See how narrow it is after the bridge? They'd be sitting ducks trying to get up that road. Even the bridge wouldn't give much protection."

"Let's get going," Charlie said behind him. There was nervous irritation in Charlie's voice. "We're wasting time hanging out here."

Leo turned and looked at Charlie with some disdain. He didn't think much of this old cop. He didn't much like cops, even ones on the take. "Not a waste of time if there's something to learn," he said mildly.

"What's to learn?" Charlie asked.

"How they fight. How smart they are about tactics. From what I see, they knew how to pick their spot. Can't let them repeat that."

"What do you mean by that?" Charlie asked.

"Nothing." Leo walked back to the truck.

They reached Anne and Jason's farm late in the afternoon. Jason had returned from working in the fields. It was an awkward meeting with Frank playing the politician, trying to sweet talk everyone into relaxing. Leo remained taciturn and quiet. Charlie interjected some down home thoughts now and again.

They discussed food production and whether or not the valley could use extra hands during planting or harvest. Frank finally steered the conversation around to the seeds but didn't get too far with Jason. He was not going to show the visitors the stockpile or agree to share them.

As it began to get dark, Anne, ever the mindful of being a good host, invited everyone to have some dinner. After which the visitors went to the barn to spend the night, not wanting to be on the roads after dark.

As soon as they had been left alone in the barn and the door had been closed, the three of them and their four guards had conducted a careful search of the interior. They had found no seed. There was nothing remarkable, just a couple of workbenches, a tool rack with hammers, several saws and other tools no one recognized hanging on it. On another larger rack there were shovels, hoes, scythes, and rakes. On the floor were some other farm implements that looked like they attached to a tractor. A corner held stacks of lumber planks in various widths and lengths. At the back wall were four 55-gallon drums, two labeled "gasoline" and two labeled "diesel". A careful sniffing and jostling had confirmed the contents. Toward the end of the search, Leo had had the guards down on all fours inspecting the concrete floor to look for spilled grain and tapping the floor, listening for any hollow sound that would give away a hidden cavity

That night, when he thought everyone was asleep, Leo stepped outside the barn, closing the door on the snores behind him. The moon was three quarters full, and its cool light filled the yard. He took three quick steps to his right, into the shadow of a tree, and listened for any sound from the house. He was glad there wasn't a dog on the property.

Now he wanted to look around the property. Perhaps there was a shed or storage bin hidden in the woods. As he made his way across the yard, a pair of eyes watched him from the second floor of the house.

Catherine was sitting at the open window when she saw Leo come out of the barn. She hadn't been able to sleep and was enjoying the soft night breeze coming through the screen. The moonlit yard always looked otherworldly to her. The night didn't scare her anymore. It had its own beauty that she enjoyed.

Sarah came over in her nightgown. "What are you doing?"

"Shhh." Catherine pointed to the dimly seen figure moving across the yard.

"Who's that?" Sarah asked in a whisper. She scrunched herself onto the seat with Catherine.

"That guy, Leo."

"I don't like him. He doesn't seem very nice."

"Me either. I'm sure he's a gangster. I saw him before, when we did the trade."

"This is creepy. What's he doing?"

"That's what I'd like to know. I want to watch him. He's up to something."

"Something no good, I'll bet." They watched in silence as Leo disappeared into the trees at the edge of the yard. "You're really taking things seriously. Are we in danger from the town?"

Catherine turned to her. "We could be. I want to do my part to keep us safe."

"I can shoot and fight, but I don't want to...and I don't want to argue with people, especially adults. How do you do it?"

Catherine looked back out the window. "I don't know. I feel responsible. Like I should be helping out. I think the battles we fought changed me. I guess I don't feel like a kid anymore."

"Yeah. You're getting married...then you'll get pregnant and be no fun," Sarah said. There was a hint of sadness in her voice. Catherine understood. Sarah was losing her big sister to adulthood. The EMP attack had distorted all children's lives, but Sarah still tried to hold on to remnants of being a kid.

Now Catherine put her hand out to Sarah. "Shhh," she said. Leo was coming back out of the woods. He walked towards the barn and disappeared around the far side of it. "So he wasn't going to the bathroom," Catherine said.

"The outhouse is the other way," Sarah said. "He's looking for something,"

"Yeah, but what? They asked about our non-hybrid seed. I wonder if that's what he's looking for?"

"Why are they so interested in that?" Sarah asked.

"If they get seed of their own, they don't have to do business with us anymore."

"Is that a bad thing? Why do we need the town?"

"If we were real partners with the town, life would be better for everyone. We concentrate on food production, the town concentrates on things like electricity, machinery, medicine, education...it all works well together."

"How'd you get so smart about all of this?"

"I listen," Catherine replied.

Sarah punched her sister on the shoulder. "Well, so do I. I just don't find that stuff all that interesting."

Catherine playfully punched her sister back. "Go back to bed. I'm going to watch for a while longer, 'til this guy goes back into the barn."

Sarah yawned. "Suit yourself, but we have to get up early tomorrow. I'm sure Mom wants to feed them before they leave."

"Probably right," Catherine said. They both knew their mother.

On his way back to the barn, Leo glanced up and saw the shadow of someone in an upper room window. It looked like the older girl, Catherine. *She's smart enough to keep an eye out on me? She could be trouble.*

Chapter 22

As soon as Lori Sue heard that Leo was out of town, she excused herself from the conversation at the militia bar. The corporal she had been talking to was disconcerted and she knew she was passing up a sure transaction that would have gotten her two days' worth of rations. She spent another minute in conversation with him, enough to leave him looking forward to a happy experience in the next couple of days. Then she stepped out onto the sidewalk, took a moment to work up her courage, and headed down the street to the hotel where the guard stood waiting.

She hadn't seen Donna for some time. Donna was important to her. Lori Sue wasn't exactly sure how yet, but on matters of survival she trusted her instincts. Donna was an intelligent woman connected to Leo, a powerful figure. That made Lori Sue want to be on Donna's good side. And it would be easy. Lori Sue had seen her sadness and distress. Donna needed a friend, and Lori Sue needed influence.

The door guard wasn't a man she knew, and she wondered if he was from Joe's gang. He turned out to be easier than she had expected; after five minutes of flirting and hinting that he might get lucky soon, she was able to cajole him into letting her in. She made her way up the stairs to the fourth floor. At the door of Leo's suite, she took a deep breath and knocked firmly.

No answer.

She knocked louder. Still no answer, but she thought she heard a faint sound from inside, an odd, clinking sound, metallic, like steel nails dropped in a pile. She knocked louder and longer this time.

"Go away, Leo's not here," came a muffled reply.

"It's Lori Sue. We met a couple of weeks ago. I haven't seen you around and thought I would stop by."

"How did you find this apartment? What do you want?"

"You're with Leo." She hadn't quite known what word to use. "I know he lives here. I get to learn a lot talking with everyone. Can I come in?"

"What do you want?" Donna asked again.

"Just to visit. Maybe we can get a drink across the street. Have girl talk. Like I said before, we girls need to stick together."

"I can't go across the street."

"Why not? Look, rather than yell through the door, can you open it so we can talk?"

She heard the dead bolt retract. Donna opened the door a few inches. She was dressed in a light blue dressing gown. It was sheer enough to see through. She wore nothing underneath. "I can't go across the street," Donna repeated, looking Lori Sue in the eye. She then made a point of looking downward. Lori Sue followed her gaze. Donna had moved her left foot forward, and above it a metal cuff was locked around her ankle.

"He locks me up when he's gone for some time. I guess he doesn't fully trust me," Donna said. Her lips pressed shut, and she turned and walked back into the room, letting the door swing further open. A chain rattled along behind her. "Close the door and your jaw. You don't need to keep it hanging open."

Lori Sue came in and closed the door. The windows filled the room with afternoon light. She followed Donna into the kitchen.

"The chain allows me move from the bedroom to bathroom to kitchen, but it doesn't reach much into the living room," Donna said. Her voice was dull and flat, without emotion. "We'll sit in here." She sat down at the little table and pointed to Lori Sue to sit across from her. "If you want anything to drink, help yourself. Don't feel bad if I don't serve you. It's a pain to walk around like this."

Lori Sue didn't know what to say. "I'm sorry...what's going on? I thought you were his girlfriend?"

"You did?" Donna's face had a hard expression on it as she looked at Lori Sue. "Guess you're not much of a judge of character. You think I'd be that monster's girlfriend? That what you thought?" She shook her head. "I'm his possession now. He thinks he owns me. How does that strike you?"

Lori Sue just stared at Donna.

"I told you to get away when we first met. Remember? Get away from this block, from these men. You didn't listen. Stupid girl. You might wind up with an ankle bracelet like mine if you're not careful."

"I'm sorry...I didn't realize. I thought you were okay with being his—"

"His slave? Certainly not his girlfriend." Donna's face now looked sad.

"I didn't know." Lori Sue lowered her gaze. She wasn't sure what to say. It had all seemed so simple when she assumed Donna was a willing partner.

"Of course not. No one knows. No one wants to know. *He has my son.* That's how he controls me and gets me to do anything he wants." She leaned forward, her eyes now blazing with anger and hatred, "Anything...do you understand?"

Lori looked at her, her bravado gone. "I think so."

Donna turned away in her chair. She seemed to sag. The fire seemed to have left her and now she just looked defeated. "What do you want from me?"

"I...I wanted to be your friend...I mean I still want to be your friend. But, honestly, it was because I thought you had influence." Donna smiled sadly and shook her head. Lori Sue almost stopped there, but a thought came to her unbidden; one that scared her. It forced its way forward until she blurted it out. "But now I think you need me."

Donna jerked back around and stared at her in disbelief. "What kind of help can you give me? Are you going to change Leo? Make him let me go? Appeal to his finer instincts? He doesn't have any." She spat out the last words.

"What about your son? You said he has your son."

"He does. I get to see him occasionally, if Leo thinks I've been good." Suddenly her eyes reignited. A new fire burned in them, not one of hatred, but one of excitement, maybe even hope. "That's it! You can visit my son. Let him know how much I love him. Tell him that we're going to be together again, soon. You can check on him, make sure he's fine. Could you do that?"

Lori Sue nodded. "Where is he?"

"He's at the school. He stays there like the orphans do. Of course you have to be careful. Not arouse any suspicion. If Leo finds out, it won't be good for either of us." Donna locked her eyes on Lori Sue. "Are you up to it? If you want to help, that's what I need."

Lori Sue nodded again, gulping inwardly.

"Let me hear you say it. I want to hear you say you'll check up on Danny. His name is Danny. Say you'll help him."

"I'll help him."

Donna sat back. "That gives me some hope. Thank you."

This hadn't been what Lori Sue had set out to do. She'd been hoping to curry favor, get access to more resources; find an easier way to survive through a connection to one of the big guys—as big as any of the top militia officers, maybe the biggest guy she knew of outside of Joe Stansky or that director, Frank Mason. Now there was nothing in this situation for her except danger. What was she thinking?

Lori Sue knew the answer to that. She was thinking of the ankle shackle and chain.

She shuddered. "Look, I'll do what you said. But what about Danny's father? Do you have a husband?"

A curtain of sadness seemed to fall over Donna's face. Her voice was flat, without emotion. "He's dead. Leo had him killed."

Lori Sue thought about that for a moment, digesting the finality, the brutality implicit in that statement. Finally she came to a decision. "I can help another way, if you want."

"What's that?"

"I've got a gun. A pistol. I could sneak that to you. You know...to use, if you need it. If things get too bad for you."

"And have my son killed? No, that won't help."

"Still, maybe you should have it around. It might make you less afraid."

"I don't have any privacy. You see how I'm dressed. It's part of his routine, no privacy, no modesty allowed."

"Maybe you could hide the gun somewhere here in the kitchen. He makes you cook for him, right? I'll bet he don't do anything in the kitchen. I bet he never opens some of those cabinets."

Donna was silent for a moment. "That might work. But you have to bring it sometime when he's gone again. I can't get it from you on the street and bring it back, not if he's in the apartment. He'd...he'd know."

Lori Sue smiled. "I'll know when he's gone. I'll get it to you. I've got the door guard wrapped around my finger. I'll probably have to give him a tumble, but I'll get the run of the building." She felt a strange surge of energy running through her. Something like excitement. It felt good. "That bastard may get his due yet...treatin' us like this. We girls got to stick together."

When Lori Sue left, Donna sat at the kitchen table for a long time. After a while she put her head in her arms and began to sob, loud, harsh sobs. They shook her whole body. For the first time she felt the rebirth of hope, and with that rebirth came pain; the pain of her loss, the pain of her situation, her degradation. But, through the pain, the kernel of hope grew. Finally she began to smile, for the first time since she had been taken. *That girl*, she thought. Help could come from the most unlikely of places.

Chapter 23

It was fully dark when Charlie left the house, still weary from his trip to the farm valley. The route out to the water mill project was more difficult than usual, because he had the unaccustomed problem of having to avoid militia patrols. They posed no danger to him, but he didn't want anyone to get word of this nighttime excursion.

When he reached the mill, there was no one to be seen. The building was black against the stars. He did not call out. He just stood there in the dark, waiting. Finally he heard someone speak from behind. He thought he recognized the superintendent's voice.

"Don't turn around. Just keep looking forward like you are." Charlie did as he was told. He heard footsteps behind him. "I'm going to put a blindfold on you. I'll lead you so you won't stumble. We have to walk a little way."

"Remember, I'm not a threat to you. No one came with me."

"We'll be the judge of that. I'm talking to you because we confirmed you weren't being followed. Do what we say and you won't be harmed. And you'll get some information."

Charlie did not resist as a bandanna was tied tightly over his eyes. His arm was taken in a firm grip. The voice was low and tense. "If we're seen, I'll tell you and leave. Keep walking for ten steps and then take off the blindfold and hide it. You can explain yourself to the militia, can't you?"

"The police force never sleeps," Charlie said.

His companion led him at a good pace. They made many turns, and he lost track of direction after they had gone a little way. After ten minutes he heard a door open and he was jostled inside. They walked up stairs that turned and turned again. Finally, he heard a door open and they entered a different space; one that echoed a little. He was guided into position and pushed down onto a hard chair.

A different voice spoke. "Don't take the blindfold off. Just listen. You can ask questions later."

For the next ten minutes Charlie got an earful. He thought that there were at least five people in the room. They took turns speaking to him, their voices all hard, giving him terse, cold information that made him increasingly uncomfortable. They told him about other people disappearing, other families taken away. He didn't recognize the names. With each new description, they asked him if he knew about it. Each time he told them that he didn't. They told him about the doctor that had disappeared last year. Charlie had thought the man left to go to another town, but now he learned that he had been wrong. He was asked repeatedly why they weren't having any town meetings to elect officials, why the militia was still running things. At length, there was a pause. "You wanted to know about Jim Bishop," the voice that had first spoken to him after his arrival said.

"Yes."

"Jim Bishop is dead."

Charlie exhaled shakily.

"We don't have a lot of good sources within the militia or Joe's gang, but we're sure of that fact. We also know he was tortured during questioning. Maybe he died from that or was killed after. That no one knows." The voice now seemed very close to Charlie's face. "He was tortured, Chief Cook. You understand?" Charlie barely nodded his head. The voice paused. "We don't know how much he told them. Did he confirm there is a resistance group? How much detail did he give them? We're sure he told them something. He was part of our group so he knew what we know. We're now fewer by three. He's dead, and because of what was done to him, two others of our group have opted to leave us and go into hiding after they heard the militia had been asking around about them."

Charlie was silent.

"You know about Jim's wife, Donna?"

Charlie nodded.

"We figured that might be the reason you were nosing around, asking questions. Did you find out what's happened to her?"

"She's been taken as a prisoner. She was seen in the militia compound."

"You know who Leo Stupek is, don't you?"

"Yes."

"I figured you would. Joe and Leo tend to go together, don't they? But maybe you don't know Leo all that well. He's worse than Joe. And Donna Bishop is not being kept in any normal detention. Seems Leo has taken her for his personal woman, his personal captive. You understand what that means? You understand just what's going on in our nice little town?"

Charlie's body stiffened in shock.

"Maybe you didn't know. Do you know what Leo does?"

Charlie just sat there.

"That's not a rhetorical question. *Answer me.*"

Charlie started at the sharp command. "He's Joe's right-hand man. He runs Joe's gang."

"Partly right. You mean to tell us that's all you know about him?"

"I don't know...I don't know what you mean, what you're asking."

"He's playing stupid," another voice spoke out.

"I'm not. I don't know what you think I should know about Leo other than that."

"Let me educate you, Mr. Chief of Police," the first voice said. "When the militia was set up, you weren't directly involved. You just kept running the police department, right?"

Charlie nodded. "Frank was to organize the militia. It would be civilian run."

"But Frank needed help so he turned to Joe."

"He had the resources," Charlie replied. "But we told him it had to be separate from his group...his gang."

"Of course you did. But Joe had Leo doing most of the work, quietly, so you wouldn't notice. Maybe that was one of the things you didn't *want* to notice. Anyway, Leo pretty much runs the militia now, and from what we can tell, it's hardly different from his gang. There's a guy in charge that Frank talks to. But no matter what it may say in the City Hall paperwork, Leo's been nudging promotions and recruitment from the beginning. The head of the militia takes his *real* orders from Leo. And Leo takes his orders only from Joe."

"I...I...didn't know," was all Charlie could say.

"Apparently there's a lot you didn't know...or didn't want to know."

Charlie just sat there in the black. He had a knot in his gut, and his heart was hammering in his chest.

He had thought that he and Frank working with Joe, who had corralled most of the resources, would help the town stabilize. He had thought that, through Frank's control of the militia, they had maintained a balance of power with Joe. But that was just an illusion. The militia and Joe's gang were both led by Leo. Joe was turning the town into a criminal operation, and he and Frank were actually helping Joe do it.

While Charlie had been uncomfortable with Joe, he had felt that Joe's taking on the role of helping the town might make him a more upright citizen, that it might somehow reform him. Now that all seemed like a foolish rationalization. A wave of shame swept over him and he felt himself blushing. Joe was treating the town like an extension of his gang. You followed the rules. If you stepped out of line, discipline came swift and hard.

"You got anything to say?" a new voice asked.

"I'm digesting what you've just told me," Charlie replied.

"So you maintain this is all new to you?"

"Most of it. And the parts I knew about, I didn't think were indicative of something wrong." His explanation sounded lame, even to his own ears.

"It's easy for you to dismiss these events. You get to live pretty nice." The voice had a hard, rough edge to it.

"Things have to change," another man said. "We can't keep supporting the authorities. Joe's only going to get more powerful as people get more comfortable. And we're helping him accomplish that."

"What do you plan to do?" Charlie asked.

There was a silence. Then someone said, "We're not sure. But I'm afraid things may get worse before they get better."

"Are you talking about an uprising? Why not bring these issues...your demands up at a committee meeting. I could get you on the Safety Committee's agenda for one of our meetings."

A couple of men laughed in derision. "And within a week we'd disappear. That what you want? Haven't you even been listening? Who's on your committee anyway? You, Mason, and Stansky? Or does his muscle Leo sit in for him? That's a joke."

"I told you this was a waste of time. Now he knows about us. Maybe he shouldn't leave, 'cause if he rats us out we're dead."

"Hold on." Charlie recognized the voice of the superintendent. "I promised him safe passage. He hasn't seen any of you, and I'm the only one at risk."

Charlie sat in the dark, looking about even though he couldn't see through the blindfold. He suppressed an urge to rip it off. If he saw them, that would only give them more of a reason to kill him. He was beginning to sweat.

"Maybe I can start lobbying for better treatment for everyone," he said. "I could promote the idea that we don't need martial law anymore since things have calmed down."

"Good luck with that," one of the men said.

"You know Stansky runs things. I don't think Mason, or you, can control him," the voice that had spoken to him longest said.

"Well, we are the civic authority in town," Charlie began.

"You don't have any power. You buck Stansky and you'll be out of a job and out digging latrines...or worse. I'm guessing you don't want to do that. So you go along."

Charlie sucked in his breath. The town was heading towards becoming a criminal enterprise. If Joe continued, he'd just kill the opposition. He had the guns, the militia, and the resources that Hillsboro survived on. Soon he and Frank wouldn't be needed. How long were they going to last? If Roper left with his troops, it might be all over for the two of them. He had to take a chance—do something.

"I've got a small group of police that are loyal to me. They still believe in the duty and honor of police work, in keeping our town safe. I'm not without support."

"How's that going to help?"

"I just want you to know that I've got some backup. I'll start by trying to change the direction of where we're going. I hear you. It may not work, but I'm willing to try."

"But not so hard as to get yourself in trouble. Am I right?" one of the men said.

"I'll try, but..." Charlie stopped for a moment as he made a decision; one that meant danger, to him and to Mary. When he continued, his voice was soft but firm. "It won't do your cause any good for me to be kicked out of the inner circle. I'll help you. I'll help you stop Stansky, somehow. But I can help better from the inside than the outside."

The words hung in the air. The room was absolutely silent.

Mary's sleep-puffy face was ashen as she stared up at him. "Charlie. This is terrible. You're telling me that Jim was killed and Donna has been taken by that guy Leo? What for?"

Charlie sat on the edge of the bed by her side, fidgeting with his hands, trying to find ways to skirt the more sordid details of what he thought was taking place. Otherwise he told her everything, right up to where he had been led back to the mill and told to count to sixty before taking off his blindfold. They talked until sunrise. Mary was scared. So was Charlie. But they both felt they should not stand idly by while the city was being transformed into something they didn't recognize; a place in which they didn't want to live.

Chapter 24

Isend the three of you out there to locate the seeds and you come back with nothing. All you can tell me is the seeds ain't in Jason's barn. You didn't check the other farms?"

Leo sat quietly in a corner, away from Frank and Charlie where they sat in front of Joe's desk. Joe's reaction wasn't a surprise to Leo. He figured he would leave the talking to Frank, who usually filled in the silences almost by instinct.

"We drove all the way up the valley road before we left," Frank said. "Saw the other farms but didn't stop. We didn't want to tip our hand...you know, get too aggressive. We were specifically told not to wander around."

"Told 'not to wander around'?" Disdain dripped from Joe's voice. "Who the hell do you take orders from?"

Joe had only been getting angrier and angrier as Frank talked, and now he was pacing and chewing hard on his cigar. Frank stopped talking when Joe leaned over his desk, his eyes blazing, putting his face close to Frank. Beside him, Charlie's face had turned white.

"Leo," Joe said in a low, dangerous voice.

Leo straightened up in his chair. "Yeah, boss?"

"Did Frank here screw this up?"

Leo looked at Frank. Frank's eyes met his, almost pleading for his support.

"No, Frank did okay, Joe," Leo said calmly. "He's a smooth talker. Was even better than usual." Actually, he thought that Frank had stumbled when the topic of seeds had come up. Frank hadn't been very persuasive with his story. "The thing was," he said, "we couldn't blow the bigger job. They were nervous, cautious. Frank made his play, but they didn't bite. There was no way to do more snooping without making them more suspicious."

Leo didn't see any sense in sacrificing Frank. Getting at the seeds had been a long shot from the beginning. And Leo had other ideas about that.

Joe ran his hands through his hair. He shook his head in disgust. "It's time to put an end to this crap."

"Whaddaya got in mind?" Leo asked.

Joe didn't answer right away. He walked over to the window behind his desk and looked out on the city, taking a deep breath. "I worked hard to set this town up," he said, his back to them. "It's my town. I've made it safe to live here. We have food, we have resources, and we have a militia for defense." He turned back to his desk and brought his fist down on it with a crash. "I did this. Not you, not the engineers, not this guy Jason. If they get in my way, I'll crush them. I want the fertile seed and I don't want to have to deal with that independent son of a bitch to get it. He doesn't get to be the town's hero. "

Everyone was silent. Joe crossed the room restlessly, scowling.

"We could raid the valley when they're harvesting," Leo suggested. "Forget finding the hidden seeds. The grain would be there for the taking, before they grind it up. Later we'd have time to find the seeds."

Frank shook his head quickly. "That could interrupt our food supplies." Frank struggled to meet Joe's eyes. "Remember how tight things were last winter? We'll have another one like that."

Joe glared at him, still angry.

"We'd get pushback from the town," Charlie said. The chief sounded cautious.

"You two are like a goddamn broken record," Joe said in disgust. "Be nice, don't upset things. I'm damned tired of being nice." He paced back and forth.

"We need to play this out for a bit longer," Frank said. He put up a hand as Joe turned toward him. "Hear me out," he said. "If you attack the valley, you'll have to kill some of them. The army won't like it. Hell, Lieutenant Cameron and that girl are a couple. Let's get the army out of here first. Let me work on Roper. Once they're gone you'll have more freedom to act...to do what you want."

Joe stopped in the middle of the room. He nodded after a moment. "All right. You talk with Roper, but don't take too long."

Charlie spoke to Frank as they left Joe's building. "Are you willing to let Joe attack these people once Roper leaves? You know that's what'll happen."

"It looks like this group doesn't want to cooperate with us. Seems to me they want to hoard the seed and use it as leverage against us. You heard them."

"So that's a reason to attack them? Kill them?"

"They're bringing it on themselves." Frank was walking quickly, angrily. Charlie had to hurry to keep up. "Why should we care about them?"

"If that happens, where do we go from there? Frank, remember that engineer Joe told us he interrogated? I think Joe killed him. I can tell you his wife's been taken. Don't you see what's happening?"

"How do you know she's been taken? The whole family could have left town. Maybe they're afraid of getting caught trying to start an insurrection."

Charlie paused. Talking to Frank suddenly felt dangerous. Telling him about Danny and about Donna being Leo's personal prisoner now seemed like the wrong thing to do. There it was between them for the first time, a lump of distrust. He only said, "People don't padlock their door from the outside if they're leaving. And they don't ransack their own apartment. Bad things are going on, Frank."

Frank came to a sudden stop and grabbed Charlie by the arm. "What the hell have you been doing? Are you snooping around in Joe's business? You better be careful."

"It's the town's business. And it should be your business as well as mine. We were once elected to run and protect the town."

"Joe wouldn't like it if he thought you were going against him," Frank said. His tone had grown threatening.

"So you're going to knuckle under to whatever Joe and Leo come up with? Leo's a gangster, you know that. And Joe came out of that same background. He's Leo ten times bigger."

Frank didn't look away. After a moment, he said levelly, "I'm playing this out for my benefit...and for the town's. If I can keep Joe acting more like a proper citizen and less like a gangster, it'll be better for all of us. Look at what we've accomplished so far."

"It's the cost that bothers me. I'm seeing it more clearly now...the lack of concern for life, the willingness to eliminate people to get what you want. Frank, do you want to be a part of that?"

Frank just shook his head. "You're not hearing me. We're protecting the town and working to civilize Joe."

Charlie remembered the way Joe had looked at Frank upstairs. He shook his head. "I don't think it's going so well." He turned and started walking.

Frank caught up with him and grabbed his arm. Charlie didn't look at him. Frank's voice almost sounded pleading for a moment. "Just don't get on the wrong side of Joe. We've known each other for years, but I can't help you if you cross Joe."

Charlie didn't answer. They walked together in silence.

Chapter 25

This time there was a red mountain bike with lots of gears in the police bicycle room. Charlie smiled at his good fortune. He rode it over to the army's compound. With Colonel Stillman gone, the encampment was a shadow of its former size. It didn't take Charlie long to find Lieutenant Cameron in one of the storefronts being used as an office.

"I need to talk to you...if you have time," Charlie said. He motioned with his head to indicate that they go outside.

Cameron got up from his desk and led Charlie outside. They walked to the edge of the compound and sat down on a concrete barricade.

"This is not easy for me to say," Charlie began. "And I could be stirring up a hornet's nest, but I think you can be trusted...from what I've seen of you, from what others say. I hope I'm right."

The lieutenant looked at Charlie for a moment. Charlie couldn't read his expression.

"You can trust me, unless you're asking me to do something unlawful. Now tell me what's on your mind."

"I talked with some people. I can't tell you who they are. They're good people. At least I think they are." He paused for a moment. "They're people I think are telling me the truth. Anyway, I've got confirmation about some of the things they told me."

Cameron waited for him to continue.

Charlie struggled to get out what he wanted to say. "Lieutenant, people are getting killed...or disappearing. People who disagree with the authorities."

"You're the police chief. You're one of the authorities, aren't you?" Cameron's tone was cool, but there was a note of surprise in it.

"I'm starting to not to think so, to be honest." Charlie took a deep breath. "Anyway, to get to the point, there are a group of people, professionals and technicians, who want some reform, more freedom, maybe elections, an end to martial law. They're talking about resistance. Maybe an insurrection, maybe a strike. They're still trying to figure out what to do. I'm still not sure how many people are with them, but they exist." Charlie went on to describe his meeting with the group. "They confirmed that one of their members, an electrical engineer, was murdered and his wife was...taken. I found his kid in the school right where he's supposed to be, but I think there's something strange about that too. And the man's wife...she's been seen in the militia compound, and I've been told she's under Leo's control, Leo Stupek, you know him? God knows what's happening to her."

Cameron's eyes had darkened slightly at the mention of Leo. "That's a serious allegation—"

"Neither this engineer nor his wife are using their ration cards, and their apartment was padlocked and torn apart—thoroughly searched. That much isn't an allegation. I investigated it. Something bad happened to them. The next part is more disturbing."

"Yes?" the lieutenant said.

"Look, Frank...and Joe...and Leo..." Charlie exhaled, then said it quickly. "They're getting ready to raid the farms in that valley. To get their seed. It has to do with the valley having some special kind of seed. Joe doesn't want to have to keep trading, and he doesn't want to wait for them to start trusting him more. So they're just going to take it." Cameron's eyes narrowed. His face grew hard. Charlie rushed on. "Part of what they're waiting for is you. They want to wait until you're gone. Frank's going to work on Captain Roper, get him to leave."

"How long have you known about this?" Cameron asked.

"Just since yesterday." Charlie looked down at the ground. "But I've known Roper's been covering for Joe with Colonel Stillman nearly from the start. Joe's been paying him off. In gold and jewelry."

Suddenly Cameron grabbed him by his collar and jerked him to his feet. "And you knew this all along?" Cameron's voice was sharp with anger.

"From the start," Charlie said with resignation. "We didn't want the army interfering with what we'd accomplished in town. It didn't seem to cause any harm..." He cut himself off and forced himself to meet Cameron's furious gaze. "I understand your anger. But hitting me won't help. I think I've been on the wrong side of things and now I want to do what's right."

"You're a two-faced, deceitful crook. And Mason's in on this as well?"

Charlie nodded. "Yes. Maybe more in than I thought." He swallowed and wondered how to explain. "We were both trying to work with Joe for the benefit of the town. But Joe's going too far. Yesterday I expressed my concern about what Joe is doing and all Frank did was warn me to be careful. It sounded wrong."

Cameron let go of Charlie. The young soldier's voice was cold as ice. "If anything happens to Jason and his family, I'll personally see you hanged...or shot."

"I want to help, if you'll let me. I'm still on the inside. The others, the group that's talking about resistance, don't think I can help, but I have access to information. They also think your numbers are too small to stand against Stansky."

Charlie looked Cameron in the eye. "And they're more right than they know. If it comes down to an open challenge with Stansky, the army will lose. If what these civilians tell me is right, the Hillsboro militia is under Leo's control, so it's all Joe's.

"You know he's stockpiled weapons, don't you? You'd be shocked by how many weapons he has. Joe's got a lot of firepower. I'm just a cop. And I've only got twenty men and women loyal to me in the force. Stansky's corrupted the rest."

Cameron sat back down on the concrete barrier. He looked out at the city, but Charlie could tell he wasn't seeing the buildings. He didn't look alarmed or enraged. His face was serious but calm, like he was figuring out what his first step should be.

"I need to think," Cameron said at last.

"Don't speak a word of this to Captain Roper. That would get back—"

"I understand you, Chief." Cameron stood. He looked at Charlie. Charlie saw cold steel and pain in his eyes. He didn't look very young now. "I have some people who I can trust as well. We'll talk again."

Cameron did not say goodbye. He simply turned and walked briskly back toward his office. Charlie guessed that Cameron would soon be conferring with his sergeant. The training manual probably didn't cover something like this.

Charlie Cook straightened his uniform and went to unlock his bicycle. He paused. *I might as well take a loop through the south side on the way back*, he thought. He mounted the bike, wobbled for a moment, and then he pedaled into the street and turned left, a policeman in his city.

Chapter 26

The Humvee pulled up to the farmhouse. A shock of excitement ran through Catherine as she saw the vehicle outside the kitchen window. Kevin, Rodney Gibbs, and Tommy Wilkes stepped out. She burst out of the door and jumped onto Kevin as he was walking towards the front steps, wrapping her arms around him. He smiled and blushed as he hugged her back.

"Looks like someone's glad to see you," Gibbs remarked.

"What are you doing here?" Catherine asked as she released her fiancé. "I didn't think you were coming for another month."

"Something's come up and I need to talk with Jason. I think the valley may be in danger."

Jason came out and greeted everyone. "Come, sit down. We're having dinner soon, you can join us."

"That does sound good, Jason, thank you."

"How did you get permission for the trip?" Jason asked.

"Remember, I'm still assigned to help the valley become more productive. So I ginned up an excuse to visit. I talked about getting an update from you on how the new planting is coming and also said I needed to check in and warn you of some outlaw activity reported around Hickory."

"But we aren't anywhere near Hickory," Catherine said.

"Yeah, but I'm being cautious. You never know how trouble like that can spread, and Captain Roper knows I have to protect the valley." He winked at her.

Gibbs, Tommy, and Jason had already taken places around the porch table, and Sarah had come out from the house and grabbed a seat next to Tommy. Kevin took the last chair, and Catherine sat on the rail next to him. Kevin began to talk. After a while, Anne called them in to eat.

After the meal, they went back out on the porch to capture the last of the evening.

"We're in a difficult spot," Kevin said. "Joe's got the militia under his control and with the weapons he's collected, we're outgunned as well as outmanned. And we can't rely on Captain Roper. I'm not sure what we can do."

Jason's voice was low and thoughtful. "It looks like the valley will have to rely on ourselves. We've done it before."

Anne thought about the battle with Big Jacks. "But this time we won't know when they're coming. That makes it difficult."

"They won't try to raid the valley before the army leaves," Kevin said.

Catherine grabbed his forearm. "If Frank Mason convinces Captain Roper to leave, then you'll be gone and we'll be alone, on our own, when they attack. What will happen to us?"

Kevin put his hand over hers. "I don't know, but I'm going to help."

At the edge of her vision she saw Rodney Gibbs turn his head and look at her fiancé for a long time.

The group talked late into the night. Finally Gibbs and Wilkes excused themselves and went to put up small, single-person tents in the dark yard. Jason and Anne excused themselves too and went inside, taking a reluctant Sarah along with them. Catherine and Kevin lingered on the porch, holding each other in their arms.

They had been silent for a long time. Suddenly Kevin spoke. "We can talk about our future tomorrow," he said. "I know I don't want to be without you. We're going to get married no matter what gets thrown at us."

Catherine looked at the man she had fallen in love with. She knew he was an honorable person, without guile, not really able to hide his feelings, at least from her. But there was something he was holding back from her.

"I'm going to wake you up before dawn," she told him. "I want to show you a special place. We can talk there...before the others get up. There'll be much the group has to talk about, but we need to have our own conversation." She kissed him long and hard and went inside.

In the predawn darkness, Catherine packed a small satchel and quietly went out to Kevin's tent. She gently shook it. "Wake up. Let's go," she whispered.

A few seconds later Kevin crawled out, yawned, and stretched. He reached back inside and grabbed his boots and put them on. As he got to his feet, he froze as a dry whisper came from the tent next to his. "Don't worry, Lieutenant, we're sound asleep. You won't wake us." Kevin silently swore. Catherine grinned.

"Follow me," she said, and led him towards the forest slope. Within moments they had entered the trees. Catherine weaved her way easily through the dark woods, avoiding the brambles and thickets without effort, finding the game trails that led them around the thicker parts of the forest. Kevin crunched and stumbled his way behind her, often getting snagged in spots where Catherine had just slipped through.

Partway up the slope she stopped. Kevin stood behind her, breathing hard.

"You're not very quiet in the woods," she remarked.

She waited as he caught his breath. "I guess I haven't had as much practice as you have. How do you see where you're going?"

"I know this part of the forest well. That helps. But I've also learned to recognize where the game moves. The deer don't like bashing through brambles or wild rose thickets any more than we do, so they go around and wind up making paths around those parts."

"I didn't see any signs of trails, certainly not in this darkness."

"They're not that obvious." She looked at the sky. "It's getting lighter. Already not as dark as it was a few hours ago. Come on, we're almost there. It's my favorite spot." She set off again with Kevin hurrying to keep up.

It was ten minutes later when Catherine led him into the secluded copse. They sank to the ground. Catherine pulled a metal canteen from her satchel. They both took a long, refreshing drink and quietly watched the dark fade, huddling in each other's arms to ward off the early morning chill. The sun had yet to break over the ridge to the east. For now the light advanced slowly.

"No one knows about this place but me," Catherine said softly. "You can't be seen from the farm and you have a beautiful view of the valley. It's not as dramatic as further up on the ridge, but that's a longer hike."

She rested her head against Kevin's chest. Their breathing began to synchronize.

"What's going to happen to us?" she said. "I didn't think you'd be going away. I guess I was naïve, thinking you'd be around forever. But you have to go sometime...since you're in the Army."

"I confess I didn't think about it either. I just knew that I wanted to share a life with you, that I wanted to be with you forever."

Catherine pulled back and looked Kevin in the eye. "I'll go with you, wherever you're sent. That's what army wives do, don't they?"

"You'd leave this valley? This beautiful place? The place you fought to defend?"

"If there's not going to be an attack. If we can keep that from happening, I would leave. It would be only a lonely place to me without you. I love it here, but I love you more. You and I have a future together. I don't have a future here without you."

They held each other and were silent.

Finally Kevin took a deep breath. "I'm not going with the Army," he said.

Catherine looked at him, stunned.

"If Roper gives in to Mason's demands to leave, he'll have proven himself corrupt. I can't...won't follow a corrupt officer. I'll call him out and let him drum me out of the ranks. I'll resign my commission if necessary. I'm staying. I'm in this fight with you...to save the valley, and maybe to save Hillsboro."

"Kevin!" Catherine almost shouted as she hugged him so hard it took his breath away. They lay back among the rocks, ignoring them, and just held each other tight.

"Can Captain Roper put you in jail?" she said after a moment.

"I don't know...but I don't think so. The Army has been too busy, dealing with the emergency to change the rules. Legally I should be able to retire. Stillman would still think that way, though he'd certainly try to talk me out of it first. And..." She heard him sigh in the dimness. "I can't imagine that locking me up is what Roper would want. He just wants to...not deal with the issues. I don't know what his game is, but I'm not interested. I've got you and I'm here. Your fight is my fight."

"It very well *could* be a fight, you know."

"I know. But it's time to take a stand. I've kind of ignored this as well. I was thinking about how successful Hillsboro was and how the army was helping it get back on its feet. I didn't see how bad things have gotten. Now they're threatening you...and your family, and the valley. Now it's become much more personal."

They were both silent, thinking about what might be coming: the danger, the fighting, fear for their loved ones, the killing again. Catherine thought about what Kevin had said over dinner about Joe Stansky. He was a dangerous enemy to have, she thought. He had the men and the arms, and he would have no reluctance about using them to get his way.

"Why do you think Stansky wants to attack us? Is it really over the seed? We told him we'll share it."

Kevin gave her a questioning look. "Is that the message you've been sending? That you'd share?"

She was stung. "Well not right away but we didn't know he'd go crazy!"

He kissed her gently. "If I had to guess, I don't think it made much of a difference." Kevin shook his head. "It's not just the seeds. He has power and wants to keep it. We don't know what's coming...none of us do. But Joe wants to be in control. I think he's afraid of the valley, Jason...and the others." Catherine gaped at him. "Don't look so surprised. You represent freedom, self-sufficiency.

"It's just because the stories got blown up out of proportion."

"No, it was more than that. And I think Joe recognizes it. Jason, your family and the rest of the valley could represent a rallying point for a revolt in the city, for people insisting on true representation and honest government, an end to martial law."

"And that would threaten his hold on power?"

"That could end it. Joe can't have that happen. When or if the national government shows up, he wants to be the man in charge, the most powerful man in the region. That could be a good thing if some corrupt form of a regional strongman were to arrive on the scene. But Joe is actually becoming that corrupt regional strongman. If he's not checked, he's going to set up a dictatorship."

"Kind of like a mob family structure," Catherine said. Kevin looked surprised. "I watched some shows about the Mafia before the power went out. They're organized like an extended family. One you can't leave or rebel against. This seems to be the same thing."

"You may have it exactly right."

As Kevin spoke, he suddenly glanced up. The sun burst over the ridge, lighting up the valley like someone turning on massive floodlights. The birds in the woods had begun to sing in the last few minutes, and now they exploded in a riot of happiness, as if welcoming the new day.

Catherine laughed at Kevin's astonishment. "It comes rather suddenly here," she said. "Let's go back. People will be getting up and looking for us."

Kevin kissed her. They both felt the energy of attraction surging through them.

"Let's get married as soon as we can," Catherine said as they stopped for breath. "Even before this battle or whatever is going to occur takes place. I want you and I don't want to wait. Who knows what will happen."

"I can arrange it with a minister in town. Considering Captain Roper's involvement with Stansky, I don't want him marrying us."

"Absolutely not." She released him and stood, hoisting the strap of the satchel back over her shoulder. "Do you think you can move more quietly on the way back?" she asked mischievously.

"I'm in the Army. We're all about shooting and breaking things."

"Well, you're going to need to know about stealth as well, so better start practicing."

With that she took off through the woods. Behind her she heard the rustling of brush and the snapping of twigs as her fiancé scrambled to try to keep up with her.

Over a breakfast of fried pork, berries, and greens, Kevin made his announcement.

"I don't know what Captain Roper will do when Frank Mason meets with him, but I've decided I'm staying. I won't leave, even if it means resigning my commission and leaving the army."

Everyone except Catherine looked at him in surprise.

"You're sure about that decision?" Jason asked.

Kevin nodded. "I'm sure."

"Well, you'll still have to go back to town. You can't just park yourself here, so we'll still have to be prepared to fight on our own," Jason said.

"You're right," Kevin said, "We can't stay here in the valley." He looked at Catherine with pain in his eyes as he spoke. "Captain Roper will expect us back. And I can't affect anything if I'm not in Hillsboro. I need to still try to head this off, have the platoon staying in Hillsboro and doing its job. Somehow."

He looked at Rodney Gibbs next to him. The sergeant was looking pensively at his empty plate.

"What about you?" Kevin asked. "How do you feel about all of this? You're not involved the way I am."

"I didn't sleep much last night." Rodney gave him a wry grin. "Really, not much since you told me about Captain Roper's involvement with Stansky and the others. I feel the same as you about Captain Roper."

"But what'll you do if he decides to move out? There's a pretty good chance he'll work something out with Mason and leave," Kevin said.

Rodney paused for a moment. "I said, when we decided to work on the farming project, that we can do some good here. Seems to me we haven't finished that work, so I'm thinking I'll probably stay. When things are better here, maybe I'll go and try to find my family, who knows?"

"This could be dangerous...for both of us. Especially if Roper decides to take action rather than give us his permission to stay."

"Yeah. I thought about that as well. Just have to see how it plays out." Gibbs stood up and stretched. "I don't have much appetite to follow someone who will cut and run."

Kevin broke into a broad grin, jumped up and clapped Rodney on the back. "I'm glad you're in this with me. Besides, I doubt we'll be seeing any retirement benefits anytime soon."

"We should let the others know what's going on before you leave," Jason said.

After the group made their way around the valley to inform the farmers of the danger approaching, they came back to Jason and Anne's farmhouse. They were all standing around on the porch; Anne went inside to get some water for everyone. When she came out, Catherine announced that she was going back to Hillsboro with Kevin.

"Why do you want to do that?" Anne asked, stopping in her tracks. She held a tray full of glasses in her hands. "You could be putting yourself in danger if what we know about Stansky is correct."

"I know, but Kevin and I are going to be married. Now, if we can. We're going to find a preacher."

"You can't get married in town, without your family," Anne protested as she set the tray down on the table.

"Don't worry, Mom. I'm going to try to bring the preacher back here. Kevin and I have decided we're going to get married, sooner rather than later. It may be weeks before Frank Mason can get Captain Roper to leave, if ever. We don't know what will take place after that, but it doesn't look good, so we want to get married now, before anything bad can happen."

"But we haven't made any arrangements. We haven't planned anything yet. I thought you'd get married at the end of the summer, when the harvest is in and we go back to town," Anne said.

"I know, Mom. But things are different now. We don't know what's going to happen between now and then."

"But a ceremony, food, location, how will we arrange all of that?"

"Do I still get to be the bridesmaid?" Sarah asked.

"Yes, you do," Catherine said, smiling. Turning back to her mother, she said with finality, "I'll go back with Kevin. We'll find a preacher and we'll arrange to bring him back here. We'll have the wedding in our front yard."

The front yard. The place where Jason had introduced himself to her mom over two years ago; the place of so much fighting and bloodshed; the place where Jason had defended her family from attackers, and where, later, the whole family had fought the raiding party from Big Jacks's gang. It had seen so much, and now it would become the spot for a nuptial ceremony, where two people would join together to begin life as a couple in a new reality.

Jason put his arm around Anne. "It's all right. I think they've made a wise decision. And we can get married as well. What do you say? A double wedding?"

Anne smiled. "That would be nice. I guess Sarah and I can inform the others and make arrangements."

Chapter 27

A few days later Jason set out through the woods. He was heading to Linville Falls to find the clan's encampment. Clayton had told him to look for a box attached to a tree near the falls where he could put a note. But Jason didn't want to leave a message; he wanted to talk to Clayton right away.

The going was rough at times, but he followed game trails wherever he could. The journey reminded Jason of his initial trek into the mountains after the EMP attack. In those early days he had been so awkward in the woods, not understanding how to navigate the wilderness, how to adjust to it instead of fighting it. Now he moved more easily and comfortably. He realized how much he had learned since leaving Hillsboro. He had become a man of the woods.

By late afternoon when he got close, he could hear the sound of the water and was able to follow his ears to the falls. On arriving, he sought out a tall tree by the river and climbed it. He scanned the forest. The camp could not be far off, not if the message box was regularly checked. Hopefully a cooking fire would be lit soon, giving him a bearing on the camp.

After a half hour of scanning, he saw smoke start to rise about a mile west of the falls. He got a fix on the direction and climbed down.

In the rough terrain, it took him almost an hour to reach the camp. Just as he was beginning to think that he had passed his objective, he stepped into a clearing and saw armed men approaching with their rifles trained on him. Behind them was a mass of tents. Jason put his hands in the air.

"I'm here to see Clayton Jessup. Is he around?"

One of the men whispered something to another who took off. The others kept their rifles pointed at Jason. It wasn't long before he saw Clayton approaching.

"What you doing here?" he asked coming up to Jason. They shook hands. He turned back to the men, "It's all right. This be Jason, the man from the valley I told you about."

"I've got to talk with you and didn't want to leave a message and wait days for a reply."

"How'd you find us?"

"Got to Linville Falls, climbed a tree and watched. I hoped I'd see smoke from a campfire since it was getting near eating time."

Clayton shook his head. "Not much we can do about fire smoke. Got to cook food." He looked around. "But I got to check on guards. You walked right in."

"I did, but I was probably quieter than most. You'd probably hear others, if there was a group and they weren't used to moving through the woods."

"Still, don't pay to be lazy. Too much to go wrong if we let our guard down."

The encampment was in a clearing about the size of a football field, irregular in shape, bending to the right as he looked at it with a dense cover of trees along its rough edge. He was surprised that he had not seen it sooner, but realized that the tall trees of the forest provided an effective screening. There were about thirty tents on platforms arranged around a central open space. At the center of the camp there was a large fire pit and logs for benches, next to a rough-hewn, windowless cabin which Jason guessed held the group's communal supplies. Numerous smaller cooking set-ups were scattered among the tents, with brackets to hold roasting spits or cook pots. Interspersed around the tents were garden plots, carefully netted to protect the vegetables from deer and smaller animals.

"So what do you want to talk about?"

"I've come to ask for your help," Jason said. For your people's help. We've got some trouble with Hillsboro."

"Trouble? What kind?"

"We've learned they're thinking of raiding us. Stansky and his gang. For our non-hybrid seed. They seem to want us out of the picture. We don't know when, but it may be very soon."

"You want us to help defend the valley? That could cost men, husbands of wives, fathers of children. Why should we do this?" Clayton looked straight at Jason.

"An honest question. There's more reason to help than just being friends with us."

Clayton took Jason's arm. "First we get something to eat and drink. Then we talk."

They walked over to a tent where Clayton introduced Jason to his wife, Lizbeth, and his two sons, Henry and Morgan. After introductions, they sat down on stools, except for Lizbeth who picked up a galvanized bucket and left them. She returned almost immediately, steam trailing from the bucket. After setting it down, she brought out a ladle from the tent along with spoons and bowls of wood and pottery. Clayton ladled the rich brown liquid into the largest bowl and handed it to Jason.

"Stewpot don't get emptied, unless we can't find game. Some months we got to go far to find game, others it's close by," Clayton said.

The stew was tasty, but Jason couldn't identify what was in it. He guessed that it had probably started out as a rabbit stew and had changed as different animals and greens were added over time.

When they were done, the two men sat on the ground cloth with their backs against a log while Lizbeth and the boys wiped out the bowls and then rinsed them with water sparingly poured from a jug next to the tent. Clayton sat quietly, looking across the camp. Jason realized that the man was politely waiting for him to explain the problem further.

He cleared his throat and began. "First, we need your help because the guy who runs the town, Joe Stansky, can bring a lot of men against us. He also knows what happened to Big Jacks's gang, so they'll be prepared. We won't be able to surprise them. Second, if we can defeat them, we can drive Stansky out of the city. The people in town will work with us as partners. We'll have more open trade. Both groups, city people and all of us outside the city, will prosper."

Clayton listened carefully, his face thoughtful. Finally he spoke. "Seems like a high price to pay for easier trading. We doing okay now on our own."

"You could be doing better." Jason looked over the camp. "This is a comfortable enough camp, but it's still camping. You got kids, you need schools for them. And other groups are going to be coming around. Other militias...or the government. They'll find you eventually. If you start raiding towns, you'll be considered outlaws. Who knows what that will bring? Here's a chance to take down a gangster and partner with a town. This could be the start of a strong regional organization that could end lawlessness in our area."

"You mean join other towns too?"

Jason nodded.

"We country folk. We don't care to live in town."

"Look, before the EMP attack you lived in the country, on small farms. There may have been federal aid, but you had to work at growing food, hunting, trapping, and you used the towns to buy what you couldn't get by yourselves."

Clayton gave him a sharp look at the mention of federal aid. "We don't take money from the government," he said with pride. "Now the towns don't have anything and there ain't no government. Looks like the tables turned to me."

Jason had to agree. Still he pressed his point. "Maybe they don't have as many things you need, but that doesn't mean the two groups shouldn't work together. It's the way it's always been done. The towns are going to get electricity going again. They're working on getting machines running, farming machines that will make it easier to plant and harvest crops. They're working to improve medicine, maybe even making anesthetics."

Clayton just shook his head.

"Look," Jason said. "The population has been reduced, you know that. So many people have died, both in the city and the countryside. Think about this." He looked intently at Clayton. "There are many good farms, productive farms, just sitting idle. They're south of here, close to Hillsboro. Your people could move onto them. They've got houses, barns, farm equipment, all waiting to be put to use. Wouldn't that be a better life than here in the woods?"

Clayton looked at him. There was a hint of interest in his eyes.

Jason went on. "I know you love the woods. The woods are there as well, not as wild or remote as up here. You wouldn't be giving up the woods so much as adding farming back into what you do, how you live." He paused to let that sink in. "Don't tell me you wouldn't like having good farm land. Your ancestors came to these mountains for new opportunities. They came for good land. Over the generations you lost the best of the land and were pushed further into the hills. In the recent past you farmed what you had, what was passed down to you. Well, now you can give your people better land to farm. Land to prosper on."

Clayton looked at the ground, deep in thought.

Jason continued, "The country is going to remake itself. I don't know how that will work out, but it seems to me you have the opportunity to advance your position, to make something good out of this disaster."

He fell silent. He had made his pitch. Altruism might not work, but he hoped self-interest would. It had grown dark while he and Clayton had been talking. Some of the older men had quietly gathered around them, intent, listening to all that was said.

After a long silence, Clayton spoke. "I talk with the others. You rest." He pointed at a lean-to shelter to the left of his tent. Jason saw Lizbeth standing up from where she had been making up a makeshift bed. "We talk about what you said. Give you an answer in the morning."

A sense of fatigue flowed over Jason. The exertion of the hike, the stress, the threat to his family's happiness and security began to overwhelm him. He nodded and headed to the shelter. As he lay down on the pallet, his body began to relax. The murmur of the men's voices came to him in the dark; the words unrecognizable, just a background sound as he drifted off to sleep.

In the morning Jason awoke to the sounds of people stirring, fires being re-lit, pots being jostled as they were set over the fires. He got up and stretched in the cool air. Clayton motioned for Jason to join him. He was sitting in front of his tent on a stool.

"We can help you. Everyone says moving to good farmland is a smart thing to do. Can't do that with someone like Stansky in the area. What you need?"

Jason smiled. He held out his hand, but Clayton didn't move. "'Fore we shake on a deal, what do you want from us?"

"I need a fighting group. I know you'll need some men to stay back to protect the others here, but I need as many fighters as you can spare."

Clayton thought for a moment. "We talked about that. We can send twenty men. All got rifles, not many pistols, but pistols won't be much good. What you want us to do?"

"Your men will help guard the valley. If or when Stansky tries to raid us, you'll be the defense at the bridge, just like the last time. If we can defeat his raiding party, then we head to town."

"You want us to go to Hillsboro? Fight there as well?"

"That's your choice, but it will take defeating Stansky back in town to make those farms safe for your people."

Clayton looked Jason in the eye. "You always been straight. You want to make things better. You fight hard." He paused for a moment, then stuck out his hand. "We in."

Chapter 28

Jason went with Catherine and the soldiers back to Hillsboro. As soon as they arrived, she and Kevin went to police headquarters and went through a directory of churches in town. Kevin wrote down the addresses and they left to find a minister. With the dangers confronting them, they both felt the press of time, but they wanted to complete this task before events intervened and disrupted their plans. Catherine was almost bubbling over with excitement at this first concrete step in their wedding plans.

Most of the churches were empty with clergy working at the food centers or the hospital, often counseling people who were feeling overwhelmed. Like others in the city, the clergy were under the strict control of martial law.

After visiting three churches, they found an older minister who was in his church. He was frail looking, slightly stooped with a shock of white hair on his head. He agreed to marry them after some discussion.

"It's pretty irregular to perform a wedding with strangers, especially strangers without much church connection. I'm not a justice of the peace and this wouldn't be a civil ceremony. It would be a church wedding." He leaned forward. "Do you understand that? It's a sacrament of the Christian faith, not to be taken lightly."

Catherine felt some alarm as she looked at him. "I'm sorry I'm not a regular church member, but these are pretty irregular times. The one minister that might know me is gone. Who knows where? There's no one left alive in Clifton Forge."

Pastor Randolph winced at her comment.

"We do live in difficult times," he said. There's a noticeable lack of support for churches these days. You'd think people would be flocking to us in these times, but I'm not seeing it." He paused to reflect. "And those in charge don't seem to want to encourage church attendance."

He seemed to come to a decision. "Okay, I'll do the wedding. I appreciate your desire to have it in a church rather than go to your commanding officer or city hall. When do you want this wedding?"

"Well, we're not sure," Catherine said. The pastor gave her a puzzled look. "There are a number of things happening right now and we don't know how they'll play out. We think we can be ready in about a week, but we can't give you a firm date yet."

"That's a bit odd. I'm not going anywhere, so let me know when you're ready. But give me a couple of days' notice." He stood up. "And I can't do it on Sunday, I have services. I'm trying to grow a congregation again, even without help from the city."

Catherine and Kevin walked out of the office. She felt a joyful spring in her step as they left the church. She put her arm through Kevin's as they walked.

"That went well, don't you think?" she asked.

"Yes." He smiled at her. "When are you planning to tell him we want to be married in the valley?"

"We'll let him know later. I didn't want to hit him with everything at once." She gave Kevin a smile and leaned her head against him. "We have us a preacher."

Looking up at Kevin, she couldn't help but notice that his smile had faded. There was a serious look in his face.

"Why so glum, then?"

"Not glum, just concerned about how these other events will turn out, that's all."

That night, when it was fully dark, Kevin and Jason left his office and went to the rows of parked vehicles. Wilkes and Gibbs were already waiting beside a turreted Humvee Kevin had chosen. They all got in, with Wilkes standing up through the hatch to man the machine gun. Kevin pulled out of the compound and drove out into the silent town. If they were seen by the militia, they would look like a normal night patrol.

"I hope Chief Cook can help us," Jason said. "We know the best plan would be to just avoid this attack, but can he change Stansky's mind?"

"It's a long shot," Kevin replied. "I don't think he really has Joe's ear. Frank might have more of a chance, but I don't think we can ask him. Not if what Charlie told me is half right."

"Captain Roper can't be willing to go along with this," Jason said. "Even if he's getting paid on the side somehow, he's not going to be a part of attacking civilians...is he?"

"I could go to Captain Roper," Kevin said. "But it's the same problem as Frank. I don't know how far he's in. I only know he's in. It may only alert Stansky that we're on to him. If Stansky guesses right, it could even have repercussions for Charlie."

Wilkes's faint voice came down from the turret. "I wouldn't worry about Chief Cook. Seems to me he got his conscience back a little late. I'd let him deal with the repercussions."

Kevin looked back at Gibbs. Gibbs raised his voice. "What you don't realize is that the *repercussions* could take Cook out of the game and we lose an important ally. Man your gun and pay attention to keeping a lookout."

"Yes sir."

"Not wrong though," Gibbs said under his breath.

They arrived at Charlie's home without incident. There was a driveway that went past the house towards a garage set to the rear. Kevin drove all the way back before he stopped. They piled out and started for the front door when Kevin saw a man holding a candle standing where the back door must be. Charlie had a quizzical look on his face, but he quickly let them in without a word.

There was a pale-looking woman in a nightgown in the kitchen with Charlie. "This is my wife, Mary," Charlie said. They all introduced themselves, and she nodded with a nervous politeness. "It's all right," Charlie said. "She knows everything."

Charlie led them into the dark dining room, where he used the candle he was carrying to light a bigger one standing in the center of the table. He motioned for them to sit, and they found places.

"Charlie, I know you told me about the plans to attack the valley, but I want to hear you tell all of us which side you're on now," Kevin said.

Charlie looked embarrassed. Mary sat next to him with her hand in his, looking at him. "I'm with you," he said. "I... Mary and I will not be a part of what's going on. I'm not proud of the fact that I turned a blind eye to so much, in order to make life easier for us." He was looking down at the table. Raising his head, he continued, "Stansky's going too far. Martial law is one thing, we had to establish control. But attacking civilians is another. He went too far when he killed Jim Bishop." He shook his head as if to clear his mind of the thought. "Lord knows if it's happened to others. I could have kept a closer eye on what was going on, but I was focused on working with Joe. We thought we had to—"

"I'm not looking for a confession. I just want you to be clear, in front of the others, where you stand."

Charlie nodded. "I'm with you," he said again.

"Now, we need your help to get us in touch with this resistance group," Kevin said.

"Are you going to start a revolt?" Charlie asked.

"Maybe, maybe not," Kevin replied.

"Chief Cook, we want to try every possible way to avoid that, but we need to be ready for a fight if we can't negotiate something with Mason and Stansky," Jason said.

"You can call me Charlie. I don't feel much like a chief of police right now," he said. Mary squeezed his hand. "All right, I'll get a message to the group recommending that they set up a meeting with you directly."

"Sergeant Gibbs will also be at the meeting," Kevin said. "He'll be another point of contact for them."

"Sergeant Gibbs. I'll tell them."

"Charlie, do you think you can find someone here in town?" Jason asked.

"Maybe. Who do you want to find?"

"Well, I have an idea...thinking about all the help we can get. Billy Turner, he's from the valley, he came to town after the trading day. He's a hunter for the town, I think, and maybe helping to make whiskey."

Kevin looked over at Jason. "Why find him?"

"He may be able to help."

"He also could be on the side of the gang," Kevin said.

"If I could talk to him, maybe in the context of inviting him to Catherine's wedding, I could sound him out to see if he could or would help."

"I don't know," Kevin replied.

Gibbs spoke up. "You said he was hunting for the city, so he's working for them. Have you heard back from him since he left?"

"No way to."

"So how do you know he's a hunter? He could be in the militia."

"No, he told me he had it lined up. He talked to Goodman during the trade, and Goodman made him an offer."

Gibb's face was grim in the candlelight as he looked at Jason. "Goodman could have been thinking about food, but it's not reassuring. The lieutenant's right. If Billy's on the side of the gang, he could expose our plans."

"I know. I'm not going to reveal anything unless I can determine which side he's on. I'm betting he has some loyalty to the valley, even though he left it."

Kevin's feelings mirrored Gibb's doubtful expression. "Okay, but be careful about this," he said.

Jason turned back to the police chief. "So, can you find him?"

"If he came after the trading, like you said, he shouldn't be too hard to find. I'll work on it."

"I need you to hurry. I can only stay here for a few more days."

Chapter 29

The next morning Charlie sent Les Hammond out to find Billy. It didn't take Hammond long to find the apartment building where Billy had been assigned a room. The problem was that Billy's room was completely empty, with the door ajar. Asking around didn't get Hammond much information. Few of the militia would even stop to talk with him. It wasn't clear what happened to the kid or where he might have gone. People who dropped out of sight like Billy often never surfaced again.

That first day Hammond reported back to Charlie around one o'clock. After hearing Hammond's report, Charlie sent him back to the militia compound to learn more. Someone had to have seen Billy. He was a hunter; he had to be bringing game to the food centers.

That afternoon, Hammond talked with the bartender at the militia bar. The bartender had heard that Billy had taken up with a prostitute named Lori Sue. It seemed that Billy had killed someone who was trying to rape her. The timing of the incident matched a corpse Hammond and Charlie remembered from a couple of weeks back. The problem was that no one knew where Lori Sue lived; she didn't stay anywhere near the compound.

Hammond went over what he had found with Charlie that evening. "I could hang around the militia bar. The bartender says she often shows up there. I could talk to her...you know, get her to take us to Billy."

"I don't think that's a good idea. She'll be suspicious. I doubt she'll believe Billy's not in trouble. Remember, he killed a man in town, and we're the police. She'd probably lie to us and get Billy to move so we'll never find him."

"What do we do, then?"

"You hang out there—out of uniform. When she shows up, follow her home. We need to know where she's staying. I'm betting Billy'll be there." Charlie paused for a moment. "You think you can do it?" he asked. "It isn't going to be like sitting in a squad car down the block. You'll have to blend in on the street."

"I can do this, Chief," Hammond said with a smile on his face. "Like being a detective."

The next morning he greeted Charlie at the station with a big grin. "Found her. She showed up and I was able to follow her back to an apartment building in a seedy section of town on the south side. It's an empty area. Hardly anyone lives there now. 'Course I had to wait until she got finished with her work at the compound, so it was a late night."

Charlie smiled. "You see Billy?"

"No, but if we stake out the place, I'll bet we'll find him."

"We'll go tonight," Charlie said.

That night Charlie and Hammond took up a position in an alley across from the apartment building. Before he had left, Charlie told another of his trusted officers to take a message to Lieutenant Cameron to meet him at his house later that night. They had been waiting a little less than an hour when they saw two people approaching the building.

"Is that him?" Hammond asked.

"It's him. I saw him with the convoy." He grabbed Hammond's arm. "We can't let them get in and close the door."

"Don't worry, Chief. The front door doesn't close all the way. I checked it last night."

After waiting a minute they crossed the street and quietly entered the front hallway. The stench of human feces hit them hard. They stopped to listen but heard no sounds above. With a hand over his face, Charlie took his little flashlight out of his jacket pocket, with its precious two batteries, and turned it on, screening most of the intense beam with his fingers. Barely breathing, they quickly climbed the stairs to the second floor.

"We'll have to check each floor," Hammond whispered.

Charlie nodded. The carpet was filthy, un-vacuumed since the power went out and now strewn with debris. They walked down the hall, being careful to not step on anything that could crunch and give them away. They listened at each door, hoping to hear if anyone was inside. Finally they stopped at one door that had no trash in front of it. The doorknob was shiny, indicating regular use. They could hear someone moving about inside.

Charlie gently knocked on the door. If this was not the right apartment, they didn't want to alert others that strangers were in the building. Someone knocking on doors at night would be alarming.

Nothing happened. Charlie knocked gently again, and did it again after another pause. Finally he heard someone moving close to the door. "Who are you? What do you want?" an older voice asked.

"It's Police Chief Cook. You're not in trouble. We just need your help."

"We haven't done anything wrong. We help, we work and do what we can. We're old, please leave us alone." The voice sounded frightened.

"You're not in trouble," Charlie repeated. "Just open the door. I just want to ask you some questions. We're looking for someone."

The doorknob turned and the door slowly swung open a few inches, stopping where a security chain held it. A white-haired man peered through the gap. "What do you want to know?"

"There's a young woman living in the building. She has a guy staying with her. We need to know what apartment they're in."

The man shook his head. "Don't know anything about that."

"Look, they're not in trouble, but I have to talk with the young man. It's important. You must know where they're living."

Again, the man shook his head.

Charlie leaned forward and looked the old man in the eye. He kept his voice low, but he put a new threatening tone in it. "You're not in trouble, they're not in trouble, but if you don't tell me, you *will* be in trouble."

"Okay, okay," the man said. "We don't want any problems. She lives on the fourth floor. She's nice enough, but we don't see her much. Don't know what apartment she lives in."

"That'll do. Now close your door and stay inside," Charlie said. "Everything's going to be fine. Don't worry."

The door closed. They headed back to the stairs. "Gotta be quiet. We don't want them to bolt now that we're almost there." Hammond nodded.

On the fourth floor they again stepped quietly down the hall, looking for signs of doors being used. Halfway down the hall, they spotted a pathway to one of the doors. They stepped close and listened at the door for a moment. Inside they could clearly hear a woman talking. Billy had to be there.

Charlie straightened up and knocked loudly on the door. Inside the talking stopped. Hammond put his hand close to the gun on his belt. Charlie knocked again.

"Who's there?" Lori Sue finally asked.

"Chief of Police. I need to talk to you."

"I ain't done nothing," she said, her voice sounding tense. "You better not mess with me or you'll have trouble with Leo."

Hammond's eyebrows rose at the name, and he looked at Charlie and soundlessly whistled.

"You're not in trouble," Charlie said. "I just need to talk with you and with Billy Turner. I know he's in there. Neither of you are in trouble, but you will be if you don't open this door."

Billy was standing in the hallway outside their bedroom, shirtless and barefoot. Lori Sue had gone into the living room with an oil lamp in her hand when she had heard the knocking. At Billy's name, her head jerked around and they looked at each other, wide-eyed.

"How's he know I'm here?" Billy whispered.

Lori Sue shook her head. "There's no one here but me," she called back through the door.

"Don't lie to me. I don't have time for it. I saw the two of you come into the building. Unless he can fly, he's in there. Now open the door." Chief

Cook's voice was firm and authoritative. It didn't allow for any delay or diversion.

Lori Sue motioned for Billy to hide in the bedroom. He stepped back into the room and closed the door, leaving a crack through which to peek. He stood in the dark, feeling helpless. There was no place to run and really no place to hide. Were they coming to take him away for killing that man? He heard the door open. Floorboards creaked in the living room. Unfortunately he could only see flickering shadows through the crack in the door.

The same voice again. "Bring him out. It's Billy I need to talk to and I don't have all night." There was a silence, and then whoever it was spoke again, his tone now a little softer. "Look, I'm doing a favor for a friend, and I don't need you making this harder. Jason Richards from the valley is in town and wants to talk with Billy. So I got asked to find him. Now it's late, I'm tired, and I don't want to mess around. Get him out here."

When Billy heard Jason's name and that he was asking for him, he came out from the bedroom. A bright light flashed in his face, and he flinched.

"There you are," said the man holding the tiny flashlight. When he lowered it, Billy recognized the police chief who showed up at the city gate on trading day. "You know Jason?" Chief Cook asked. Billy nodded uncertainly. "He asked me to find you. He'd like to talk with you, tonight. It's important, and I said I'd help, since he organized the trading."

"What's he want to talk to me about?"

"Dammit, boy! I don't know. Just get your stuff and let's get going. I don't want to take all night with this."

Billy turned and went back into the bedroom to pull on his shirt and grab his boots. He heard Lori Sue declare, "He ain't going anywhere without me. I'm his girlfriend and I ain't lettin' him go off with you. If this is some kind of trick, I'll kick somebody's ass."

Billy stopped in his tracks, his boots in his hands. He'd never thought any girl would want to fight for him. A flush of pride went through his body.

He went back out into the living room and sat down on the sofa to pull his boots on. "We was gonna eat, when you knocked. We ain't had anything to eat since morning," he said to the police chief.

"I'll get you something to eat. Let's go."

When they reached the sidewalk outside the apartment building, the other policeman spoke quietly with the chief and then walked briskly away. The chief led them in a different direction. No one spoke. They walked in silence. Lori Sue kept close to him, and Billy put his arm around her.

After a while, their journey took them into a section of town that Billy had never seen before. There were individual houses; most looked as though they were occupied, with no broken windows or doors hanging open. The yards were overgrown and unkempt, but everything looked distinctly neater. Occasionally a window glowed with a hint of fire or candlelight. They had been walking for perhaps a half hour when the chief led them into the driveway of a bungalow with a large oak tree in the front yard. In the back, at the end of the driveway, was the familiar shape of a Humvee. Chief Cook led them to the front door, knocked softly twice, then put his key in the lock.

The living room was lit by several of the thick tallow candles similar to the ones he'd seen in the militia building. Several people were sitting around the room. Catherine's boyfriend Lieutenant Cameron and Sergeant Gibbs were sitting on a long sofa, along with a younger soldier Billy recognized from the trading convoy. Across from the sofa sat a thin, worried-looking woman he didn't recognize. Jason was sitting in a straight-backed chair smiling at him.

"Hello, Billy," he said.

Chapter 30

H i, Jason." Billy tried to sound nonchalant. "What's so important you want to see me tonight?"

Before he could answer, Lori Sue stepped forward beside Billy. "I'm Lori Sue," she said, giving Jason an aggressive look. "Billy here is my boyfriend. I don't know what the hell you want, or how you can get the chief of police to run your errands, but he hasn't done anything wrong and you better not mess with him or you'll be messing with me." She stood there, all five foot five of her. "I may not be that big, but I fight hard and nasty. I've had a lot of experience dealing with men who try to mess with me, so don't you."

Sergeant Gibbs started to grin. Lori Sue saw the grin and turned to him. "You think I'm funny? I've had to deal with assholes like you before. You stay out of this."

Billy was starting to get embarrassed, although Lori Sue's clear statement of their relationship felt good.

Gibbs held up his hands. "Miss Lori, I'm not laughing at you. But I think you're getting off on the wrong foot."

She just glared at him, looking ready to fight. "It's Lori *Sue*," she said.

Jason finally spoke up. "I asked Chief Cook to help me find Billy. I want to invite him to a wedding...my daughter's wedding." He looked at Billy. "Lieutenant Cameron and Catherine are getting married, maybe next week, and since I was in town, she asked me to find you and invite you to come. You're a big part of the valley and your dad gave his life defending it. We'd be honored to have you there."

Lori Sue turned to look at Charlie standing behind them. "Shit. Why the hell didn't you say what this was about? You got me all worked up over nothin'." Turning back to Jason, she continued in a friendlier tone of voice. "I'm sorry about yelling at you, but I got to defend what's mine, if you know what I mean."

Jason smiled. "I think I know about defending what's mine. No offense taken." He got up and extended his hand. "I'm Jason Richards and I'm glad to meet you."

Lori Sue grinned and took it.

"Mary, these two haven't eaten all day," Chief Cook said.

The older woman replied, "Oh, we can do something about that!" She got up. "Let's go into the other room."

She took one of the candles and led them into the dining room with a huge table. Charlie followed, bringing in the other candles. Billy and Lori Sue took chairs next to each other. Mary disappeared into the kitchen, but she returned a moment later bearing two large plates which she set in front of Billy and Lori Sue. The plates were filled with macaroni noodles in an unfamiliar sauce that held bits of meat.

"Go ahead," Mary told them. "We've all already eaten." They both began wolfing down the food as Mary went back to the kitchen and brought in another plate for her husband.

"Wow, you sure do eat well," Lori Sue said between mouthfuls.

"This is a lot better than we get at the food centers," Billy said.

Mary smiled and nodded her head as she took the empty chair to Charlie's right. Nobody around the table spoke as they ate. Billy barely noticed the quiet.

When Billy, Lori Sue, and Charlie had all finished eating, Jason broke the silence. "Did you get the job you talked about?" He nodded. "So how are you doing here, in town?"

Billy shrugged. "I can't say I like it a lot. There's too many rules. But since I'm a hunter, I get to do a lot on my own. I can be out in the woods. It's better than the city, which is dirty and noisy." He looked at Lori Sue on his right. "All in all it ain't bad, though. 'Specially since meeting Lori Sue."

"He saved my life," Lori Sue said. Everyone listened intently as she went on to describe the incident and how Billy's crack shooting had saved her. Billy felt a little embarrassed and worried. He didn't know how that information would sit with the chief of police. He could tell nothing from Charlie's expression. "He's gonna teach me how to make whiskey too so I don't have to work the streets."

"Sounds like you want to do the right thing when you see it," Kevin said.

"I guess."

"Billy, what do you think of the militia?" Kevin asked.

Billy looked cautiously at Charlie Cook. "I don't know," he said. "They're all right, I guess."

To his surprise he saw Charlie smiling at him. "You can speak openly here. I'm no fan of the militia and neither is anyone else in this room."

"Really? You're part of them, ain't you?"

"No, the police are separate. We don't have any ex-gangsters or looters on the police force. So feel free to speak your mind."

"Why you want to know what he thinks?" Lori Sue asked Kevin.

"I'm the U.S. Army. I want to get his perspective on the situation. There's some friction between us and the militia some times."

"Well, I don't really like them," Billy answered. "They ain't like you. After I shot that guy trying to rape Lori Sue, his buddies tried to beat me up, maybe kill me. Didn't seem like the officers gave a damn, 'bout the shootin' or 'bout me nearly gettin' murdered on the sidewalk. I got to be on the lookout for them all the time now."

Jason asked, "How about you, Lori Sue? Do you think things are going well?"

Lori Sue didn't answer for a moment, and Billy looked at her. She was studying the candlelit faces around the table. "You're asking a lot of questions...all of you," she said. "You didn't bring us over here to just invite Billy to the wedding. What do you want?"

"Well, I do want to invite Billy to the wedding...and you, too," Jason replied. "But I'm worried about the town. We have to do business with them, so I want to get more information, good or bad. No one here is going to pass anything you say on to anyone else. It's for us and the other valley farmers, so we can better know what we're dealing with."

"I can tell you stories," Lori Sue said. "You know that guy, Leo?" She looked at Charlie, who nodded, his face darkening. "Well, he's a piece of work, or a piece of shit, really. He's dangerous, a killer, someone you don't want to mess with. A while ago I found out he's keeping a woman, Donna's her name—"

Mary's eyes suddenly widening. Charlie grimaced and turned to her, taking her left hand in both of his own.

"She ain't there 'cause she wants to be," Lori Sue continued. "Leo's got her chained up like a slave. I mean a real chain. And that ain't all. Got her kid under his control and uses him to make her do what he wants." She shook her head. The room was silent. "Piece of shit," she said. Her face was hard as she looked at Mary. "We girls got to stick together. It's one thing to give a guy a tumble and get something in return, hell it's fun sometimes...at least till I met Billy." She put her hand on Billy's arm. "But it's bad when someone tries to make you a slave. That ain't right."

Billy was shocked. She had not told him anything about this. "You shouldn't go near Leo," he said.

"It's all right. I'm careful, but I have to help her. She ain't got nobody. I'm visiting her kid to check up on him, let her know how he's doing. I even snuck my 9mm to her, 'case things get real bad."

"This is worse than I thought," Charlie said. He put his arm around his wife.

The group was silent for a while.

"You ain't gonna get me in trouble for telling you all this, are you?" Lori Sue asked.

"Absolutely not," Charlie said. "No one will know you told us. Not unless you tell anyone else."

"I ain't telling them bastards anything, and neither is Billy."

Jason leaned forward and studied Billy and Lori Sue for a moment. "We'd like to help. Help both of you and this woman, Donna, and her kid. Will you help us do that?"

There was a long silence in the room. Finally Lori Sue spoke up. "How are you gonna help?"

"What do you want us to do?" Billy asked.

"We think we can change who runs the town," Jason said. "There are people in town who want to help change things. You can be part of that. In the process, we can save Donna and others like her."

"You talking about a revolt?" Billy asked in astonishment. "Cause if you are, they got too many guns and too many men."

Kevin spoke up. "No open revolt. Not unless we have to. But we can organize, collect resources, and be ready to change the balance of power if we get the chance."

Billy shook his head. "I think you're all crazy. This is...this is a whole *town*. I ain't gonna tell anyone, but you're gonna get yourselves killed."

"That was your daddy's first response," Jason said softly. "But he came and helped, and you did as well. And we won."

Billy turned to him with an angry look in his eyes. "Yeah, and he died doing it."

Jason's eyes were sympathetic, but they did not waver. "I'm sorry about that, I really am. But you didn't die...*and we won*."

"Look," Kevin said, "if this group gets more powerful, no one will have any freedom. Lori Sue could be put in a brothel, her freedom taken away. You think they'll listen to you? You say you're going to teach her how to make whiskey. What if one of the bosses, Leo or someone else, says no, he's got people to make whiskey, he wants her in a whorehouse, servicing the men? What're you going to do then?"

Billy could think of nothing to say. He could feel Lori Sue's body grow tense next to him. He stared back at Kevin.

Kevin went on. "Right now you think you got the run of things, you've got the best of the situation even though you have to keep ducking that guy's friends. You think you can keep doing what you like best. But don't fool yourself. Being able to do what you want is not where this is headed. That isn't what Stansky has in mind. He wants everyone doing what he wants...or what Leo says to do."

"On top of that," Jason said, "they're planning to attack the valley, to steal our seed."

Billy couldn't hide the shock he felt. Jason's eyes bore into him. "They don't have seeds that breed true. They just have hybrid seed, and they don't seem interested in waiting until we can share with them. And now it looks like their talk of wanting to cooperate was just a pack of lies," he said. "Charlie here tells us they're set on attacking us. And I expect that attacking us means killing all of us. If they can get non-hybrid seed of their own they think they don't need us, so we're better off dead."

"That don't make sense. Why would they do that?" Billy asked.

"Because the valley represents freedom," Kevin answered. "An alternative future to what Stansky's planning. You didn't see the crowds when we went around to the food centers on trading day. They were all excited to see Jason and Anne."

Jason nodded, his eyes on Billy. "They'd like to get us out of their hair and they'd like to get our seed. That's enough for them to kill everyone in the valley. These are people you know, people who have stood with you, people you fought alongside of. Are you going to let that happen?"

"I don't know." Billy squirmed in his chair. His mind raced. "Don't know what I can do to help."

"I'll help," Lori Sue said unexpectedly beside him. Billy turned to look at her. "I don't know if I can do anything, but if I can help shove a stick up Leo's ass, I'll do it." She turned to Billy with her eyes afire. "You should be in too," she told him. "I know I'm not gonna let someone put me in a whorehouse like that. No way. That bastard Leo, keeping Donna chained up like that. That's fucked. We girls got to stick together."

Billy felt as if he were falling, the ground crumbling away under him. Life had been pretty good, even if he had to keep a sharp eye out for the friends of the guy he had killed. He had Lori Sue, and she had opened up a world of female delights for him. He was completely in love with her; she was good looking, exciting, and she made him feel special, like no one ever had before. They ate pretty well, and they had a place of their own. Now it all seemed ready to come apart.

He finally looked back at Jason. "Is Catherine really getting married? Or was that just to get me here?"

Jason laughed. "Yes, she's really getting married and she wants you to be there. But now you know it wasn't the only reason to talk to you tonight."

Chapter 31

*U*h oh, *what do we have here?* Captain Roper thought as he looked across his desk at the four serious faces. Seeing Jason surprised him; he'd had no hint that he was back in Hillsboro. But his real concern was Charlie Cook. Charlie knew all about his involvement with Stansky, the bribes, the cover-ups. Roper couldn't have that coming out in front of Cameron and Gibbs. Roper kept his features expressionless. Charlie's face was the same.

But had it already come out? Not if the Chief was still looking out for his own hide. Either way, the thing was to play this as if it hadn't.

And then there was the surprise they had brought him.

"It's going to happen after Mason gets you to pull the platoon out," Lieutenant Cameron told him. "I don't know how soon, but, based on what I know of Stansky, I don't think he'll wait long at all. He sees this business with the seed as an obstacle, and he sees the valley farmers as an obstacle. He doesn't like obstacles. And he can get everything he wants right away if he just takes the valley and kills everyone in it."

Roper let the lieutenant finish explaining. Knowing Joe, his own estimate matched Cameron's. *That son of a bitch.* How was he going to play this out?

"What makes you think I'll go along with Mason?" he asked when Cameron stopped.

"Frank seems to think you'll agree," Charlie said. His choice of phrasing was interesting. It looked like the policeman was going to play along and not expose him.

He raised his eyebrows. "I would only leave Hillsboro if I got a direct order from Colonel Stillman, or if I felt things were stable enough that our presence wasn't needed."

"It seems that you're getting ready to make that call, sir," Cameron said. "I get the impression that you feel things are under control here and that we can move on. I know you didn't like getting left here."

"What I *like* is irrelevant, Lieutenant," Roper said. He looked harder at Cameron. "I do my duty, as I expect you to do yours."

"But now you know what'll be behind Mason's request when he makes it. How does that fit into your assessment of the situation? Seems to me that planning to attack and murder civilians makes his leadership criminal in nature."

"You're getting ahead of yourself," Roper said. "And why," he said turning to Gibbs, "are you involved in these discussions? Your job is to keep the troops in line, to carry out orders. I don't remember elevating you to strategic planning."

"Sir, Sergeant Gibbs is here because I asked him to be. He can give us valuable information on our own readiness and strength in the event that we have to oppose the town's authorities. Ultimately, if we decide they're acting criminally, we have to take over."

Roper ignored Cameron and focused on Gibbs. "Sergeant, you are dismissed. Please see to the platoon. Make sure everyone is inspection-ready. And while you're at it, get me an inventory of our materiel and prepare a report on our battle readiness. That will be helpful while I discuss strategy with the Lieutenant here."

Gibbs saluted and left the room.

"Sir, that wasn't called for. Sergeant Gibbs has been invaluable throughout this deployment," Cameron said.

"Do not question me, Lieutenant. Gibbs has a job to do. I sent him to do what you should have done immediately after hearing of this threat. I'm surprised you didn't realize that. It seems as though you've become sloppy in carrying out your mission."

Cameron stiffened but didn't respond.

"You," Roper said, turning to Jason. "I don't know what you're doing here either, beyond the fact that you seem to have become a local hero. I'm afraid that doesn't qualify you for sitting in on military strategy discussions. Even though Lieutenant Cameron seems to want to include you, I have to ask you to wait outside. My officer and I have important matters to discuss. The Chief of Police can stay as a representative of local law enforcement. Since you don't have any official title, I can't include you in those discussions."

"My family and I are going to be on the receiving end of this attack, so I have more than a little interest in the discussion."

"Nevertheless, this is a military discussion with my junior officer here. No civilians allowed."

Jason gave the captain a long hard stare. Roper didn't flinch. Jason finally stood up and with a glance at Cameron, left the room.

"So you're going to take action on what we told you?" Charlie Cook asked when the door closed.

"No. I'm going to wait to have this conversation with Frank that you say is coming."

Charlie shifted uncomfortably. "I'd appreciate it if you don't let on about what you know. He'll know it came from me."

"Are you concerned about upsetting your comfortable arrangements?" Roper asked blandly.

"No more than others might be," Charlie replied. He gave Roper a pointed look. Roper understood the threat implied. *Fair enough*, he thought.

He leaned comfortably back in his chair. "I'll get back to everyone after Frank talks with me...if he does."

"Sir," Lieutenant Cameron said, in a voice that failed to conceal his anxiety. "He *will* talk with you. Probably pretty soon. I urge you to not give him an answer until we can discuss our options."

Roper gave Cameron a reassuring smile. "I'll play this by ear." He let a trace of grim concern into his face, then looked at Cameron and said sharply, "You get with Gibbs. I want a full inventory of our situation. And I want it by tomorrow."

With that he dismissed the two of them.

He sat in his empty office, *Joe, what the hell kind of mess are you creating?*

The next day Jason rode back to the valley with Kevin and Tommy Wilkes, who sat in the back. Gibbs had stayed to complete the task Roper had given him. Captain Roper had quickly approved the trip. "I don't want him hanging around the compound. He's not part of our decision-making." He gave Cameron a stern look. "Diesel is a scarce commodity. After this trip, I don't want you ferrying those people around anymore."

Lieutenant Cameron was barely an hour on his way when Frank Mason came to visit Captain Roper. Roper welcomed the politician with an enthusiastic handshake and offered him a cup of some precious but vile-tasting coffee. He watched Frank carefully during the usual pleasantries. It didn't take Frank long to come to the point.

"Larry, don't you think it's time for you to move out? I'm sure your men could be better utilized somewhere else."

Always the slick one, thought Roper.

"I haven't been given any orders to move yet," he replied, feigning a note of surprise.

Frank looked at him pleasantly. "I know," he said deliberately, glancing back at the closed door, "but there's not much more payoff we can send your way. I'm thinking you need to find new fields to plow."

Roper smiled and spread his hands. "I still provide you guys cover. My weekly reports to Colonel Stillman keep him happy. He thinks he has a thriving community back here, fully under control with everything going well. You still want that kind of report to go in, don't you?"

Frank's tone became a little sharper. "I'm thinking we're past needing any kind of report being sent in. We're self-sufficient and under control. I'm thinking if Stillman knew that, you could get reassigned. Somewhere you could do some good."

"Somewhere I could do some good? Why, Frank. I think you just want to eliminate my share."

"That's the problem. There isn't much of a share of anything left. There's no more gold or jewels, that's all been picked over. We're now just stocking weapons, ammunition, food and fuel...plus rebuilding our infrastructure. Not much loot for you in that."

"Not much for you either. What're you going to do?"

Frank had a thoughtful look on his face. "I'm in it for the long run," he said. "Stansky's not too smooth, he's a gangster after all, but he's the reason Hillsboro hasn't come apart...a big reason why we're not starving—"

"A big reason why you've gotten wealthy."

"Maybe so, but it's more than that. In spite of having to act harshly sometimes, we're doing some good. And Hillsboro is able to protect itself and have a say about its future by being strong and organized."

Roper laughed. "Don't give me that horseshit. Save it for the civilians. I know you, it's all about power, power and wealth. You and Stansky are two of a kind. He's just willing to break the law. *You* only want to *bend* it."

Frank actually seemed to look insulted. "I don't expect you to see it from my perspective, but this is my home. I've spent my career here."

"So has Stansky. That doesn't make either of you upstanding citizens."

Frank just shook his head. "So what do you believe in? What inspires you? Your future isn't here in Hillsboro. Where do you want to end up?"

Roper just stared back at Frank, his smile fading.

Frank continued. "How do you see this playing out? This situation, what's going on all over the country? At least I'm home and want to make the best of that. Where do you wind up?"

"Where I wind up is my business." Roper said. He glanced out the window, taking in the parking lot where they were encamped, the empty stores and deserted roads. It was a dismal place.

"Well, the game seems to have run its course here. At least for you."

"You *telling* me to leave?" Roper turned back to Frank.

"I'm not telling you to do anything. But I am telling you that Joe thinks it's time we were on our own. He's not interested in prolonging the situation. Now, before you get all worked up, he's paid you well for your help, but it's not needed any more. Time for you to get a new game going."

"And if I decide to wait? You know I can't just move around on my own."

"You have to convince Stillman, we know that. But that shouldn't be hard. I hope you'll make that happen and we all can move on."

"And if it doesn't happen?"

Frank shook his head. He glanced down at the floor and then back at Roper. "You know I can't fully control Joe. You know how much firepower he has. You have a delicate position here. I wouldn't push it. Take what you got and get going, that's my advice."

"Stillman would not be happy to hear his officer being threatened."

"Stillman would also wonder why he'd been receiving such glowing reports if things were going to shit here." Frank let that sink in. "You see, your reports put you in a bit of a corner. The best way out is to move along, put Hillsboro behind you. Whatever happens *after* you leave can't be pinned to you. Think about that." He stood up. "I'll come by tomorrow to see what you've decided. I know you'll do the smart thing...you always have."

After Frank left, Roper sat behind his desk, thinking. He felt trapped. If there weren't a clear threat to civilians, he'd load up the platoon and move out. He knew there was little else to milk from Stansky and Mason.

He thought about what he wanted to do. The army had been his career. Before the EMP attack he had been getting close to becoming a major. All that had been put on hold as the army scrambled to get itself under control and then begin to pacify the countryside.

A good job in Hillsboro could lock up that promotion. But to what end? Was the army going to be a solid career again? In the old days he had envisioned going on from major to lieutenant colonel. If he had topped out there, he could have easily retired. He would have had enough years at that point for a full pension, and he could have gotten a lucrative job consulting with the government or military—essentially getting re-hired to do what he had done as a colonel.

None of that seemed so sure now. If the country didn't recover soon, it could split up. The reports were that China was on the West Coast. Mexico had taken control over much of the Southwest. Some cities had fallen under the brutal control of some of the larger gangs. New York City was a war zone. St. Louis was controlled by a gang. New Orleans was in the middle of a gang war. Chicago was a mess. No, the real possibility was that the United States as he knew it, as everyone knew it, was over...at least for some time. There'd be no lucrative, easy retirement for now...if ever. The army itself was in danger. It was structured for emergencies and its organization had saved it, but it couldn't keep functioning forever without an economy supporting it. There was a real possibility of the military coming apart.

Hell, even the gold and gems he had amassed could turn out to be as meaningless an investment as paper money and U.S. bonds, if the infrastructure and economy didn't recover. Going to Panama or somewhere else south of the border might be the only sensible thing to do. There was nothing really holding him here.

But attacking civilians...that was a problem. Was it too late to stop Stansky? Maybe get him to back off, work out some compromise with the valley? It didn't take a genius to see Hillsboro was doing well compared to other small cities. Maybe it *was* run by a gangster, but he had improved safety and living conditions. Could he, Mason and Cook convince Joe to make some kind of peace with the valley? At least so he could depart cleanly?

But there was Leo. Leo was a killer. Not as smart as Joe, but even more deadly. Leo would relish the use of force; he wouldn't be advising compromise.

Still, should he give it a try? What was in it for him, a clear conscience?

Damn it. He smiled at the harsh irony of it all. If he hadn't known about the attack, his decision would have been easier. But he did know, and now he had to figure out what that meant to him.

Chapter 32

Joe Stansky stared out at the dark city from his office, high above the silent streets. He tried to imagine the city with electrical power back—the dark buildings lit, communication restored, refrigeration operational again. Life would become much closer to how it had been before. His position of power would be solidified and Hillsboro would be the dominant town in the region.

But that wasn't happening. Work had slowed on all the power projects. The cable project wasn't reaching its targets on cable and wire production, the waterpower project seemed stuck in low gear, and the generator rebuild team was getting few units completed. Hell, he wasn't sure how the technicians could tell if the refurbished units would work, since there was no way to drive them in order to test their output. The town, to Joe's frustration, was still stuck with old gas or diesel generators that burned precious resources for the limited power they produced.

He had asked his men to find out what was going on, and they had come back with long, technical explanations that were pretty much unintelligible. A few questions had shown him that his men had understood almost none of what they'd been told. Frank had gone down to the projects as well, and it was clear to Joe, when he reported back, that he understood just as little.

The projects were all interconnected; if one was delayed, it affected the functionality of the others. The generators were waiting on wire, the waterwheel would be just a big toy when it was finished if it didn't get its generators, and without the cable there would be no way to distribute the power. If all the projects were delayed, it would make the hope of power restoration look like a futile dream.

Frank reported a loss of enthusiasm among the technicians that had been present for some time. Joe had his doubts that it was due to technical problems. He had a lifetime of ferreting out lame excuses. Now his instincts told him something more than obscure technical problems was causing the slowdown.

He was not fuming; he'd gone through that phase earlier. Now he was thinking about his next steps. So what to do about the hold-up on the electricity?

Some of the technicians seemed happy. With Joe's approval, Frank had been effective at working out ways to reward them for their cooperation and expertise. They got special benefits for working on the infrastructure—more food, better quarters, and their spouses got exemptions from having to work on other projects.

But some of them were not on board. There was a subversive element, plotting to undermine martial law. And this slowdown in progress seemed to be a part of that conspiracy.

Why was it so hard for people to accept his authority?

He had made things better in town. Hillsboro was in better shape than any community they had been in touch with, big or small. And a regional structure would solidify everything. With that in place, and with a little more time to expand and train his militia into a military grade fighting force, he figured he'd be in good shape when the feds showed up.

Captain Roper could have been helpful there, but Joe knew Roper's type. Roper wasn't going to jump on any offer to run Joe's army. That would be too much work, and he'd be under Joe's authority. No, Roper would take the easy way. Joe would do it on his own.

Electricity. That was the key. If Joe could just get the technicians on board for long enough to get that going, the people would settle down. Life would be better and people would accept his leadership. Feed them, protect them, make life easier, and he could do what he wanted. As far as Joe was concerned all they had to do was go along.

A surge of enthusiasm went through him. If he kept moving faster than others around him, just like he'd done right after the EMP attack, the sky was the limit. The civilians of Hillsboro, they would be his gang members, his elite. That was how this would play this out. His citizens would be on the inside, part of the gang, when they spread their control to other towns. Joe smiled at the thought of a city-sized gang with him as the leader.

He walked out into the hall and found the guard half-asleep behind the receptionist's desk.

"Wake up," Joe snapped. The man jerked upright in the chair, fear on his face. "Go get someone to find Leo and Frank Mason and bring them here."

The man looked at the clock on the wall as he stood up. It was ten minutes past midnight.

"I don't give a damn what time it is, so don't open your mouth. Just do it."

"Yes, sir," the man said, and he ran down the hall toward the door to the stairwell. Joe went back into his office, smiling.

Three minutes later he heard an engine and watched headlights splash on the empty buildings across the street as one of the cars burst out of the parking garage and turned right, disappearing around the block.

Around twenty minutes later the sound of an engine announced the car's return. He saw the headlights through the window as it pulled up to the front of the building. Joe sat down behind his desk and waited for the two men to appear.

"Don't you ever sleep?" Frank asked as the men entered Joe's office. He looked sleepy, his clothes rumpled. Leo just sat down quietly.

Joe looked at Frank coldly. "Don't be cute. I got no time for cute. You're here because we need to move forward. The electricity project isn't going well. All I hear from you is some technical crap which don't mean a thing to me."

Frank took the other chair, frowning. "It doesn't mean much to me either, but it seems to be why progress is so slow."

"It could also be just a way to hold things up. The ones who don't like my authority would like to keep the electricity shut off. Not so it looks like they stopped it, just so it looks like we can't deliver. They know if we get the lights on, people will be happier with my running things."

Joe stood up and ran his hands through his hair. He allowed a slight smile to cross his face. "It's actually pretty clever, the way they're doing it. We don't know how to bypass them and get the work done. We could complete the waterwheel project. It's mostly grunt work. But for the rest of it we need the experts, and without them the waterwheel is useless. They seem to have us in a position where we gotta take their word on things. They could string us out for years, maybe."

Joe's smile faded. He sat back down and leaned forward. When he spoke again, his voice was hard. "We don't have time to wait. Who knows when the feds might show up? Which brings me to a conclusion. I want the town in better shape by then. I want other towns under my control by then. I want a larger, better-trained militia by the time anything calling itself the federal government comes nosing around us."

"What makes you think they're going to show up soon? You hear something?" Frank asked. Joe could see he was getting nervous.

Leo didn't react at all. He sat relaxed, patient in his chair, waiting for Joe to make his point.

"I haven't," he said. "But it doesn't take a genius to figure out they'll come around. Shit, the *army* has. There's still a U.S. Army, and I'm bettin' there's a government behind it trying to regain control. If the army can let them get reorganized, the next thing you know we'll have some government official show up with soldiers. Or Homeland Security." The last name he spat out with disgust.

"Well, we shouldn't be too quick to do anything. I'm waiting to hear back from Roper. I think—"

"He'll go," Joe said impatiently. "There's nothing for him here. You just need to make sure he doesn't think he can squeeze me for more. He's got to go now or face the consequences."

Frank's eyes widened. Leo glanced at Frank, and the ghost of a smile touched his mouth.

"Now these technicians," Joe continued. "I think it's time we made an example of a couple of them." He turned to Leo. "I want you to pick out two of the uncooperative ones. Try to get the ones involved in the slowdown, but, if you can't, just pick out any two. Do it quick. We'll put them on trial, in front of the whole town, and convict them of subversion, not helping their fellow citizens, sabotaging the public good. Then we execute them, publicly." Joe paused for effect. "The rest will get the message, and we'll be seen as being on the side of civic progress...and," he looked hard at Frank, "as not allowing anyone to stop us."

Leo sat calm and still, like a statue. Frank looked distressed.

"We haven't done that since the early days, when we caught looters," Frank said after a moment.

"You afraid to do it now?" Joe asked.

Fear showed in Frank's eyes. "I just don't like upsetting people."

"I don't like people disobeying me," Joe answered coldly. "This works," he swept his hand around the room, "because people do what they're told. They have to understand that. And they have to understand they better not cross me. This group seems to have forgotten that fact. It's time to remind them who's in charge. And while we're at it, we'll show the rest of the town as well. They won't miss the message. And then we'll turn the lights on." He smiled. "The sooner we get the electricity going, the happier everyone will be. They'll follow my orders when they see how good things can be. I'm not letting a few traitors think they can screw with me and get away with it. We're past that."

He went on without waiting for a reply. "Leo, get this done, tomorrow, first thing. Bring Charlie along, I want to be sure where he stands." He locked eyes with Frank. "And, I expect you to get Roper out of my hair. You make that happen, quick, 'cause Leo's next job is taking care of the valley. With them out of the way there won't be any heroes and we'll get all the seed we want."

Frank looked surprised.

"That Jason's been back since the trading, maybe more than once. Why is he coming around? Seems to me the valley is sticking their nose in where it don't belong."

"Are you sure about this?" Frank asked.

Joe got up. He walked around his desk to where Frank was sitting, leaned over him, and stuck a finger in his chest. "I'm sure about one thing. Things ain't going right and I'm going to change them. You better understand that. I'm tired of all your whining, Frank. Be careful you don't become a problem for me." He let that sink in. "Now go get some sleep, both of you. Tomorrow we act."

Chapter 33

The next day Charlie had only just gotten into work when he heard the rumble of a vehicle pulling up in front of the police station. The sound was rare enough that it caught his attention immediately. He went to his office window and looked down on an old white van. He guessed it must be a militia vehicle, although he couldn't see any markings from his vantage point.

He walked out of his office and started down the stairs. Leo Stupek was waiting at the bottom.

"Hate to interrupt your day, Chief, but you need to come with me. We've got a security issue to deal with."

"What's the problem?"

"A security problem, militia business but I want to be sure law enforcement is on the same page." Leo's look made it clear that Charlie was required personally.

"I'll get my coat," Charlie said.

The white van had been crudely converted into a cross between a militia patrol vehicle and a paddy wagon, with a wire grille welded behind the second-row bench seat, partitioning off the back half of the vehicle. The bench seat was occupied by two stern-looking militia with rifles. The front passenger seat was empty. Charlie climbed in.

"So where are we going?" he asked as Leo started the engine.

Leo didn't say anything.

Charlie waited. It was clear that Leo wasn't going to answer.

It soon became plain that they were headed out to the water mill. Leo remained silent throughout the whole ride. When they arrived, Leo parked in front of the main entrance. Work had already begun for the day; from inside the mill came sounds of voices, hammering, and boards being sawn. Charlie got out, and the two militiamen piled out of the side door. Leo was already standing at the entrance, looking idly in at the construction. The building itself appeared largely finished. Most of the workers were clustered around the supporting structure for the millstones.

Charlie went over to Leo, tension rising in his gut. "What are you doing here, Leo?"

"Detective work, Chief. Detecting evildoers. Something you should have been doing." Leo's eyes were alight, a smile flickering on his face. After looking around for a moment, he called the two militia over and pointed to a middle-aged worker hammering a beam onto the support structure. "Take him," Leo said in a flat voice. They stepped over to the man and quickly grabbed him. "You're under arrest," Leo called.

"What?" The man looked astonished. The militiaman behind him was handcuffing his hands behind his back.

"Did you think you could fool us forever?" Leo said to the man.

"What are you doing?" Charlie asked Leo in a low voice.

"Making an arrest, Chief."

"For what? What did he do?"

"He's part of a plot to slow down and sabotage the electrical project. He's a subversive, trying to keep the town from recovering."

Charlie fought to conceal his shock. "You got any evidence for that? I haven't seen any," he replied, trying to keep his voice calm.

"You wouldn't," Leo said, grinning. "But we'll soon find some."

The man was shouting that he hadn't done anything wrong as they wrestled him towards the van.

"Who is this guy?"

"I told you. A subversive."

"Do you even know this man's name?" Charlie asked.

Leo yelled, "Hey you!" The pair of militia stopped dragging the man. "What's your name?"

"Dan!" the man said. "Dan Overbeck!"

Leo turned back to Charlie. "That's the man we're looking for."

"Stop this. This is illegal," Charlie demanded.

"I got orders from Joe."

"Well, then take him to the jail. That's where he belongs. I'll keep him locked up until I find out what's going on."

Leo didn't answer. The man was shoved into the van and the rear doors slammed on the protesting suspect. Charlie swore under his breath and got in.

"I haven't done anything!" Overbeck kept yelling through the grille. He was practically screaming. "Nothing! Chief, take me to the police station! Have them take me to the regular police station!"

Charlie's head was spinning.

He thought at first that they were going to the militia complex downtown, but they pulled up in front of the wire and generator repair building. Leo and the two militiamen got out. By the time Charlie had gotten out and walked around the vehicle, Leo was already informing a baffled young man in coveralls that he was under arrest.

There was nothing that Charlie could do. The militia threw the technician in the back with the other prisoner.

"This isn't right," Charlie protested again in the van. "You don't have a warrant to arrest these men and there isn't any immediate probable cause. You have to at least take them to the station and put them under my control."

"We're under martial law," Leo replied as he drove at high speed through the empty streets. He was ignoring the traffic signs and careening around the corners. His eyes were bright; an excited expression on his otherwise dour features showing that he was enjoying the experience. "The militia doesn't need a warrant, you know that. And we don't have to go through you."

"Then why the hell did you bring me along?"

"So you can see how things are going to be, since you don't seem to have a clue. Joe wants to know which side you're on. I'm wondering myself."

"I'm not on the side of indiscriminate arrests, that's for sure."

Leo gave Charlie a menacing look. Charlie avoided looking at him by glancing into the rear. Leo's men were peering through the grille, watching the prisoners rolling around as the van lurched through the corners. "We're going back to the militia's holding cells," Leo said. His voice suddenly sounded oddly officious. "I'll get to the bottom of this subversive activity. Your department doesn't seem to be able to conduct a real investigation."

When they pulled up to the building that contained the militia detention cells, Leo ordered the men to put the prisoners in separate rooms out of earshot of each other. They bundled out, but Leo didn't move. He turned to Charlie. His eyes were dark, with no more amusement in them.

"This was a lesson...and a test," he said, in a cold tone that sent shivers down Charlie's spine. "I got to report to Joe that you don't seem to want to go along with how he's running things in town. Seems like you're becoming a problem, like you're not on the same page. After all the special considerations, the loot you accepted, I'm surprised."

"If that's what this is all about, you can have it all back."

Leo smiled at him. "And the food you ate? It don't work like that, Charlie. You're in and you can't get out. You better think hard about your situation." He turned to glance at the men being half-dragged into the building. "I know something's going on, and I'll find out what it is. Those two will know something. I'm thinking you might know also. You might know more than you let on."

"I don't know what you're talking about. I just know that you're interfering with police work. What you did here today is not about defense of the town."

"Oh yes it is. Everything is about the defense of the town. That's the beauty of it. Your department isn't needed." Leo began to grin; an evil, sinister grin. "Now you got to wonder, do we need you...or your wife?"

"I'll walk back to headquarters. I don't need a ride from you," Charlie replied through his clenched teeth, shoving his door open.

"Think hard about what I said," Leo called after him.

Chapter 34

The announcement went out in the mimeographed paper that was posted in all the food centers. It said that two men, Peter Caldwell and Daniel Overbeck, had been caught subverting the restoration of the town's electricity. The paper portrayed Caldwell and Overbeck as using their technical knowledge to hold the good citizens of Hillsboro for ransom for their own gain. The notice included an order that all residents gather at the downtown sports arena on the morning of the following Friday to be told about the plot. All attendees would receive a coupon entitling them to a double serving at their next visit to a food center.

Everyone in Hillsboro knew what electricity would mean. Not just better lighting. Electricity meant energy: the ability to use power tools again, to pump water from wells, to heat homes. It meant getting the phone system going, the return of radio. It meant X-ray machines and dentists' drills. It meant refrigerators. Everyone remembered how things were before the EMP attack; electricity would mean a return to much of the normalcy of that time.

People who didn't know either of the accused men were angry. The few who did know them were confused. Neither Overbeck nor Caldwell seemed to be the sort to engage in such criminal selfishness. Both men were married; Overbeck had two children. They were thought of as hardworking, solid citizens who were interested in getting the town back on its feet.

On the day selected, the arena began to fill up by around nine in the morning. The announcement had specified ten, but since the EMP attack time had become less precise, and few wanted to find out what missing this mandatory meeting might mean. The city government delayed the start of the meeting until the flow of new arrivals had ebbed to almost nothing.

People filed into the arena; on the stage were two rows of seats for the VIPs. The director of safety and the chief of police were sitting in the middle of the row. Leo Stupek sat at one end, next to the stage stairs. There was a hum of generators running just outside the arena, providing power for stage lighting and sound.

Finally a single figure appeared on the stage. It was Joe Stansky, dressed in a dark suit. He carried an electric bullhorn.

Joe looked out at the crowd for a moment, waiting for the crowd to quiet down. When the arena was silent, Joe began to speak. He did not bother to introduce himself.

"We come a long way," he said, the amplification accentuating his gruff tone. "When the EMP attack occurred, I set out right away to grab all the resources I could find. Most of our officials didn't know what to do. If I had waited for them, we'd have missed out on lots of stuff—stuff that would have been looted. Take a look around." He paused, not lowering the bullhorn. "You all made it through that first god-awful winter. You didn't starve. I'm the reason you didn't starve. I saw what was needed and made sure we had it. While others were trying to figure out what had happened, I secured our future. I didn't wait for anyone to tell me how to do it. I just did it my own way." His voice boomed through the bullhorn. "I made sure our town was not overrun by refugees from the larger cities. You remember that fall and the following spring. It was me that forced us to put up the barriers. You worked on them, and they kept us safe."

It was the first time many in the crowd had heard of any of this. They stared at him with new interest. "Since I was getting all of this done, Frank Mason, as you know, made me Director of Resources." Joe lowered the bullhorn. He let the pause stretch, watching the crowd. A few confused people began to clap uncertainly, then he raised the bullhorn again and the silence returned.

"As of now," he said clearly, "I'm heading the Safety Committee. With me in charge, we're going to make Hillsboro stronger. I'll get the electricity going again and I'm not going to let anyone stop me."

There was a smattering of applause. Astonishment showed on many faces. Behind Joe, Frank Mason's head jerked suddenly to the right, toward where Leo sat. Leo just smiled back at him.

Joe continued after a moment, his voice suddenly harsher. "Now there are two prisoners coming out in a minute. They were arrested five days ago. They've confessed to their crimes." Joe paused a moment, then continued more slowly. "Confessed to trying to sabotage the electrical project." He stared out at the crowd, as if he were trying to make eye contact with every one of them. His face became red. His voice throbbed with righteous anger. "I want you to see them. I want you to *see* the people who wanted to keep your life from getting better. My militia found them and captured them. I'm working for you, for Hillsboro, and I'm not going to let anyone get in my way to make this a better place to live."

He was shouting now. He went on raging against the saboteurs, against the very idea of them. "Not just stealing. *Trying to make things worse!*" he roared. "This is worse than looting!" He continued on about his commitment to not allow anyone to get in the way of progress in Hillsboro, about how he had protected and would continue to protect the town. As he spoke, a smattering of applause broke out now and again as some people seemed to respond to his message.

Finally he turned and gestured to Leo, who nodded to someone below. Two men in loose orange prison uniforms were brought up onto the rear of the stage, each between two burly militia guards. Their legs were shackled, their hands cuffed behind their backs, and they moved in a slow, awkward shuffle as they were guided forward between the seated VIPs to the front of the stage to Joe's right. They were barefoot, and their heads were shaved. There were no obvious bruises on their faces, but they appeared to be in pain.

Joe put the bullhorn to his mouth again. "Before I sentence them, I want you to see them. The men who wanted to destroy your future." He turned to the pitiful prisoners and shouted through the bullhorn, "Do you confess to trying to sabotage the electrical project?"

The men stood with their heads bowed.

"Do you?"

The two men nodded their heads.

"Say it into the microphone," Joe commanded. He walked forward and held the bullhorn up to Caldwell's mouth. He got a barely audible "Yes". Reaching past him, he held the bullhorn in front of Overbeck's face. Overbeck's "yes" was almost a moan.

"You heard 'em. There's no doubt about what they did." Joe turned and walked a few steps to his left, shaking his head in disgust. Then he turned and pointed dramatically at the men. "For trying to hold Hillsboro back, trying to overthrow the government and cause civil disorder, I sentence you to death by firing squad."

The crowd gasped. There hadn't been an execution in Hillsboro for nearly three years. In the desperate days just after the EMP attack, the Safety Committee had held public executions of looters in order to create a deterrent and to impress the new rules of martial law upon the people's minds. As the emergency had ground on and on, the militia still had looters shot, but without any public display. They had been summarily gunned down and their bodies buried in unmarked trenches. Now public executions had returned.

"The execution will take place outside after this meeting," Joe announced coldly. "Take them away." The militia led the men to the back of the platform and down the steps. Leo stood up and followed them.

Charlie leaned over to Frank. "This is wrong," he said beneath the sound of the crowd. "There wasn't any trial."

Frank kept looking out at the crowd, his mouth set in a grim line, his face pale. "They confessed, didn't they?" he answered in a strained voice. "Joe knew what was going on, you didn't."

"It looks like they were tortured, beaten."

"I didn't see bruises on their faces."

"There don't have to be bruises on their faces and you damned well know it. They didn't get a trial, Joe just pointed a finger. Why don't you stop this?"

"Why don't you?"

"I don't have any power," Charlie said.

"Neither do I." Charlie watched Frank swallow hard. Frank's face showed a mixture of fear and resignation. His voice was quiet and shaky as he continued. "It's time to decide where you are. Joe wants to run things his way. He doesn't seem to need either of us much anymore. If you want to stay safe and keep your comfortable life, you better get on board. He's got big plans and doesn't want anything...or anyone getting in his way."

Charlie clamped his jaw tight and got up to leave. Joe was speaking again, but he'd heard enough.

When he got outside, he saw Leo leading a procession of militia and the two orange-clad prisoners on the sidewalk that ran along the side of the arena. At the corner of the building was a weedy area that had held decorative plants years ago. Charlie saw two tall, dark posts that had been driven into the ground in front of the arena wall.

Charlie walked quickly towards Leo. At Leo's direction, the militia began to tie Overbeck and Caldwell to the stakes.

"Leo!" Charlie shouted. Leo turned toward him, his eyebrows slightly raised.

"Leo, I want these men released to my custody. I'm giving them a twenty-four hour stay to see if they want to appeal their so-called convictions." Charlie closed the distance and stopped in front of Leo, glaring into his eyes

He could see the disdain in Leo's expression. "You don't have any authority here, old man. If you know what's good for you, you'll shut up and leave. You make any more trouble and you and your wife will regret it."

The militia gathered in a menacing semi-circle around Charlie. The condemned men just looked at Charlie with hopeless eyes.

Charlie didn't move.

The disdain in Leo's eyes slowly turned to something like disgust. "Go. Before I have my men put you on a stake and execute you. You can consider yourself retired." Leo suddenly shoved Charlie. Charlie staggered backward a few steps. Some of the militia started for him, but Leo put up his hand to stop them and turned his back on Charlie.

He motioned to the militia to continue tying up the condemned men. A firing line was being formed under the direction of a militia officer. Only one of the militia kept an eye on Charlie, standing slightly apart from the others and holding an M16 pointed at his chest.

There was nothing that Charlie could do.

He turned and started to trudge away. More people had begun emptying from the main entrance. Many of them were trying to slink away, but Charlie saw lines of militia blocking their paths, keeping them corralled to the street in front of the arena. *Joe's going to make them watch. Drive home the point.*

Suddenly there was the sound of heavy engines. Two of the Army Humvees came into view and rushed through the militia lines, stopping along the curb near Charlie. He saw Lieutenant Cameron in the lead vehicle, with Sergeant Gibbs driving and more soldiers behind them. The other vehicle was just as full. Cameron's Humvee had a .50 caliber machine gun on top with a soldier manning it. Charlie ran over to Cameron as the lieutenant stepped out.

"What's going on?" Cameron asked.

Charlie stammered out a hurried explanation. The street was now filled with civilians from the arena milling about, unable to leave. The prisoners had now been tied to the stakes, and ten of the militia had moved back twenty paces and were now arranged into a firing line facing the stakes.

Cameron reached back into the vehicle. "This is an unlawful assembly," he shouted out through his loudspeaker. "I order you to disperse, and I want those men tied to the stakes to be brought over here. I'm putting them under my control as a representative of the federal government."

The line of militia looked to Leo, who held out his hand and said something to them. He turned towards Cameron and shouted, "You got no authority here. This is a civil matter and it's being handled by the militia."

"We let you enforce local laws and regulations. But when it comes to capital punishment, I take over. And since they're charged with sedition, which is a federal offense, they come under my authority. Release these men."

As Kevin was talking, the militia on the street were moving in to surround the two Humvees. Kevin looked around the crowd and inwardly cursed as he spotted two shoulder-mounted rocket launchers aimed at each of the vehicles. *I should have gotten my men out right away,* he thought. Even without the rocket launchers they would be sitting ducks as they emerged. There were about forty militia with automatic rifles pointed at the two vehicles. His machine gunner would not last long, even though he could do a lot of damage with the .50 caliber. The rocket launchers sealed his disadvantage. The crowd was silent, scared of what was about to happen. The militia kept their rifles aimed at him and his Humvees. No one moved.

"What are you going to do, Lieutenant?" Leo called. "Looks like you're not in a good position. You see those two rocket launchers aimed at your vehicles? If you try anything they'll open fire, along with the rest of my militia. I think you better leave."

Just then Kevin noticed a small knot of militia approaching from around the corner, coming from the back entrances of the arena. Walking amidst the guards were Frank Mason and Joe Stansky.

"What's going on?" Frank asked, his voice harsh and strident in the hush on the street.

"The lieutenant here thinks he has jurisdiction over these condemned prisoners," Leo said.

"This is a federal crime. These men are to be put in my custody," Kevin said loudly.

"These men are just like looters," Frank replied. Kevin could hear his voice shake as he spoke. "They're depriving the town of its rightful resources. They can be, and are being, handled just the way we deal with looters. This is not an army or federal issue." Beside him, Joe Stansky's eyes were cold and dark.

"Keep them covered," Leo shouted to the militia in the street. He grinned at Kevin. "You can stay and watch, but this execution is going to take place. If you attempt to interfere or your men attempt to get out of their vehicles we'll open fire."

Inside the Humvee Sergeant Gibbs growled, "We drove right into a fucking trap."

Kevin turned back toward the open window behind him. "It's suicide to jump out and fight," he said quietly. The savage look on Gibbs's face showed the sergeant's frustration at being outmaneuvered. Looking over the front fender, Kevin called out to Leo, "I'm putting you on notice. If you execute these men, I'm going to arrest you for murder...along with you, Frank. You can keep them in your custody, but until Captain Roper discusses this issue with Mason and Stansky, these men are not to be harmed."

With that, he motioned to the rear vehicle to back up out of the crowd. He opened his door and threw himself back into his seat. "Back to base," he gritted out. He'd get Roper fired up at this affront. Roper would draw the line and put Stansky in his place. A communication to Colonel Stillman could result in a larger force showing up, with some heavy firepower, and all three of those men getting arrested.

Gibbs pulled the Humvee away from the curb, the second Humvee following. In his rearview mirror, Kevin saw Charlie Cook looking after them. As they passed out of the main crowd and headed down the street, he heard the crash of the rifles.

Kevin pounded his fist on the dash, over and over. "Damn them! Those bastards. They wouldn't wait and let this end sensibly."

Gibbs's hands had the steering wheel in a fierce grip, his face still contorted in a fury. "It's Stansky. He's showing everyone who's boss."

The executed men slumped on their stakes. The crowd shrank back. After a moment, the militia let them quietly disperse.

Most people were sickened and frightened. Many tried to believe that these had been bad men, men who wanted to hold Hillsboro back for their own gain, but, to most people, the prisoners had only looked pitiful.

Others feverishly rationalized that this demonstration had been necessary to keep order. If two malcontents had wanted to subvert progress, well, they had gotten what they deserved. These were hard times, and they called for hard measures. Joe Stansky was right. No one should be allowed to hold back progress, and Joe was going to make sure Hillsboro progressed.

For most, there was now a large lump of fear in the back of their minds. Better not get out of line. Better not draw attention to yourself. Just do your job and keep quiet.

Things will get better, and you don't want to get in the way of progress.

Chapter 35

Roper looked up in surprise from the readiness report Gibbs had compiled as Lieutenant Cameron and the sergeant stormed into his office.

"What's up?" he asked. Both Cameron and Gibbs appeared to be very agitated.

Cameron answered with a barely suppressed fury. "Stansky's group just executed two men...in front of a forced audience. Apparently he had some kind of mock trial in the arena and convicted them of sabotaging the electricity project."

"How did you find out about this?"

"We got word of a gathering at the arena. Didn't know what it was going to be about, but it was supposed to be the whole damn town. We were *damned* late finding out about it. I took two Humvees and some men to check it out. When we got there the men were outside, tied to stakes with a firing squad lined up."

"And you didn't stop it?" Roper looked hard at his lieutenant.

"We rode into an ambush. They surrounded us and they had two rocket launchers pointed at the vehicles."

"Rocket launchers?"

"Looked like MK153s. No way they brought those for anybody but us." Cameron's voice was still full of anger as he continued. "I told both Leo and Frank that the men were not to be harmed until you could meet with him and Stansky. They could hold them, but they were not to be harmed. When we left, we heard shots, so I think they carried out the execution."

Roper put his head in his hands. "Christ almighty," he muttered. "What the fuck are they thinking?"

Gibbs spoke in almost a growl. "Looks to me like they're taking off the gloves. Stansky must think he doesn't need to pretend, and I'm not sure we can oppose him with the firepower he has."

Roper looked up at the sergeant. "Sergeant Gibbs, I keep finding you in the middle of officers' discussions. Why the hell is that?"

Cameron spoke quickly and coldly. "Captain, at the risk of sounding disrespectful, that's a bullshit comment."

Roper turned to glare at his lieutenant. Before he could speak, Cameron continued, "We don't have the luxury of standing on protocol. Sergeant Gibbs is experienced and deserves to be in this conversation."

Roper leaned back in his chair. "All right, I'll deal with the disrespect later." He turned to Gibbs. "So do you have some wisdom to impart to us?"

"Not now, sir," Cameron said. "Right *now*, I suggest you call Colonel Stillman and get him to send some reinforcements here. We need to arrest these guys and put a stop to this. It's gone too far."

"First things first, Lieutenant," Roper said, his voice icy and full of authority. "That means information. I've gone through this readiness assessment and now I'd like to hear what we're up against."

He watched Cameron choke off a response. The lieutenant knew that he was right; they needed to have a clear understanding of their position. Roper turned to Gibbs. "*Rocket launchers*, Sergeant?"

"Yes, sir. And a hell of a lot more." Gibbs went on to talk about rifles, machine guns, grenade launchers, mortars; whole armories stripped. Roper had noticed the town militia had improved their weaponry with M16s, but now he began to realize the true tenuousness of his position.

"Sir, that's why we need to contact the colonel," Cameron said.

Roper sighed. He couldn't play the charade out much further. "There's a problem with that," he said heavily. "I've lost contact with Colonel Stillman."

"Since when? Cameron asked.

"Since about three weeks ago."

His two subordinates stared at him. "How can that be?" Cameron asked.

"I don't know. The radio has power, but the signal doesn't seem to be getting out and nothing's coming through. I'm only getting static."

"Crap," Cameron said under his breath. "Why didn't you do something about it?"

"What the hell was I to do? I've noticed how powerful Stansky's gotten. I can count the men. They've put up with us only because they think I'm radioing in cheery reports once a week to keep Stillman happy. Would it help to let everyone know the radio doesn't work? Maybe ask Mason to find me a technician to fix it?"

"Cheery reports?" Cameron said. "So you're covering for them?" Roper felt a sudden chill as he realized what he had just let slip. "And leaving Stansky alone to do what he wants. Which now includes executing what might be innocent people."

Roper turned and looked out his window, trying to collect his thoughts. "Why the hell does he go and do that?" he muttered.

"To terrify the population into submission," Sergeant Gibbs said. "I saw it in Iraq and Afghanistan. It's an old technique used around the world, if I might be so bold as to add to this conversation." The last was said with more than a hint of sarcasm.

Roper turned back and scowled at Gibbs.

"Sir," Lieutenant Cameron said slowly and clearly, "I'm going to be straight up with you, even if you don't like what I'm about to say." Roper looked at Cameron, unsure of what would follow.

"Chief Cook has split with Stansky," Cameron said. "He had a long conversation with us. We know that you've been on the take from Stansky. Getting things in exchange for looking the other way and, as we find out now, giving Colonel Stillman your 'cheery reports'."

"That's a large accusation," Roper replied. He tried to sound sarcastic, dismissive, "coming from a Hillsboro cop that's probably dirty."

"Captain," Sergeant Gibbs said. Roper noticed that Gibbs had moved over to his left while he had been talking to Cameron. "There's no time to dance around this. You know what Lieutenant Cameron's saying is true. Don't waste anyone's time denying it. The issue for me, for the lieutenant, and for the other soldiers in this platoon, is what're you going to do about it?"

Roper sagged in his seat, a sense of defeat sweeping over him. "I don't know what there *is* to do about it," he said in a low voice.

"From where I stand, you have some options and so do I," Cameron said. "You can take a stand with us and do your duty, or you can try to leave, bug out, desert your command." The lieutenant stared at him for a moment. When Roper didn't respond, he went on, "I have three options. I could arrest you and hold you for court martial. I could let you slink away, with anyone who'll go with you—I've thought it over, and anyone who'd go with you under these circumstances is someone that I do not want in this unit. Or I could forget about your collusion with the enemy if I think you'll do the right thing."

Roper stood up, his eyes blazing in anger. He was ready to reassert rank on his unruly lieutenant when he saw motion in his peripheral vision. Gibbs had drawn his .45 and aimed it at his chest. He stopped still.

"This is insubordination. I'll have you up on charges," Roper said in a tight voice.

"I'll be happy to stand for those charges," Cameron replied. "I think I'll be able to produce evidence of your collusion. I'll have Charlie's testimony, and I'm sure to find some loot you've collected. You probably weren't taking IOUs. It's here and I'll find it. Now if you're asking me to arrest you, I will."

"It won't go so well. You'll have dissension in the ranks. Not everyone thinks you're so wonderful. Some of the men will be loyal to me. They'll think this is goddamned mutiny." Roper's mind was swirling as his rage grew. He stopped to try to think what to say next. "If you try to take me prisoner, not only will you trigger a split in the ranks, but I'm going to be a burden to you as a prisoner." He paused to let that sink in. "You're better off with me just leaving."

A look of dismay crossed Cameron's face at Roper's declaration of willingness to leave. Roper gave him a cold smile. "While you're thinking this over, remember, if you shoot me, you'll have a rebellion of your own."

"I hoped you'd do the right thing," Cameron said. He shook his head and sighed. "I can't believe it has come to this. You know this will all come back on you. You'll never get away with it. Even if I let you go for now, you'll be considered a deserter and shot."

"Who'll report me, you? You're staying here. You'll never survive a fight with Stansky." Roper picked up Gibbs' report from his desk and waved it at Cameron. "We don't have enough firepower to stand up to him. I'm not interested in becoming a statistic...MIA or KIA. I'll take my chances on my own. And the smart troops here will know damn well that this situation is precisely what a strategic retreat is for. Your best bet is to let me leave with those who want to go. That way you won't have any dissenters in your ranks to worry about. The fools that want to stay and be martyrs can do it. You're welcome to them, Lieutenant."

Doubt flickered in the lieutenant's eyes. Sergeant Gibbs's face darkened. He looked like he just wanted to shoot Roper and be done with it.

Roper allowed a slight smile to show. He seemed to have turned defeat into victory. *A strategic retreat.* Roper liked the sound of the phrase. It would play well when he met up with Stillman, and there wouldn't be any witnesses to say otherwise. If Stillman chose to come storming back here, guns blazing, he wouldn't take time to listen to any stories from Stansky or the others. And if Stillman didn't come back to Hillsboro, that was even better for Roper.

Cameron stared at Roper and spoke crisply. "Sergeant Gibbs, take his sidearm. If he resists, shoot him." He drew his own pistol.

Roper looked at Cameron in some confusion.

"Against what my emotions tell me, I'm going to let you leave...with whoever wants to go, after I've explained the situation to them. You get one truck. And you don't get to take your loot. That's blood money and you'll never see it again. If it wasn't for you giving these bastards cover, we'd have intervened a year ago and Stansky wouldn't have gotten to this point." Cameron's face was red with anger. He stepped around Roper's desk, opposite Gibbs, and moved close to Roper's face. "You could have exposed all this to Colonel Stillman while we had the upper hand, the firepower. No, you let him depart, thinking everything was fine, and then you let your men, the men you took an oath to lead and be loyal to, fall into an indefensible position. You disgust me."

The slap was like a gunshot. Roper never saw it coming. He reeled backward, catching himself against the desk.

"You just assaulted a senior officer. That could get you a long time in the stockade." Roper felt his lips swelling, felt blood dripping down his chin.

"No, I didn't," Cameron said. "I just subdued a prisoner who was trying to escape. Isn't that right, Sergeant Gibbs?"

"That's the way I saw it, Lieutenant," Gibbs replied. He stepped forward and shoved Roper back into his chair.

Cameron spoke to Gibbs as if Roper weren't present. "You go find some handcuffs."

"Yes, sir."

Cameron stepped to the rear of the office and opened the door to a utility closet. There was a sink with a drainpipe running through the wall. "We'll cuff him to the pipe. He'll be safe and quiet here. What you do next is find Wilkes and collect all the men you're *certain* aren't going to side with Roper. Have them quietly assemble with their weapons. Tell the others you're assembling a team to arrest Frank Mason. The ones who are in on the graft probably won't want anything to do with that."

"What do we do about the others, the ones that might end up siding with him? You want to let them go? And are you going to let this piece of shit go?"

"Much as I don't want to, he's right." Cameron scowled down at Roper. "I don't want to have to worry about him, or the other men. We've got a hell of a fight coming and I don't know how it's going to play out. But it's not going to be easy—and we're not going to wind up becoming martyrs like this asshole says." Cameron stared at the office door for a moment. "I think we get the men we're sure of armed up, then we assemble everyone. The others won't have their rifles since they're in camp. You see to that. Then I'll address the whole platoon, tell them what's been going on, and give them the choice—stay and fight with us, or leave and throw their lot in with Roper."

"What about the ones who choose to stay? Do I let them have weapons?"

Cameron thought for a moment. "No. They need to remain unarmed. At that point, the men we *know* are loyal to us will be keeping the rest under guard. No one moves. If any of them aren't telling the truth, they won't have a weapon until the others have left with Roper." He shook his head. "I don't think anyone will want to fake a desire to stay and be stuck here if they really want to go. There's no upside for them."

Roper was seething with indignation. "You can't send us out without weapons. We have to be able to defend ourselves."

The look he got from Cameron was dark and dangerous. "I can do whatever I want to do," Cameron replied.

"There may be men who go with me because I'm the senior officer," Roper lashed back at Cameron. "Because they see your actions as mutinous. They don't deserve to be cast out with no ability to protect themselves."

Sergeant Gibbs looked over at Cameron.

"Go find those cuffs," Cameron said calmly. "We'll figure this out as we go."

Chapter 36

Some of the assembled soldiers were beginning to look apprehensive when Lieutenant Cameron walked out onto the asphalt to address them. The men standing on the periphery of the group with rifles, on the other hand, had different expressions, carefully blank; Sergeant Gibbs had spoken to them. By the time Cameron was halfway through his recitation of Roper's misdeeds, a few of the men started glancing around nervously at their fellow soldiers holding M16s.

Ten men held weapons. Twelve men were unarmed; two of them were men that Gibbs had said he didn't trust; the others he was unsure of.

"Captain Roper is in his office. I have put him under arrest," Cameron concluded.

The men stirred uneasily.

Someone shouted out, "You got any evidence for your charges?"

"Whoever asked that question, step forward," Cameron said. No one moved. "I'm willing to answer questions, but I will not answer anonymous questions shouted out from a group. If you have a question, step forward and ask it."

The group slowly parted, leaving a man standing alone. It was Specialist Atkinson, a thin, dark-haired man. Atkinson looked at Cameron belligerently. "So you gonna arrest me 'cause I question what you're doing?"

"No, Specialist. I'm going to answer your question. I've got the testimony of Charlie Cook, the chief of police here in town. He attended meetings between Captain Roper and Frank Mason, in which they discussed the Captain's fees, meaning his cut of the loot collected by Joe Stansky's gang, and the nature of the Captain's services."

"Well, he ain't here to tell us himself, is he?"

"No, and I don't have time to assemble a courtroom level of evidence to present. But Chief Cook is my main witness, and we have a respectable pile of gold and jewelry found in the captain's quarters."

Atkinson shook his head but said nothing more.

"Now here's the deal," Cameron said. "Some of you are not part of the special detail just announced, and you are not armed. That special detail is not going out. It's covering you. Consider yourselves under guard for the moment. Do not attempt to disperse. Sergeant Gibbs has given these men orders to shoot anyone attempting to leave this assembly."

He watched as the men stirred and began to grumble. The volume of dissent grew. Someone shouted, "You can't keep us restricted, we haven't done anything wrong." Cameron did not bother to identify the speaker this time. He simply stared at the group until the commotion subsided.

When they had quieted he said, "I can do what I've just done, and you are required to obey my orders. Absent Captain Roper, I'm the senior officer here. Now to get back to the plan, as of this moment we face a serious strategic problem that constrains my options as acting commander. I will not have the time nor the men to keep Captain Roper under guard pending reunion with battalion command. Nor will I have time to be looking over my shoulder at this platoon and worrying about who might be disloyal to me. The reason is that, very shortly, we will be engaging a force superior in numbers to our own—the militia of the city of Hillsboro."

Dead silence.

"I have just told you about the corruption of the city government. That government is now preparing to attack and murder some civilians outside of town. This unit is going to do something about it."

A babble of voices arose from the group. Cameron spoke over the confusion, quelling it. "I need every soldier I can trust. And I cannot afford to have any soldier I cannot trust, no matter the circumstances. Due to these conditions, I am going to turn Captain Roper loose, send him out of town. To make it back to Colonel Stillman, if that is what he chooses to do. Any soldier who does not agree with the actions I've taken, who wishes to continue to follow Captain Roper, can leave with him. Those of you who remain will be in a fight for your lives...and the lives of the civilians we are all pledged to protect."

"You just gonna throw us out of town, on foot?"

Cameron didn't pause to single out the questioner, although he was certain that Gibbs was on it—the word 'us' had been loud and clear.

"I'm going to give Roper and anyone who leaves with him a truck, with a full tank of fuel, one full fuel drum, and food for a week."

"What about weapons? You can't throw us out without any way to defend ourselves."

"I can. And in the case of Captain Roper, I ought to. The captain made his choices and they were the wrong ones. He can now be judged complicit in the deaths of two civilians and in the deaths of others yet to be identified."

"This is all about your girlfriend, isn't it?" Private Jensen shouted.

"Soldier, you have just made your decision to leave with Roper. Sergeant Gibbs, make sure that man is on the truck." Cameron's gaze swept the group. "Now, before I was interrupted, I was about to say that I will allow one rifle per soldier. The weapons and the ammunition will be locked in a case. Those of you who choose to leave will be escorted out of town under guard. The escort will give Captain Roper the key when they break contact. If the truck stops or anyone disembarks while still in sight of the escort, we will open fire on you. If we encounter you in the field after you leave, you will be considered enemy combatants and treated accordingly."

He turned back to Gibbs. "It's time to separate this group into who's going and who's staying." Before he could speak further, another soldier shouted, "What can we expect if we stay?"

Cameron paused. After thinking for a moment he responded, "That's a good question. The best way to answer it is to remind everyone that we are soldiers. Our job is to put ourselves in danger when required, to protect our country and its citizens. Sometimes that mission is hard to discern, but we still carry it out. Here at home, in the present crisis, it can be even more confusing, but not in this case. We have direct threats to civilians from a criminal group that is running this town. The mission is not hard to see.

"We are going to put ourselves in harm's way to protect the civilians, probably leading to a fight to liberate this town from the group that controls it now. The fight will be dangerous, it may not succeed, but we will set out on it anyway. I have an experienced sergeant to help lead us, hopefully to victory. This may be the only time you'll ever get a chance to sign up for a mission instead of being told you're going on one."

A couple of men laughed. The man that had asked the question responded, "Where do I go to stand?"

Quickly the men began to shuffle around. When it was done, five men had gone to Sergeant Gibbs and said they wanted to stay. The other seven were standing together, having chosen to leave with Captain Roper. Cameron kept his face immobile. He had hoped for more but this was about what he had expected. He knew that at least two of the seven, and perhaps more of them for all he knew, were dedicated soldiers who simply remained unconvinced that he was right to have relieved the captain of his command without a formal investigation or trial, even in the current circumstances. Finding themselves corralled at gunpoint did not make them think better of the Lieutenant's actions.

And he suspected that some of them figured traveling with Roper and having some means to defend themselves was almost certainly a better proposition than going up against Stansky's gang.

There was nothing to be done about it. Cameron needed a force he could rely on.

Gibbs put the seven dissenters under guard in one of the storefronts. Cameron went to three loyal soldiers and told them to get one of the transport trucks ready. Then he headed back to Roper's office. The sooner Roper and his contingent were gone, the sooner Cameron could start thinking about what they were going to do about the threat. The threat was no longer only to the people in the valley. What remained of his platoon was now just as much in danger.

As the men dispersed to their tasks, he heard something. Engines. Close by. Many. He looked around with a flash of panic, and stared. A line of old cars and vans with police insignia were making their way slowly into the encampment lot.

Chapter 37

Charlie walked hurriedly through the streets towards police headquarters. His clothes were soaked with sweat. Dark thoughts swirled through his mind. He felt he had come very close to being shot back at the arena. He was not sure now that getting shot wouldn't still be his fate after the day's events were over. Would Leo recommend taking him out? Would Joe have already come to that conclusion? He could take no comfort in the thought that Frank might stick up for him. Frank had made it clear that Charlie should not oppose Joe, that Frank couldn't help his old pal if he did. Charlie didn't know where the day's events might lead. What he did know was that his instincts were screaming at him to act quickly; to not assume that he could carry on like yesterday. Today things had changed, and if he was to avoid a terrible fate—for him and Mary—he had to act decisively.

When Leo had come to take him downtown to the arena that morning, he had told the officers he was still sure he could trust to stay close to the station. He had wanted them available if he needed them. Leo's attitude had made him suspicious without knowing why. Now he understood. But his earlier orders to his people had given him a possible way forward. As he hurried on, a plan began to form in his mind.

When he arrived at the station, Charlie went quietly around to his ten loyal officers individually. "When I send the others down to the arena, you stay put. Don't ask me why, just don't go. Be busy, be out of sight, but don't leave." They all gave him surprised looks, but none of them said anything.

After Charlie had spoken to all of them, he went back to the ready room. "Higgins!" he called out.

"Yes, sir?" Higgins was the only police lieutenant on the force these days. He was bald, wore steel-rimmed round glasses, and had a tall, lean build. He had been a serious cop, hard on perps, harder than Charlie liked. He was also pretty much devoid of conscience and had been corrupted early by Joe.

"I need men down to the arena," Charlie told him. "Pronto. That's a hell of a big crowd, and things are a little more exciting than expected. You take Brodsky, Vance, Brown, and Smith." There were only five cops on his untrustworthy list in the station; the rest were out in the streets. "I want you to go down there and help the militia. They don't know about handling crowds, and I don't want a bloodbath. Show them how it's done."

"Should we take the cars?"

"No. Gas is too limited and the militia has vans to stuff people into if you have to arrest anyone. Grab the bikes, they're almost as fast, and get your asses over there. Pronto."

"What about rifles? Shouldn't we take our riot gear?"

"Dammit, I just told you the militia is there in force. Your job is to keep it from getting out of hand, keep civilians from getting shot. Now hurry or you'll be too late."

After the five officers left, the others that Charlie had spoken to began to gather in the ready room. They all had quizzical looks on their faces. When they were assembled, Charlie spoke to them.

"We're moving to the army camp. I want you to gather all the weapons from the building and load them into the vehicles." He looked at Les Hammond, "How many vehicles do we have here right now?"

"We got four cars and one van. There's six cars out on patrol right now."

"That'll do."

"What's going on?" another officer asked.

"Lots. Maybe a revolution. We don't have time for me to explain now, but Leo Stupek just told me I was finished. And that may mean any honest cop is finished."

"Holy cow!" someone muttered.

"Gather up all the gear you can find and let's move. We may not have much time before the militia shows up."

"There's a fight coming," Charlie told his ten police officers. They were standing in a large tent that Cameron had led them to after running out to meet them. Charlie related what had gone on at the arena. "I'm probably now considered part of the opposition. Most of you will get put in that same category. Stansky will allow no resistance to whatever he's planning. He's ruthless, as is Leo Stupek. They'll eliminate everyone who opposes them. I'm sorry to have put all of you in this position where you and your families may be threatened, and I know you just want to do honest police work, but that's where we're at. I made a decision...and Mary supports me in it. We're not going along with Stansky turning the town into a criminal enterprise."

Charlie took a deep breath. "The days of being on the fence, trying to do the right thing while accepting some of the wrong things we saw, are over. With Stansky, that won't be one of the choices. We'll either be part of his militia—there won't be any normal police work anymore—or we'll be eliminated." He looked hard at his officers, one by one. Eight men and two women. Half of them had families, he thought. Could they make the hard decision? Would they? "You can join with Stansky...or you can join the opposition. There's no middle ground. I brought you out here to be able to give you the choice. But you have to make it now, there's no time to lose."

Many in the group looked stunned. They glanced around the tent. Charlie noticed many eyes settling on Cameron, who was standing to one side watching the group, waiting for him to finish speaking.

"I could see this coming," Les Hammond finally said. "I think we all could. Just didn't think it would happen this sudden."

"I didn't sign up to be a gangster. Chief, I joined to do police work, to fight crime," Hank Ames said.

"What about our families?" Barbara Thomas asked.

Charlie looked over at Cameron as he spoke. "I don't know. But if you decide to stay, throw in with me and the army, we have to do something fast. There's no plan here. Events are happening fast, so we're figuring this out on the fly."

Mike Ortez recited a list of ten other names and asked about them. These were officers who he thought were loyal to Chief Cook.

"We'll have to assign a couple of you to intercept them and ask them which side they want to be on. I'd like to give them a chance to join us rather than leave them stuck with Stansky's men," Charlie replied.

"Things are changing here in camp as well," Cameron said. "I'm Lieutenant Cameron. I have just taken over command of the platoon. Captain Roper is under arrest and we are separating our men into those who want to follow me and those don't."

Murmuring arose among Charlie's officers.

"Give me five minutes to talk with Chief Cook," Cameron said, and he motioned to Charlie.

"What's going on here?" Charlie asked when they had stepped out of the tent.

"I confronted Roper, after we were ambushed downtown. I told him I knew what had been going on with him and Mason and Stansky."

"Why the hell—?"

"Let me finish. It was time to pick a side. That scene downtown meant Stansky was taking the gloves off. I couldn't let Roper play it as if nothing bad was going on."

"So what do you do now?" Charlie asked.

"I've decided to let Roper leave with any men that want to follow his command."

"And you're staying? How many men do you have?"

"Fifteen."

Charlie blinked at the number. Even with the addition of his own people, it would be a very small force to oppose Stansky's militia. This was beginning to look hopeless. "So what do we do now?"

"I'm going to take the men loyal to me and leave with Roper and his men. Act like we're all leaving town. That's what Mason and Stansky expect to see."

"But where does that leave us? I brought these officers here to join you. And now you're leaving?"

"We can't stay here. This compound is indefensible. On top of everything, Stansky has mortars. He can just lob them on us until we're wiped out. We have to retreat, connect up with the valley. You know they're going to be attacked, so we need to defend them. Then we can plan an assault on Stansky."

The feeling of security from having arrived at the compound melted away to nothing. "But how will we fight them? You're leaving us alone to deal with Stansky?" Charlie waved his hand at the tent behind him. "These officers stayed loyal to me and now they're in danger. We've got families here in town that are vulnerable."

"You can leave with us," Cameron said. "Send your cars to collect them all, fast."

"And when are you leaving?"

Cameron looked around at the activity going on in the compound. "Probably not until tomorrow."

Charlie shook his head. "That's too long. If Stansky or Leo figure out we went here, they might attack us right away." Charlie knew his outburst at the executions might have already triggered orders to the militia, putting all his loyal officers at risk. He struggled to clear his head.

"Chief Cook, I'm sorry, but everyone who isn't behind Stansky is in danger, no matter where you're staying. If you're not on board with his agenda, for him being the absolute authority, you're in danger. Given what Leo told you, I think you made the right move."

The lieutenant stared across the compound for a moment. "Can your officers stay in the city? Change where they're living and hide out? There's lots of empty buildings around town. They can help train those dissidents you met. That group may be the fifth column of fighters we need."

Charlie thought about it. "We can do that," he said. *If we're very lucky*, he thought. They'd have to move fast, collect their families and disperse. The technicians could help his men hide later, but at the start they just had to get gone; find unoccupied places without preparation and get into them without being seen.

"Have everyone get back into civilian gear, but keep their weapons."

"Okay, we'll do that." There was no time to argue and he couldn't think of a better plan. "But how do we get in back touch with you?"

Cameron shook his head. "Damned if I know. I'm making this up as we go along. I'll find you."

A thought struck Charlie. "We'll connect through Lori Sue."

"That's perfect. Mark her address on my map of the city." Cameron took him over to one of the storefronts with a long folding table in the middle and several maps laid out on it. Charlie made a careful X on the Hillsboro map and printed the address in tiny letters next to it.

Cameron reached past him, grabbed the map, folded it, and put it in his vest pocket. Then he spoke quietly. "There's one other pressing issue. Maybe you can help with it. We have to raid Stansky's arms cache. We have to try to get any mortars and other heavy weapons we can find. Not only could they take us out, they could do a lot of damage to the city. Stansky may not care about that, but we don't want to defeat him only to have the town in ruins."

Just then Gibbs came through the door. "We won't have Roper's group packed up before sunset. Not if we do it right."

Cameron sighed. "All right. Keep them under guard. The delay won't hurt. We're going to pack the rest of the platoon as well. Everything. The escort is going to be all of us. I want to keep an eye on Roper until we're well away from town. I don't want him circling back and spilling our plans to Stansky."

Gibbs took the news in stride. "That's going to take an extra day."

"Frank and Joe will see we're prepping to leave. They'll wait." Cameron gestured for both Charlie and Gibbs to sit down. "We have to figure out how to deal with the weapons Joe has. We have to get as many of the larger weapons out of his hands as possible. We'll also need rifles to arm the civilians, and ammunition...as much as we can take."

"Before or after we leave?"

"After we're out of here."

Gibbs stared thoughtfully at the desk. "That's tight. I can leave a small team behind. Very small. Too small for a real fight." He turned to Charlie. "Maybe we can add in some of your police. If they could help get us in quiet, that's even better."

Charlie nodded his head. "I know where the weapons are stored. And you're right, we can't assault the building, but if we can get in quietly and have a truck to haul the arms away, we can do it. How many do you want?"

"Let's talk to your people," Gibbs said.

Sergeant Gibbs looked levelly at Charlie's wide-eyed group. "If we can do it as a burglary, I think we can spare Specialist Wilkes and one other soldier. The advantage of Wilkes is that he knows some of the militia. He could get up close to them. He could pretend that he wants to stay in town, not leave with the squad, and needs to buy a weapon."

"I can work that game with him," Hank Ames said. Charlie was surprised. Hank hadn't seemed to be a big risk taker. But he was grinning. "I know a lot of those militia guys. They probably think I'm on Stansky's side. I can say I'm helping this guy out, since he wants to desert from the army. I'll say he gave me a bottle of whiskey to introduce him to someone who can get him a weapon. The guards get something nice too. So he'll have to bring a bottle of booze or something. If we can get close, we can take them down."

Gibbs smiled. "Captain Roper's hoard contains a few likely possibilities."

He turned toward Charlie, his smile fading. "Can he pull this off?" he asked while his expression meant, *Can we trust him?*

Charlie looked back. "Positive."

"It's a plan," Lieutenant Cameron said. "Sergeant, go find Wilkes and see if he'll volunteer. Charlie, pick another officer to go along. We'll send four total."

Chapter 38

Two days after he had gotten back from visiting the clans in the north, Jason was cleaning his M110 sniper rifle at the kitchen table, always to Anne's annoyance. She and Sarah were out visiting Claire Nolan, a widow whose husband had died defending the valley. Before she left, she had given strict instructions to Jason to cover the table with a generous cloth and had made him promise to clean up his mess afterward. Though he had been engrossed in the work, he saw a flicker of movement out of the kitchen window and instantly looked up to see the clansmen from up north emerge silently from the tree line and cross the open front yard.

He went out to meet them. It was mid-afternoon and the sun was hot. Jason invited the men up to the porch, which was partially shaded and protected from the day's heat. The men crowded up on the porch, some of them sitting on the floor and the steps while Clayton and a few others took a seat at the table.

Catherine was home, and she got some venison jerky and dried apples out of the pantry. She and Jason carried out three bowlfuls to pass among the men. After making sure the men all had something to eat, he sat down at the table with Clayton.

"We gonna set up at the bridge?" Clayton asked.

"It's the best place," Jason replied.

Catherine stepped out to join the conversation. "They've seen the bridge, they've heard the story. Won't they know how dangerous the bridge and the gorge are for them? I'm wondering if they won't try to find another way in."

"She be right," Clayton said with a nod.

"I can't say she's not," Jason said ruefully. "And speaking of the visit, that guy Leo was quiet, but I get the feeling that he's smarter than he looks. I'll bet he took a really good look at everything. We now know he's the one who runs the militia for Joe. He's the general." He rubbed his temples. "But the problem for him is he still doesn't have an alternative. There's no other way in."

"They's other ways in." Clayton pointed in the direction of the afternoon sun, towards the far side of the valley. "Over the west ridge they's a bark road that goes up and over. See that saddle?" Clayton pointed to the western ridge "Not very deep, but the road goes over the ridge there."

"How do you know that?" Jason asked.

"We know these woods."

Catherine nodded. "He's right. I hiked part of that before the EMP attack and I came across an old road."

Jason frowned. "Can you get a vehicle over the road? Many of them aren't passable."

"Four-wheel drive could make it," Clayton said.

"Damn." Jason thought for a moment. "Would it be on a map?"

"Don't know about any maps," Clayton responded.

Jason closed his eyes a moment, then shook his head. "We don't have enough forces to split the group. We've got to assume they probably don't know about that road. Hell, I didn't. We have to go with the bridge. They know the bridge is a dangerous place, so they'll try to avoid it and the road completely—they'll try to cross the river and climb the ridge through the trees. That technique almost worked in the last battle."

Catherine had a pensive look on her face. "If you're wrong, the whole valley will be wide open. That endangers Tom, Betty, Claire, John and his wife and kid. They're all exposed."

"What's the alternative?"

She was silent for a moment. Jason watched her stare over the valley. When she answered, her voice was calm and cool. With a pang of regret he realized it was not the voice of a teenager; that part of her life was now gone.

"I don't like it, but I don't have a solution. How long do you think we've got before they get here?"

"No way to know. We figure Stansky's going to push Roper into action this week, and after the army's gone he'll attack pretty quick. It may come next week, if not earlier."

Catherine shook her head. "What a crappy situation," she said quietly.

"It is what it is. Ain't nothing to do about it." Clayton said. There was a note of stoic acceptance in his voice, but beneath it something deadly.

Charlie's loyal officers and their families made their way across Hillsboro. They moved deliberately along many different streets that diverged widely from each other, angling wide of their eventual destination before changing course, or passing it entirely and then working back toward it. Some walked with partners and families, some walked alone. They did not hurry, despite the tension.

The return of the police vehicles to the headquarters lot had gone unobserved. The corrupt officers they had left behind would not immediately discover that the weapons were missing. The irregularity of the extraction of the children from the school wouldn't be reported immediately, and only later would it be connected to the disappearance of

Charlie and his loyal officers. Charlie figured there would be a delay of a day at least before any special word went out.

The spouses and families of the officers were afraid, but they handled the trip better than Charlie expected. Within the bags they carried were the firearms collected from headquarters. All the absconding members of the force had changed into civilian clothing.

And so Charlie's loyal contingent made its way into the neglected south side of the city, along streets lined with more and more uninhabited houses and abandoned structures, and came at last to the neighborhood around Lori Sue's apartment. Each new arrival was beckoned to from doorways and alleys, brief instructions were passed on, and as the afternoon went on the people Charlie could trust vanished from sight.

Charlie and Mary took the empty apartment next to Lori Sue's. Two of his people moved into rooms in the same building. Hurried consultation with a surprised and irate Lori Sue had gotten him suggestions about places for his people in the neighboring blocks. She had warned him that she was only telling him where she hadn't noticed any sign of life, that she hadn't actually searched the buildings. It didn't matter; it was all he had.

He and Mary had brought along their supply of extra food. He was happily surprised to find that all of his people had been saving some of the extra food he had surreptitiously been diverting to them and had brought at least some of those reserves with them. There would be no immediate problem with hunger, and he hoped that between Billy and the insurgents they would have at least a somewhat steady food supply. His officers could not show up at the food centers any more.

Lori Sue told Charlie, "You all got to be careful coming and going. You tell everybody. If the militia sees lots of activity here, they'll come snoopin' around. We don't need that. And no noise. None. *Specially* the kids. You tell 'em, you hear me?"

Charlie nodded dutifully. Lori Sue was highly opinionated, and, in this case, her opinion was correct. Discretion was the rule of the day.

Although he could not see very far ahead, he knew what his next step had to be.

Charlie waited till dusk and then set out again. He dared not take a direct route to the generator and wire factory; that was too risky. So he set out on a circuitous path. After reaching the factory, it took him a half hour of wandering around near the building before he connected with one of the conspiracy's lookouts. Going there unannounced was dangerous, but he had no choice. Events were moving fast and he had to make contact and bring them up to speed.

He was led blindfolded to another secret room to talk with the leaders. From the sound of their voices, they seemed both frightened and encouraged by the news he gave them.

When the discussion finally quieted and sorted itself out, the conspirators all agreed they would stay where they were and keep on working, but now more intensely, abandoning their slowdown. Stansky would think the executions had achieved the effect he wanted. For a while, he would not watch them so closely.

Charlie told them he would get weapons to them. He didn't elaborate as to how. He told them it was better to keep information compartmentalized while things were so dangerous. He didn't know where the technicians lived, and they didn't know where he lived. It was a good situation to maintain, given that Charlie and his group were about to be hunted.

With no more information to impart, Charlie begged off staying longer. The group could discuss their strategies without him. He was exhausted from the day's events and just wanted to get back to Mary.

He was old, he acknowledged to himself as he was led back out into the streets and his blindfold removed. This was a young person's game he was playing. *But you have to play the cards you're dealt, isn't that what Frank said?* Charlie had picked his side—his cards—and now he needed to play them out as best he could.

He made his way carefully back through the dark streets, ever watchful of being spotted by a patrol. He felt on edge, exhausted after the long stressful day. When he got back to the apartment, he lay down next to his wife and fell fast asleep.

Before dawn, Charlie was up with Hank Ames and Les Hammond, heading to the army camp. They were in uniform in case they were seen by any militia. They concentrated on moving normally, but they took a roundabout path that steered clear of downtown. With their precautions, they were able to reach the platoon headquarters undetected. The tents were being taken down, and supplies and gear were stacked neatly on the pavement, categorized and ready for loading. Men were moving in and out of storerooms and supply tents, adding to the piles in the parking lot.

Tommy Wilkes and another soldier were waiting for them in one of the storefront offices. Wilkes introduced his companion as Specialist Terry Jackson.

Wilkes and Jackson were wearing T-shirts and blue jeans. Charlie could see a sheath knife in Wilkes' belt, and he spotted the tell-tale bulge of a pistol stuffed into his jeans. Jackson had his service rifle and magazine packs.

They went over the plan again, but it was a brief conversation. The job was set for the evening of the next day. Hammond would bring the police truck and wait near the facility for the signal that entry had been secured. Everything else was an ambitious blank. While Hank knew the general layout of the building, where the different types of weapons were kept was another matter. There was no way to know how many men would be on guard either, inside or out. The raid would have to be played out as the action dictated.

With the morning not yet old, they slipped out into the city. The four that were going on the mission would find their own place to hide through the next thirty-six hours. The platoon would pull out of town the next morning, apparently with all its soldiers, leaving an innocently empty compound. Two alleys away from the base, Charlie shook hands with each of the four. There didn't seem to be anything else to say.

Chapter 39

The army's packing up," Frank stood in the doorway to Joe's office. Leo was sitting inside. "They should be out of here by tomorrow. Next day at the latest."

"I heard," Joe told him. "Looks like you were successful."

"Sometimes it takes a politician to get things done, to convince people where their best interests lie," Frank replied. He looked proud of himself as he took the seat next to Leo. He tipped his head at Joe. "You should remember that when the federal government shows up. We'll need to do a lot of convincing to make them see they should work with us."

Joe smiled. "So that's the plan? Get them to work with us?"

"Better that than replacing us...or us going to war with them. When that day comes, we want to be put in charge by the feds, just like the army let us remain in charge. We need to be the solid, helpful structure in place. Then we can keep this operation going." Frank spread his arms out as if covering the town.

Joe's smile broadened. Frank never stopped lobbying for putting himself into every deal. Joe knew that Frank saw his future as being the middleman between Joe and whoever showed up.

"What's up with Charlie?" Leo asked Frank. "You seen him since he put up that show at the execution?"

Frank shook his head. "I haven't seen him. I can check on him, but from the line he took with you at the execution, I don't think he's on board."

"That's no secret. Leo told me what went on." Joe leaned towards Frank. "You know anything else?"

"He talked to me in the arena. I didn't think too much of it when it happened. I thought he was in shock from the announcement, running his mouth...but now I guess it was pretty clear. He tried to convince me that we should take a stand against you."

"He did? And what the hell did you say?"

"I told him that the valley had brought this trouble on themselves and I wasn't going to let them interfere with the town's progress."

"So, he tried to recruit you to double-cross me?" Joe said. His anger began to rise. "I'll deal with him later. I want to get ready for this raid. We got everyone keeping their heads down here in town, now it's time to take care of the valley."

Frank asked, "What do we do with the police?"

Leo smiled at Frank. "Half of them are on our side. I'll just put them in the militia. The others we'll eliminate."

"Forget the cops for now," Joe growled. "Frank, you go over to the electrical project and check on them. I expect to see an improvement or we'll have another trial. Make it clear."

"I will." Frank replied. Joe kept looking at him. After a moment, Joe nodded slightly. Frank got the point. He rose stiffly and exited the office.

"So when can you hit the valley?" Joe asked Leo.

"In a couple of days." Leo frowned. "Maybe. I got to think more about the plan. The bridge goin' in is a dangerous place. We got a problem if it's the only way in."

"Well, don't take too long. I want you to head out the day the army leaves." Leo looked back at him from under his heavy brows without answering. Joe stared at him for a moment, then sighed. "Okay, figure it out, but don't take too long. Let's get this done so we can concentrate on our projects here in town with no interference."

"Why you want to see Leo's woman? That ain't healthy, and it ain't healthy for me if you get caught."

Lori Sue looked up at him and giggled. She'd been working on the door guard for a half hour, and she could tell she was getting through. His reluctance was one thing, but the eager flush on his face was something else.

"Aw, Reggie, I won't get caught, and you can always say that I must have slipped through while you were taking a pee around the corner." Her voice and smile continued to tease him. "You have to do that sometimes, don't you?"

"Not now I don't, you got me all excited. Damn, we should just go around the corner for a minute."

Lori Sue smiled and stepped back from his groping hands. "I don't want a quickie. I want to do it right with you. Get the full effect."

"You'll get it. Just come around tonight when I get relieved."

Lori Sue made a sad pout. "I'd like to but I've got some bigwigs want me tonight. Fact is, they got me scheduled for most of the week. My ass is gonna be tired by the end."

"Shit. They get all the breaks."

"Much as I like you, and how you're helping me, I got to make a living." She gave Reggie her most soulful look, promising delights to come.

His voice trembled. "So why you keep seeing her?"

"We girls got to stick together. She's got a kid at the school. Leo don't let her see him much, so I stop by and let her know how he's doing. It makes her feel better." Lori Sue decided it was time to move, before Reggie got nervous again. "Now I better go. Don't want Leo to find me here." She quickly stepped through the hotel entrance as the guard reached for her.

Donna answered her knock almost instantly. She had an eager look on her face.

Lori Sue slipped inside. "How much time we got? The guard said Leo just left a little while ago."

"He said something about going to see Joe. I don't know how long it'll be. You shouldn't stay long." Lori Sue headed for the kitchen. Donna followed her, dragging her long chain.

They sat down at the table. "I'm bettin' that's an important meeting. He's going to be doing something big pretty soon."

"What do you mean?"

"He's getting ready to attack the valley," Lori Sue said.

Donna looked blankly at her.

"You don't know? The valley where those farmers are from. The ones that came to town."

"Oh yeah, Leo said something about them."

"Well, Joe doesn't like them. He wants to go get rid of them."

"I thought they were bringing food."

"It don't matter. Stansky thinks they're a threat to him. He's boss of Hillsboro now, taken over and he's going to get rid of anyone in his way. He went and had two people shot last week, and made everybody watch. And he wants those farmers out there gone. They're friends of some people here that don't like Stansky." Lori Sue grabbed one of Donna's hands. She wanted to give the woman hope. "There's people here that are starting to work against him. They're starting to link up. If the valley don't get wiped out and if the army can help too, we may be able to get rid of Stansky and Leo."

"Maybe I can get free," Donna said.

"You will. I'll help you. We girls got to stick together."

Donna nodded and kept looking at her. "What else do you have to tell me?"

"Oh, I got to see Danny again," she said.

Donna's face lit up. "How is he?"

"He's okay. Healthy. I think he needs more sun.

"Did you tell him I love him?"

"Every time. He said he misses you..."

Chapter 40

Clayton's people had set up camp in the orchard again. Catherine stood at the porch rail looking out at the tents and canopies, her mind drifting away from the conversation going on behind her.

Seated around the porch table were Jason and Clayton, joined by Tom Walsh and John Sands. Tom was a Vietnam veteran and no stranger to battle. John, who lived farthest up the valley, had been an architect. He was married with a seven-year old daughter. He had little knowledge of fighting, his first battle having been the one where the valley defeated Big Jacks' gang. The experience had taught him that fighting was necessary when reason would not prevail.

As they talked about placement of men, how long they would have to wait, whether they could have scouts that could signal when Leo's men approached, Catherine kept thinking about the back door; the bark road over the saddle to the west.

It didn't feel right to leave it unguarded. The road was over a hundred years old and unused…but it existed. That fact was enough to continue to worry her. It had taken substantial effort carve it out of the mountain side. She had hiked part of it before; it was rough, but not impassable. It had to have been mapped at some point and might still be seen on older maps—tax or property maps. She didn't know much about any of that, but logic indicated that since the road existed it was on a map somewhere.

Leo was no fool—a killer, but no fool. He'd check. He would want to find an alternate way into the valley. He'd look for maps. The thought chilled her; she shivered in the morning's cool.

Finally, she spoke up. "I can't get past the idea that Leo will try to find another way in and that road will be on some map somewhere. We shouldn't leave it unguarded."

The men stopped talking. Everyone turned to her.

Finally Jason replied, "We already agreed that we can't split our forces. We just don't have enough men, and we aren't sure if Kevin will be here before the attack comes."

She looked steadily back at him. She was now calm in her conviction. "I know all that. But that's our back door and we're leaving it unguarded."

"I have to bet they don't know about it," Jason said.

"That's what worries me," Catherine replied. "There's got to be maps in town. Old ones that will show that road, and it's possible Leo will find them. He's not stupid. When he plans this attack, he'll want some maps. You said he would want another way into the valley. And that Frank guy...he probably knows where to look."

Jason looked at her for a long time. She saw his face grow darker as he saw the danger.

"Do you have any solutions?" he asked.

She nodded her head slowly. "I do. But don't interrupt when I tell you. Hear me out."

As she assembled her thoughts, she became aware of her mother standing in the doorway listening.

"I'm the best shot in the valley next to you," Catherine said to Jason. "You need to lead the main group at the bridge. What if Mr. Jessup picks his best marksman and the two of us go up to the saddle and guard it."

Jason started to object, but Catherine put up her hand. "Please, let me finish. We'll act as snipers as well as spotters. We'll set up multiple shooting positions, each one a fallback. We'll be sniping, slowing them down, retreating when our position gets too hot and then slowing them some more. When we can't do any more, we can melt away into the woods. They won't find us."

"You could be overrun. You can't stop them, you already said so."

"I said we'd slow them up. If they come that way, we give the valley time. Those waiting at the farms will hear the gunfire. They'll know the attack is coming from the west."

"What if it comes from both directions?" Clayton asked.

"If it does, we've got big problems, but aren't we better off taking some of them out and slowing them down? Everyone who isn't fighting can head for the woods, the others will be ready. And we can keep attacking them from the sides."

Jason was looking doubtful. Catherine continued, "Look, you know I'm the best shot. You taught me how to set up ambushes in the woods. I know how to fight like a sniper, from a distance. It's how I saved your life, don't forget. And I'll have Mr. Jessup's best shooter with me. We know the woods and how to move in them. We can harass them all along the way. You said yourself that a sniper can hold up a much larger force with lethal shooting."

"Until he's discovered and neutralized," Jason said.

"Or falls back, melts away into the woods only to show up in a new spot pinning them down again. Remember, they'll be on the road, in the open. We'll select spots that have sight lines to the road. They'll be in the open, not us."

Jason turned to Clayton. "How far can your best men shoot?"

He thought for a moment. "Don't get long shots in the forest, you know that. Hard to say. If it was open, across fields," he paused, looking down into the valley, "I'd say one of my men could hit a can down there, along the fence." He pointed down the drive to the barbed wire fence across the valley road.

"That's about a hundred and fifty yards," Jason said. "That should be far enough. Catherine can make that shot and more." He turned to Catherine. "You'll have to set up ahead of time to maximize the distance you can shoot from."

Anne spoke suddenly. "You'll be out there all alone, without anyone helping you."

Catherine looked at her mother. "Mom, I'm going to be out there somewhere fighting. I'm not staying out of this battle. But I think I can be most helpful in this role."

"You're right," Jason admitted. "Slowing them down, giving the valley warning with the shooting, that all helps. If that's the only way they're coming, then we can regroup and attack them while they're distracted by you. If it's a two pronged attack," he paused, "then God help us, but, like you said, we're better off knowing than not."

Lori Sue knew she had to leave. She had been in Leo's apartment for an hour and Leo would be coming back soon. Donna kept hungrily asking her more about Danny, what he had been doing in school, if she could bring Donna some of Danny's school work.

Finally Lori Sue interrupted Donna. "Look, when Leo goes to attack the valley, he'll be gone for a couple of days at least. I'll get you out of here and we'll pick up your son from the school."

Donna blinked. It seemed hard for her to focus on any hope beyond news of her son. "How will you get me free? I'll have that ankle cuff on. And where will we go?"

Lori Sue got up, anxious to be gone. "I'll figure something out. I'll bring a chisel or a hack saw. And don't worry about where we go, I can hide you. I know lots of hiding places in town...lots of empty places. And folks who can help." She stopped for a moment to think. "Course I got to give that dumb doorman a tumble. He's getting damned impatient to collect his reward for letting me in. Promises ain't cutting it anymore."

Donna was looking at her. Lori Sue saw her expression brighten. "Oh bless you!" She wrapped Lori Sue in a big hug. Then she pulled back. "But you better go. If Leo catches you here, you'll get thrown in prison, or worse."

"Got that right,"

They walked to the door. As Donna turned the doorknob, Lori Sue heard the stairway door at the end of the hall open. Donna jerked back her hand away from the knob like it was on fire. "Oh God, it's Leo," she said, panic in her voice.

"Shit!"

Donna looked around frantically. "Quick, here in the closet," she whispered.

"Won't he open it?"

"I'll stop him, I'll do something. Get back in the corner, get some coats in front of you!"

Lori Sue shoved herself through the coats to the back corner. The closet door closed silently, and she was enveloped in blackness. She heard the door open and then Leo's voice. "What are you doing at the door?"

"I heard you coming. I was going to open the door. I missed you this morning. You left before I got up."

There was the sound of the deadbolt turning, a rustling and murmuring, and then Leo's voice again. He sounded pleased. "Let me take my jacket off," he said.

Lori Sue shrank back into the corner. She was concealed from the waist up, but she knew her legs had to be in plain sight. All Leo would have to do was look down and he'd see her. Her heart raced. Her body wanted air, but she didn't dare breathe.

"I'll take it," Donna said.

"That's okay, I'll just hang it up." The closet door opened. The pounding in Lori Sue's chest increased. Could it be heard? It was so loud in her ears. She saw Donna's arm reached in and grabbed a hanger off the pole, and the door drifted half-closed again. "You're being awfully helpful," Leo said. "Haven't seen you like this before. What's up?"

"I just missed you. I'd like you to take my shackle off." Donna's voice became sultry, provocative; a voice Lori Sue had never expected to hear from her. "We can go into the bedroom and have some fun. You've been good to my son, so I want to be good to you."

"I might just take your ankle cuff off if your attitude keeps improving."

"I just want you to be happy." The inviting purr continued in Donna's voice. Donna's slim hand slipped the hanger hook over the closet rail, and the darkness returned. Lori Sue heard them recede, the chain clinking along the carpet.

Later, when Donna's cries of passion rose in a crescendo, Lori Sue pushed her way out of the closet, quietly unlocked the door, and slipped out.

Later, when Leo's appetites had been satiated, he wandered naked from the bedroom to the kitchen. Donna followed him out, and then she thought of the front door with the deadbolt now unlocked. Her heart jumped in her chest. She had to keep Leo from seeing that; he'd know something was up.

Pushing down a surge of panic, she grabbed him round the waist and pulled him back toward the bedroom. "You've got me so excited, I want some more of you," she gasped, panting from the surge of adrenalin.

Leo looked down at her and smiled. "You've changed," he said. "I think you're starting to enjoy our relationship." He followed her into the bedroom and grabbed her, pulling her down onto the bed with his body hovering over her. His face held a wicked smile as she looked up at him and trembled.

She was pretty sure she could wear him out and get a chance to lock the deadbolt while he slept.

Feigning excitement and willingness was still distasteful, but she had gotten better at shutting down her emotions and acting her part as the submissive, excited woman. It had been necessary to survive and appease Leo. Now she was beginning to hope it might be the price of a chance at freedom.

Chapter 41

Clayton went into the encampment in the orchard and picked a boy to be Catherine's partner and brought him back to the porch. He was about sixteen, tall, rangy and unkempt, with shaggy light brown hair. Clayton explained the assignment to the boy, pointing towards the western ridge. When Clayton was done, the boy just nodded and looked curiously at Catherine. His eyes were hazel, and Catherine noticed that they looked very sharp and clear.

"This here's Burdett Early. We call him Bird," Clayton said.

Catherine reached out to shake Bird's hand. He responded awkwardly, almost shyly. Yet there was a calm presence about him.

"What kind of rifle do you have?" Jason asked.

He unslung it. ".30-06," he said.

"How many shots?"

"Five rounds in the magazine."

"That's not many rounds," Jason said.

"I got six shots total and extra mags," Bird said. "Takes only a second to change 'em out. Course, when I'm done, I got to reload them."

"That's a bolt action," Catherine said. "Can you fire fast enough? We'll have to put a lot of shots out when we get the chance. Can you cycle your shots fast enough?"

He smiled shyly, but there was no hesitation in his eyes. "Shoot as fast as you want," he said. "Fast as need be."

"How much ammunition do you have?" Jason asked.

"Fifty rounds."

"We can give you some extra rounds," Jason said. "Tom and I are shooting .223 rounds." He turned to Catherine. "You should use the M110. You've practiced with it. It's more accurate at long range and delivers more punch."

"It's pretty heavy. I'm comfortable with my rifle," Catherine said.

"Yeah, but you'll be shooting longer distances now. It's a better tool for the job."

"What about Bird? Shouldn't he upgrade as well?"

Bird looked anxious for the first time. "I don't want another rifle. Mine's just fine."

Jason shook his head. "Bird's .30-06 will punch about as hard as the 7.62mm M110. Both hit harder than your .223, especially at a distance. The .30-06 is accurate, and if Bird's used to it he should keep it."

Catherine thought to argue, but Jason was right. The M110 was a better tool for the task.

Jason handed her a well-worn notebook. "You've looked at this before. Use it when you've set up your positions." The book contained tables of scope adjustments for distance and windage.

He went over with her how to take the average height of a male, around five feet ten inches, and estimate the range using the binoculars with their ranging scale in the lens. Next, he reviewed how to adjust for distance using the tables in the book. Adjustments could also be made for how many degrees up or down she was shooting. It was somewhat intimidating, but Catherine had been exposed to the information before.

"Now positioning," Jason said. "It's vital to your survival. Remember, your job is to fight from a distance. You're outnumbered. You have to always have a back door, a retreat path, and a new position to set up again and continue shooting. In a direct confrontation, you lose, so make them fight you on your terms, and *never* up close."

Early the next morning, as the sun rose, Catherine and Bird started walking up the valley road. They wore backpacks carrying two days of trail food and one hundred rounds of ammunition each. Catherine carried the M110 slung over her shoulder. Strapped to her waist was her 9mm pistol. Bird had only his rifle. They trudged along the road in silence. Bird didn't seem the talkative sort, and Catherine was enjoying the quiet of the morning.

The sun warmed them as it rose in the sky, and they soon began to feel the heat of the day. When they came near the end of the paved road, they veered off to the south and began to hike up the slope.

The road was difficult to detect where it joined the pavement. It was heavily grown over with grasses and small willow shrubs. A close inspection would reveal the traces, but a casual observer would not notice it. The paved valley road ended in a turnaround as it approached the west slope. What one didn't see through the thicket was the old road connected off to one side. Unless you knew it was there, your eye would not pick out its faint path.

They worked their way through the trees, staying close to the deepening gorge on their right. The old two-track road was off to their right, across the gorge. It came over the saddle on the west ridge and wound its way down into the valley. They were ascending the south ridge, with a ravine separating them from the western slope. They were looking for outcroppings or clearings that would give them clear sight lines to the road as it came over the top and down the ridge across from them.

During their climb, they detoured to the right to look for the old road and to check their altitude. The road was sometimes hard to pick out. The trees covered it under their canopy for long stretches

"We're only going to have clear shooting at the switchbacks," she commented as they stared through the trees. The road took a serpentine route, snaking down the slope and turning back each time it came to the gorge separating the western and southern ridges.

"Got to make the shots count," Bird replied.

"Yeah. Let's get higher, so we can start shooting while they're further upslope. We have to take full advantage of each switchback."

"Might make them stop and think before each turn," Bird offered.

They turned back to their uphill climb. The day grew hotter as they worked their way uphill. Both of them were soon sweating and swatting at flies that harassed them.

When they had climbed well over halfway up the slope, Catherine stopped at an outcropping that was shielded with a few trees and mountain laurel bushes.

"This is a good spot. We're not far below the west saddle. We can shoot at them as they come over the ridge. They'll be skylighted against the horizon."

Bird shook his head. "That ain't good."

"Why do you say that? It's a clear shot at them where they're most exposed."

"We shoot at them at the top of the road, they just back their trucks down out of sight, leave 'em, and spread out through the woods. That's what I'd do. We won't know where they gone."

Catherine thought about that. "So we have to wait for them to get over the ridge? That means we don't shoot until that switchback about fifty yards downslope from the top."

"We start there. If they jump into the woods, we'll see the direction they gone. I don't think they'll be very good in the woods, so we can fight them that way too."

"I hate to let them get further into the valley, but you may be right."

They stepped back from the edge of the outcropping and began to set up their shooting positions. They cut some brush and wove the branches through the laurel to better hide their position, and they piled up stones for shooting rests. When they were finished, they moved down the slope and searched out two fallback shooting positions that had sight lines to the other exposed switchbacks on the bark road. By the time they were done setting those up, the day was ending.

They climbed back to the first position to spend the night. Each had a blanket and a ground cloth. They would alternate sleeping and keeping watch. There was no way to know when the attack would come.

If it came at night, Catherine hoped the attackers would be using their headlights to light their way.

For now, she and Bird settled down to dried venison and water, accompanied by some early blackberries they had packed. After they had eaten, they got as comfortable as they could among the rocks, nestled in their blankets and ground cloths, their backpacks under their heads.

With the sun gone, the cool of the night began to advance. Even in summer, the nights often remained cool in the mountain valley. There was no question of a fire. The buzz of insects from the day had faded with the sun. Stillness surrounded them like a thin blanket, soft and loose. Over it an occasional hoot from an owl could be heard in the distance. Frogs began their ritual croaking somewhere below in the ravine.

As the first stars began to show, Catherine thought about Bird. He was the only teenager she had come into contact with outside of the valley after the EMP attack. It made her think about school and the normal life that had ended. "Do you miss school?" she asked.

"Nah. Never liked it much."

"Did they call you Bird there?"

"Yeah. Everybody did."

"So they called you Bird Early in school? Did that cause you any problems?"

Bird looked at her. His face was scowling. "You mean like changing it to 'early bird'...getting' the worm?"

"Yeah. I'm not making fun of it, Bird's a nice name really, but I know how kids can be. I got kidded a lot in school."

"I got that. Got in some fights over it."

"That why you didn't like school?"

"Some. I didn't like sitting in a chair all day...being inside."

They were quiet for a while, with only the sounds of the forest intruding on their silence.

Finally Catherine spoke again.

"You miss the power being on? I mean how much it's changed our lives?"

"Not so much. I like what I do now...being in the woods and all...you know, huntin', fishin', trappin'. I always liked that. Now I get to do it every day."

Catherine thought about that for a while. "I kind of miss going to school...learning things."

"Bet you had a lot of friends. You're pretty. I didn't have many friends. Most looked down on kids like me."

Catherine smiled at him. "Thank you. I had a few friends, but not that many. A lot of the kids were more popular than me. I was pretty quiet."

"Quiet's good. Most people talk too much anyway."

"Some of the kids looked down on me and my sister since we came from this valley. They really treated Billy bad."

"Who's Billy?"

"Billy Turner. He's my age. He moved to Hillsboro two months ago."

"I think some of us are related to him. I heard Clayton talk about it."

"I didn't know that. Turners have lived in the valley for a long, long time." Catherine thought about Billy. "He's a country boy like you, that's for sure. But he wasn't always nice...like you are. You have an honest look and nice, clear eyes. I like that."

Bird looked down at the ground, grabbed a stick and began to poke around with it. "You got a boyfriend?"

Catherine smiled. "Yes. We're getting married as soon as this fighting's settled."

"Pretty young to get married, ain't you?"

"Not really. Times have changed. I'll bet you got some girls eyeing you."

Bird snorted. "Maybe. Some of 'em just too fussy for me." He looked up at Catherine. "They not be like you. They can't shoot and take care of theirselves. I like that you can do that."

"Most boys don't, I think."

"Well, I do. Not sure I'll find a girl like you."

"You'll find a girl. Maybe you just have to teach her how to shoot and hunt. Jason taught me."

There was an awkward pause.

Catherine tried to change the subject. "You think they'll come this way?"

"Can't be sure, but I think you right about watching this road. It's what I'd do if I was to attack the valley. 'Specially since they know how you fought at the bridge. Bet they don't want any part of that."

"Then we have to stop them." Catherine felt the burden of their task pressing down on her. If her fears were proven right, they would have to significantly slow down the attackers until help could come. It was up to her and Bird to keep them from hitting the farms, killing their friends, and destroying what they had all built.

She wanted to steer the conversation back to lighter things, but the import of the moment pressed other thoughts from her mind.

Bird said, "Look, if something happens to me, you get out of here. Don't try to save me and get yourself killed."

"Nothing's going to happen to you. We'll just shoot at a long distance and keep out of sight. I doubt they can shoot all that well."

"Still, I don't want you to get hurt...or worse, caught by them. No tellin'
what they'd do."

Catherine had faced down outlaws that had killed, raped, and even
participated in cannibalism. In that fight she had known the fate that
threatened her, and it had only made her fight harder.

She spoke in a quiet tone. "We'll both be all right. I've been up against
even worse than these." Her voice sounded so sure of itself, but there was a
kernel of fear inside her that tried to grow and take over her confidence. She
pushed it down.

She yawned and stretched out her arms. "Okay then, you go to sleep,"
Bird said. "I'll watch first."

"All right, but wake me. I don't want you to stay up all night. We both
need some rest."

Chapter 42

Lori Sue and Billy lay in their bed, spent from making love. Billy savored the feeling of intense satisfaction coupled with a deep relaxation. He had found a girl that liked him, that made love to him, that respected what he knew and what he could do. He was calmer now when they made love. Lori Sue had shown him how to please her. And she certainly knew how to please him. He rolled over toward her and propped himself up on his elbow, "I love you, Lori Sue," he said quietly.

"That rhymes," she said with a giggle. "Maybe you could write a song about me."

"I doubt it. I ain't good with words. But I'm sure glad I found you."

"Me too," she answered.

After a moment she turned over to put her face close to his. "You know we been talking about what we can do after Stansky's gone. I know you don't want me to keep doin' what I'm doin'—"

"I don't like you seeing other guys...now that you're with me."

"I know. But the way things are now, it's what I gotta do." Lori Sue put her fingers to his lips to keep him from responding. "But after, things'll be different. I'm thinkin' we can start a bar and restaurant. You can hunt for the food, make the moonshine, and I can run the place. I used to work in a bar before the power went out. We'll have good food to eat, lots to drink." She went on, excitement building in her voice. "We'll have sawdust on the floors. It'll be warm inside and smell like beer. I'll find us a cook and some guys to play country music. People will come and drink and dance and have a fine ol' time. We'll make lots of money."

Billy looked up at her. Her eyes were gleaming, excited. She grinned at him. "Whaddaya think? Want to do it?"

Billy looked at her, this honky-tonk girl who had opened his horizons, made him feel wanted, accepted. "Yeah. I'd do that with you." He figured he'd do almost anything she asked him to.

Lori Sue fell onto Billy and wrapped her arms around him, wiggling her petite body all over him, trying to connect every part of her skin to him. "We'll be famous...and rich!"

Billy smiled as his body started to respond to her embrace.

Suddenly a thought came to his mind. "What will people use for money? How they gonna buy the food and drinks?"

"Oh, they'll get money going again. There's people know all about that stuff, you'll see. We can't just keep tradin' things, it's awkward. So people will get paid to work on projects, they'll come into our bar and pay us to eat and drink, and we can buy what we need with the money, so you can keep hunting and making liquor. It'll all work out, you'll see."

Billy thought it sounded good, but he couldn't quite picture how all that would get started. Still, it had to start again sometime, he supposed. The prospect of living his life with Lori Sue warmed his whole body. He began to run his hands over her back and bottom. She responded to his touch, and soon they were lost in kissing and nuzzling one another, the rush of the vision now replaced by the rush of their bodies enjoying each other.

They lay entwined in their bed; a nest safe from the world outside. A pale light from the moon came through the window. The city outside was dark. Some of the empty buildings might never be lit again. Grass and weeds grew in cracks along the streets and sidewalks. Broken windows went unrepaired, with the rooms behind them laid open to the elements, becoming homes for birds and bats. In the empty quarters of Hillsboro, the desolation advanced with nothing to slow it down. Wildlife crept back into the city, taking over abandoned spaces even within the great curve of the wall, while the people huddled together in the smaller inhabited parts of the city and worked to keep the decay at bay, at least on their own blocks. The hopes of Lori Sue and Billy warmed them in their nest, but the outside world seemed indifferent, even impervious to their plans.

Later in the night, after they were spent, Lori Sue was talking about Donna and her plans to get Donna free when Leo was away.

"I don't want you to go back there. It's too dangerous," Billy said.

"But I gotta help her. She's got no one. I'll go when Leo leaves to raid the valley. I'll be all right."

Billy just shook his head, but he was beginning to fall asleep. "I still don't like it," he murmured.

"You just help me find a hacksaw or a chisel. I'll be okay."

In the morning light, the column of Army Humvees, troop trucks, and tankers moved slowly through the main gate in the rough city wall. Frank had gotten there a little beforehand; he had parked his car a block away from the barrier, not wanting to create any disturbance with his presence. There was nothing further he wanted to say to Captain Roper. Roper was leaving and that was all that mattered. They were free of the Army. *Finally.*

Now Frank and Joe could finish getting the city under control. Once they took out the valley and got the proper seed to start their own farming, Frank figured that the internal dissent would wither. If it didn't, a few more executions would do the job. It was distasteful, somehow more so than it had been in the early days after the attack, but he could see how effective it had been. His visits to the water mill and the wire plant had given evidence of that fact. The technicians were more focused and were working harder. No one seemed to talk about the executions, but their effect had been a renewed burst of productivity.

Soon they would get the power back on. The unpleasant actions would then be forgotten. And as he and Joe solidified their dominance over the other towns, as they rewarded their own citizens with increased security and more food, as they reestablished normal patterns, the people would fall in line. All anyone had to do was obey the authorities. Frank would make sure life got better for everyone.

He smiled as the last Humvee drove through the barrier and disappeared down the road. All the obstacles were fading away.

Then his thoughts shifted to Charlie, and he felt his smile waning. He had worked closely with the man for so many years. No, Charlie was not as politically sophisticated as Frank, but Charlie had managed to navigate the world of policing crime without using a scorched-earth approach. And Charlie Cook had always been willing to follow a path that didn't upset the power structure. As a result, the criminal elements in town, while not defeated, had been contained and didn't impact the lives of the ordinary law-abiding citizens. Charlie's easy hand had kept life calm in Hillsboro. Since the EMP attack, Charlie and his department had been a calming influence just by being seen still doing their jobs; Chief Cook had become a reassuring symbol for the town that normalcy wasn't dead. But now Charlie had dug in his heels. The man seemed to have taken sides...the wrong side, Frank thought. What to do about him?

Frank knew that Joe was capable of eliminating Charlie without hesitation. It was an uncomfortable thought.

Still, they had a future to secure, one in which Frank would play the prime minister to Joe's king. Frank knew that, when the feds showed up and it came time to navigate those tricky waters, Joe would need him more and more. He would come to recognize Frank's value, and Frank would ultimately gain a large share of power.

As much as he liked Charlie, he couldn't let the old man get in the way of that goal. Charlie had had his chance and had turned his back on it.

A gray pall came over Frank's vision.

It was Charlie's decision, he thought regretfully. He couldn't do anything about what would come next.

Frank sighed.

Chapter 43

The army convoy made its way slowly through the abandoned outskirts of Hillsboro, heading east away from town. Captain Roper sat with the men who remained loyal to him in the back of their transport truck. Roper's mouth was set in a thin line. He was angry at being stuffed into the back like a non-com, and the awareness that the truck was being driven by Lieutenant Cameron's men grated on him.

He thought they might have gone about thirty miles when the truck turned and came to a stop. After a couple of minutes the back opened. Lieutenant Cameron and Sergeant Gibbs were there, with soldiers behind them.

"Captain Roper, step out, please." Cameron said. "There is a formality."

Roper rose with an effort and made his way to the back of the truck. He stepped down and looked around. They were in the parking lot of a gas station and restaurant, now long abandoned. The convoy filled the lot, with the tankers strung out along the highway outside the entrance.

"This way," Cameron said. Gritting his teeth, Roper was escorted to the door of the restaurant by two soldiers. The lock had been broken long ago and the door opened stiffly. Cameron, Gibbs and Roper stepped into the restaurant. Behind them a soldier took up a position guarding the entrance with an M16. Cameron led the trio to a square table at the rear of the dining area. He motioned for Roper to take a seat and then took one across from him. Gibbs sat to Roper's left, Cameron's right.

"We need to sign some documents to make our separation legal," Cameron said.

"I don't think I'll be signing anything," Roper said evenly. "You can do this, but when I report to Colonel Stillman you'll be labeled rebels, you know that."

Cameron continued as if he had not heard. "I have here a document I typed out last night. It says that you are granting me, Sergeant Gibbs, and all the men with us, listed here by name, an honorable discharge from the army so that we may remain in Hillsboro and participate in its reconstruction. We will have reservist status, but will now be able to enter into civilian life."

Roper stared at Cameron. "You're nuts. I'm not signing anything like that. You're screwed, but you brought this on yourself."

"I think you will sign the paper," Cameron responded. He held up an old camera. "You know what this is? It's a film camera. And I have some good 35mm film. The other day I photographed all the loot that you got from your collusion with Stansky. The army will be able to develop the film. I feel certain that you'll find the pictures extremely difficult to explain. I also have the signed testimony of the chief of police, witnessed by another police officer. In it Chief Cook testifies about personal knowledge of payoffs to you, about your active involvement in covering up Stansky's looting and even about your demands for a larger share in exchange for your contribution, namely hiding Stansky's activity from your commanding officer, Colonel Stillman."

Roper felt his anger rising. All his work was for nothing. All his fortune that would have gotten him to South America with enough wealth to live like a king was now gone. And, on top of that, he had to give this impertinent lieutenant a free pass after the man had destroyed his plans.

"Do we have a deal?" Cameron asked.

"It's my word against yours in the end," Roper growled.

"Your word against my evidence, the sworn testimony of the town's chief of police, and the testimony of Sergeant Gibbs."

"And if I don't sign? What are you going to do?"

Cameron turned to Gibbs, "What do you think, Sergeant? What should we do with Roper and his men?"

Gibbs looked at Roper. The sergeant's dark face was hard and unyielding. "I fought in Iraq and Afghanistan. I got shot. I saw men get maimed and killed. I served under some good officers and some not so good officers. But I never served under someone who would lie and deceive to line his own pockets. I *heard* about that crap, but I only got to experience it here, in the States, under your command. If I had my way, I'd stand you up against a wall and shoot you for consorting with the enemy—"

Roper laughed sharply, trying to sound contemptuous. "That's a fancy word, Sergeant. You know what it means?"

"What *I* mean is that you should be tried for dealing with the enemy, dereliction of duty, lying to your superior officer, undermining the mission, and a host of other charges if I had time to think of them. For all of that, you should be shot." Gibbs' voice was full of loathing. "You disgust me. You've violated all I hold dear about my time in the army."

Roper stared at Gibbs.

Cameron nodded. "Sergeant, if we don't shoot Captain Roper, do you have any other suggestions?"

"Sir, if the captain does not sign your documents, in my opinion we can't afford to let him go. Even with as much as we've got on him, he's not worth a lick of extra risk."

Roper clasped his hands together to keep them still. He began to shift uncomfortably in his chair, while he tried to keep his voice level. "You kill me, you'll have to kill all the men who chose to come with me."

Gibbs said to Cameron, "I suggest we find a remote building and lock them all up. We'll separate Roper from the rest of the men. We can leave them there for some time. Maybe after a week, we ask the men if they want out…without their captain. Or would they like to remain locked up with him until Colonel Stillman comes back?" Gibbs paused and almost smiled at Roper. "I'm betting they'll want to go free and leave the captain to his own fate. Especially when they know he could have spared them the whole ordeal."

"Not a bad idea," Cameron said.

"You're just digging yourself a bigger hole," Roper said. The shaking in his voice betrayed him.

"I'll take that chance. We've got enough evidence against you to give us cover either way. Of course, you can sign these documents to make our separation official and legal and then head off with a truck and some supplies, just like we told you in Hillsboro. It's your choice."

Roper just sat there. It was a bitter pill, but he was out of options.

Cameron pushed back his chair and stood up. "We don't have all day. It's time to make up your mind. Sign and leave with some resources, or don't sign and get locked up. Your call, Captain."

Roper sighed. He would take the easier route. Revenge wasn't worth making his personal situation more difficult. "Give me the papers."

Chapter 44

When word got to Leo that the Army was gone, he gathered his men. He had prepared a list of twenty-five names. They all knew how to handle weapons, they were all experienced fighters, and none of them would be shy about killing civilians. He had chosen the list with care; they were some of his best men.

He wanted to strike quick and hard, leaving no complications to trail behind him. He'd take a few of the valley residents alive so that they could tell him where to find the seed. He'd tell them that this was just business, that he had no reason to hurt them if they gave him what he was after. After they told, they would be eliminated. Joe hadn't mentioned survivors, and Leo saw no sense in leaving any. There would be no one to tell any stories about what had happened there.

The men he brought were equipped with military-issue M16s. The four pickup trucks waiting for them had already been loaded with packs heavy with ammunition. In addition, Leo was bringing along three M60 machine guns, one M2 heavy machine gun, and three mortars. After loading supplies and ammunition, and filling the gas tanks, it was early afternoon by the time they left Hillsboro, and would be night before they arrived at the valley entrance.

They drove through the countryside, with Leo in the lead truck. He had a map, which he consulted as they worked their way along the county roads towards the valley. It was near dusk when he stopped the caravan at a crossroad. They had not yet arrived at the little village of Clifton Forge.

He got out and his captains piled out to gather around him. "We'll split up here," Leo told them. He spread out his map on the hood of the pickup. "I'll take three trucks and head west. I found an old road that goes into the valley from the west." Leo pointed to one of his captains, a man who had distinguished himself in the early battles with desperate refugees. "You'll take one truck with five men and head to Clifton Forge. You wait there until about two hours before dawn, then you head to the valley entrance."

"We'll be headed into an ambush for sure. Big Jacks's gang was killed there, and he had a lot more than six men," the man replied.

"You think I don't know that? You stop a mile before the bridge, cross the river, and climb the ridge. You don't go over the bridge, idiot, you go around it and attack the guards from behind. If you run into too much resistance, you retreat. Your job is to keep them focused in that area while we go over the west ridge. We'll come down and join up with you. We'll sweep through the valley and take out the bridge defenders. They won't expect us to come from behind."

"We get any mortars?" the captain asked.

"No, you got to be able to move fast. You take one M60 with you. The rest is rifle work."

As it grew dark, Leo led the three trucks to the west. Looking over his shoulder, he could see the headlights of the fourth truck moving along the road to Clifton Forge.

Clayton and his men moved through the gathering evening on the ridgelines, setting up their defensive positions above the road where it led in from the bridge to the south. They were positioning themselves as Jason had done during the battle with Big Jacks's gang. Only now Jason had more shooters available to him. After carefully making sure everyone was in position and properly spaced, Jason and Clayton hiked away from the bridge. The narrow canyon shallowed with the ridges sloping down to the valley floor as they got further away from the bridge. They saw Tom emerging from the trees on the other side, coming across the road to join them.

Tom didn't look happy. "I doubt they're going to come over the bridge," he said.

Jason sighed and nodded. "Yeah, I know."

"They going to come up the ridge. In the woods," Clayton said.

Tom scowled. "That could be either side. We can't be sure they'll come from the direction of Clifton Forge."

"We put out some scouts on either side," Clayton said. "In the woods, east and west of the bridge."

"We don't have enough men to spread out all over the woods," Jason remarked.

"Don't need many," Clayton said. "Just a few to fire some shots, let us know where the attack comes from."

"That'll be dangerous for the scouts," Tom said. "There'd only be a few against who knows how many."

"Not if they know how to move through the woods. My men can do that. They can shoot and melt away."

"I get it," Tom said. "If they can keep retreating, we'll meet up with them. Then we have a shootout in the woods. I'm betting we're better at that than any city militia."

"How many guys do you need?" Jason asked.

"Just two on each side," Clayton answered.

As night fell in Hillsboro, Tommy and Hank Ames walked along the dark sidewalks toward the militia warehouse. As they got closer, they passed the police van parked on a side street. They could barely see the figure inside wave at them through the window.

At the corner of the side street, before turning on to the broader road where the warehouse entrance was located, they passed Specialist Jackson. He was crouched down behind some steps of a building on the corner, his rifle in hand. There was a flash of a smile and a thumbs-up from him as they walked past. Jackson would be backup with a clear shot at the guards if things went wrong.

They emerged onto the street, crossed it, and walked towards the warehouse entrance half a block away. There were two guards out front.

"Who's there?" one of the guards called out as they approached.

"It's me, Hank. From the police department."

"What the hell are you doing here? This ain't your area."

"Yeah, but I got a business proposition for you."

"What's that?"

"This guy." Hank laughed and shoved Tommy forward. "He quit the army, didn't want to go with them. He wants to buy a weapon. Says he'll pay me if I can hook him up."

The guard sounded amused. "So whaddaya want me to do?"

"Sell him a rifle, or something. Hell, you make money, I make money. No one will know."

"What's your name?" the other guard asked Tommy.

"My name ain't important. What's important is, I can pay with gold," Tommy said.

"Gold. Really?" The second guard's voice sounded interested.

"Why don't you just join the militia?" the first guard said. "You can get a rifle for free, and regular meals as well."

"I just quit the army. I ain't interested in joining another group. Following orders and stuff."

The second guard leaned forward, his quiet voice beginning to sound eager. "So, we sell you one, you can't stay here. Can't have you knocking people off in town."

"Ain't planning on sticking around. I'm heading out on my own. Going to get back to my family. Now you want to sell me a rifle or not?"

"Why don't he buy one from you?" the first guard asked Hank.

"'Cause we don't have that many. Someone would notice a missing rifle. Shit, I figure you got hundreds in the warehouse, so who'd know if one was missing? And if anybody notices, it's like someone counted wrong in the first place."

"Okay, what you got?" the second guard said.

Tommy took out the two gold coins and a gold necklace, held them up so a faint glint could be seen. "What'll this buy me?"

The guard looked at the gold with a greedy eye. "That real?"

"The weight says so. You want to feel, you gotta show me something."

"That'll get you a rifle and some ammunition. Won't be our best, but it'll work."

The second guard turned toward the door. The first guard looked at him dubiously. In that instant Tommy and Hank struck. They grabbed both guards. Hank stuck his pistol in the side of the guard who had spoken to them first. Tommy pulled his knife and stuck it against the other man's neck.

"Don't make a sound or I'll slit your neck open. Open the door."

"You shoot us, you wake up the other men and they'll kill you," the first guard gasped.

"Don't need to shoot you. I just slit this guy's throat and then slit yours. Then we take the keys and go right in.

"Reach down, slowly, take your keys and unlock the door," Hank ordered.

"Either of you yell, you both get your throats cut," Tommy said.

The second guard complied. Tommy and Hank shoved the men inside. It was dark and silent; they seemed to be in a small anteroom that opened up into what they sensed was a larger space.

There was a sudden small, bright light. Hank had snapped on a small flashlight and put his hand over the beam to let out only a sliver of light. "Rechargeable batteries," he said as Tommy looked at him in surprise.

They could now see that the back of the room had a large opening with the main warehouse beyond. An immense space with shelving that faded away into the dark.

Handing Tommy the flashlight, Hank quickly handcuffed the two guards to a steam radiator. Tommy went over to them and whispered, "You don't have to die, but you will if we run into any problems. Now I'm going to ask you a question and I want a straight answer. If you lie to me, I'll slit your throats now and I won't have to worry about you. Got it?" The two guards looked terrified.

"Okay, here's the question. How many other guards are there and where are they?"

"There aren't any," the second guard said in a quavering voice.

"You're sure now. None at the other doors? Remember your life depends on the answer."

"There's no other man-doors," the first guard said. "Just rear loading bay doors, four of them. They're big roll doors and they don't open from the outside. You gotta open them with the chain hoist from the inside. It's a pain with no motors."

Tommy looked at Hank and nodded. Hank slipped back out the door, closing it gently behind him. Ten seconds later Terry Jackson came in, his rifle at the ready position in front of him. They waited in the dark.

Many long minutes later, Tommy heard the low mutter of the police van's engine pulling up outside the door. A moment later the door opened, and Hank and Les Hammond joined them.

Tommy left Hammond to watch the two guards while the others quietly went through the warehouse. It wasn't hard to find anything. The weapons were stored for easy access. They collected arm-loads of M16s, and they found two M60 machine guns with cans of 7.62mm ammunition. Those went straight out to the van. Boxes and boxes of 5.56mm ammunition for the M16s were loaded into the increasingly heavily laden van. Tommy figured they had a couple of thousand rounds of rifle ammunition. His only concern was that he could not find any mortar tubes or rocket launchers. He did find some mortar bombs, which he took. At least they wouldn't be available to the militia in a fight, and the platoon had mortars that could use them. An hour later they had the van fully loaded and riding low on its suspension.

Before they left, the men stopped to look at the guards handcuffed to the radiator.

"Should we just leave them?" Tommy asked.

"You'll never get away with this," the guard who had been eager for the trade said. "We know who you are." The other guard's head snapped round toward his partner, horror on his face. "Shut your mouth," he hissed.

"So we better kill you so you won't talk," Hank said.

"Maybe we *should* finish them off now, since they know you," Tommy said.

Hank pondered the proposition. "They'll be found sometime tomorrow. If they're alive, they'll tell everyone, so I can't be seen again. The whole militia will be looking for me."

The guard who was clearly more intelligent said, "Listen, we won't say anything. You don't have to kill us. That ain't right and you know it."

"Funny, you talking about what's right," Tommy said. He looked at the two hapless men. They stared back. Killing them would be the simplest solution. He could imagine Sergeant Gibbs making that call. He couldn't imagine Lieutenant Cameron making it. Cameron would say they were called to a higher standard. "I don't know. It doesn't feel right to just shoot them or slit their throats."

Hank looked at the guards. "You're right. I guess it's your lucky day," he said to them.

Tommy cut the shirts off the men and tore them in half. He stuffed wads of fabric into the guards' mouths and tied the other strips around their heads to hold the gags in place. "That'll keep them quiet 'till someone comes in the morning. Gives us a little more time."

With that, they left. Tommy locked the door behind them and then dropped the warehouse keys down a storm grating. Hammond started the van and they drove away through the dark city.

Chapter 45

Early the next morning, before the sun came over the eastern ridges, Catherine and Bird woke up to the sound of gunfire. It was far off, fading in and out in the slight morning breeze. They were instantly awake.

"The bridge," Bird said. "They attacking there. Maybe we should go help."

"That would take too long," Catherine said. "By the time we got there it would be all over." She paused. "And I don't think we should abandon our post. They could be attacking from both directions."

As she was speaking, they both heard the sound of engines above them. About a minute later, the dark, rectangular shape of a pickup appeared against the sky.

"There, at the top of the ridge," she called out.

Bird grunted. Two other silhouettes came into view, one after the other. Catherine and Bird took up prone positions on the ground. They put their blankets under their rifles to give them a firm support.

After a moment, they were able to see the three pickup trucks quite clearly. They moved downward from the pass for twenty yards, angling to the left, and disappeared into the trees. Now the two teenagers would have to wait for them to appear at the next switchback where it showed like an exposed elbow.

The first shot would be a long one, about three hundred and fifty yards. The switchback after that would bring the road back closer to them, within two hundred yards. Their fallback shooting positions below maintained a range of one hundred and fifty to two hundred yards.

"This is a long shot. Are you good with that?" Catherine asked.

"I'll figure it out. Make sure you get some good first rounds in," Bird said, "With that fancy rifle and all."

Catherine smiled to herself. *Just shooting targets, that's what it is.* Somehow this seemed easier than the desperate fight at the bridge.

It had taken some time, but Leo had finally found the old road. They lost a couple of hours dismantling a barrier blocking the entrance. Steel posts had been planted in the ground to block vehicular access to the old track and large boulders prevented going around the obstruction.

The road beyond had been left alone to return to nature, but here in the mountains growth was slow. Very little vegetation had grown on the rocky bed of the road. It was passable, but the journey up was slow. On two occasions they had to use the four-wheel-drive truck to pull the other pickups up over some boulders that had pushed up through the bed of the road.

Leo started fuming. He had wanted to be down in the valley by dawn. Now the day would find him at the top, just starting down. He would be late to join up with the fake assault going on at the bridge. He had to get down there before the defenders figured out the main attack wasn't coming at the bridge. When they did, they would know where to look next. They knew the valley, and his element of surprise would be gone.

Finally he saw the top of the pass ahead. There was enough visibility that Leo stopped the group just short of the ridge and ordered all the headlights turned off. In the dim predawn light the trucks finally crested the ridge and started down the valley side.

Leo noted with satisfaction that they would be under tree cover for most of the way. And the road seemed more passable on this side of the slope, maybe because they were now going downhill. Things were looking up.

Catherine and Bird waited for the trucks to emerge at the second switchback. They had their rifles trained on that spot. Catherine had estimated the distance yesterday when they had set up their position. Now her scope was dialed in. There was barely any breeze. She was ready.

"You take the first shot," Bird said. "You probably more accurate than me at this distance."

Shoot the lead driver to stop the truck. It was what Jason had told her. In their fights with the gangs she had seen it in action twice. She repeated it to herself as she emptied her mind of everything but the switchback she saw in her scope.

There was motion, and then the lead truck was squared to her, in the middle of the corner, the windshield in her sights. Catherine squeezed the trigger. The rifle's loud crack was accompanied by a sharp kick against her shoulder. A huge hole appeared in the windshield. She heard someone cry out, but she didn't think that she had hit any of the three dim shapes behind the glass squarely. Bird now fired, smashing in the top left corner of the windshield. The sound startled Catherine. She quickly refocused and fired again, and this time the glass blew in immediately in front of the driver. She saw his torso flung backward and then falling forward over the steering wheel. The truck straightened out in the middle of the turn and rolled downslope to bang into a boulder on the edge of the road. A man was already out, dashing for the cover of some boulders. He must have jumped out of the passenger side with the first shots.

Bird had switched his aim to the trucks that followed. His initial shots were off target, but he quickly zeroed them in with deadly effect. Another man was scrambling out of the lead truck where it had come to rest. Catherine shot him. The first man had already made it to the rocks and cover. The other trucks had stopped. Men were scattering to the sides of the road or getting behind the pickups.

Gunfire was beginning to come from the caravan, but it was unfocused. The raiders didn't know where she and Bird were.

Yet.

Leo looked out from behind the rocks. He had thrown himself out of the truck as soon as the first shot had torn through the cab. He tried to pinpoint where the shots were coming from but could only see woods.

He turned and shouted to the men to get the machine guns from the backs of the pickups. *Lucky they weren't in my truck*, he thought. One of his men opened the tailgate of the second truck and crawled into the bed. Lying flat on his stomach to stay out of sight of the snipers, he pulled the M2 back to the tailgate. The gun crashed onto the dirt road, the man slipping down beside it. It was a heavy gun, Leo knew, weighing one hundred and twenty pounds with its tripod. The man stopped at the back of the truck, clearly not wanting to risk dragging the gun across the open ground to the cover of the rocks and trees. Leo approved. If they lost that gun in the open, they'd die one by one trying to get to it.

Others had retrieved the M60s, which were considerably lighter. The last of his men scrambled to cover along the side of the road.

"Look for the muzzle flash when they fire," Leo yelled. "Don't waste shots if you don't know what you're shooting at."

They were on the edge of a steep, wooded ravine carved by runoff from the ridge. The ravine had forced the road to turn away, the builders snaking their way up the ridge, always seeking the easier path. Leo studied the slope across from the switchback. Somewhere on the other side of the ravine, a couple of hundred yards away, was the sniper...or snipers. He couldn't tell how many there were. Suddenly he saw a flash, then a second, followed by the reports. The granite knob near the upper part of the opposite ridge, that's where they were. It looked like two separate shooters.

"There!" Leo shouted out to the others, pointing to the ridge. One of the men stood up to get a better look and was dropped by a bullet. Leo swore. He couldn't afford to lose many men here. "Get that M2 going. Light up that rock," he yelled.

"Cover me," another man shouted back. His companions fired a fusillade of shots at the outcropping. The man grabbed the M2 and staggered across to some rocks near Leo, half carrying, half dragging the heavy machine gun.

Leo liked the M2. It fired a .50 caliber round, a massively lethal projectile, capable of penetrating an engine block. It could chew up trees, rocks, and concrete walls. Its rate of fire was slower than the M60, but the M60 only fired a 7.62 mm round, and the M2's deeper sound evidenced the enormous firepower being sent downrange.

The man wrestled the heavy machine gun around. A bullet screamed off the boulder just above his head. He began to fire. The M2's rounds peppered the outcropping, shattering the rocks, tearing though the brush. There were no more shots from the ridge. Whoever was up there had no choice but to keep their heads down. Leo jumped up and shouted, "Everyone back in the trucks! Get them round the bend and back in the trees!" He ran to the lead truck, threw open the driver's door, and dragged the dead man out. Then he jumped in, reversed the truck, and sped around the corner. In his rearview mirror he made out the second truck in line jolting forward and stopping to pick up the man with the M2. Then he was away, with the other two trucks following.

Chapter 46

The stream of bullets blasted the granite, sending shards flying in all directions. Catherine and Bird were peppered by the fragments. They shrank back from the violence, putting their heads down to protect their eyes.

When the firing stopped they looked at each other. Both had blood running down their faces and arms.

"Are you okay?" Catherine asked.

Bird nodded. "You?"

"Yeah." She wiped her face with her sleeve, then she looked at the sleeve and took out a scarf and tied it across her forehead to keep any blood from running into her eyes. "They got around the corner. We'll have to hit them at the next switchback."

"Should we move position?" Bird asked.

"Not sure. They know where we are, but this is a good shooting spot. Maybe we try one more round here, then move. We've got two more positions."

Before the next switchback Leo stopped the trucks, well back in the cover of the trees. He had his men set up a mortar and sent one to the edge of the trees to spot for them.

They didn't know how to aim it. There hadn't been a chance to train out of earshot of the city. Joe hadn't wanted the army to learn what he had.

"Aim it the best you can and then adjust. The spotter will call out where you hit."

"How we get over the trees?" one of the men asked.

Leo pointed. "Set up across the road to give you some clearance. Adjust the angle as you go." They quickly moved the mortar.

After it was reset, one of the men manning the gun asked, "Okay, I got an angle. I just drop the thing in?"

"That's it. Then get back from it," Leo said.

The first round slid down the tube. There was an explosive *whomp* as it fired. Everyone flinched. A few men put their hands over their ears. A few seconds later the sound of an explosion shook the air.

"You're too high, it's hitting way down the slope," shouted the spotter.

The subsequent rounds began to zero in on the rock outcropping.

"We got to go," Bird yelled. They were pressed flat to the ground. They had heard the mortar firing and had watched the explosions, each one further up the slope, closing in on the outcropping. Catherine had thought at first that the mortar bombs were not well aimed and would not be a real danger, but now the rounds were getting close to their position.

When another blast hit upslope and to their left, spewing dirt and chunks of rock over them, they jumped up and dashed back away from the ravine. They ran through the woods, slipping and sliding on the incline, to get some distance between themselves and the mortar explosions. Once they were back far enough from the edge, they worked their way down to the second shooting position.

Both were dripping with sweat when they arrived. Catherine panted, "They'll either figure they knocked us out or scared us off after we don't return fire."

"We got nothin' to shoot at with 'em back in the woods. Gotta wait till they come out in the open."

"Here, let me tie something around your head," Catherine said. "You don't want blood getting in your eyes." She took out her knife and cut off some of Bird's sleeve and wrapped it around his head. Then she straightened her scarf on her forehead. Bird watched her.

"That's a mean gun they got," he said at last.

"It sounds like an M2. A .50 caliber machine gun. We have one we captured from the bridge battle."

"Sure tears things up. We need to take it out."

"If we can."

Bird looked across to the switchback. "So we wait. We closer now."

"Yeah," Catherine replied. She picked up the M110 and checked her sights.

After seven rounds, Leo called for a halt. The mortar had scored three hits to the shoulder of exposed granite across the ravine. The spotter reported no sign of activity. If the shooters had stayed in the shelter of the rocks, they had probably been killed or they had run off back into the forest.

Still, he wanted to be careful. The other switchbacks along the road below would probably be just as exposed. But now he was even more late, and frustrated. He needed to get down off this old road and onto the paved section.

He went to his captain. "When we get to the next switchback we'll stop before we get out of the tree cover. I want the machine guns out, the M2 and the two M60s. You and three others go forward to the switchback. Set up those machine guns. Then we'll move. You see any firing, you pin them down and we'll get the trucks around the bend. You can hike down through the woods to meet us."

Catherine and Bird saw the militia moving up, two on each side of the road. The men were carefully stepping from trunk to trunk, never quite exposed enough for a sure shot. After a moment of watching for more, Catherine decided that there were only three or four coming on foot. They stopped short of the open corner and dropped out of view.

"Trucks be coming," Bird said.

"They'll try to pin us down. We'll have to make our shots count."

"We can move around more here," Bird said. He pointed to the trees above and below their position. "Maybe we spread out. They can't get at us so easy."

The two separated. Catherine crawled uphill for ten yards and found a good tree to lie behind. Bird headed down the slope and lay down behind some mountain laurel that would screen him from view.

Nothing moved for perhaps a minute and a half. Keeping very low, Catherine slowly adjusted the position of her M110.

Then there was a sudden roar, engines accelerating hard. As the trucks reached the exposed switchback, Catherine opened fire. She put five quick rounds into the cab of the lead truck, hitting the driver in the chest and head. The passenger jumped out and dove for some rocks at the side of the roadbed. Bird fired below her, and Catherine saw the second truck's windshield shatter and its passenger get flung against the door by the bullet. As the second truck slewed around the corner, Bird's .30-06 boomed again and one of the men crouched in the bed of the truck fell on his side into a splash of brains and blood from his own head. The militia around him were peering wildly over the side of the truck bed, looking for the shooters. They were thrown sideways as the truck jerked to a stop, blocked by the immobilized lead truck. Behind it the third truck could do nothing but stop as well. But now the gunners in the trees had had time to find Catherine and Bird.

"There, further down the slope!" someone shouted.

"Shoot, shoot!" came a panicked reply.

The thunder of the M2 began, and dirt and rocks sprayed in a line up toward Catherine. Two other machine guns joined it. She threw herself back behind the tree trunk.

The machine guns swept the area. It seemed that Catherine and Bird hadn't been pinpointed exactly, but the gunners were sweeping back and forth, giving them only an instant now and then to snap off return shots before they had to duck and cover. There wasn't time to aim. Catherine had to rely on a quick look for each shot.

Then she heard the thump of the mortar firing. *Oh no!* She couldn't see the mortar. The shell exploded down the slope between her and the trucks, well short. Ten seconds later came another thump, and the explosion was back behind her. Catherine realized that they were bracketed. The next round would land very close.

"Bird, watch out," she yelled over the din of the firing and flattened herself on the ground behind the tree.

The next explosion came, loud, behind them, closer to Bird. Catherine heard a cry of pain. She crawled quickly backward, away from the edge, and scrambled down the slope to find Bird. He was lying behind the laurel bushes clutching his side. A red stain was spreading across the bottom of his shirt, and blood was squeezing out between his fingers.

"You're hurt," she exclaimed.

Bird looked at her. "I'm sorry," he said. "Didn't get low enough."

They heard the mortar fire again. Catherine spread herself over Bird as they waited for the impact. It hit uphill from them. Shrapnel screamed over their heads.

"We have to get out of here," Catherine shouted, "Away from the ridge."

"Not sure I can move."

"I'll help you. We have to get back." She remembered Jason's admonition. *No fighting to the death. Move back when you're pinned down.*

She pulled off her jacket and then took off her shirt. Bird looked away as she knelt over him wearing only her bra. She tied her shirt tight around his waist in an attempt to stem the flow of blood. Then she pulled her jacket back on.

"We've got to get back from the ridge. Hold tight," Catherine said. She put her hands in his armpits and began to drag him back further into the woods. When she had gotten ten yards from their shooting position she said, "Now grab my hand. I'll help you up." She got her legs under her, took hold of Bird's left arm, and hauled him to his feet. A painful grunt forced its way through his teeth. They stumbled together through the forest, away from the edge of the ridge. When they heard another *whomp* of a mortar round being fired, they dropped to the ground. After each detonation, they got up and staggered on.

Leo realized that no more shooting was coming from the opposite ridge. He had the men move the trucks around the bend and back into the cover of the trees. He wanted to press on instantly, but the lead truck had a flat tire, and he dove in to change it himself. He told two men to smash out the remains of the broken windshields with their rifle butts.

With the tire changed and the windshields cleared, the trucks began to move forward again. Leo fumed. He could shut down the snipers, but they seemed to come back at every switchback. At this rate he would be hours late and the element of surprise lost. Still, he had to go on. He had seen the machine guns and the mortars in action now, and he knew that he had the firepower to overwhelm the valley. Once he got down there.

Chapter 47

When the very first signs of dawn began to appear in the sky, Leo's skirmishing party waded across the river and climbed up the slope beyond. They had stopped a cautious distance downstream from the bridge and had encountered no initial resistance. When they reached the top of the ridge, they began to move through the trees towards the road.

They were not used to the woods, and they stumbled along in the predawn gloom. The brightening of the sky in the east did little to relieve the darkness. Twigs snapped. Branches slapped at their faces. Fallen logs caught at their legs and tripped them. One of the men began to mutter about their bad luck to have been chosen to slog through the river and then these miserable woods.

The two lookouts from Clayton's group heard them well before they saw them. The lookouts separated, moving about twenty yards apart, far enough to give them separate firing positions. Shortly, indistinct figures began to emerge in the dim light. Six of them. Clayton's lookouts fired. Two men fell, both shot in the chest. The other four dropped to the ground and hastily snapped off blind shots into the dimness.

Lying in the brush, the machine gunner flipped the safety off on his M60 and began to fire, blindly spraying the area ahead. A round hit one of the lookouts and spun him to the ground. The other man crawled over to him and began to drag him back. The wounded man struck his hands away and motioned him to go. He had a hole in his chest that was going to kill him within the hour. His rasping breath left nothing for talking. The other understood, and, after a long look and pat on the shoulder, he faded back and took up a position thirty yards away.

The attackers, realizing they were no longer taking fire, got up and began to move forward. The wounded lookout managed to work himself back into a shooting position. He shouldered his rifle with much difficulty and fired off another round, and another attacker dropped. The others ducked for cover and again began firing blindly into the woods. After a moment, with no more shots fired back at them, they began to advance again. This time the retreating lookout took out another one. The attacking party was now down to two men. The captain had been the last to die.

The machine gunner sprayed the woods ahead of him with multiple bursts of automatic fire, and the two men slowly began to advance again.

They sensed that it wasn't a large group that had fired on them, but they went more slowly, wanting the protection of the woods they had been cursing moments before.

No more shots came. They passed the wounded lookout without seeing him. The other lookout was already on his way back to the main body of defenders. He had seen enough to be satisfied that this was only a scouting party or a decoy attack, and he was anxious to give his report and get help for his friend.

Back at the ridge near the bridge, the men heard shots coming from the woods to the east. Jason's breath sucked in through his teeth. "Here we go," he said to Clayton. He started towards the woods.

Clayton grabbed his arm. "Could be more comin' up the other side. Give it a minute."

Then they heard the staccato of a machine gun.

"We've got to redeploy towards the woods," Jason said.

Clayton didn't let go. The shooting stopped.

"Don't sound like a full attack," Clayton said. "One machine gun, maybe five or more rifles, two of 'em my boys."

There was another burst of gunfire, the rifles mixed with the machine gun, and then the woods went silent again.

Tom approached the two men with a confused look on his face. "What's going on?"

"We trying to figure that out," Clayton responded.

Just then they saw a figure running towards them through the woods. There were shouts along the ridgeline to hold fire. Jason saw that it was Enoch, one of the men Clayton had chosen to scout, more like a boy really. They watched him sprint toward them, and someone waved him toward where Clayton was standing. He ran up to Clayton, already talking. "It were six men, one with a machine gun. Henry got hit. 'Fraid he won't make it. They's only two left, but they got the machine gun still with 'em."

"You're sure there's only two left?" Jason asked.

The boy nodded. "Saw 'em drop. I came back to get help for Henry."

"A decoy attack?" Tom asked.

Clayton told Enoch, "Grab Willy and Donny and go finish them off. Bring Henry back out." The young man nodded and ran off.

Suddenly more shots were heard, much more distant, from up the valley. Then Jason heard a boom, deeper, louder. The hair on the back of his neck bristled.

"They're coming in from the west," he shouted.

"We need to go!" Tom yelled.

Clayton shouted to Enoch, "Go, do what I told you. Then stay here in case any try the bridge." He turned and snatched up his rifle. The hill people and the farmers were already a scattered tide of motion from their places along the ridge. Clayton waved furiously at the peering figures that had risen from cover on the ridge across the gap, and after a moment they began running too.

Jason left Clayton behind. He pelted along the trail that traced the top of the ridge. It might be more than ten or fifteen minutes before all the fighters made their way down to the pickup trucks that were parked around a bend in the road, out of sight of the bridge. And every minute meant they might be too late to the real fight.

Remember what I told you, he thought to Catherine. *Remember.*

The mortar rounds stopped. Catherine and Bird were nestled together on the open forest floor, perhaps a hundred yards away from the ridgeline. Bird could go no further. The militia could not come looking for them; they were on the other side of the ravine. They would head down into the valley and attack the farms. It was up to Jason now. She held Bird in her arms. His breathing had become labored.

"Didn't mean to get hit," he said in a hoarse voice. "Sorry I let you down."

"You didn't let me down. You did good. I hope the others are on their way. They must have heard the shooting."

"Bettin' they heard. Them mortars are loud. Nasty when they hit." He stopped. She could see that he had to gather his strength to speak again. "You think we did enough?"

"Yes," she told him. "We did what we set out to do. Help will be coming soon."

He didn't answer.

Catherine sat up, careful not to jostle him, and set about trying to tighten Bird's bandage. She could see that blood was still seeping out of him.

She told him, "We'll rest here now, but we'll have to move down the slope to get help."

"Not sure I can move."

"Just lie still for now. Rest. I'll help you when it's time."

The defenders' convoy raced up the valley road. Jason felt a growing fury inside. He glanced over at Tom whose face was set hard. The same thoughts circled round and round in Jason's mind, over and over. The enemy had invaded, come down from the west, just as Catherine had predicted. Were Catherine and Bird alive? Glancing in the mirror, he could sense a blood lust growing among the clan. They were ready for battle, ready for killing. He could feel it.

The tree line neared. They reached the end of the pavement. The road here had been widened to make a turnaround area. There seemed to be nowhere to go. Jason pulled to a stop. The other pickups stopped behind him.

He looked over at Clayton sitting by the window. "Where's the road?" he asked.

Clayton didn't say anything. He got out of the truck and looked around at the bushes and trees that faced them.

"Where the hell is the road?" Jason said again, leaning out of the window.

The heavily treed slope climbed upward ahead and to the right of them with no sign of a road. To the left was flatter ground covered with tall willow bushes creating a thick screen.

"Off to the left, through the willows," Clayton said, pointing.

Jason looked at him. "That doesn't look like a road. Are you sure?"

"I be right."

"How'll we get the trucks through there?" Tom asked.

"I go ahead, lead the way on foot. You follow. The trucks be able to drive over the willows and we got plenty of men to push if they get bogged down. It's low only for a while and then climbs and turns to the right." He swung his arm in an arc. "It climbs around this knob in front of us."

"Man, I don't see that," Tom said.

"Can't from here. We too close. Trees cover too much." Without another word, Clayton set off into the willows.

Jason cranked the wheel to the left and started forward. "If we start spinning, jump out and push. We can't get stuck," he shouted back to the men in the bed of the truck.

They forced their way through the willows. The ground was flatter and softer and the men had to get out to push the trucks forward. Soon the ground rose, and, sure enough, as Clayton led them forward the remains of the old road began to emerge on the forest floor.

Clayton got back in the truck. Jason could now follow the path with no guide. The going was slow, the men had to jump out at times to push, but as they climbed the road became clearer with less vegetation growing over it.

"Now I understand why I never noticed the road," Jason muttered. He worked the steering wheel back and forth, guiding the truck over the rocks, trying to avoid the larger ones and not get the undercarriage hung up. "We need to find a place to stop them. Up here where there's no options but the road."

They drove up the dirt two-track. Ahead was a sharp left turn with a dense line of trees blocking the sight line around it. Jason eyed the corner carefully and then stopped well short of it and angled the pickup across the road. The other pickups did likewise without having to be told. If you were coming down the road you wouldn't see the blockade until you rounded the corner.

Everyone got out of the vehicles and the men began to fan out into the trees on both sides of the road. Jason chose the upslope side. He found a place behind a large oak that had fallen some time ago. From this spot he'd be able to get a partial view of the enemy coming.

Suddenly he noticed that there was no sound of gunfire. He closed his mind to what that might mean.

"You think we'll have long to wait?" Tom asked next to him.

As he spoke, they heard the engines of the vehicles coming down from the ridge.

Chapter 48

Leo decided to charge around the next switchback. The snipers must have moved to new positions when he had hit them with the machine guns and mortars. This time he decided to risk not stopping. He had to get down off the dirt road.

He lowered his head and accelerated and tore around the exposed corner, gravel and dirt flying out from the tires. He wrestled with the steering wheel to keep the pickup from sliding off of the road and down the embankment. If the snipers were going to shoot, speed was his friend; he couldn't go slowly. But this time no shots came. The other pickups were roaring right behind him. He heard a loud bang as one of the pickups careened off a boulder on the side of the turn. And then they were back into the cover of the trees. Maybe they had killed the shooters with the mortar rounds. Leo felt a rush of relief. They had to be getting near the bottom. Soon he would be starting his vicious run through the valley.

The three pickups were going at a furious clip, slewing back and forth on the rough dirt road. They dodged the rocks bulging out of the roadbed as best they could, bouncing over the others with the men in the back holding on for dear life.

No more stopping, he thought savagely. He kept the accelerator pressed down. The pickup careened around the next corner and Leo slammed on the brakes as he saw the trucks blocking the road ahead. The men in the back were thrown about in a tangle of tumbled legs and bodies. The pickup behind him rammed into the back of his own, slewing him to the left. The third truck just managing to stop without hitting the second one. Before his truck came to a stop, Leo dove out of the cab. He knew this was an ambush.

Suddenly furious rifle fire erupted from both sides of the road.

"Out!" Leo shouted as he ran in a crouch towards the rear truck. His men jumped down from the pickup beds but were exposed to the deadly crossfire. One dropped like a sack of laundry, and another fell and hung slumped over the bed wall, the back of his skull blown open. The screams from the other side told the same story. Leo heard the two M60s start up on the other side of the truck, the downhill side.

The worst place they could stay was in the middle. "Downhill!" Leo roared, dodging between the second and third pickups. He ran crouched low, bringing his rifle up and firing blind, hearing bullets slamming into the pickup behind him. He passed bodies, looked to his left and saw more. Maybe half of his remaining fifteen men were already killed. The two machine gunners were fanning the trees as they ran into them, suppressing the shooters there. His men followed, firing their M16s and screaming. They dove into the cover of trees on the downward slope. Leo saw a valley defender break from behind a tree trunk ahead and dash back into the brush. They were pushing the defenders back with their superior automatic rifle fire.

Inside the trees they had some cover from the shooters on the other side of the road. But they would follow in seconds. Leo kept running and firing. The men who had made it into the trees were doing the same. They paused under cover, fired, and moved forward as they continued to drive the defenders down the slope. They were keeping better order than Leo would ever have expected. The ambush was half reversed. As Leo moved downslope, adrenaline pounding through him, the image of the carnage back at the road rose up in his mind. *Where had all those men come from?* He had estimated that the valley had less than half a dozen men to defend it. Now there seemed to be twenty or more men, all armed and seemingly all good shots.

He heard a machine gun start up behind him, uphill. Leo almost stumbled in shock. The defenders had a machine gun.

It was firing in short bursts, spraying the woods in an orderly pattern. Bullets tore through the leaves. Leo dropped behind a huge log and knew the lightning charge was over. He saw his men vanishing from view ahead of him as they dove for cover. Anyone caught without the protection of a substantial tree at his back during one of the bursts was in danger of being taken out.

Leo risked a look back around the bottom of the dead tree. He could still see the trucks, his own and those blocking the way, and he watched as some of the defenders began to cross the road. They would attack his men from behind, his men could no longer run ahead, and the shooters downslope would just now be realizing that they could turn around. He and his men would be caught in a pincer with no way out.

The defenders only had to be careful to not shoot their own men. Leo could only hope that they *would* do that.

He opened his mouth to get his men to keep moving forward—it was their only chance to avoid being slaughtered until they found a place where they could somehow turn the whole battle around—and then he realized that he had no way to do that. The rush had been spontaneous, a result of panic. With fire coming at them from both sides, no words would get them to stand up and advance. With that realization, he knew the attack had gone all wrong. It was doomed.

He didn't hesitate. He made a decision. He was not one to fall on his sword, to die for his commander when the fight was futile. His decision made, he turned around and began moving. He carefully worked his way to his left, angling back up the hill, until he thought he was to the rear of any of his men. The firing intensified. He began to circle back toward the pickup trucks. If he could get to the rearmost one, after the uphill defenders had crossed the road, he could escape back over the west ridge.

The shooting intensified even further. Men were screaming. He knelt behind a tree at the edge of the road. He heard a machine gun thundering away behind him.

They've all crossed over into the woods. Maybe he had a chance.

Leo got up and sprinted across the bark road to the last truck, leaping over the sprawled bodies. He jumped into the cab, twisted the key, the engine roared to life, and he reversed it with all four tires spitting dirt. He drove backward up to the blind turn as fast as he could go, spun the truck around at the corner, shifted gears, and was tearing up the two-track when the first defenders got back to the road.

"Let him go, whoever it is," Jason said. "We probably can't catch him, and I don't want to waste time trying. We have to find Catherine and Bird."

"Let's hope they're alive," Clayton said.

"How are we going to find them?" Tom asked. He had just come up from the slope below and given Jason the body count.

"That's the question," Jason muttered.

"You kill 'em all?" Clayton asked Tom.

"We got five prisoners. They surrendered."

"Not sure I'd take prisoners," was Clayton's response.

"Bring them up here, on the double," Jason said. "They may know where Catherine and Bird were positioned."

Tom called down the hill. More of the defenders were coming up, and after a couple of minutes, five men in militia uniforms were dragged and shoved up to the road. Tom oversaw tying their hands behind them and had them sit down on the side of the road.

Jason went to them. He focused on the largest one, a stout bearded man with the stunned look of defeat in his eyes "You ran into some snipers. Where were they shooting from?"

"What you gonna do with us?"

"Hurt you if you don't answer me. Where were the shooters? Where did you encounter them?"

The man frowned. He looked as if he was struggling to gather his thoughts. "They shot at us at two places. They hit us two or three times...I don't remember how many."

"Where? Where did they hit you?"

"On the corners. Where the road turns away from the ravine. It's exposed on the turns."

"Which ones?" Jason shouted.

The man's face pinched in concentration. "The second one coming down from the ridge, and the others after that."

"How far back up is that?"

"I don't know. We didn't get fired on for the last two, I'm sure of that. What you gonna do with us?"

Jason ignored his question.

He grabbed Clayton and headed to the second militia pickup where it sat mashed against the one ahead. "Tom, get the men together and bring the captives down to the valley road. Then clear this road. From what this guy says, Catherine and Bird had to be to the left, across the ravine. We'll drive back up to try to find their position. If we can locate them, we'll have to get all the way down to the bottom to climb up the slope they're on."

Chapter 49

Catherine and Bird listened to the gunfire below. There was a lot of rifle fire, and Catherine thought she could make out the sound of a machine gun. It seemed strangely harmless so far away. She did not hear any mortars.

Finally everything went quiet.

"You think they won?" Bird whispered.

"Don't know," Catherine said. "I'll go back with my rifle and spotting scope and see if I can tell what's happened."

Bird nodded. He had little strength for words.

Catherine ran through the woods. Their last sniping position was uphill. She heard the sound of a single truck roaring up the hill. It sounded like it was moving fast. The sound faded. She ignored her fatigue and jogged through the trees and brush, pushing uphill, her breath coming in harsh pants. She desperately hoped they had won the battle. She had to get help for Bird. She had tried again to tighten the bandage, but blood was still seeping out from under it.

She came out not far from where they had last shot at the trucks. She could hear another engine approaching. She knelt quickly and studied the road through her spotting scope. There was a pickup truck racing around a lower switchback, heading uphill. It looked shot up. It wasn't one of the valley pickups. She thought it was one of the ones they had been shooting at earlier. It disappeared into the trees.

She waited. The truck reappeared at the last switchback where she and Bird had fired on the convoy. It stopped. Two men got out. They were looking in her direction. It was Jason and Clayton.

She jumped up and waved her arms. At first the men didn't see her. Frustrated, she unslung her rifle and fired a shot in the air. They saw her instantly. They waved, and Jason cupped his hands around his mouth and yelled something that she couldn't make out. She swung her arms in a circle to indicate they should come to her. They stared. "Bird's shot! He needs help!" she shouted. Frantically she pointed back to the woods and swung her hands, beckoning them to come. Finally Jason and Clayton jumped back into the truck and it turned around and sped off downhill.

Catherine ran back down through the trees to Bird.

He was lying where she had left him. Her shirt was fully soaked with blood.

"Bird, they won!" she exclaimed.

He looked at her with dim eyes.

"Come on, Bird. We got to get down off the ridge. They're coming to help. You're going to be okay."

"You go," Bird said his voice now weak and hoarse.

"No. I won't leave you. We'll get you out of here. You're going to be okay."

"I don't think so." He looked down at the bandage. "Lots of blood. Too much."

"No! You got to get up. Help is coming. You have to hang on."

Catherine gently slipped her hands under Bird's armpits and started to lift. "You help me, Bird Early. Don't you quit. You aren't a quitter!"

Bird groaned, but he struggled to gather his legs under him. Soon Catherine had him on his feet. She pulled his right arm over her shoulder and they began to stumble down the hillside. Catherine kept searching for the easiest terrain. Bird was not going to be able to climb down any rocks.

As they worked their way down she tried to keep Bird talking, keep him focused.

"I'm sorry I got hit. I messed up," Bird said.

"No you didn't. It could just as easily have been me."

"Glad it wasn't you. I like you. Wish I had a girl like you."

A wave of anguish rushed through her. "You'll find one. She'll help you get better and you'll have a long life together. You just hang on. We're going to get you some help."

After a while they heard a shot below them. Catherine shifted her hold on Bird enough that she could get out her 9mm. She fired two shots in the air.

"They're coming," she told Bird. They began to struggle downward again. After ten more minutes they heard another shot, closer this time. Catherine immediately fired two more rounds.

Then she felt Bird sagging. She began shouting, "Here we are! Hurry! Bird's been hit. He needs help."

Bird's legs gave out and he sank to the ground with a groan. Catherine guided him down, and he lay back on the sloping ground. She knelt down next to him and took his face in her hands.

"You hang on, Bird. Don't you give up." She had tears in her eyes as she spoke.

Bird looked at her with sad eyes. "I'm tryin'. It hurts some." His eyes began to lose focus.

Catherine held his head firmly in her hands. She put her face close to his and began to exhort him again. "Don't quit. Don't you leave me," she shouted into his face. Tears streamed down her cheeks. She turned from Bird to shout out, "Over here! Hurry! Bird needs help!"

It seemed to take far too long until there were shouts nearby, and then Jason, Clayton and two of the clansmen came into view below. They ran up to her.

"Are you okay?" Jason asked.

"It's Bird. He got hit by some shrapnel. He's bleeding badly. Please don't let him die."

Clayton shouldered in past her and bent over Bird. She almost toppled backward.

"Bird, you hear me?" Clayton shouted.

Between Jason and Clayton she could see Bird nodding.

"We got to put pressure on the wound," Jason said to Clayton. "He's lost a lot of blood." Catherine felt a stab of guilt. The two of them stripped to the waist and they doubled their shirts across the wound, pulling them tight around Bird's lower torso. Finally it looked as if the flow had been stopped, or nearly so.

After a moment's consultation, the four men knelt down beside Bird. Clayton was at his head, Jason at his feet, and the two bearded clansmen knelt beside him, one on each side. The two men laced their arms under his torso and clasped hands. Clayton supported Bird's head and Jason took his feet. They gently lifted him up. Bird's face was pale, but he made no sound. The four of them began to carry Bird down the ridge. Catherine carried Bird's rifle as well as her own and went ahead of them, pushing branches out of their way.

She asked once, "Did you get Leo?"

"No," Jason said.

"No?"

"Tom checked the bodies. Didn't see him. Someone took off in one of the trucks. Maybe Leo."

The going was slow and painful. Bird grunted whenever the men stumbled on the uneven ground. Finally they came down onto the flat ground. The paved road was only a short distance away. Ahead they saw a cluster of pickup trucks, two of them looking well shot up. The rest of the fighters were waiting for them.

The four men gently laid Bird down on the grass just short of the asphalt. He was barely conscious. Catherine leaned the rifles up against one of the pickups and went back to where Bird lay. Clayton carefully tugged the makeshift bandages to one side. The shrapnel had torn a deep, jagged gash in his side. It was no longer bleeding much, but, looking at it now, Catherine realized it was much deeper than she had thought when she had been hurrying to bind it up on the slope.

"You think the shrapnel's still inside?" Clayton asked.

"Only way to tell is to probe the wound," Jason said in a low voice.

"You do that?"

When Jason answered, he sounded uncertain. "He's pretty weak," he said. "But, if there's metal in him, we need to get it out. It could keep cutting him inside." He looked up at someone in the small crowd and said, "Get me some water. I need to clean my hands as best I can."

The crowd shifted. Jason gently loosened the layers of cloth and pulled them completely open around the wound. Catherine looked at Jason's large hands, dirty from the fighting and scrambling he'd done. She took a deep breath. "Let me do this. My hands are smaller and cleaner."

Jason looked at her. She could feel the dried tears on her face, but she wasn't crying now. She felt a stubborn will gather within her.

"Can you do this?" Jason asked her. "You've never done anything like this before."

Catherine nodded.

Jason shook his head. "Go rinse your hands as best you can," he said quietly. "Then just reach in. You can move things around gently. If you find metal, you have to be careful to pull it out without cutting him more."

Catherine looked grim. She struggled out of her coat and laid it behind her, heedless of the onlookers. Someone above her handed a deerskin water bag, and she splashed water over her hands and then rubbed them together, flapping them dry in the air. She turned to Bird who was looking at her. "I'm going to check for metal," she told him. "If there's any inside you, we need to get it out."

Bird gave a weak nod. "It don't hurt now. That's odd."

Catherine took a breath and held it. She moved closer to Bird, leaned over him, and put her right hand to the red tear in his side. She slowly worked her fingertips into the wound. Then her fingers. He was so warm. Her hand was partially inside when she felt something hard and twisted. She looked up at Bird. "I found some."

"Be careful," Jason said close behind her. "Don't yank and don't force it."

Catherine grimaced. She gradually slid her fingers around the metal. "I got a grip on it."

"Go slow," Jason said.

She nodded. Her mind was focused on what her hand felt. Everything seemed magnified to her hand's touch. She only belatedly realized that she was staring into Bird's eyes. Now she saw him as if for the first time. He was staring back at her. "It don't hurt," he said. "You doin' a good job."

He smiled.

Slowly, slowly, Catherine began to work the metal shard out of Bird. When she felt resistance, she paused, moved her hand slightly, and then started again. And then the shard was out, in her hand, and a new spurt of blood shot up her arm.

"Nooo!" Catherine shouted. She threw the piece of shrapnel to the ground.

Jason pulled her back from Bird. She put her hands to her face to wipe the sweat away but only smeared herself with warm blood. She rubbed her bloody right arm across her body, trying to clean it, but only succeeded in smearing her bare midriff. Jason had gotten shirts from the people around them, and he was working over Bird, struggling to bind his wound again. Catherine shuffled around the men and knelt down close to Bird's face. She took his head in her hands, putting her face close to his.

"You hang on, Bird. We got the metal out. You're going to be all right."

Bird looked at her. "Thanks," he said in a barely audible voice. "Wish you were my girl. You somethin'."

"*You're* something. Some girl's going to get a prize in you, Bird Early."

Bird turned his head, his eyes searching. They found Clayton. "I'm sorry," he said. "Didn't mean to get hit like this. Mortars are somethin' else. Bad."

"You save your strength," Clayton said. His voice was gentle. "Just stay with us. We'll stop the bleeding and get you to..." He stopped abruptly.

"Ain't gonna make it. I'm done." Bird's voice faltered. "Too much blood...too much gone."

"No," Catherine told him. Her voice threatened to break down. "Stay with us, don't give up. Don't let them win." She was sobbing now. He turned his face back to her, and she bent over him.

"Can't...goin'...can't focus."

He looked back to Clayton who was leaning over them. "Tell momma I'm sorry," he said, and he exhaled and his eyes went blank.

Catherine buried her face in his chest and cried. Gentle hands pulled her back. Clayton leaned over and slowly wiped Bird's forehead and closed his eyes. No one moved or made a sound, except for someone toward the back of the group who could not hide his weeping.

Chapter 50

Finally Catherine got up. She was not crying now. Her face grew dark and hard. On the other side of the road, the five captured men sat on the ground with their hands tied behind their backs.

"You!" she shouted. She strode across the road. "Why'd you come here? What did we ever do to you?" She pulled her 9mm out of its holster as she approached the men. "Which one of you fired the mortar? Which one of you killed Bird?" She pointed her pistol at them. "Was it you?" she yelled at the nearest man. She jammed the 9mm against his temple, and he flinched, shaking his head wildly. She put her pistol against the next man's head. He tried to shrink away from the barrel. "Was it you? I should shoot you all!"

"Catherine," Jason said coming up to her, "These men have surrendered."

Catherine kept glaring at the prisoners. "These men killed Bird. They deserve to die." Her voice was dark with a deadly intent.

"No they don't. This is not fighting, defending yourself. It's execution...murder."

She saw that all the defenders were looking at her. She wavered, and then emptied her pistol barely over the heads of the prisoners. They threw themselves sideways to get away from the gun. When the slide slapped back and stayed open, the weapon empty, she holstered it and turned and went to the truck where she had put the rifles. She grabbed the M110, grabbed her jacket, and stomped off down the road toward the farms. "Catherine," Jason called. She heard Clayton say, "Let her go. She got to grieve. She got to get over her angry."

And then she was alone with the sound of her footsteps.

Leo drove fast along the winding highway back to Hillsboro, going as quickly around the dead vehicles as he dared. He had no illusions about the final outcome in the valley. His remaining men had either surrendered or been killed. The ones who had surrendered would spill their guts about whatever they knew. Thankfully they didn't know much.

Leo also knew that this wasn't the end. The valley wouldn't let this attack go unanswered. There would be a response, and it might come soon.

And the farmers were better equipped now. Behind him the .50 caliber M2 rode in the back of the truck, but the bed was otherwise empty. The farmers had his mortars, not to mention three new machine guns.

Leo ended jobs well. This one had not ended well, but—Leo's face broke into a grim smile—this job was not yet ended. He had to get back to Joe, so they could prepare for what might be coming next.

As he drove, he resolved to find Charlie and kill him personally. The valley had known they were coming. Charlie must have been the one who tipped them off.

But where did they get the extra men? He thought, over and over. Those men had tipped the fight against him.

They weren't from town. Hillsboro was full of sheep.

It suddenly came to him that it must have been that hillbilly group that had come along with the farmers to trade. But they didn't live anywhere near the valley. Had Jason Richards recruited them? *How?*

He remembered seeing the hillbillies at the trade meet. Even unarmed, they'd had a rough and untamed look about them. But he hadn't thought about having to face them when he attacked the farmers. They were a formidable fighting force, and he had overlooked them.

Trouble.

Still, how *much* trouble? His militia back in town outnumbered them, even if they joined in an attack on Hillsboro. He still had more weapons than they did, even with what he had lost in the valley. And he now knew about the extra fighters. He'd be ready this time.

Catherine stomped down the road, her fury undiminished. She had put on her jacket, now covered with dirt and blood. It was unbuttoned, and her bloody midriff showed through the opening. Her hair was wild and caked with blood, Bird's blood. Her face, stained with tears, blood and dirt, was now set in a fierce frown as she looked down at the pavement.

She was not thinking, only feeling the anger coursing through her body. With no plan, her steps took her towards her home farther down the road. She heard engines ahead and looked up to see a convoy of military vehicles approaching. The sun was high in the sky and heat ripples were rising from the dark macadam.

When the trucks were close, they stopped in the middle of the road. Kevin jumped out of the lead Humvee. "Catherine!" he shouted as he started towards her.

"You're too late," she yelled.

He stopped five paces in front of her. She saw Gibbs exit the other door of the Humvee and stare at her with a concerned look on his hard face.

"Catherine?" Kevin said again.

She looked away and started to walk past the Humvee. The other vehicles were stopped in a long line, and everyone was staring.

Kevin reached out to her, but she brushed his arm away. "Where were you?" she said.

"I—"

"We had to fight them by ourselves! Bird and I had to try to hold them off when they came over the west ridge."

"I came as soon as I could. It took some time to deal with Roper. Catherine, are you—"

"You were too late. We had to fight without you and a friend got killed"

Kevin's face was filled with concern.

"Are you wounded?" he asked.

She shook her head.

"Tell me what happened."

"Ask Jason." She jerked her thumb over her shoulder. "I don't want to talk now." She turned away from Kevin and started walking. He didn't follow. The men in the other vehicles stared wide-eyed at her as she marched past them.

A few moments later she heard the engines start. The convoy moved ahead and the sound diminished away with distance.

She walked towards home, alone with her thoughts and the sound of her boots thumping on the pavement.

She crunched up the gravel drive to the farmhouse and when she got to the front yard the front door burst open and her mother came running out.

"Catherine!" she screamed. "Oh God Catherine, are you hurt? How bad is it—"

"Mom!"

And then her mother's arms wrapped around her. "Oh baby, you're all bloody! What happened? Where are you hurt?"

"Mom, I'm fine," she said, pulling away. "I'm fine. It's not my blood. It's Bird's blood."

"Oh, Catherine!" Anne tried to pull Catherine back into her arms, but Catherine's body was hard and unyielding. She heard running footsteps from the house, and this time her sister screamed her name.

They were in the kitchen. Anne had taken Catherine's coat off and was washing the blood and dirt from her body. She related what had happened. Telling the story only increased her anger and grief; someone had to pay for Bird's death.

"Everyone did the best they could," Anne was saying. Her voice was patient and gentle. "That mortar could just as easily have hit you as Bird."

"If Kevin had come earlier, it wouldn't have happened," Catherine said. Her voice was still agitated. "He would have attacked them and they wouldn't have been able to fire mortar rounds at me and Bird." Her whole body shuddered. "He didn't have to die."

"What's going to happen now?" Sarah asked. She was sitting across the table, watching them both. Catherine could see not only her sister's concern, but puzzlement as well. She didn't understand. "Will they attack us again? Over some *seeds?*"

"I don't know. But I know what I'm going to do." Catherine stood abruptly and pushed her mother's arm away. Grabbing her backpack, she ran out of the kitchen and up the stairs to her room.

She threw her backpack on the bed, rummaged quickly in the closet and her chest of drawers for some clothes, put a shirt on, and stuffed more into the pack. She carried it back downstairs.

"What are you doing?" Anne asked in the kitchen doorway. Catherine didn't answer. She went to the corner of the living room and grabbed her Bushmaster and some boxes of ammunition. "Catherine," Anne asked again. "What's going on? Tell me."

"I'm going to get the man who's responsible for Bird's death."

Sarah pushed out past her mother. "You're not going to town, are you?"

Catherine looked at Sarah, her anger and grief, still in a mixed-up swirl, radiating through her body. "He's not going to get away with this," she said. "He had to be with them. I'm betting he led the attack. He's hands-on. But nobody found him after the ambush. I think he ran when the fight turned against him. I heard a truck drive up the ridge after the battle. I'm going to find him and kill him."

"Who do you mean?" Sarah asked.

"Leo."

"No you're not," Anne said in alarm.

Catherine looked at her mother. "He killed my friend. Bird didn't deserve to die...none of us deserve to be attacked like this."

"Why won't they leave us alone?" Sarah asked. Her voice sounded plaintive and irritating to Catherine. "We could get along with everyone in town, if they would just leave us alone."

A wave of fatigue passed over Catherine. She let out a sigh. Tears threatened again. She set down her backpack and rifle on the floor and stumbled past Anne and Sarah to her seat.

"They want power over us," she heard her mother say. "At least the ones in charge do. That guy Stansky, and Frank Mason. Somehow we represent an example they don't want the rest of the town to see. They are so afraid of losing power that they can't have anyone see how we live. On our own, independent...free."

"That's so stupid," Sarah declared. "What do they get out of it all? How does that make anything better?"

"I don't know that it does," Anne replied. "I just know that people in power seem to want to hold on to power and grab more for themselves. Getting more power and control becomes the goal, not helping others with their power."

"Well, I'm going to do something about it," Catherine said. "I'm going to end it. Cut the head off the snake and the body will die."

Chapter 51

There was a roar of many engines piling into the yard outside and coming to a halt. Catherine tensed. Anne and Sarah ran out of the kitchen. She was alone. She took a deep breath and got to her feet. She went into the pantry and grabbed some dried venison and fruit. She was putting the food into her backpack when the men came into the house. Kevin was there, and Jason, with Clayton and Gibbs close behind them. Kevin looked at her warily.

"Where are you going?" Jason asked her.

"You know," she replied. "To town."

"You can't go off by yourself, half-cocked—"

"I'm not going off half-cocked. I'm going to kill Leo. He's the one responsible for Bird's death."

Jason took a deep breath. "We have to plan this out as a team. I can't have you doing something on your own."

His answer only fed her anger. She glared back at him.

Clayton's calm voice cut in. "We all upset over Bird's death, but others got killed today," He stepped past Jason. His eyes bore into her, calm but completely unrelenting. "More of my kin, my folk. You don't know them, but they all have families, same as Bird. All their families, and Bird's mother, how do you think they'll feel?"

Catherine scowled angrily at him, but he never wavered. She finally dropped her eyes. What he had said began to penetrate. How many had he lost?

"Point is you ain't the only one upset." Clayton looked beyond her. His face remained placid, but his eyes had a fierce and dangerous look. He stepped past Catherine and turned, crossing his arms. He looked at the others. "What we do now?" he said in the same calm voice.

There was a thoughtful silence. Catherine digested Clayton's words. Bird had been kind and thoughtful. He had liked and appreciated her. In their short time together, they had bonded, whether because of their similarities or their mission. Now she realized others had been affected as well. Others had died as well. Suddenly she felt the selfishness of her actions, wanting to act out on her own to salve her own private hurt.

She still wanted revenge, to make Leo pay, and certainly Clayton felt the same way. But maybe the best path to that lay in sticking together.

"We attack," Jason said. His voice came out crisp and resolute. "The sooner the better. Giving them time will only let them get their defenses organized."

Catherine and her mother looked at him.

"He's right," Gibbs said. "Don't let them regroup. You've dealt them a big blow. Let's follow it up while they're in some confusion."

"What about their numbers?" Anne asked. Everyone could hear her uncertainty.

"Their numbers are reduced after today," Gibbs said.

"But you're taking on a *city*," Anne said.

"Most in the town are non-combatants. It's only the militia we have to go against," Gibbs replied.

"Don't they still outnumber us? Badly?"

"Ma'am, they may outnumber us, but can they outfight us?" Gibbs replied. "I'm betting Leo used his best on this raid, seeing as he knew about your battle with Big Jacks and his gang."

"The militia is not well trained," Kevin said. "Adequate for the action they've seen, dealing with civilians and disorganized bandits, usually not in large numbers. They can all handle weapons, they're all capable of killing, but they're not disciplined, and they don't have any idea of battle tactics."

The others were nodding.

"We move quickly, and get the locals involved, we could finish this quickly," Kevin said quietly. Catherine heard a professional certainty in his tone.

"Are your men in?" Jason asked Clayton.

Clayton's face remained calm, but his eyes were burning. "We in," he said. "We got to make them pay for killing Bird and the others. Make 'em fear us."

Jason exhaled. His face showed fatigue but his eyes were dark—warrior's eyes. Catherine had seen it before. "So we do this, and we do it fast."

The sun was nearing the west ridge when the valley defenders set out for Hillsboro.

Tom Walsh was not with them. He had agreed to stay behind and guard the prisoners. Assisting him in this were Anne, Sarah, and his wife, Betty. They would be taking no chances until the others returned. The men were kept separated in Tom's barn, and constantly tied up. They would be fed by their captors; their hands were tied behind their backs, and the bonds would not be loosened. They would have an uncomfortable few days.

The valley's attack force numbered thirty-five. There were fifteen soldiers, plus Lieutenant Cameron and Sergeant Gibbs. Clayton also had fifteen men from his two clans, for a total of sixteen, and Jason and Catherine were the only fighters from the valley itself. No one questioned

Catherine coming along. She had proven herself in battle, and, in any case, she was not going to be denied her opportunity to avenge Bird's death.

She rode silently with Jason in one of the pickup trucks with Clayton in the cab.

They raced over the back roads in the gathering dark.

Finally Jason spoke up. "We'll have to find a way to get into town. We can't just show up at a gate."

"We sneak in some way. Got to meet up with the town folk," Clayton said.

It took a moment for Catherine to bring her mind back to the present. She didn't want to talk, but things had to be dealt with; their lives depended on it. She said, "Maybe a small group can get through the wall and connect up with Chief Cook and the civilians. Then get the rest in? According to Kevin, the town's barrier walls are porous. Both he and the militia had to keep dealing with refugees and bandits who'd gotten in. Not a rush but it kept happening. There's got to be a way through."

"If we do it this way, who do we send?" Clayton asked.

Catherine responded, "I can go with Sergeant Gibbs and maybe another soldier."

Jason turned to look at her. "Why you?" he said. "That's too dangerous."

She looked at him: a man she admired. She had looked up to him from the beginning. At one time she had even thought she was in love with him. He had saved her life and had taught her how to fight and defend herself. It was Jason who had given her the freedom of self-confidence. And she had given back to him; she had saved his life, twice.

Yet what he said now didn't make sense to her. He was trying to be the protective father, sheltering her from danger. Even in the face of convincing evidence that she could take care of herself, that she was a capable warrior.

"I suppose sniping the attackers who were firing machine guns and mortars at us wasn't dangerous?"

"That was different," he said. "Now you're going into the nest, into the lair of the enemy. Your shooting skills may not help you there—"

"They won't?"

"Catherine, I love you. You know that. I think of you and Sarah as my own daughters. I know you can take care of yourself, but I can't help worrying about you."

"I'm trying to understand," she told him. "But it doesn't make much sense when you consider what I can do, and what I've...what we've...been through."

He looked back at the road, and she saw his jaw muscles clench. She wasn't sure if he was angry or frustrated. "I'll try to keep my protective instincts in check, but it's hard to think of you as just a member of our fighting team.

Having you in harm's way scares me, somehow more than before. Maybe it's because we didn't have any choice in the matter before."

Then his expression hardened, and he turned it back to her. "But here's what's important. We have to fight with a plan. That means you can't be a rogue actor. You've got to go along with whatever plan we come up with. Can you do that?"

Catherine thought about that for a moment. "I can do that as long as you allow me to be in the fight, to use my skills." She paused to sort out her thoughts. There was one thing that really mattered. "And I want to kill Leo. That's personal for me."

Jason sighed.

They drove on, each lost in their thoughts about what was to come.

Chapter 52

L eo? He's got something going on," the bartender said, polishing the bar. "Something special. He's not even in town right now."

"What?" Lori Sue blurted. She covered quickly. "No one's ever not in town anymore, Hank. It's not like anyone goes to Vegas. Where would he even *go?*"

"Out with some kinda task force. Bigger than a patrol. Don't know what the deal is, but there's talk that maybe those farmers who came for the trade visit are gonna get a visit of their own. Maybe the goods weren't as advertised or something." Hank shrugged.

"When'd everyone find out about this?" she asked.

"Word got around during the day. People didn't see Leo around and noticed some of the men gone. Seems to have been kept pretty quiet. What's it to you anyway?"

Lori Sue gave him a big smile. "A girl in my line of work needs to know what's going on."

"A girl in your line of work needs a strong back...amount of time you spend on it." The bartender gave her a nasty grin.

"Shove it up yours," Lori Sue retorted and gave him the finger. "You're just jealous 'cause I don't give you a tumble."

"Don't worry about that, dear. I ain't looking to catch a disease."

"You don't have any worries there. Since you probably aren't getting any action." She smiled at him.

"Go to hell," he said, his smile turning to a scowl.

"See you later, Hank. Stay out of trouble." She turned and left the bar.

Outside she stopped to think. Leo was gone. She'd already lost a day. Her biggest problem was that she didn't have a hacksaw or bolt cutters. She'd need those to do anything anyway. Lori Sue cursed. There was nothing to do but head back to her apartment, find Billy, and make him get the tool she needed. Leo was probably going to be gone for two or three days, so she could spring Donna tomorrow. She put her frustration aside and started walking.

Well before the deserted houses thinned out, Jason pulled his pickup to the middle to block the street and stop the convoy behind him. He, Clayton, and Catherine got out and went over to the Humvee with Kevin and Rodney in it. The night was dark and overcast, a cool wind blowing from the north. They spoke in whispers, even though they guessed that they were still quite a way from the barricades.

"We can't go any closer. They'll have men at the barricade," Kevin said.

"And they'll know we're coming," Jason said. "Remember that pickup that got away? Whoever was in it had most of a day's head start on us. Whether it was Leo or not, I think we have to assume the town is alerted."

Rodney spoke up. "Since there are only two main gates, it wouldn't be hard for them to really be ready for us."

"They've got a .50 cal machine gun." Catherine said. "I heard it when they fired on me and Bird."

She could barely see Rodney's head nod in the darkness. "You don't forget that sound," he said. "And who knows how many M60s. A .50 cal would stop the whole convoy and scatter it."

"I think we have a small group head off to the barricade," Kevin said. "Climb over it like other refugees do, away from the guarded entrances."

"What about the rest of the group?" Clayton asked.

"We've got working radios," Rodney said. "We can join up with Chief Cook. He's probably at Lori Sue's place, or she knows how to get hold of him. He'll know how we can get our main force in."

"That's going to take time," Jason said.

"Yeah," Kevin replied, "but if we take that time, I'll bet we'll get all our men in without any losses, along with our gear. And they won't know we're inside until we attack. If we just go at the main entrance with the whole group, we'll probably be engaged while we're still outside. We don't want that."

Rodney looked out into the dim jumble of rooflines and trees. "I'm thinking the group should head to our right, towards the west side. That'll take them away from the entrance."

"I should stay with the main group, so you should sneak in," Kevin said to Rodney.

Catherine spoke up. "And I want go with him."

Kevin looked at her. "I don't like that."

"You said you needed to stay here, and so should Jason. Clayton doesn't know the townspeople all that well. I'll be able to communicate with Lori Sue, and I think I can do a good job if any convincing is needed to get all of them on board. This will be easy compared to today."

"She makes a point," Clayton said.

"I still don't like it," Kevin said. "At least you should take a second soldier. Three isn't too large of a group."

"I'll take Bradley Thomas," Rodney said. "He's a solid soldier. And he can be quiet." He turned and walked back toward the looming rectangle of the big troop truck.

A few moments Rodney returned with Specialist Thomas, followed by Kevin with three helmets in his arms. Mounted to the front of each were strange, boxy constructions, each with a single stubby lens pointing forward—night vision goggles. "These should help you navigate your way through the barrier."

"Good call," Gibbs said. He took two and handed them to Thomas and Catherine.

Catherine put her helmet on and it flopped down over her eyes. "It's too big," she said.

Kevin reached for the helmet. "I'll find a smaller size," he said and headed back to the truck.

In a minute he was back without a helmet. "Couldn't find a small, so I got this headlamp harness." He held out a webbed harness. "It goes over your head. This strap goes around your forehead, this one goes over the top. I can clip the goggles onto the harness. Put your ball cap on backwards and then put the harness over the cap."

Catherine tried it on, and Kevin attached the goggles up at the top of her forehead and adjusted the straps until they were held securely. "That feels good. And it isn't heavy like the helmet."

"Okay, let's gear up," Kevin said. "Catherine, do you want an M16? It has an automatic fire switch."

"No, let me keep my Bushmaster. I'm used to it."

"One mag in your weapon and take four more with you," Rodney said. "Now the radios."

Kevin reached into the Humvee and pulled out two handheld field radios.

"How do those still work?" Jason asked.

Kevin smiled. "Protected circuits. They're rechargeable with a crank charger."

Rodney and Thomas put on their helmets. Kevin showed Catherine the switch to turn on the goggles. She flipped them down over her eyes and gasped. "Oh wow. It's so bright. I can see everything."

"That's the idea," Kevin said.

"And it's all green." Catherine flipped them up and stared around in the dark. "That makes such a difference. This will be easier than I thought."

"We can only hope," Rodney said.

"You better go," Jason said gruffly. "We're losing the night standing here."

Catherine reached for him and gave him a hug. "I'll be careful," she said.

"Thank you," Jason replied.

Then Catherine turned to Kevin, who stood there expectantly looking at her. There was a residue of confused anger still in her, anger that had no object. Her words were tight in her throat. "You be careful," she said, her voice coming out more stiffly than she meant it to.

Kevin nodded. "You be careful too," he said.

Chapter 53

The shapes of the convoy vehicles quickly disappeared into the dark as Gibbs and the others rounded a house. They were in a suburban area of empty houses, long deserted. With the goggles the walking was easy. At first there was little to worry about as they quietly made their way through the abandoned neighborhood, while keeping an eye out for patrols or sentries. But soon they crossed the street with the single line of ruined houses on the far side that were partially dismantled and entered the zone that had been cleared of all buildings. There was little cover now and they could see the wall. They dashed from hiding spot to hiding spot in a crouch, hunting for the few concealment points left in the open area, avoiding the open basements that now lay uncovered and filled with stagnant water.

"I hope the militia doesn't have these goggles," Catherine whispered to Gibbs.

"We have to assume they do," he replied.

At each hiding place, they scanned the area ahead. As the rubble wall came closer, they could see no sign of guard posts along its top or along its base, for as far as they could see along the curve.

"They're concentrating on the entrance points. We should be able to climb over without being detected," Gibbs said after a long look to left and right.

When the wall was built, the town kept things simple. All the smaller roads into town were just blocked by the rubble.

"We'll need to find a thin point to bring the convoy in. A place where we can just shove the rubble aside," Gibbs said.

"You think we could find a place like that?"

"I don't know. Maybe Charlie Cook knows." Gibbs sighed. "Everyone might have to climb over like we're going to do."

"You like that gamble?" Thomas asked.

"Better than getting caught and engaged in a firefight outside of town. That's what Stansky'd like. We'll have to find a spot or do it the hard way."

"Tough choices," Thomas said.

The wall was about seven feet high at the point they were approaching. It was not as imposing as it had been around the main gate, there were no car bodies in its base, but it looked dangerous. Here it was really more of a construction trash pile, built up of building rubble, concrete blocks, rocks, lumber, metal beams, gravel, and miscellaneous debris. At any time one part of it could come loose as someone climbed it, burying them, or perhaps the whole thing would sag into a new point of stability, crushing anyone caught on it. Catherine suppressed a shudder at the sight. At night, without the goggles, it would have been nearly impossible to scale without incident.

They covered the last thirty yards in a dash. There was no cover. Gibbs looked up for a moment; he grabbed something and began to climb. Catherine and Thomas started to climb as well, but a soft whisper stopped them. "One at a time."

Catherine went next with Thomas last. A cascade of rubble followed him as he descended and the three were inside. They looked around at the buildings, clearly illuminated by their goggles. The houses stretched out along the blocks, with larger buildings visible in the distance. No hints of candlelight showed in any of the windows.

"Where are we?" Catherine whispered.

"Not exactly sure, but I'll get my bearings as we move into town. Don't worry. I've got Lori Sue's address and I'll get us there. Just have to get some street names so I can orient myself. This way." He led them quickly across the street and along it to their left.

They kept to the shadows, staying close to the buildings, and carefully scanned the intersections. The street crossings exposed them to anyone who might be keeping a lookout. Occasionally they heard the sound of a vehicle far off across town, but none came in their direction.

"We get close to Lori Sue's place, I'm betting we'll run into some of Chief Cook's men," Gibbs remarked.

"Dangerous?" Thomas asked.

"Could be. They'll be skittish about anyone moving around at night. We got to not look like a militia patrol."

"Will they recognize us?" Catherine wondered. "If they think we're militia, they'll just hide...or shoot at us."

"We have our uniforms on," Thomas said.

"Won't help much in the dark," Catherine said.

"Both of you quiet down. Less talk, more listening," Gibbs said in a harsh whisper.

After seven blocks of walking south and then east, the environs had become discernibly more neglected. Gibbs stopped and took off his helmet. "Take off your helmets," he told them. "Hook your arm through the strap. Let's all take our rifles and hold them under our jackets."

They moved more openly as they approached their objective. Suddenly Gibbs stopped them again.

"Catherine, take off your cap," he whispered.

"What?" She wore a billed cap, with her hair in a ponytail to keep it out of her face.

"Take it off. And let your hair down. I don't think there are any females in the militia, so if anyone sees you, they'll know we're not them."

Catherine turned to look at him, "You think that will help?"

Gibbs shrugged. "It won't hurt."

They walked on, searching for any sign of light in the buildings, listening for any sounds as they went. Except for distant sounds, nothing disturbed the dark and quiet of the night.

"This could get us killed," Thomas complained. "It doesn't make a lot of sense."

I've got an idea," Catherine said.

The two men looked over at her.

"Why don't I just call out for Chief Cook? We can't really hear what's going on in Stansky's section of town so they shouldn't be able to hear us. When we get close to the building, I could identify us and call out for Chief Cook."

"We could try that. Militia raiding parties don't announce themselves," Rodney said.

When they got to the block that contained the right street number, Catherine began to call out. Just before they reached the building, they heard someone shout, "Stop! You're covered from multiple positions. Don't reach for your weapons. Identify yourselves."

"I'm Sergeant Gibbs. I'm with a squad led by Lieutenant Cameron. With me are Catherine Whitman and Specialist Thomas. We're here to connect with Chief Cook."

"What's your mother's name and your sister's name?"

Catherine spoke up. "I assume you're asking me. My mother's name is Anne and my sister is Sarah."

"Wait where you are. Don't try to leave the area."

Some five minutes later, which seemed like hours to Catherine, the front door of the apartment building opened and two men stepped out. As they approached, she could recognize Chief Cook from his white hair.

He came up to them and shook Rodney's hand enthusiastically. "I'm sure glad you found us. Is everyone in the valley okay? Did you and Cameron get there in time?"

Gibbs hesitated. "We got there late, but the valley prevailed. Most of the raiders were killed or captured, but one escaped."

"We've haven't seen any increase in activity in town. They may not know about the outcome yet," Charlie said.

"That's what we're hoping, but they will by tomorrow. We have to get the rest of the men inside the wall, tonight if possible."

"Come on," Charlie said. "We'll figure out the best place to get through. Back to your places, everyone."

He led them across the street into a three-story building that looked as if it had housed offices. They followed him up a dark flight of stairs and into a large room that was even darker. There was the sound of a match, and then they saw Charlie leaning over the growing glow of a gas lamp. After lighting it he moved across and checked the curtains that were tacked across the windows. The lamp sat on a large table in the center of the room, and spread on the table was what Catherine immediately recognized as a huge map of the city.

Gibbs stepped closer and looked at the map. The wall was drawn in as it curved around the city. The downtown area was marked, showing the central area of Stansky's offices, militia compound and warehouses, and that part of the map was densely annotated with handwritten notes. The whole area was noted as 'Militia HQ.'

His eyes followed the broad stroke of the wall, marked with a heavy black line. Along the western arc there was a break in the line. It was close to the river. He looked up at Chief Cook. Their eyes met. He was already nodding.

"That's the best place to enter." Charlie said. "The wall petered out at that point. It's tricky through there. They're going to dig out an old canal that ran through there. It used to divert flow off the river to feed a water mill. The city's rebuilding the mill as a hydropower plant, so they need the flow, but that means they can't wall that part off. The city keeps a small guard force there, two men. Where are your people?"

Gibbs leaned over and pointed to the main road heading north out of Hillsboro. "We stopped somewhere along this road, well before the checkpoint. Didn't want to be heard. The trucks are pulled back onto a side road for concealment."

Charlie looked at the map. He took a pencil from the end of the table. "The cleared area starts about here," he said, putting a mark on the road north of the mark for the wall. "Since you hadn't reached it yet, you're somewhere north of this point."

Gibbs pointed. "We walked to the west of the road to get across the wall." He traced his finger along the map, like a hound trying to pick up a scent. He mumbled to himself, "We walked three blocks before coming to the cleared space." Gibbs's hand stopped circling and zoomed to the wall. "Bet we crossed here, and I'll bet the convoy is located about here."

"That's good enough." Charlie began to draw a path through the network of roads, keeping the line well back from the broad black bar of the wall, until he got close to the break. "That's the route they should take. Now how do we tell them?"

Gibbs smiled. "We have radio contact with the convoy," Gibbs said. He took off his pack and pulled out his radio.

Charlie looked surprised. "That's great!" He stared at the device. "It's a wonder it still works."

"Hardened circuitry and hand-cranked chargers. It's low tech but it works."

"Do your people have a map of town? He asked."

Gibbs nodded in assent.

"You should get them going. With the trucks it will take some time. Those are small roads, and I can't speak for obstructions." Charlie looked at his watch. "I don't think they can make it before dawn."

Chapter 54

Just before dawn, Charlie set out with Les Hammond and four other officers for the guard post at the gap. The morning shift for the guards began at sunrise, so he and his men would wait until after the changeover. That might give them as much as eight hours before anyone noticed something amiss.

After neutralizing the guards and securing them in an abandoned shack, Charlie took one of the men and walked him away from the group. He sat him down amidst the rubble, out of eyes or ears of everyone else.

"What's your name?" Charlie asked the man.

"Steve."

"Steve, we got a situation here. It's dangerous for you. For all of us, really. So I'm going to ask you a few questions and you're going to have to make a decision."

Steve looked at Charlie suspiciously "We were told you weren't in charge anymore."

"Forget what you were told and listen. I don't have a lot of time. Leo and the militia, the group you're a part of, tried to murder the valley farmers, the ones who came to trade with us earlier this spring. The militia was defeated. Of the three truckloads of men who left, only one man got away. The rest were killed or captured."

"Why should I believe you?"

He gave Steve a serious look.

"Just be quiet and listen," Charlie said. "I'm giving you a chance to save your life. You keep interrupting, it won't work. Right now you're talking to someone who thinks like a cop. Lieutenant Cameron is coming with some soldiers, and if you and I don't have an understanding by the time he gets here, he'll decide what to do with you. This is now a war situation. You're essentially a prisoner of war. The lieutenant knows we don't have room or time to hold prisoners of war securely. You might try to escape, and you know what happens to prisoners who try to escape?" Charlie leaned closer. "They're shot. You get my point?"

Charlie saw the fear come into Steve's face.

"You have the option to join our forces or remain a prisoner. If you don't join us, after we defeat Joe you will be put on trial as a militia member, and I don't think the townspeople will go easy on militia members."

"What do I got to do?"

"Stay on guard duty, and when the next shift comes on, don't let them know we brought these men in."

"What if you lose? I'll be killed by Stansky's men. He's got a lot of men."

"We got a lot of men also. The valley people, the army, some mountain clan people, the police. And all of these people know how to use weapons and fight. They're not amateurs." Charlie let that sink in. "But if we do fail, I figure you'll have a chance to talk your way out of any problems. You can say you were disarmed and forced to say what you said. Hell, no one may even figure out how they got in."

"I don't know—"

"You have one minute to decide," Charlie said, looking at his watch. "I can't spend more time with you, and I don't even know if Cameron will want to talk. You seem like a decent guy, Steve. Are you on the side of killing men on trumped up charges, like what went on last week? Are you on the side of killing civilians, the people in the valley? Women and children?"

Steve looked down at the pavement and shook his head. "Nah, can't say I am, but I don't want to get myself killed either."

"So what's it going to be?"

Steve looked up at Charlie. "I guess I'll put in with you. You're holding the cards."

"That'll do for now," Charlie said. He motioned with his pistol for Steve to get up.

He walked Steve back to Les. "I want you to stay with this guy. We'll unload his weapon. When the next shift arrives, you can explain that the other guard took sick and you filled in. That'll give us another 8 hours."

"What about the other guard?"

"Gag him and cuff him in an abandoned building. We'll get him later and turn him over to the insurrection."

A half hour later the convoy came through the opening. When they were through Charlie directed them to be dispersed into the alleys in the abandoned part of the city. Soon the convoy and fighters disappeared. Charlie walked back to his headquarters. He felt energized like he hadn't felt in years. *All this may not work, but it's good to be on the right side of the fight.*

Chapter 55

Leo finally saw the rubble wall ahead of him in the dark.
He had taken more than twice the time he had estimated to get back to Hillsboro. Coming down from the ridge on the outside, he had had a flat tire which had taken some time to change. Once he was on the paved road his larger problem had emerged—the damage to the truck included a leak in the radiator. The pickup had started overheating. The first time he had lost two and a half hours until he had found a plastic detergent jug in an abandoned house, and then, after he had made his way back to the truck, he had had to walk a quarter mile to a pond to fill the jug. After three trips to the pond he had been on the move again, this time with the filled jug beside him. The temperature needle had climbed steadily, and two hours later he had been looking for another water source. By the third stop, night had fallen. By the third stop, night had fallen. He was exhausted but knew he couldn't sleep. He filled the radiator and pushed ahead, determined to make it back to town that night.

After Leo had pulled through the stunned cluster of guards at the outer gate, he drove the bullet-riddled truck straight to headquarters without thought of food or a change of clothes. It was still night and Joe would not be there so he leaned back in the truck and tried to sleep. The sun would wake him and he would talk to Joe first thing in the morning.

Joe stared at him while he related what had happened in the valley. Leo knew he wasn't looking very good; he was dirty, disheveled, sweaty, and not very calm. When he finished his explanation of events, Joe exploded into a fury.

"You got a bunch of idiots," Joe shouted. "They couldn't defeat those farmers? With all the weapons you had?"

Leo had remained standing. He had noted that Joe hadn't told him to sit down. He didn't think Joe was going to take his anger out on him, but he couldn't ignore the fact that he had been the leader and he had failed in his mission. The best he could do was to explain *how* things had gone wrong. "Wasn't their fault, boss," he said. "They're solid guys. I picked the most experienced. The thing was, we got hit before we could surprise them. And they had those hillbillies. We didn't expect that. There were a lot more men than we anticipated. They're damn good fighters. Good shots."

He grimaced. "They guessed we would come over the west ridge. Hell, they had some snipers slowing us up as we came down the ridge. And they figured out the attack at the bridge was a diversion, so reinforcements came before I could get off the dirt road and into the valley."

Joe slammed his hand down hard on the desk, glaring at Leo. "Shit. It's all excuses. I don't need excuses, I need results. And you better deliver. I waited until the army left, but what the hell did I gain by waiting?"

Leo said carefully, "Joe, we got to consider another possibility now. Those people might hit the town."

Joe stopped moving. Very slowly, he cocked his head. "What did you say?"

"I think they're going to be looking to attack us. The whole town."

"Hillsboro? You got to be kidding." Joe said.

"You know I'm not. We tried to annihilate them. They understand that. They won't let that stand. They'd just be setting themselves up for getting slowly picked off by us later, over time."

"So they'll come after us? Me? Everyone?"

"They won't be looking to knock off a patrol or give us a spanking. They'll be looking to take us down, you and me."

"We'd wipe them out!"

"We didn't do that yesterday. They're good. They won. They're full of themselves now and they got those hillbillies with them. And that's gotta make a time factor too. Jason has to act before those guys go back to their hills." Leo leaned forward to press his point. "We just tried to kill them. Would *you* give somebody a second chance to come back and do it right?"

Joe's eyes had turned to ice. After a moment he said, "No, I would not."

"Me either. The farmers might, but the hillbillies wouldn't. And they'll come at us while their blood's up."

Joe walked around the desk and came up to Leo. Joe's face was still flushed with anger. Leo held his place. He had seen Joe enraged before and knew it was best to stand still.

"If you're right, we have to get ready. But they'll be on our turf now." Joe's voice was strangely calm.

"What I'm thinking."

There was a new light in Joe's eyes. It wasn't pleasure, but it glinted with excitement. Leo knew Joe was a fighter. Now that fierce, manic energy was shining in his eyes.

"Go get our defenses ready," Joe said, his voice still calm. "Whatever you need. Whatever you think." He stepped up close to Leo and put his finger on his chest, not a jab, but a statement of authority. "And you better not let me down this time."

His voice left no doubt as to what Joe meant. Leo quickly turned and left the room.

He went straight across to the militia block and collected his top people. He told them what had happened and what to expect.

He ordered the men to begin barricading the downtown area to wall off the center blocks. A square, made up of the militia block, the block diagonally across from it that was the base for Joe's organization, and then the blocks that made the other two corners. They would create a secure fortress there and not try to defend the whole town.

"Do we need to do that?" one of the captains said. "Can't we deal with them outside the gate?"

Leo gave the captain a baleful look. "I do the thinking," he said. "You get it done, just like I told you."

He sent them out and settled himself at a table to study a giant hand-drawn map of the new Hillsboro. His mind churned, turning over and over the events of yesterday. He was trying to get a better sense of what he was up against. He didn't want to underestimate them again.

The curving line of the wall around the new Hillsboro was a good defense. A nice protective wall, an open killing field outside, a defensive pinch at the two gates. A buffer to hold back an assault while he pummeled the attackers from inside the barricade or gathered a large force to go out and crush them. But the attackers wouldn't waste their forces trying to smash through the gates. They'd want to find another way.

Would they infiltrate slowly, over time? Leo knew people could get inside in small numbers; the wall was porous. His militia dealt with that every week as desperate people outside tried to slip into town. But could a larger group do it?

The wall wasn't perfect all the way around. No wall that had been built that way could be. There was even the river on one side. There were too many possibilities.

And his militia was not as big as the wall. He couldn't man it along its whole length. If he tried, they'd be spread so thin that the attackers could punch through at the place of their choosing.

The wall was useful to keep out refugees, but it wasn't defensible against a focused force, especially if they had explosives.

Got to assume they'll beat the wall.

He could go outside, ambush them on their way. But they had many choices of back roads to use besides the highway. And it would be too big a gamble to split his forces up. He wouldn't send a small force out. It would have to be twice the size he had used yesterday. And if they got past, the numbers still in town would be too diminished to stop them. If there was time, he could get clever and work out a more complicated plan that might deal with those problems, but his instinct told him he wouldn't have much time.

And as Leo thought about it, he realized stopping them from getting into Hillsboro was not the way to go. Having them inside could give him an advantage.

The idea was to smash their smaller force with his larger one, wasn't it? He knew just where they'd be going. They wanted to get at Joe and him, and they had to concentrate their forces to do it. They didn't have enough people to be stupid. They wouldn't bother with an unimportant target. They'd go right for downtown.

And that's where he'd be waiting; with his superior force.

Leo forced himself to get up and go back outside to check on how well his defense instructions were being carried out. Fatigue was catching up to him. Except for a couple of hours of rest on the road, during which sleep never came, he hadn't slept in two days. He walked the compound perimeter, thinking about the fight to come, looking at the defenses.

He had instructed his men to move dead trucks and trailers into the main roads leading into the two square blocks comprising the headquarters area. There was the bank building which held offices, the militia living quarters, and the building that doubled as a militia prison. Mixed in were two empty lots, one filled with tanker trailers holding precious reserves of gas and diesel fuel. Another building was used as a storage facility for all the supplies they doled out to the civilian population. Leo had ordered that the armament warehouse be emptied and all supplies of arms and ammunition be brought into this central compound.

Men were pushing cars and trucks into the intersections. Leo was encouraged to see that his captains had found some jersey walls and hauled them to the makeshift barriers. They would provide strength to the barricades. The mix of vehicles and material created ugly but effective deterrents to any attackers and gave his men ample shooting positions.

As he saw the progress on the defenses, Leo's mind turned to the hotel, a block and a half beyond the barricades. His living quarters were going to be too close to the battle zone. There was no telling what damage might occur in the fight to come. He had been busy working on how he would win the next encounter, but now his mind went down a different path.

What if things didn't go so well?

Leo liked having options. When you ran out of options you ran out of life. He wasn't one to cut and run, and he felt confident in the fight to come. It would be on his turf; it would concentrate the attackers against his superior numbers. All indications made Leo feel he could deal a lethal blow to the valley—but Leo wanted options. He decided it was time to move Donna and himself to a new location.

One that no one would know about.

Leo found one of his captains. "Get me a pickup and a man. I'll need them for the rest of the day."

The man nodded and ran off. Five minutes later a militia soldier returned behind the wheel of a 1960 Ford.

Leo jumped in and had him drive to the hotel. He got out and grabbed the door guard. "You're going to help this man move my things. And you're not going to remember where you move 'em to, you understand? Anybody wants to know where I'm staying, you don't know. They gotta ask me."

The door guard looked alarmed and said, "Yes sir."

Leo turned to the militia soldier as the man came around the truck. "Did you hear me?"

"I heard you. No talking."

"All right, the place you'll be going is on the south side." Leo had picked out an empty condo building in an empty part of town a long time ago. It was part of his always having options. Leo gave them the address, and the sergeant repeated it.

He fished out his key ring and worked the apartment key off. "You take my stuff and move it. There's a woman in my apartment, she's part of my stuff. You unchain her, you don't lose her, you don't mess with her, and you chain her up in the new place." He took the new, smaller key ring out of his pocket and handed it to the sergeant. Two keys, one for the shackle, one for the padlock on the other end. He locked eyes with the man. "You understand me?" The man nodded. "These are for the chain. When you're done, you bring 'em right back to me."

"Yes sir."

"I'm going to assign you to guard the building door. You'll be there till I tell you different. Do a good job and you'll get promoted when this is all over."

"Yes sir!"

Leo turned on his heel and left them with the truck. His fatigue began to rise again. He tried to shrug it off. There was still much to do. The central defense area was a bustle of activity. Leo smiled to see that his captains had even thought to find some sandbags to fill in the gaps. The attackers were going to be in for a big surprise.

Chapter 56

With the combined forces of the valley along with their armaments safely hidden, Charlie took Cameron and Jason into an apartment building, with an appalling smell inside the door, and led them straight up the stairs. They put down their loads in Charlie's own apartment, where Mary greeted him nervously. Then they headed over to the headquarters office that Charlie had set up across the street.

"Have the men bed down where they can in the other rooms. The carpets are not too uncomfortable," Charlie said.

When they entered the headquarters room, it was already crowded with Gibbs and Catherine waiting for them.

"Are you in touch with the insurgents?" Jason asked Charlie. "We have to meet with them and work out our next steps. We're vulnerable just sitting here."

Clayton nodded. "Don't like waiting around. Bet they be getting ready."

Charlie looked at the mountain man.

"Charlie," Jason said, "this is Clayton, he's the leader of the clansmen who helped us defend the valley. You may remember him from the trading day. They're joining our attack. Got fifteen sharp-shooting men."

"Glad to meet you. Your men will be a big help. I'm Charlie Cook, once the chief of police here in town. Not sure what I am now. I've got fifteen good cops to help with the fight and we've got some citizens who will fight with us." They shook hands. Charlie turned to Les Hammond. "Les," he said, "You go visit our friends and get one or two of them to come join us. Steve Warner, if he's available.

"Sure will, Chief," Les said.

As Les left the room, Tommy Wilkes came walking in. Wilkes was grinning. "Hi Lieutenant," he called out in a jaunty voice. Alongside him was Specialist Jackson.

"Wilkes!" Cameron called out. "Jackson! I assume from the big-ass grins on your faces, you were successful."

"We got the goods," Wilkes said. Lots of rifles, lots of ammunition." His smile faded a bit. "We didn't find any mortar tubes or MK153s, but we grabbed some 60 mil mortar rounds."

Cameron turned back to Charlie. "Have you distributed the weapons yet?"

Charlie nodded. "I distributed the rifles, but no ammunition. I didn't want anyone jumping the gun and starting to shoot. They've been practicing with empty weapons. We had to stay hidden until you guys got here."

Lori Sue looked up as Billy came into the apartment, and she saw that he had a pair of bolt cutters in his hand. He did not immediately move to give them to her. He looked at her unhappily. "I don't like you going over there. It's dangerous enough anytime, but if you get caught with bolt cutters, Leo's gonna have you shot...or worse."

"Billy. I'll be careful. You know that. Now give me the cutters so's I can get over there and free Donna. Leo's gonna be back anytime. This is my best chance."

"I should go with you."

"No. You got to be with the others when they plan the attack. You got a lot of inside info on the militia. We decided to help in this fight. That's how you help. And getting Donna free is how I help." She reached out her hand again. "Now gimme the damn cutters so I can do this. You ain't making it any easier."

She saw his resolve sag. He held them out and Lori Sue grabbed them. "Don't look so glum. I'll be careful. By tonight I'll have Donna back here with me and we'll all be ready for whatever tomorrow holds." She smiled and reached up to kiss him long and hard. Billy responded. She knew he could not resist her kisses. What she had not told him was that she couldn't resist his either. *Better to not let him know all that.* The thought was a habitual one, she was unused to opening herself up to anyone, but it bothered her. *One day I'll tell him.*

"No one's here," Reggie said when he saw Lori Sue walking up to the hotel door. It was late afternoon. He didn't sound in a good mood.

"What do you mean? Where'd they go?" Lori Sue asked. She had the bolt cutters hidden under her jacket.

"Moved. To an unknown location."

"She ain't coming back?"

"Doubt it. That mean you're not coming around anymore? I'd hate to think that."

"I need to tell her about her kid. She asked me to do that."

Reggie shrugged. "What can you do? You try to help and someone just ups and leaves."

"She didn't leave on her own. You helped, didn't you? You know where she's gone. You can tell me, I'm Donna's friend."

"Not supposed to. This time Leo made it personal, like he knew something was up. I ain't going against him. He'll kill me, or have me beaten. I don't want that."

"Leo ordered the move?" Her heart sank. "When was this?"

"This morning."

Damn. He's back already.

"Well, you can tell me. Hell, I ain't gonna tell anyone, I'm just being friends with Donna." Lori Sue sidled up to Reggie. "Did I ever get you in trouble? Come on, no one will know. And I'll sure appreciate it." Her voice dripped with erotic possibilities.

The guard shook his head. "Not this time." He looked at her with a sour expression on his face. "Besides, you're all promise. You never deliver. All I got was a quick kiss and feel."

Lori Sue sighed. She knew this time would come. "You're right. I haven't taken care of you, but you know how busy I've been. Look, I can make it up to you right now if you tell me where to find Donna." Before Reggie could say no, she grabbed him by the arm and tugged him along the street toward the alley. "Come on, you'll enjoy this." She shoved him forward and slipped off her jacket, dropping it to the ground over the bolt cutters.

It didn't take long. She led him back to the entrance.

"Wow that was hot." He had a surprised look on his face. His attitude was different now. *It's so easy*, she thought.

"You help me and I'll make sure you're happy. Now where did they move?"

"To the southeast side of town. Ain't many people there." He gave her the address.

"Thanks."

"You goin' there now?" Reggie's brain was starting to re-engage and he seemed worried. He gave her a sharp look. "You better not let anyone know how you found the place."

"You can trust me."

"When are you coming back? I'd sure like to try that again."

"Not right away. I'm pretty busy, big boy, but you'll get more of what I got, don't worry."

He smiled.

Leo's back. How'm I going to pull this off? Lori Sue left Reggie at the hotel entrance and walked back towards the bar. She had to step aside repeatedly for hurrying workers. Men shouted at one another, shouted at her to get out of the way. They were pushing, dragging anything they could find—desks, large copiers—into the streets to close them off. Lori Sue decided to walk around the perimeter to see what was going on.

Along the way she ran into some of her militia customers. "What are you doing down here?" The officer who had given her his pistol asked.

"What am I usually doing down here? I'm working."

"Ain't no work for you today or tonight. Everyone's too busy."

Nobody would talk to her. She looked at the developing fortress and shivered.

Then she saw Leo.

She was just passing an opening in the barrier, and she was in a position to be able to see down the middle of the four-block compound. Leo was far down the center street, by the bank building, but she recognized him instantly. He was giving orders to two nervous-looking militia officers. Then he jumped into a pickup and drove off.

Ain't gonna get Donna today. He may be headed back to his place.

She decided to head back and tell the others. They'd want to know about this.

When she got back to her apartment Billy wasn't there, and the nearby rooms were empty too. She dropped the bolt cutters in her living room and ran across the street. The guard inside the door looked at her curiously, but he let her run past him and up the stairs.

"Hey," she said as she burst into the room. Everyone stopped to look at her. She was surprised to see Billy there, but first things first. "They're walling in the downtown area. They know you're coming." She began to explain the preparations she had observed and what she had learned from the militia officer.

"They're not reinforcing the defenses at the perimeter wall?" Lieutenant Cameron asked.

Lori Sue glared at him. "I don't know, maybe they *are*. I wasn't *out* at the damn perimeter wall. But I know they're making up the blocks around militia territory like a fort."

"Damn," Jason said. "Do they know we're in?"

Sergeant Gibbs frowned and rubbed his chin. "They can't know too much if what they're focusing on is fortifications. That says they don't know where it's going to come from and they don't know where to hit us. Maybe they're guessing, or just being cautious. But it does say they're not putting their faith in their wall, which is disappointing." He shrugged. "I think we can say at least that they're sure we're coming. Maybe they even suspect we're already inside."

"But they don't know we're here, the army," Cameron said. "They think the full contingent left. They won't be expecting any large weapons; heavy machine guns, mortars, grenades. This gives us a big advantage."

As the men discussed Lori Sue's new information, Billy took her aside.

"So, you all joined up?" she asked him.

"Guess so," Billy said. "Right now it's pretty boring. They've had me pointing out things on the map, sayin' what building in the militia area is for what, and then they all argue. You didn't get Donna?"

"She wasn't there anymore. Leo moved her to a place over in the south side. I think it's almost as empty over there as this part of town."

"Leo's back?"

"Yeah. I saw him. He's directing the defense work. I can't go get Donna tonight in case he goes back there. I told you, I'm being careful."

"You shouldn't go there at all, now he's back."

"I can do it tomorrow. He'll be downtown all day from the looks of what's going on."

"No, no. This ain't right. Wait 'til after the battle. It's too dangerous."

Lori Sue whispered to him, "You don't know how this'll come out, you said so yourself, back at Chief Cook's house. We're on this side, 'cause we head close to Billy's. "They could lose, we could lose. Then it's every man for himself. If ain't gonna support someone like Leo." She looked around and then put her I can get Donna out, no one will know who did it. We'll just get along like we did before, only Donna'll be free. If we lose the battle, there's no way to free Donna. We free her now, that's a poke in the eye for Leo and we'll just act like we was with the militia all along."

"You think we'll lose?"

"It's what you said. And besides, it makes sense. We help this group how we can, but we make sure we got a plan if things don't work out."

"Then why risk helping Donna?"

She gave Billy a long, serious look. "We girls got to stick together."

The two sidled their way back to the group to listen to the plans.

"How many men you got?" Clayton was asking a man Billy didn't know.

"We have about fifty," the man replied. He looked subtly different than anyone else in the room. He was dressed like a city man, in a maroon dress shirt and gray pants.

"How many can shoot?"

"Maybe thirty have shot before, but they've all been practicing. We haven't fired the rifles, but we've gone over the M16, how to aim it, how to load the magazines, change them, switch fire modes, what to do if they jam. They'll do all right. This is their fight."

Clayton gave the stranger a non-committal look but didn't say any more.

Cameron turned to Billy. "I'd like you to go out this evening and scout the defenses. You should be able to move around without being challenged."

Lori Sue looked sharply at Cameron. "You don't believe me? I seen it all today."

Cameron turned to her. She could see the surprise on his face. "This is too important to go with just one report. I want more detail. Billy can tell us what has developed since you saw the defenses." He turned back to the group. "He can corroborate what Lori Sue reported with any updates, then we'll have the best info we can get. We can attack tomorrow after getting his report." The rest agreed.

"Well, then you better also recheck that Leo's back," Lori Sue said irritably. "'Cause I saw Leo too."

The whole room looked at her in surprise.

Chapter 57

As they walked back over to their apartment, Billy spoke ruefully. "I wanted to spend the night with you, but now I got to do this scouting. Damn! Things are gonna get hot tomorrow. Sure would be nice to have a chance to love some with you."

Lori Sue hugged his arm as they crossed the street. "That'd be nice, but we'll have plenty of time for that, no matter how tomorrow works out. You just be sure to take care of yourself tomorrow. Don't you go getting shot."

"I'll be all right. But I still don't like you going back to Leo's place to get Donna. You should just stay here."

"I told you. I'll be okay. Leo's going to be gone all day tomorrow. He'll be working on the barricades. I'll have Donna back here before evening."

Billy shook his head in doubt. "I want you to wait for me. I'll go with you tomorrow after giving Cameron my report."

Lori Sue rose before dawn. She knew that she had to leave before Billy got back from his scouting mission. Otherwise they'd have a big fight, and she didn't want that. She was naturally stubborn, and she was committed to freeing Donna. Billy had shown surprising stubbornness of his own in not wanting her to go back. There was no reconciling the two. Better to just go and get it done. There wouldn't be a fight when she got back with Donna, having stolen her from that monster, Leo. It would have been nice to see Billy off before the attack started, but this way was better. Get this done and get the hell back here while everything else was blowing up.

"You got that 9mm I gave you?" Lori Sue asked Donna.

"It's stuffed inside of one of Leo's shoes, behind some socks. It's a pair I've never seen him wear, but I made sure they took all his shoes," Donna replied. She smiled for an instant. "They listened. They're scared of him."

"I'll bet he's gonna be downtown until this fight is over," Lori Sue said. "I'll get your gun. Let's also get you dressed in something other than that nightie. We may have to run for it."

"Get me loose first. I've got some clothes. I saw them when I got moved. But I haven't worn anything but this and a house coat to go across the street."

"Bastard," muttered Lori Sue. "Hold out your leg." She pulled the bolt cutters from her jacket and began to go to work on the shackle. "Damn. These ain't big enough. That's some hard-ass metal." She was squeezing the handles together as hard as she could and moving the jaws back and forth to try to gouge out the metal of the cuff. It was barely leaving a mark.

"Just try to cut the chain. We can get the cuff off later."

Lori Sue switched to the chain. "That ain't much easier." She kept at it, grunting with the effort.

"Let me help," Donna said. "I'll grab one handle, you grab the other, and we'll try to push them together."

It worked only for a moment, then the cutter slipped sideways and they rapped their knuckles together.

"Ow! *Shit* that hurts," Lori Sue shouted.

"Shhh."

"Who the hell's gonna hear? The only guard's down at the main door." Lori Sue jumped up and looked around. "We got to get you free somehow. We could be here all day gnawing at that damn metal."

"Oh God. He's going to come back before we get done. I know it," Donna said. Her voice began to rise in panic.

"Don't get hysterical on me. He's probably not coming back today."

"But he might. He might check up on me before the attack. I can feel it."

"Will it make you feel better if I get that gun?"

"Yes. Hurry."

"Then we got to figure something out with that damn chain." Lori Sue went into the bedroom. "Where're his shoes?" she shouted back to Donna.

"In the far closet. There's some shelves on the floor for shoes."

Lori Sue got down on her hands and knees and poked around the closet floor. It was too dark to see anything. She pulled out a pair of shoes. No gun. Another shoe, then another. Still no gun. *Shit. Did he find the gun?* If he had he'd be coming back, coming back for her. She reached back into the closet and pulled more shoes out. Finally she felt the gun. She reached into the shoe and pulled the 9mm loose from where it was jammed into the toe.

After retrieving the gun, she checked it. It hadn't been unloaded. *He didn't find it!* She could imagine Leo playing a trick like that. She ran back to the hall near the door where she had left Donna sitting. Donna looked up at Lori Sue with tears in her eyes. "Give me the gun and you get out of here," Donna said. "He's going to come. I can feel it. And he'll kill you. I'll use the gun on him when he comes."

"You ever shot someone?"

"No."

"You ever shot a gun?"

"No."

"You won't stand a chance. Look." Lori Sue pulled another pistol out of her back waistband. "I got a gun too. Picked it up after I gave you mine. I wasn't gonna go without." She shoved it back into her pants. "And I shot someone once. Some cowboy who thought he could manhandle me into some sex. Came following me out from the roadhouse out on Vickers Pike, couple of years before this shit happened. He grabbed me but I got free and ran across the parking lot. He made the mistake of comin' after me, so I shot him. Hit him in the shoulder. He went down and started bawling, 'Why'd you have to go and do that?' 'Why?' I told him, 'Why'd you come after me, you dumbass? Serves you right—"

"*Okay*, let's hurry," Donna said.

Lori Sue put the jaws of the cutter over a link of the chain, with one of the handles on the floor. Then they both pressed down on the other handle together. They were pushing with all their strength, sweating and puffing in their exertion. They didn't hear the key turn in the lock. .

The door swung toward them.

"Need the keys?"

Leo put the key he was holding in his pocket. Smiling, he pulled out a small key ring. "It's easier than trying to cut through high-strength steel. The shackle and chain are not wimpy decorations. Nothing cheap like that for my girl. I got her quality gear."

They were frozen in place. They stared up at Leo.

"Don't I get a welcome home?" He shook his head slightly at Donna. "The last time you were all over me, wanting to make love. Now you're trying to get loose? And who's this?" He pointed at Lori Sue. A smile played at the edges of his mouth, but his eyes were dark and malevolent. "You got a girlfriend? Without asking my permission? Maybe I should add her to my collection."

He stepped forward and shut the door without taking his eyes off them. "Slide the bolt cutters over to me...on the floor. Don't get up," he commanded as Lori Sue started to move.

"I was just trying to make her more comfortable," Lori Sue said. "That shackle around her ankle chafes, in case you didn't notice."

"That so?" Leo replied. "I wouldn't get smart with me. It could get painful for you. I don't think she'll be doing much without that shackle for some time, now that I've seen this." He switched his gaze to Donna. "And I thought I could trust you. I thought you were coming around."

He moved, and Lori Sue tensed, but he just stepped around them and into the living room. He turned a chair partway round, so that it faced them, and sat down. "I'm now curious," he said. "All that loving the last time. Was that just an act?"

Donna didn't answer. She just stared at him, her eyes wide with fear.

Leo abruptly bellowed, "Answer me!" His cool veneer cracked, and his rage was now plain to see.

Donna flinched and didn't answer. Lori Sue's mind was on Donna's gun. He hadn't seen it; in the struggle with the bolt cutters, Donna had actually ended up half-sitting on it. But as soon as Donna moved, he would see it.

"Don't yell at her," Lori Sue said. "Ain't you done enough? You're just a bully. I seen guys like you before, pushin' women around, makes 'em feel big—"

"I told you to hold your tongue." There was no pretense now. "That's gonna cost you." Leo stood up.

Lori Sue jumped up. "I ain't afraid of you," she said, even as she stepped back.

"You will be." Leo said. He stepped forward. His speed caught her off guard. He moved shockingly fast.

Lori Sue's 9mm was in her hand in a flash, but it felt slow as he reached for her. She fired. The bullet grazed his side. He lunged at her. Something small and silvery spun from his hand. She pulled the trigger again as he grabbed the weapon and the shot went into the wall. Before she could get off another shot he twisted the pistol toward her, almost ripping it out of her hand. His hands squeezed tight over hers, he turned the gun and the pistol fired again.

A huge fist slammed into her stomach. She couldn't stop herself from falling backwards.

"Stupid bitch. Serves you right," Leo said above her.

Above her she saw Donna standing, one arm out, with a pistol in her hand. The gun fired with a sharp explosion of sound and flew out of Donna's hand back toward her ashen face. Leo staggered sideways, looking at Donna in surprise. Lori Sue felt him trip over her legs. He fell out of her view, her gun thumping on the carpet.

She saw Donna almost leap over her and stoop to snatch something up. It was the little key ring. She heard Leo groan and begin to roll over. Donna crawled back past Lori Sue and twisted around, trying to insert the key into the shackle lock. Her hands were shaking badly, and she couldn't seem to make it work. *No, shoot him*, Lori Sue wanted to say, but the words wouldn't come out. She could see Leo now, slowly getting to his feet. He'd be on Donna in a moment. There was the click of the lock springing open. *The gun!* She wanted to say, but Donna forgot it and leaped for the door.

Leo lurched overhead. "Come back here, bitch. I ain't done with you." His voice harsh with rage and pain.

Lori Sue saw the door fly open, and heard the sound of running feet, and she was glad.

Chapter 58

It was morning. The map room was just starting to fill with people for the final meeting when Catherine saw Billy run in. The boy looked around wildly and saw her and Jason; he ran over to them, almost knocking over one of Charlie's people in the process.

"Billy!" Jason looked at him in astonishment.

"Lori Sue's gone to rescue Donna. At Leo's place." Billy's face was flush with frustration and alarm. "I told her to wait, but she don't listen. Left me a note. I got the address. Leo moved to the south side. He's back in town. She could run into him. We got to help her."

Jason stared at him. "Billy...we've got to get ready for the attack. It has to be quick and effective. Before Joe gets things more organized. Before he finds out we're in town and *we're* the ones who get hit."

Billy looked at Jason in surprise. "You ain't goin'? I thought you was my friend."

"Billy." Jason rubbed his hand over his face. "Lori Sue should have waited, like you said. I can't jeopardize the mission for her."

"So you say." Billy's expression soured. "I helped you when you asked me to. Thought I'd get some help in return. Fat lot of good that did me." He started for the door. "Guess I'm gonna have to do this without any help."

"Wait," Catherine called out. "I'll help you."

Billy stopped and turned to her.

"Catherine, we just talked about this last night," Jason said sharply. "You can't go off on your own, do your own thing."

"Yeah, but this is different. A woman's in trouble, another one went to help, and now Billy, a valley neighbor, needs help to go to them...*and Leo may be there.*" She stared back at him, driving it home. "You remember what I said, I get to take Leo out. This may be the best chance we have. And he's boss of the whole militia. If I can kill him, they'll be disorganized. Cut off the head of the snake, the body dies."

"It's what my pa said," Billy said.

Jason just looked at her.

Catherine continued. "When we're done, I'll link up with you, or find that rooftop and start sniping. I can do a lot of damage from up high."

Kevin said quietly. "Can we talk privately for a moment?" He looked alarmed.

She looked at him grimly, but she nodded. They stepped out into the hallway and walked to the stairs.

"Catherine, don't do this. It could be suicide for you."

"You're telling me to not help two other women? One of them Billy's girlfriend?"

"Think about the larger picture, the battle to free this town. It's one of the reasons I stayed behind."

"I thought you stayed behind for me."

"You know I did. And now we've both gotten caught up in the town's battle, in ending this, freeing up the town and trying to make a more normal life...for us and everyone else."

"That's what I'm trying to do. Help Billy's girlfriend and rescue a woman." She stepped close to Kevin and tapped his chest. "You think she'll have a normal life as Leo's captive?"

"Catherine..." Kevin looked pained. "Why are you angry? Is this about Bird's death?"

"Yes, I'm still mad about Bird's death, but this is about lives. And this is a chance to get Leo. I need to do that for Bird...and for myself." She gave him a sharp look.

He touched her shoulder. She could see him hesitate. Then he sighed. "I see I won't talk you out of this."

"No, you won't."

"I can't go with you. I have to—"

"I know. I know, Kevin."

"I just fear for you. It's natural."

"And I'll fear for you when you're in the battle. It'll be in the back of my mind, but I'll try to block it out so I can fight better. I've learned a lot about fighting...about needing to empty your mind of everything except the moment, about controlling the fear. You know what I'm talking about."

She reached up around his neck and pulled him close to her. They kissed, long and deep. His arms were tight around her.

"This is hard," Kevin said.

"Yes."

Catherine saw Billy standing impatiently behind Kevin. Jason was with him. "Leave the M110 here," Jason told Catherine. "The Bushmaster will be more useful to you. When you're done, come straight back. We'll be ready to go in about ninety minutes."

Catherine nodded. Without a word, she and Billy went to grab their weapons.

Chapter 59

Catherine stuffed four extra magazines in her jacket pockets. She could see Billy's pockets already bulging with his five-shot magazines. With no more words, the two headed down the stairs and into the streets. It was now midmorning. She had gotten only a couple of hours of sleep during the wait for the rest of the group to arrive. Fatigue was beginning to attack Catherine's focus. She fought it off. *Time enough to rest when this is done.* The chance to find Leo and kill him drove her, pushing her fatigue aside.

They made their way towards the address. Billy walked a short distance ahead of Catherine, a few steps out into the street, so if a patrol came by they would see him first. They saw two patrols, groups of four men each. None reacted with alarm to Billy walking with his rifle slung behind his shoulder; it was clear that they knew him by sight. One of the patrols actually stopped to talk to Billy for a moment. Catherine had plenty of time to duck into a basement stairwell.

She heard Billy say, "You're joking."

"Not joking," she heard a voice reply. "Reckon you can forget about hunting for a while. They'll probably be telling you to join up with us. They think the attack will come anytime."

"Who would be stupid enough to attack us? The whole city!"

"It's for real. Knew three guys they pulled out to go on the valley raid, and they sure didn't come back. Bet you get assigned to the barricades. I'd try to avoid that if I was you." A couple of the others nodded.

"I will. You be careful then."

"You know it."

Catherine emerged, her mind focused on the tension she had heard in the man's voice. *They're going to be ready.* "I hope they don't have a chance to start using their heavy weapons."

They hurried on through the streets.

"They that dangerous?" Billy asked.

Catherine shuddered. "You don't want to be on the receiving end of a mortar shell. There's no place to hide."

"Bad, huh?"

"Yeah. I was trying to crawl into the ground, laying there so flat so nothing would hit me. You just don't know where it'll hit and how the shrapnel will spread." She shuddered again at the memory. Her mind swung to Bird. "I don't want to talk about it. We've got something to do. Go lead on."

When they got near the building, Billy told Catherine he should approach the guard. "The guard will be focused on me. I should look like I'm coming up alone."

"Wait till we see the place. Maybe there's no guards."

When they came to the right street they carefully peered around the corner. The condo was half a block away, on their side of the street. It was a white stucco building, set back, with a U-shaped driveway. The front doorway jutted out from the rest of the wall, and, sure enough, there was a guard. He was seated on the steps, his rifle propped against the railing next to him. He looked bored. Catherine and Billy backed out of sight.

"Okay, then." Billy thought for a moment. "Why don't you go around the block in back and work up close from the other side. It looked like there was another driveway going down the far side of the building."

"What are you going to do?"

"I'll just walk up like I'm allowed to be here. I can ask the guy what he's doing way out in this part of town. If he asks, I'm heading out to do some hunting."

"Don't start until you see me in position, okay?"

Billy nodded.

After making her way around the back of the building, she saw Billy come into view, walking casually along the sidewalk. Billy turned onto the driveway and walked towards the front door. Now she could see the guard. He had stood up and grabbed his rifle. He stepped forward to meet Billy.

"Who're you?" he called out.

Catherine began to crawl along the wall, behind the bushes. She had to get closer.

"Name's Billy Turner. I hunt for the city. What're you doing way out here? Hardly anyone lives in this area."

"Question is, what are *you* doing out here?"

"Right now I'm looking for my girl."

"This look like anyone hangs around here?" Catherine heard tension in the man's voice.

"She said she was headed here. To see a friend. My girl's name's Lori Sue."

Catherine kept moving forward. Now she was up to the corner where the entryway extended a few feet outward.

"Lori Sue?" The man repeated the name.

"That's right. She's friends with Leo's woman. She come by?"

Catherine moved out to the end, holding her breath. There was a large shrub beside the entrance. She stopped behind it. She was now within five yards of the guard.

"Oh, yeah." The guard snickered. "Yeah, she did. You're her guy? Lucky dog. She's hot."

"She still here?"

"Yeah, she went up a while ago. I let her in. Why not? No one said not to. Didn't really expect anyone to come by. Then Leo showed up. He said not to let anyone in, so you're out of luck now. Lori Sue may be out of luck too, if Leo thinks she's messing around with his property."

"Shit! I got to get in there." Billy moved towards the door.

The guard stepped in front of Billy. "No you don't. It's locked, and Leo said no one gets in." He pushed Billy back. "So get lost or you'll be answering to Leo."

Catherine took three quick steps and was at the guard. She pressed her 9mm into his back. "Don't move, don't turn around or you're dead."

The guard started in shock. Billy reached behind him and drew his own pistol from his waistband. He leveled it at the man. "Give me the keys, or I'll kill you myself."

The guard took out the key ring and handed it to Billy. "You're in a heap of trouble," he said, in an effort at retaining control.

As Catherine stepped around him, he looked at her in surprise. "You're that girl. The one from the valley. How'd you get here?"

She ignored him as Billy unlocked the door.

"Shoot him," Billy said. "We got to hurry, Leo's up there."

"I can't shoot him. It'll make too much noise."

"Good point," the man said.

Catherine kept her pistol aimed at his chest. "I will, though, if you try anything."

"We can't turn him loose." Billy was dancing around on both feet, in a panic to get to the apartment. "Turn around," he ordered the guard. When the man turned Billy whacked him on the back of his head. The man fell unconscious.

"Why'd you do that?" Catherine asked.

"No time to do anything else. We got to get up there."

They ran for the stairs.

"He's in five-thirty," Billy said his voice harsh with anxiety.

When they got to the fifth floor, they stopped to catch their breath on the landing.

"What's the plan?" Billy whispered.

Catherine slipped her carbine off her shoulder and pulled the charging lever back, chambering a round. "We bust in and shoot Leo. I don't have any fancy plan. Stay low and don't shoot any females."

Billy nodded.

They heard two shots, fast, and then a third.

Catherine gasped. Billy's eyes opened wide. He grabbed for the doorknob and threw the door open. Another shot shook the air. To the left there was a long hallway, bright skylights spaced along it. The shooting came from that direction.

Billy broke into a dead run, and Catherine was right beside him.

They heard a door open far down the hall, and then a woman in a pale blue nightgown stumbled out and ran towards them. She was barefoot. Her eyes were wild.

"Leo!" she shouted. "He's got a gun."

The woman was almost on top of them when Catherine saw Leo stagger into the hall. He had a gun in his hand. The woman was blocking her line of sight.

Catherine gave her a violent shove to the side. The woman crashed into Billy. They both went down in a heap beside Catherine. Catherine dropped to one knee. Leo fired off a wild shot in their direction.

Catherine's sights swung across Leo's torso. She fired. He lurched back. She thought she had hit him in the stomach, but he was still standing. She fired again and saw the second round hit his shoulder. The pistol spun out of his hand. He dropped to his knees. He reached out, trying to find the pistol, while he glared at Catherine. His face was ugly with pain and rage.

"That was for me," she shouted at him. "This is for Bird."

And she shot him in the face. His head was flung backward, and his body sagged after it. He lay slumped in a heap with his legs folded under him, what was left of his face staring at the ceiling.

Billy was already up and running toward the apartment. He ran past the body without even looking.

Chapter 60

Lori Sue lay in the short hall just inside the doorway, a red stain of blood spreading out from under her and soaking into the beige carpet.

"Lori!" Billy shouted as he dropped to the floor beside her. "Oh my God, you're shot."

She looked up at him. It took a moment for her to find her voice, but when she spoke she sounded almost normal. "You came. I'm glad. I ain't hurt bad...I'll be okay now you're here."

"You're bleeding."

"Yeah. From my gut. Guess I wasn't so good at shooting Leo. He turned the gun on me."

Billy cradled her head in his arms. He looked up as Catherine and Donna Bishop came in. "We got to stop the bleeding." His voice was filled with a desperate intensity.

Donna stumbled past them and disappeared to the left. She was back in a moment carrying an armful of towels. She knelt down across from Billy. Her face was very pale, but she spoke with a mother's authority. "Help me press these to her side to stop the bleeding. We get that under control, we can get her to the hospital."

"Thanks, Donna," Lori Sue said. "We girls got to stick together." Her voice was softer, without its usual sharp edge.

"I'll go and get some help," Catherine said above them. "We have to get her to the hospital."

"Hurry," Billy said, but he could already hear Catherine's footsteps receding quickly down the hall.

He told Lori Sue, "We'll get you some help. You're gonna be all right. Damn, I wish you hadn't gone."

"Had to go...promised. Gonna be all right. We're gonna be all right." She paused to gather her strength. "Leo?"

"Catherine shot the bastard. He's dead in the hall."

Lori Sue sighed. "That's good. Glad he's out of the way." She turned her head towards Donna. "Now we got to get your son out of that school."

"I'll get him later," Donna said. "He'll be all right, Leo can't hurt him. We have to help you now." She looked down at the towels, and Billy saw the red seeping through. "Billy, hold them tight. We have to control the bleeding."

Billy groaned out loud. "I'm trying. I don't want to hurt her by pushing too hard."

"You ain't hurting me." Lori Sue reached up and touched his face. "I love you, Billy Turner. We gonna have a good ol' time when this is over. We gonna make lots of money with our bar. Everyone'll come, you'll see."

Billy could feel tears streaming down his face. "I love you too, Lori Sue. We'll have the best bar around. People'll come from all over."

"Yeah," she said. Her voice was getting softer, breathier. "I know how to work a bar. I'll show you too. You do the huntin', make the liquor. I'll even teach you how to make drinks. I can work the tables." Billy just nodded, staring into her face as she looked up at him.

"It don't hurt bad. I'll be fine." She paused and seemed to gather her strength. "You want kids? I'd like kids someday."

"Sure, we can have kids. Don't know much about raising them, though."

She smiled. "It ain't hard. Just do what comes natural. Course, we got to make the bar work first. That's how we'll support them. How many you want?"

He shrugged. "I don't know, two, three? Can't think about that now."

"Hope it ain't a lot. I ain't a big girl." She started to breathe harder. "Just thinking about it makes me horny. Sorry, Donna. Something about having babies with Billy just turns me on. That happen to you?"

Donna smiled back at her. "I guess so, when we did it...you know, conceived. I only got to have one child with Jim."

"I'm sorry for you. I'll have an extra for you. You be their grandmother? We could make you one."

"I'd be proud to be their grandmother...or maybe their aunt."

"Aunt Donna. That's good." She looked back at Billy. "See we already got us a family. She can babysit when we need to be alone...you know, when we get horny. Damn, I can't wait."

Lori Sue's grin looked brave.

"Shouldn't we get Lori Sue to a bed...or couch? She'd be more comfortable."

"I don't think we should move her," Donna replied. "It might make the bleeding worse."

"I ain't hurtin'. You being here makes it okay. Just hold my head and keep telling me you love me. I need that now." Lori Sue grabbed Billy's shirt and looked hard at him. "You tell me every day we're together, promise?"

Billy nodded.

"You're gentle, that's good. Promise you'll tell me you love me every day and never beat me."

Her words tore at Billy's heart. "I'd *never* beat you. I *love* you. And I'll tell you I love you every day of our lives."

She relaxed and sighed. "I like that. Plus it'll get you more lovin'. I got lots of tricks still to show you." Her face turned serious. "I got to tell you something. In case things don't go...in case I forget. Come close."

Billy put his face close to hers, making a small, private place between them, shutting out the rest of the world.

"I'm sorry for whoring around. I know it made you sad. You didn't get mad or hurt me, but I hurt you. I shoulda stopped when we got together. It was just easy to do, and it made it easy to get things I thought I needed..."

"It's all right—"

She put her hand to his lips. "It ain't. I'm sorry, but that ain't happening anymore. I'm your girl all the way. Nobody gets my lovin' but you. You're my man and I'm your gal."

"Yeah. That's the way it is...the way it will be."

She reached up. "Kiss me, Billy. I miss your kisses."

He kissed her gently.

"Don't hold back. Your kisses give me energy. I need that now."

He kissed her harder as she did her best to respond.

"You got to breathe," Billy said, breaking off the kiss.

"Kissin's like breathin' for me," she replied, but she was panting when their lips parted.

The towels were getting redder. And wetter.

"We need more towels," Billy said. His voice was desperate.

Donna got up and was back in seconds with more, along with a couple of clean sheets. When she changed them out she gasped at the heaviness of the towels. Billy could sense their weight, as if he were lifting them himself.

"It don't hurt," Lori Sue said.

Billy clamped both his hands on the fresh cloth. He found himself speaking. "Run and get help. Maybe Catherine didn't make it." He was beginning to panic. Donna looked at him. "I can do this," he said, making his voice sound calm. "Get some help. You know where the hospital is. Go."

Lori Sue reached up suddenly and grabbed Donna's arm. "Go, do what Billy says. Girls got to help each other out."

"We stick together," Donna said, her voice sounded choked with tears. Donna bent and kissed Lori Sue on the forehead. "I'll be back as quick as I can," she said. "Stay with us, don't quit. Don't give up. Remember, you're a fighter."

Lori Sue smiled.

Donna got up and ran out. Billy heard her footsteps fading down the hallway. He thought of her trying to get to the hospital, braving the militia. Could she bluff her way through them? He thought of Catherine, probably still on her way—where? To the hospital, or had Catherine gone back to

Charlie's people to get help in transport? There could be no help closer at hand they could trust. His heart bled.

He bent his head close to Lori Sue. "You stay with me. You gonna be okay. We're gonna have that bar...all the things you want." Another groan came out of him. "I ain't never figured I have someone like you. You can't die. You can't leave me."

Her voice was so calm. "Remember when you saved me? It scared me so when that guy stuck his knife into my neck. Scared me just as much when you shot him...right over my head. You coulda killed me, but you was a good shot."

"I remember."

"Why'd you take that chance?"

"Didn't think about it. They wasn't treatin' you right."

"Were you nervous? Shooting over my head like that?"

He shook his head. "I took harder shots than that hunting. I knew I could make that shot."

"I'm sure glad you did." Lori Sue started to laugh, and it turned into a cough. "That woulda been a hell of a thing, if you had shot me."

"Don't say that. I never would have missed."

"Lucky for me. I think I fell in love with you that night. Or I decided I wanted you around. You had somethin' I wanted."

"I fell in love with you that night," Billy said to her. "I never experienced anything like that before."

"Yeah. I was your first." She smiled at him. "It was fun, wasn't it? It's always been fun with you. Never felt like that before with anyone else. Sometimes a rush, but never fun and with a good feeling after. You know what I mean? Course you don't. I'm the only girl you ever had...I like that. And you'll be the only guy I'm having from here on out."

He had been listening to her voice growing weaker. It seemed to him that he had never listened to anything so closely.

She had been holding her head up a little, but now she sagged back.

After perhaps twenty seconds she spoke again. "This ain't workin', Billy. Don't think I'm gonna make it till help comes."

A terrible dark wave had been building in Billy, and now it broke. He shouted, shocking himself with his intensity, "Yes you will. You hold on!"

"Don't yell at me. I'm tryin'. Just hold me and kiss me."

He started kissing her face, her cheeks, her forehead.

"Mmmm, that's nice."

He kept kissing her, kissing her chin, her neck, her face. Nothing in his world now but holding her tight and kissing her. He felt her slowly relaxing.

She whispered, and he heard the smile he felt under his lips. "We gonna have a bar and a big family...big as you want, Billy...I love you."

And she breathed her last and went limp. He kept kissing her face, crying harsh tears, calling her name out over and over in choking sobs. He had to keep squeezing the sodden towel, he could not let go, so he leaned down against her and rocked her with his whole body, his hands straining beneath him, refusing to let her go, refusing to acknowledge that she was gone.

"Hang on, hang on," he kept repeating, mixed in with, "I love you, I love you."

But she could not hear his words.

Chapter 61

Catherine rushed back to the planning room. She had given up on going directly to the hospital before she had gotten down the stairs; she didn't know how fast she would be able to get any help to come back with her, and the important part was to get Lori Sue there. Maybe the police had a hidden vehicle that she could use.

Her hopes were dashed as soon as she got back. Everyone was still there, she found the conference still in progress, but Charlie told her that even the van that had been used in the armory raid had been dropped off back at the station. "We didn't want to show our hand," he said.

"But I need some help," she exclaimed to Jason and the others. "We've got to get Lori Sue to the hospital."

Jason looked at her with a pained look in his face. "I've got to get this attack started or we're all in trouble."

Catherine turned. to Kevin, "How about you?" She could see the conflict in his face.

Jason spoke, "Why don't you go with Catherine? Rodney and I can get everything ready on this end. Just join us as soon as you can."

"All right. You know how we're dividing up the forces. I'll take some first aid supplies and after I'll meet up with the north attack team."

"Bring a morphine injector as well," Rodney offered.

"Catherine, take the M110 with you as well," Jason added. "We're running out of time."

Catherine nodded and she and Kevin left the room.

They set out on a jog with their rifles concealed under coats as well as possible. They were lucky and saw no patrols. On arriving at the condo, they saw Donna approaching the entrance with a nurse. The nurse was carrying a folding stretcher under her arm.

"You went to the hospital," Catherine exclaimed.

"Yes. Billy asked me to go, he wasn't sure you'd make it through any militia."

They went through the door and quickly climbed the stairs. They burst out into the hallway and started down it. The nurse gasped and stopped at the sight of Leo's body.

"Keep going," Catherine said, shoving her forward.

When they got to the open door, they found Billy rocking Lori Sue in his arms on the floor. A loud keening sound was coming from him.

Everyone stopped and stood still.

Finally Catherine slowly approached him and touched him on the shoulder. He flinched, growling like a feral cat. "Don't touch her. Stay away!"

Everyone backed up.

"We brought help," Catherine said, her voice coming out in a shaky whisper.

"Don't need your help. You too late!"

She straightened and looked back at the nurse.

"Let's wait outside," Kevin said.

"Billy, I'm so sorry," Donna said in a broken, choked voice beside Catherine. Catherine took her arm and pulled her away. They went out into the hall.

Donna was sobbing. She sank down against the wall, her face contorted with grief.

"Billy lost his dad," Catherine mumbled to her. "He's got no one. This may be too hard for him to take." Donna looked at Catherine in confusion, and Catherine remembered that Donna didn't know Billy at all. Donna only knew Lori Sue.

She looked at Kevin. His eyes were full of sorrow, but his expression was firm. "I've got to go," he said. "We can't help Lori Sue now and I have to get on with this battle. Leo may be dead, but the militia is assembling their defenses. If we wait, more people will get killed in the fight. We've got to attack as soon as we can."

Catherine looked at her fiancé. "I know. You go. I shouldn't leave Billy now." She closed her eyes for a moment, then met his gaze again. "Tell me your plan so I can join you. I'll come as soon as possible."

Kevin glanced toward Donna and the open door. He stepped closer to Catherine. "We're dividing into two attack groups," he said quietly. "Both groups will consist of members of my squad and clansmen. This arrangement will balance the clan's shooting ability with our larger weapon capacity.

"Charlie's going to lead the civilians." He grimaced. "Not the best soldiers, but we need the bodies. And they'll be fighting for their town, as well as their own lives. I'm putting some of them in the attack groups and some to go after the patrols out in the city. That'll give us two groups of about twenty-five to thirty fighters each."

He led her a short way down the corridor and knelt. He took out the street map and spread it on the floor. "My group will be on the north side.

Rodney and Jason will come in from the south." His finger traced the approach routes. The barricaded blocks had been thickly outlined in pencil.

"And I go on a roof here," Catherine said. She knelt with him and pointed to a block to the west of the pincer attacks. "I can snipe at the militia and try to keep them pinned down while you're attacking. I'll be a block away, but if they have mortars I may be able to spot them and take them out."

Kevin nodded. He folded the map quickly. "Sure you'll be able to find a good rooftop?"

"I'll find one."

He touched her cheek, and then he rose. "Be careful."

"You do the same," Catherine replied. She felt a sudden swell of sadness. "I love you."

He smiled down at her. "I love you too," he said. She saw his eyes go behind her to the doorway, and pain crossed his face. Then he turned and hurried toward the stairs.

She remained on one knee watching him stride down the hall. Then she turned and got up and went back to the room. The nurse had come out and was standing awkwardly next to Donna.

Catherine went back into the apartment, with Donna following. She sat against the wall and motioned for Donna to do the same. She sat to wait for Billy to finish his grieving.

Finally Billy stood up and carried Lori Sue back into the bedroom and laid her down on the bed. He had stopped crying some time back, and a grim purpose had begun to fill the emptiness inside him. He felt them come into the room behind him.

"You take care of her?" he asked.

"I will." Donna replied.

"I'll be back. I'm goin' huntin' now. Gonna kill that man responsible for all this mess. Man who started up the killin' again. Cost me my pa, now my girl."

"Billy, let me tell you what's going on," Catherine said behind him. "There are plans, and the fight is going to begin soon."

"You can tell me, but I know what I'm gonna do. I know where he stays. I'm going after him."

"Who are you going after?"

He finally turned his gaze from Lori Sue. "Stansky."

"Can we work together? I don't think you should just run into this battle by yourself. You might get killed. You could be caught in a crossfire."

Billy shook his head. "I'm huntin' alone. You do what you gotta do. I'll do what I gotta do." He glanced around for his rifle. It was still out in the front hall where he had dropped it. He moved past Donna, and Catherine stepped in front of him.

"Billy, let me help."

He stood there, looking at Catherine. The sight of her penetrated the darkness growing inside him. This was a girl he had known growing up. There was a bond between them. They had never been close, but they had been part of the valley, and they had both fought to defend it from Big Jacks and his gang. That day had only been two years ago, but it seemed to him now that they had only been children then. The killing and the hard decisions since the EMP attack had put childhood behind them both. He didn't see the young girl anymore, and the boy in himself was gone.

He shook away those thoughts; there was no time for them. This was a time for fighting, and revenge.

"You do what you gonna do," he told her again. He didn't speak harshly but there was no give in his voice. "Don't follow me. No one's waiting for me, I'll do this by myself."

Catherine sighed. "At least let me show you how the attack is going to take place. I don't want to see you get caught up in the middle of it. Here. I'll show you in here."

She turned and led the way to the kitchen. Billy reluctantly followed. She was hunkered down on the floor tiles, scratching lines on the floor with a kitchen knife, showing Billy where the attacks would come from. He took it in mechanically.

The map gave Billy an idea. "I can go in opposite of where you'll be. Like using the back door."

"That might work. But you should take a carbine, not your hunting rifle. Take the guard's weapon. You need to be able to shoot faster than you can with your bolt action."

That made sense. He nodded and turned to go. He stopped at the door to the bedroom and took a last look at Lori Sue. Then he headed out, picking his rifle up from where it lay beside the bloodstain on the carpet. He would hide his own rifle in the shrubbery along the edge of the apartment building.

He didn't expect to live to retrieve it.

Catherine pulled on her pack, slung the M110 sniper rifle on her back, and picked up her Bushmaster carbine. She turned to Donna Bishop. "Are you sure you want to stay? This was Leo's place. Someone might come by."

Donna looked at Catherine. "I'm going to take care of Lori Sue," she said. Her voice was dull and soft. She had changed out of the gown into a dark blue sweater and jeans.

"Do you have a weapon? You should have a pistol at least. In case one of the militia comes in."

Donna nodded and picked up the 9mm lying on the floor. Catherine looked at the way she was holding it. "Do you know how to use that?"

For an instant the woman's tired eyes lit up, and her voice was sharp with anger. "I *shot Leo* with it."

Catherine just nodded.

"Will you win?" Donna asked. There was something—an almost apologetic pleading—in her eyes. "Will this be the end of people like Leo and Stansky?"

Catherine ignored the first question. There was no point thinking about that. "I don't know. Probably won't be the end of bad people. But with him gone, we've got a chance to make a normal life again." Catherine looked at the carpet for a moment, gathering her thoughts. Then she looked Donna in the eye. "I don't know how many bad people there are out there. You're older so you should know. They probably crop up everywhere. And I don't know if we'll ever have a real country back again.

"So we have to build something good right here and help it grow," Donna said.

Catherine nodded. She picked up her carbine again. "It seems to me that the more good people we can bring together, the more we can run our lives with respect and the less chance bad people will have to get power."

She turned to the door. "I gotta go. No more talking."

Chapter 62

Catherine ran down the stairs and crossed the lobby to the entrance, past the guard who was just regaining consciousness. She didn't even look at him. She did see that his pack had been tipped on its side, and the M16 carbine was gone. Billy had taken it, and whatever extra magazines had been in the pack. If she ran into a patrol there would be no talking her way out of the encounter but she needed to move fast. She had to get to the spot she had picked.

Her backpack and the M110 made an awkward combination bouncing on her back. While jogging through the streets, she tried to keep a mental picture of the map in her head. She was passing through unexplored territory.

Coming around the corner of a block, she surprised a small militia patrol. Five men turned towards her. "Stop!" one of the men shouted.

Catherine spun and ran back around the corner. Shots rang out. She sprinted down the block. She counted down the seconds she thought it would take the militia to make it to the corner. A third of the way down the block she ducked into a doorway that shielded her from the street. The entrance was made of granite. She dropped to the ground, hoping anyone aiming for her would be focusing higher up. She peeked around the edge, with the tip of her rifle leading the way. There were three men just coming onto the street.

Catherine didn't hesitate. She put her sights on the one farthest out in the road. Her shot hit him in the chest, knocking him backwards. Before he hit the ground she brought her aim back to the middle one. She hit him in the gut. He staggered back and slumped to his knees with a loud groan. The man nearest the corner had now reacted and Catherine's third shot missed him as he ducked out of sight.

Can't stay here and get trapped. Catherine jumped up and ran further down the block, looking for another doorway to hide in. Nothing. But one building was set out further than the others. She ran past it and stepped into its shadow. It provided a few feet of cover. She swung her rifle around the corner of the building and watched the street. Nothing moved. There was just the dead man in the street and the one dying on the sidewalk. She watched for tense seconds that dragged into a couple of minutes before she concluded that the third man had decided to go another way, not wanting to risk getting shot.

Better get moving.

She turned and ran down to the next intersection. She would go around the block and continue, but she would move more carefully. She didn't want to risk another encounter. The sound of the gunfire would have carried, and now someone knew she was on the streets. Other patrols might be more alert and she might not have the ability to duck and run next time.

She made her way around the block and cut across into an overgrown parking lot.

A half hour later she got to the building.

Billy ran through the streets. He had a lot of distance to cover to get to the east side of the downtown area housing Stansky's headquarters. His fury drove him. He was not trying to be stealthy. He actually looked forward to an encounter; it would give him an opportunity to lash out with the automatic weapon he was carrying.

As he started down one block, a patrol of six men stepped into the intersection. They shouted for him to stop. Billy had the M16 set to automatic. He began firing short bursts as he ran towards the men. The unfamiliar weapon tried to jump and climb in his hands. He tightened his grip and kept it under control, sweeping the men in short bursts as he ran at them. Two of them went down before the rest began to return fire. He zig-zagged a little but kept going at a full run straight at the men and kept firing. Two more men went down and the last two turned and fled across the intersection. Billy ran past the fallen men as the others disappeared down the side street. He ignored them. He would not be diverted from his mission. His focus was getting to the headquarters and Stansky. He wanted to be there and find him when the attack began.

When he had gotten well east of the downtown compound, he turned and headed north two blocks before turning back to the west, more carefully now. The run and the fight had burned off some of the craziness. He walked, and he kept a sharp eye out for any patrols, always noticing where he could duck for cover if a patrol came by. When he was two blocks out, he came to his first clear view of the barricade in the street. There were heads and rifles poking up along it. *Too many.* Stansky had a sizeable group to defend his compound.

Billy stopped. He didn't think he had been seen. But this route wouldn't work, and staying around could get him shot. He carefully backed up a block and headed north. He would go two blocks and then try another smaller street going west. Maybe he could find a weaker, less heavily defended place to get into the compound. He turned onto a narrow side street, but again, within two blocks, he saw that it was closed as he neared the compound. The barricade here consisted of three cars lined up across the street and sidewalk.

It looked like a hasty assemblage, but it was probably adequate for a minor side street. It would slow down any motorized assault while providing cover for the militia to fire on the attackers jammed in the narrow passage.

Careful to stay out of sight, Billy found a niche with a door set into it and sat back. He was breathing heavily; sweat covered his face and arms. His initial recklessness fueled by his rage had dissipated, replaced now with a hunter's cunning. He had to figure out a way to get inside the compound and then find Stansky.

After some thought, he decided he would wait until the attack began. The extra confusion might allow him an opportunity to get inside the barricade. Would Stansky be in the thick of the battle or would he hang back at his headquarters? Billy pondered that question as he waited for the attack to begin.

When Catherine got to the block she had chosen, she entered it through a narrow alley. She stopped at a tall building. There was an alley door. It had two small windows in it, with vertical bars over the glass. Catherine thrust the butt of her rifle between the bars of the window; the third whack broke the glass. After knocking out the shards, she carefully slipped her arm inside. It was a tight fit, but she was able to reach down and flip the dead bolt.

The door opened onto a stairwell. She closed the door behind her, so that it would be less likely to be noticed, and headed up the stairs. Her only source of light was the alley door windows, but the stairs were a back-and-forth pattern she could navigate in the growing dark as she ascended. At the top, the tenth floor as she counted, she opened the stairwell door and entered a corridor. She was at one end. There was a window at each end which dimly lit the hallway. Doors lined both sides, most of them ajar. More light came from them.

How do I get on the roof?

She walked down the hall, trying the knobs of the doors that were closed. None were locked. All but two of the doors opened onto offices. The only exceptions, at the midpoint of the hallway, were the restrooms. Catherine peeked in both, but it was too dark to see anything. There was nothing here.

She headed back to the door to the stairs and went back onto the landing.

She had not yet released the doorknob when she made out another door in the wall to her left, the side across from the stairs, just past the door she was holding. She stared at it. There was a sign on it. There was very little light coming from behind her, but the letters were big and blocky, and after a few seconds she was sure what she was looking at:

ROOF ACCESS ONLY

She smiled.

Looking closer, as best she could while holding the hall door open, she could also see that the door had a heavy padlock on it.

She went back out into the hallway and looked for a janitor's closet for anything she could use to pry the lock. She found nothing, so she returned to the stairwell. She wedged open the door with her cap to let light into the stairwell. She retreated four steps down the stairs and lay down against them with her head and rifle peeking over the landing. Then she aimed her carbine at the padlock and fired. The shot broke the lock and the bullet ricocheted off one wall before embedding itself high in the opposite wall.

She retrieved her cap, hurriedly pulled open the door, and climbed the metal steps behind it. They ended in a small landing with a door that opened to the roof.

The dazzling sunlight blinded Catherine after the darkness. She waited in the doorway for her eyes to adjust. She put her cap back on and pulled the bill down over her eyes. She wished she had sunglasses. *Shooting east so I should be okay*, she told herself.

She stepped out onto the roof. It was a wide, flat expanse of beige gravel, broken only by the hut she had just emerged from and two air-conditioning units to her left. Ahead of her, she could see the top of Joe Stansky's bank building jutting up in the distance. Along the edge of the roof there was a low parapet about three feet high. It would provide good cover for shooting.

She laid her carbine down just inside the door of the hut, crept to the wall, and knelt down behind it. She peeked over the parapet. From the roof she had an excellent view of the downtown area.

Pulling out her spotting scope from her backpack, she scanned the barricades Stansky had erected. Her position was only one block from the edge of the four-block barricaded area. The rooftops in the block ahead of her were low enough that Catherine could see most of the barricades to the south and north. From her height, she had a perfect view of the space behind them. She could see men moving around, bringing out supplies and ammunition. Further back, her view of the compound was interrupted by the bank building and by another, shorter building across the center street to the left of it, which she understood to be the militia headquarters.

Two other buildings gave her concern. They were similar in height to her building. One was to her left, at the northwest corner of the barricade, exactly where the northern attack would hit. The other was just to the right of the main street running up the middle of the compound. It was at the edge of the compound nearest her. It cut off some of her view to the right, although Catherine felt confident she could see enough of the barricades on that side to help the southern attack.

Joe's bank tower rose above all. It was at least eight stories taller than her rooftop. Its lower stories were half-hidden by the right-hand tall building that faced toward her, but she could see the ground floor entrance on the street that ran up the center.

Catherine stiffened. Next to Joe's tower, in the middle of the street, three men were setting up a mortar.

Looking carefully, she could see three other mortar emplacements in the street, closer to her than the first one she had seen. They were surrounded by low mounds of rubble and debris. To shield the mortars from street-level gunfire, she thought.

She looked for more. In the middle of the block to the right she could see part of an empty lot. As she watched, two men carried mortars out into the lot, while two others followed with loaded wheelbarrows and shovels.

She remembered the mortars on the slope, and a violent shiver went through her. Joe's people were ready.

They'll need spotters to be effective.

Her alarm at seeing the mortars now turned to a more immediate concern. She focused on the two tall buildings to her left and right that were the same height as her own.

Sure enough, there were figures moving about.

On *both* rooftops.

She hunched down behind the parapet. *How would they communicate with the mortars?* She didn't know but they had to be dealt with.

They were looking down, watching the streets beyond the barricade. They hadn't seen her come out on the roof.

She turned and sat back against the wall to contemplate her position. The spotters would be armed. If they discovered her, they could take her out, or they could keep her pinned down enough that she would be effectively neutralized as a sniper.

She might not even be able to get back to the stairs so she could find a new position. She glanced back at the stairway door. This was a big roof; the door was twenty yards from her position, and she would be out in the open once she moved back from the parapet wall.

Maybe even if she crawled. The two rooftops looked to be the same height as the one she was on. She could not see the surface of their roofs beyond their parapets, but could they see hers? It was impossible to be sure.

Getting back to the door would be a dangerous gauntlet to run, with a high probability of getting shot. She knew she could make such a shot. Could they?

She dared not assume that the men on the rooftops would be lousy shots.

And if they saw her now, with the streets quiet, it would be simple for them to send a group straight to her building.

Whichever way it went, she might never get into the fight.

She ground her teeth. She could cause serious disruption in the militia's defenses. When the attack started, the confusion would mask her initial shooting. The battle would allow her to keep shooting into the barricades. Effective sniping could pin down a lot of fighters. She and Bird had slowed down three truckloads of armed men with some well-placed shots and the fear of more. Slowed them down enough that they had never reached the farms.

I'll have to take them out first. Otherwise they'll pin me down.

But not until the sound of her shots would be covered.

She settled in to watch and wait.

Chapter 63

Leo was missing. Leo had set up the defenses. He was the guy who had been studying this kind of thing, strategy and tactics, ever since Joe had put him in charge of taking over the militia and running it. He had gone off to take care of some business, something about his woman, and he should have been back already.

That worried Joe. It wasn't like Leo. Not when there was serious business to be done.

Let alone this.

What no one but Joe and a few others had known was that Joe had a few working military radios. He had gotten them from the armory raids.

Joe and Leo had kept the existence of the radios a deep secret, even from the militia. The devices had stayed safely stored away in a private area in Joe's tower, charged but hidden. The radios represented too much of a potential surprise advantage to risk wasting for trivial reasons.

But Leo had seemed sure that a big problem was about to appear, and over the years Joe had learned to listen to him. He had gone to bed the previous evening mulling over Leo's preparations, and he had woken up early that morning thinking about the radios. If the threat really was as serious as Leo said, then there was no point in holding onto their ace in the hole. It was time to pull it out while the game was on. So the first thing Joe had done that morning was to take four of the radios and send two of them out to the guards at the two main entrances, with instructions to keep in constant touch with him.

He was barricaded into his downtown area with most of his men, but he was nervous. A street fight, a shooting or a robbery, he was good at that; used to it. But this strategic maneuvering for what could be a major battle left him uneasy. He needed Leo.

Joe had finally sent a patrol out with another radio to fetch the SOB. The patrol had gone to Leo's hotel apartment and discovered that Leo had apparently moved to other quarters. Now they were looking for him. Joe could understand the move; it made sense for security, but why didn't he know about it? The guard at the hotel had just come on shift and said that Leo had moved somewhere "on the south side." They were headed that way now.

When Joe got a hold of Leo, he was going to let him know he was pissed. But this was so unlike him that Joe couldn't shake an uneasiness growing inside.

The radio on the desk squawked again. Joe scowled at it and picked it up. "Headquarters. We just got attacked."

Joe tensed. "Which gate are you? How many?"

"We still didn't find Leo. But we got hit. There's only two of us left."

It wasn't either of the gates. It was the men he'd sent after Leo. "Who hit you?"

"One guy. I think it was that guy from the valley that Goodman hired to hunt. Looks like he's changed sides. Or else he's gone crazy."

"Who?" Joe said incredulously. He tried to remember. He thought he remembered something about whiskey. An expert. *Someone from the valley.* He swore. That was another wild card he didn't need. "Did you get him?"

"No, he's gone, headed east far as we can tell. We got no idea where Leo is. You want us to keep looking?"

Joe growled out loud as he paced across his office, the radio clenched in his fist. *Leo, you bastard, I need you!*

"Keep looking," he ordered. "Southside section. You don't find anything in another hour, come back. And don't lose that radio."

A live courier came in to report. Distant gunfire had been heard far across the city, location unknown; it had ended after less than a minute. No details about it. Joe nodded and wondered dully if it had been the same incident or another one. He was tempted to order a patrol out to investigate, just to do something, but he didn't think sending men all around town made sense with an attack coming. *Damn it!* Leo had the plan. He needed him here.

He waited some more.

The radio came to life. "Hello! Headquarters, come in!"

Joe thought he recognized the hoarse voice. "Headquarters here. Did you find Leo?"

"No! But we've got this guy! He says he was a guard for Leo and he was attacked!"

"What?"

"He came running right at us. He says he was at Leo's and a whole bunch of 'em went upstairs. I still don't know where he was, but they all went upstairs and this guy says there was a firefight, and then more of 'em kept going upstairs. They all came down except Leo... I think Leo's—"

The sound of gunfire reached the windows of Joe's office.

The two militia officers by the door stiffened and looked at each other, and one turned and ran out toward the stairs. Joe rose from his chair and moved to the window. The gunfire continued. It seemed to be coming from two directions.

The battle was on.

Chapter 64

When the gunfire erupted, Catherine rolled over into a kneeling position and brought her rifle up on the parapet. Now she watched the rooftop to the left through the rifle scope.

She could see two men from the chest up, sitting just behind the parapet. They were frantically looking around, trying to pin down exactly where the shooting was coming from. Catherine slowed her breathing and let her aim steady. One of them stood up with a pair of binoculars. Catherine squeezed off a round. The rifle barked and kicked back at her. The man fell sideways, hit in the left temple.

She quickly looked for the other spotter. He had disappeared. She kept the rifle scope trained on that spot for a few seconds, and suddenly she caught a double glare, right at the top of the parapet. Two lenses were reflecting the afternoon sun back at her. She sighted on the glare and squeezed off a second round. The light disappeared. Catherine watched for a few seconds more. She saw nothing.

Could still be keeping low. No. He's dead. Move.

She turned to the second rooftop to the south. Through her scope she saw a head appear, she thought with binoculars, but only for a moment before it disappeared. She could see no sign of anyone else. *Bad luck.* The noise should have covered her shots, but a spotter must have been looking the right way to see one of the men in the north building go down. Now one or more men were searching for her.

Then a round hit the parapet four inches to the left of her gun, chipping the decorative cement cap, spraying her with fragments of concrete. She dropped below the edge and quickly moved to her right, scrambling on her hands and knees, keeping below the cover of the parapet.

Someone over there can shoot!

The corner of the roof was close. When she got to it she caught her breath and then brought her rifle up and over the wall in one quick move. As she swept the opposing roof with her scope a shot rang out and she heard the sharp, short whistle of a bullet going over her head. She ducked down. She was on the defensive. The other sniper had control of the field of fire, scanning and waiting for her to stick her head up. *Only one shot at a time. Maybe it's just one guy...* She scrambled back to her left, keeping below the parapet. The other corner was a long way off. She kept crawling. Near the middle she stopped. She was panting, her body began to shake from the flush of adrenaline. *Can't shoot like this.* But she needed to get the advantage back; not be on the defensive. Taking a deep breath, she swept the rifle smoothly up over the parapet and had just put her eye to the scope when the brick a foot below her exploded. Fragments of brick showered her face and forehead as the shot rang out. She dropped down just as another bullet whistled over, right where her head had been.

Catherine rolled over on her back, clutching her rifle, her body shaking. *He can find me before I can settle my gun down and zero in on him. That last shot would have killed me.*

After a moment she took a deep breath and began to talk to herself. *Need to pop up where he's not watching. Got to have a chance to aim. He can see this whole wall. He can shift his aim to me faster than I can find him.* The open space above the parapet was death.

Rolling on her side, she looked around to see what other possibilities presented themselves. To her right, the parapet ran along parallel to the street. Midway back along the edge it jutted out sharply to accommodate the entrance below. The step-out gave her the possibility of coming up from behind the parapet where the shooter would not be looking.

At least not for a few seconds...

Catherine slipped her arm through the rifle strap and nudged the M110 onto her back. She crawled to her right. It seemed to take forever to get to the corner. And then she began to crawl back towards the stepped-out section. She dragged herself on the gritty roof surface. The farther back she got from the parapet, the greater the possibility the enemy could spot her. The skin on her back seemed to itch and tremble, waiting for the shock of a bullet slamming into her.

And then she got to the stepped-out section and twisted around the corner.

When she was in place, she leaned back and settled herself down. *You've got one chance, don't blow it.* If she could get the other shooter on the defensive, she might win the duel. She forced herself to say aloud, in a low voice that didn't quite shake, "He's not that good of a shot." *He's pretty good.* "But not *that* good. Or you'd be dead." It was true. "He missed you three whole times." Her voice had firmed. Only his second shot at the same place had been right on. He was only okay. She felt a grim smile grow on her face.

She rehearsed the motion in her mind.

She swung her rifle over the parapet and swept her scope across the wall on the other building. There was the shooter's head, watching for her along the wall she had just left. She fired. She saw a puff of dust burst from the concrete a foot below him. He vanished. Nothing now showed above the wall.

He probably didn't know where that shot had come from. She had turned the tables and now had the dominant position in this deadly back-and-forth game. Catherine swept the wall with her rifle, peering through the scope. She would have to be quick and accurate. If the head presented itself, a rifle would be coming up. She would have to take enough time to make a good shot, but not too much time. The other shooter would be aiming too. If they both aimed well, whoever shot first was going to win. She pushed those thoughts from her mind and forced her breathing to slow. Panic now would only cripple her. She shut off her fear and forced herself into a calm state. *Just shooting at targets.* Forget about the fact that the target could shoot back; just don't take too long to get off your shot.

A rifle appeared with a head partially visible behind it. From this angle the sun didn't give her a reflection from the other shooter's scope. Catherine centered in on the target, giving herself a split second extra to aim. *This one has to count.* When she was sure she squeezed the trigger. The head exploded and the rifle flew into the air and bounced over the edge.

Not letting her guard down, she began to scan the edge of the parapet again. *One more time.* Suddenly, back from the edge, she saw a figure duck around the corner of the stairway access. It was too quick for her to get off a shot. Catherine sagged back against the wall of the parapet. She had won the first round of her battle. Her body shook as the realization flooded her. She had been less than a second away from being killed...twice. Instead of her head exploding, the other shooter's had.

Get a grip. The battle's not over. There was more to do, but her first threat had been eliminated.

She got to her feet and ran in a crouch back to the east parapet, the spot where she had started. As a sniper, Catherine was literally and figuratively above the fray. In the intensity of the duel she had blanked out the battle going on below her. Now she knelt at the parapet and scanned the fight for the first time.

To her right, far across a stretch of single-story buildings within the compound, she could see the south-facing barricades. She could not see any attackers, but she could see the militia firing down the street. On her left the shooting was louder and much closer. The northwest corner of the compound was there, and Catherine could see militia moving behind the barricade. Some were standing and firing; some were shifting their positions. They looked disorganized to her. The gunfire was going on sometimes in a flurry, sometimes intermittently. There were a lot of long bursts of automatic weapon fire, wasteful and disorganized, but among them she could hear shorter bursts and single shots. She guessed the more controlled shooting was coming from the attackers. The militia seemed to be just blazing away on full automatic without aiming or perhaps even seeing the enemy, hoping just to hit something through sheer volume. From the military, the gunfire was more controlled and organized.

It sounded as if the northern attack had almost reached the fortifications themselves. Catherine snatched up the sniper rifle and ran left to the northeast corner of the building. The fight came into view.

Here and there she could see the Army soldiers moving toward the compound. The glimpses startled her eye, because they were more widely scattered than she had expected. They were making their way along three different streets that, unlike the grid in other blocks, ran diagonally toward the corner of the barricade. Even now there were still many abandoned cars parked along the curbs, and the soldiers used them as cover, alternating between them and door alcoves. Sometimes getting pinned down, sometimes advancing. Kevin was somewhere among the attackers.

Something bright crossed the scene, and one of the abandoned cars spouted flame and rocked sideways, fragments flying. The sound of the blast reached her almost simultaneously.

She jerked her gaze back to the barricade. There was a man with a rocket launcher standing just inside the corner of the barrier. As she watched, he raised the tube and sent another streak of fire down the street. The explosion this time burst open the front of a building along the street, and she saw five of the attackers abandon their positions and scramble back in retreat amidst a new barrage of militia fire.

Catherine brought her rifle up and located the man in her scope. The horizontal distance and the windage were the same, but now she was shooting down eleven stories. Not wanting to shoot high, she moved the crosshairs downward slightly, and squeezed off a shot. The man was turning to yell something to another fighter when the bullet caught him in his hip, shattering it and twisting him to the ground. The rocket launcher clattered to the pavement.

Other militia looked up in Catherine's direction and began to fire wildly. She ducked behind the parapet and moved to her right along the wall to another position. She heard a few rounds smacking into the side of the building, mostly far down, and a few whining high overhead.

Did they see me right away? Shouldn't the sun be in their eyes?

They might have just been shooting blindly, but she knew she presented a tiny dark lump in the line of the roof. She had to remember that.

Catherine felt a wry smile tug at her face. If they were shooting at her, at least they weren't shooting at the attackers. She hoped Kevin's team would realize what was going on and take advantage of the distraction she had provided. The enemy shooting at her was almost as big a victory as her killing them. It meant the attack could move forward.

Again, she took a deep breath. She knew she had only a moment to acquire a target and get off a shot. Those guys couldn't all be bad shots. The more time she spent exposed the more chance she had of getting hit. Her rifle swung into position and she found a target—any would do—fired and dropped behind the parapet. She thought she had seen the man go down. There was a pause in the shooting and Catherine again swept her rifle over the parapet and got off another shot. She missed, but she stayed up and took another, aiming at a man just picking up the rocket launcher. He dropped, shot in the back, and lay on top of the weapon.

Then she scrambled towards the left corner of the roof to repeat her actions. The intensity of the street attack had now increased. The attackers had realized that Catherine was distracting the defenders. The soldiers on the street resumed their advance. The militia fire being directed toward Catherine's building dropped off to nothing; the defenders could see the main threat coming toward them at street level. She could see the smart ones huddling down close to the packed obstructions, trying to keep out of Catherine's line of fire, even though it reduced their view of the approaching soldiers. The foolish ones exposed themselves to better shoot back at the attackers. Catherine went after those targets.

Both sides had machine guns in action. The approach streets were deadly. The attackers' progress slowed. Distantly Catherine was aware that the southern attackers seemed to be taking their time reaching the compound as well. Perhaps the attack was stalling on both ends.

Catherine ground her teeth. She had to focus on this end. With the militia's attention turned towards the street, she concentrated on finding the machine guns and targeting their crews. After she had taken out two of them, the attackers were able to move forward again.

Suddenly she heard the percussive *whoomp* of a mortar firing.

She'd forgotten the mortars.

Chapter 65

Lieutenant Cameron directed the slow but steady advance towards the barricade, thankful that the street was still littered with cars. Someone had made a tactical mistake to allow such cover to remain. He only hoped that the defenses would be softened up by the time they reached the barrier. He didn't relish hand-to-hand fighting at the ramparts. Too many men would die.

Then the car across the street exploded with a concussion and a flash of fire. For a second he was confused. Then it came to him, *rockets*! Debris flew through the air. The street filled with the acrid smoke of burnt metal and paint.

"Move to the buildings," he shouted. "They've got a rocket launcher. The cars are not safe."

The men ran for the more substantial cover of the buildings. Some of them had to shoot open the doors. The second rocket hit one of the buildings and Kevin saw two men fall.

The men began to retreat along the street, sprinting from doorway to doorway. Kevin tried to slow the retreat. A half block farther back they sheltered. The mountain men looked to Kevin. They were used to fighting in the woods. This street fighting with heavy weapons was new to them. While they were good shots and brave, they were out of their element.

"We got to move forward again," Kevin shouted. He could see the acknowledgement from his soldiers. They understood. The barricade had to be taken, the wall breeched.

Kevin stepped out and sprinted forward to the next doorway. He could hear shots but there was little coming down the street. Certainly not with any effectiveness.

Catherine! There were no further rockets incoming as well. He waved his arm and the men began to move forward again. The shots from the barricade were less intense now. They could advance.

Then the mortar rounds began to hit the street.

They exploded in the street two blocks from the defense line. Seconds later another mortar bomb landed near the first one. It looked like they were going to work their way up and down the streets, scattering the attackers and making them take cover in the buildings.

Again, the attackers pulled back and took shelter in the buildings. Kevin grabbed Tommy Wilkes.

"Move to the rear and get our mortars in action." He handed him a radio. "I'll spot for them. We'll hammer away at the barricade while we're pinned down."

"How are we gonna advance? If they keep up?"

"Maybe Catherine can take them out, if she's got eyes on them. Get going and let's return fire."

Tommy took off at a run down the street.

Catherine quickly looked back at the center of the compound for the origin. Men were moving around the mortar near the bank tower. The three mortars closer to her on the street looked to be screened from the northern attack by the tall building to her left.

She aimed carefully. The nearness of the mortar to the intersection at the center of the compound gave her a better read on the distance. She need to take out the crew and then try to hit the weapon itself. If she didn't knock it out they could just move it up the side street to the south, out of her line of fire, and probably still be in position to bombard the northwest corner.

She exhaled and stroked the trigger. It was her longest shot yet, and she expected to have to correct her aim, but the man dropped. The rest of the mortar crew scattered for cover. Catherine's next shot hit the mortar tube, knocking it to the ground. She hoped she had dented the tube and rendered the weapon inoperable.

A flare of light across the diagonal to her right caught her eye, and the booming sound reached her a moment later. Half of a building façade had collapsed on one of the approach streets to the southern barricade. A great cloud of dust rose. They were using a rocket launcher over there too.

No one was up and moving around any of the three other mortars on the main street. She scanned the compound. In the empty lot in the middle of the block to her right, the two mortar emplacements she could see were surrounded by busy figures. As she watched, they began firing rounds towards the southern attackers.

She growled under her breath and took aim at the one slightly nearer to her. Her distance estimate was rougher now. The first shot struck the pavement short. Luckily the men didn't notice. The second shot was high. Her third shot hit home and one of the militia spun away from the mortar to the ground. The other two stayed at their positions, one adjusting the angle of the tube, the other reaching for a rocket. She took out the man who was loading and the other one dove for cover. The other team on the lot had now taken notice and was trying to hide among the heaps of rubble.

She was causing enough disruption that the return fire had significantly increased.

Suddenly she saw a rocket headed her way.

She threw herself flat to the roof as the rocket hit the parapet thirty feet to her left, shattering a section of it. Shards stung her face and arms. She felt blood on her left cheek. Before she could respond the building shook from another blast below the parapet.

There would be more. And possibly mortar bombs. Catherine shuddered at the thought. It was time to leave the rooftop.

She got up and dashed back to the roof-access. Another rocket round smashed into the parapet behind her. She yanked the door open, stooped to grab her carbine where it lay, and ran down the steps to the door out to the main landing. After the brilliance of the roof she was totally blind, but she dragged her fingertips along the wall until she found the knob of the hallway door. She opened it and ran down the hall until she came to the room where the rocket had hit. It had blown in a short section of the exterior wall and shattered the tall window on the right side. With half its wall blown away, the office was open to the outside.

The smashed office held four desks, two of which were destroyed by the rocket blast. Another had been turned over and one still sat upright. It was heavy, a government-issued metal piece, built like a tank. She dragged it over towards the opening, its front facing the street. She was about to push it all the way up to the verge, when she caught herself.

Muzzle flash.

She needed to be ten feet back to hide her firing.

She grabbed an overturned chair and pushed it up to the desk. She put the M110 on the desk. Opening one of the desk drawers, she pulled out a handful of fat file folders and stacked them on the desk. She adjusted the folders until she had a good shooting rest for her rifle.

She took a long pull of water from her canteen and sat down in the chair. How odd it was to be sitting at a desk. But instead of doing paperwork, she was using the paperwork to shoot people.

Stay in the moment.

Stray thoughts pushed aside, she went to work, dealing death from the tenth-story office.

Chapter 66

Leo was not coming. It was hard for Joe to absorb. Leo had always been his most capable and trusted lieutenant. He could be trusted to get things done, to make problems disappear, to take care of challenges to his organization. Even when Leo had returned alone to report the surprising defeat in the valley, Joe had never seriously doubted him.

From the report he had gotten, there could be no doubt Leo was dead. How it could have happened, Joe couldn't imagine. Leo was physically strong, but, more importantly, he was ruthless. Who had done it...and how?

Joe snorted. Leo was gone. He would have to direct the fight himself.

He smiled a grim smile, one without humor. So be it. He had always understood a fight.

The militia officer who had left his office returned, looking white around the lips. Joe didn't know his name, or the other one's either. Leo would have known. "They're attacking on two sides," the man said. "The north and south. I don't know how many there are—"

"You know who's in charge of those sections?"

The man nodded, his eyes still large with fear.

"Find them. Tell them to get their machine guns going. We'll start firing the mortars. Now go!"

The man turned and ran out of the room. Joe turned to the other man, "You go to all the other sections. Tell them what's going on and to hold their places and watch. They may come under attack shortly."

The man started to leave.

"Wait!" Joe called. "You're going to be my runner to give me info on what's going on. After you make the rounds, you come back to me and report what you saw and heard. Then you'll go out with any instructions I give you. Got it?"

The man nodded and disappeared through the door; Joe heard him running down the hall.

He picked up the radio and pressed the button. "Calling the gate crews, this is Joe Stansky. We are under attack downtown. Do you have any action at your gates?"

"No sir. Nothing going on at Gate One." The man at Gate Two also reported no action.

Joe thought about that for a moment. *How did they get into the city?* He shook his head. It didn't matter.

He decided not to recall the guards at the gates right away. The attack downtown could still be a diversion, although it seemed too large for that to be true. Meanwhile it was time to run this show from the main office down on the ground floor.

The office and the expanse of lobby were mostly empty. He ground his teeth. Upstairs there was too much delay, but down here he couldn't see anything. He needed more runners. He needed to send out spotters to report back to him. He heard two deep, coughing explosions, not much further than a block away, he thought. *His mortars. That's gotta help.*

There were sudden shouts outside the lobby. Joe wheeled toward the doors as a militiaman stumbled in. "We lost a mortar!" the man gasped.

"What?" Joe shouted, frustration turning to fury "Where?"

"Right out there! Right outside the door!"

Joe took two quick strides forward and grabbed the man. "How did you lose it?" he demanded.

"Sniper," the man said. "Shot one guy. Hit the mortar tube. It's bent. Can't use it."

"Mr. Stansky?" A new voice. "I'm supposed to be a runner—"

"Good!" Joe roared as he turned to the new man. "Go out there and run find some officers in the fight. Tell them Joe Stansky wants to know what the hell is going on. What's happening at their location and what they're doing about it." He began to calm down. "Don't use the front door right now. You're liable to get your ass shot. Go back out through whatever door you came in. When you get some answers, get back here and tell me."

The man ran for the back hall. Joe cursed to himself. The deadly sound of gunfire was thick outside. Maybe he should be there, in the thick of things. But he might lose overall understanding of what was going on. He cursed to himself. Leo would have known how to balance that. Right now, better to stay where he was.

Besides, his backup preparations were here.

And this isn't a good time to be on the street. He paced and waited for the runner to come back.

Suddenly a militia sergeant threw open the glass doors and threw himself into the lobby. He started to run for the stairwell, but he saw Joe in time. "Mr. Stansky," he said. "There's a sniper."

Joe's hands clenched into fists. He waited for the man to continue.

"A good one. Took out our spotters on the west side buildings, and we haven't got any more up there yet. Our people at the northwest corner are sitting ducks. Trying to hide under the parked vehicles and the barricades. She's jamming up the whole defense."

"She?"

"That girl from the valley. Someone got a look with binoculars and they said they thought it was her."

"That damn girl," Joe mumbled to himself. "So you know where she is?"

The man nodded. "Rooftop. Building a block away from the west side. It's got the perfect—"

"Damn it! Blow it up. Blow the hell out of her! Direct some rocket launchers and anything else on the building—mortars, use them."

"Mr. Stansky, the attackers are only a block away, the mortars are slowing them down—"

"*She's* slowing us down. You say all our guys are doing is hiding. Take her out! Blow that roof up." The sound of another mortar explosion came through to Joe as the sergeant left. Even without spotters, someone was going ahead. A moment later a sergeant ran in through the door.

"Sir?" It was the sergeant. The man was shouting over the noise of the battle. It wasn't that loud in here; maybe he was still half-deaf from the noise outside.

"Yeah!"

"The rooftop with the sniper. We hit it with two rocket launchers. We smashed the whole edge of the roof and the upper floor. A bunch of times. We thought she was taken care of, but now we're being hit again. This time we don't know exactly where it's coming from, but it's still from the west. We can't see heads or any muzzle flashes."

"She's still there," Joe growled.

"Could be in a whole different building now—"

"No, she didn't have time. Take three mortars, go after that building. Level it if you can. I'll knock her out and shut her up," Joe shouted.

"The other three mortars are firing outside the barriers again, but they're blind. We're not doing great for spotters. The attack's coming down side streets, and anyone tryin' to get a good look is risking getting shot."

"You take out the sniper, we can help spot for the mortar crews."

When Jason and his assault team got within two blocks of the south barricade, he brought up his mortar team. He only had one so he wanted to make good use of it. They had plenty of rounds thanks to Wilkes and Hammond.

"Send rounds to the barricade. We need to take out the defenders and blow some holes in it," he shouted.

The mortar team quickly zeroed in on the barrier and began to pummel it with explosives. They rained mortar bombs down on the barricade, some landing on it, some in front, and some behind it. The latter probably killing and maiming the defenders. Holes began to appear in the defense as some vehicles were ripped open and concrete barriers were shattered.

Under cover from the mortar barrage, Jason's team advanced another block. Jason was hot, dirty and the scene reminded him of Iraq only this time he was not sniping from a rooftop but down in the action. *I hope Catherine is okay.* He was glad she was doing sniper duty.

His advance was slowed as the militia began firing mortar rounds. They were not aimed well but some hit the street, exploding with damaging results. The men shot open doors to the buildings to find shelter.

Joe had been pacing the lobby again, more happily this time, listening to the mortars with pleasure. Spotters at the street level were helping. Suddenly the sergeant appeared again looking desperate. "They've broken through part of the barricades on the north side," the sergeant told him.

Joe stopped in his tracks.

"What happened?" he yelled at the man. The distant gunfire was increasing, sounding closer than before.

"They started firing mortars at the barricade! Blew some of it wide open and drove the men back. Some of the attackers got through! There's a firefight right outside the bar right now!" The last sentence was almost a scream. Joe saw that the sergeant was getting hysterical. He fought for calm.

"Take some men from the south and send them to help."

The man looked at Joe, eyes wide in fear. "They're using mortars on the south too. I don't know how long the barricade will hold out."

Joe ground his teeth. He stepped forward and grabbed the man by the shoulders. The man's eyes focused on Joe. Joe raised his voice, making it hard and sure. "Then tell them to fall back and take up a new position. Get some rocket launchers, mortars, and machine guns going. You got to drive them back."

The man looked doubtful.

"That's the job. Now do it. Get moving!"

The man stumbled away and plunged out the door.

Joe's head was swirling. There were too many elements for him to coordinate. Where were the men from the entrance checkpoints? Damn! He hadn't called them back to headquarters. He picked up the radio.

"Gates One and Two, this is Stansky, come in."

"Gate One here," came the reply, accompanied by static. "Gate Two, what's up?"

"Both of you fall back to headquarters. We're under attack. Gate Two, you come in from your position to the northwest-corner barricades. Hit 'em from behind. Gate One, you circle around to the south and come up on Market Street. They're attacking on that street, trying to come right up on the bank building, but they won't be expecting you to come up behind them. Hurry, both of you!"

Would they get here in time? He cursed himself for forgetting to call them in before. He was fighting on two fronts. He tried to think about what to do next, what the plan was, but he didn't have a clear picture in his head anymore. With the attack from the north breaking through, the battle line had disintegrated. He could hear more and more shooting as he tried to think. As the intensity grew, so did Joe's doubts.

Chapter 67

Catherine's sniper fire was now even more effective than before. She could see how the battle was changing, and from her elevated position she could attack targets that were out of view from the ground level.

Suddenly there was a deafening blast. The whole room shook. Dust and broken acoustic tiles rained down from the ceiling. *A mortar*, she thought. Then there was another blast. And another.

How many could the roof withstand before it collapsed?

What if one of those large air-conditioning units fell on me?

Her skin began to crawl. With so many shells falling, it was only a matter of time before...

Catherine fought down her panic. It was time to go. She slung her carbine behind her, picked up the M110, and left the office. Her iron grip on her fear kept her walking normally for the first few steps, but then panic began to rise up and she dashed for the stairs.

As she shoved open the door to the stairs and threw herself through, a terrible white light flashed with a huge explosion. Debris flew around her, hitting her, and she was thrown forward as if someone had slammed into her back.

And then somehow Catherine was picking herself up off the half landing where the stairs changed direction halfway down to the next floor. Her ears were ringing. She could hear nothing else. Looking back up the stairs she saw the increased brightness shining down from the open doorway above.

Catherine forced herself to get up. She had to get away from those terrible explosions. She stumbled down the stairs, touching down on only every third or fourth step, more concussions continuing above and causing the steps to shake under her feet. She passed landing after landing. *Not far enough.* Finally she stopped on the last landing before the bottom and pushed open the door to another hallway with multiple offices.

Her ears were still ringing, but her panic had left her, and she seemed only to be coated with thick white dust; she was not hurt. *I'll try to set up here.* She was determined to work this position as long as she could.

Billy watched the barricade as the battle began to rage a few blocks to the west of him. The men he could see behind the obstructions were distracted. As he watched he saw some of the militia leave. Only two remained. This was his moment.

He decided to approach the barricade as if he was one of them. He *had* been, until recently. Maybe one of the men would recognize him. He would be taking a chance on getting shot before he could tell them who he was, but it was worth a try. Thoughts of Lori Sue drove him.

He slung the M16 over his shoulder. Stepping out from the corner, he raised his empty hands and shouted at the figures he could see between the tractor-trailer and the Cadillac. "Don't shoot. I'm Billy. I'm a hunter for the city. I've been trying to get back to the compound. I want to help."

The men leveled their rifles at him, but he kept yelling and walking towards them with his hands high in the air. "Don't shoot," he yelled over and over.

Finally one of them shouted back, "Who the hell are you?"

"Billy. I'm one of the hunters for the city. Leo hired me."

"What're you doing out there?"

"I was coming back, no luck today and heard the shots. I'm trying to get back in so I can help. I'm a good shot. Let me through, I can help."

"Keep your hands in the air and don't do anything tricky," came the reply.

Billy walked up to the barrier and slipped between two cars.

"Where's everyone else?" he asked.

One of the men looked at him as if he had asked something stupid. "Someone ran over and said we had to help. One group of the attackers broke through." He pointed west.

"Shit," Billy replied. "That ain't good."

"You right about that. You going over there?"

"That's where I can help, sure." Billy unlimbered the M16.

"Good luck," the second man said. His voice sounded shaky.

"Say, where's Joe? He running the defenses?"

"Just get your ass over there. I don't know where he is."

"Just may need to check in with him. He may want me to do some sniping from a roof."

"He's at his headquarters still, I think," the first man said. "The bank building."

"Better get over there," Billy said.

They nodded, staring at him.

Billy turned and trotted off down the alley in the direction of the gunfire. He ducked around a corner as soon as he could.

He didn't know what to do. It would be stupid to get caught up in the battle. He wanted to just charge the headquarters building, firing away until he ran into Joe and shot him. Of course he would be shot as well. The problem for Billy was that there was too big a chance he would get shot before he could kill Joe.

He needed to be smarter, he thought. More like Jason. More like a hunter.

There came a moment when Joe stepped back from trying to direct the battle. He had lost control of it.

The news from the runners kept getting worse. The barricades on the south side hadn't held either, which meant that the boundary no longer mattered. Enough attackers were inside now on both sides that the ones that followed could come through the gaps in near safety, and the attackers were coming down multiple streets to enter a general firefight. There was no massing of militia into a concentrated defense, despite Joe's repeated demands. Mortars were now not effective. The other side was not massed into a large group. The battle was multiple small groups of fighters, some with machine guns, some without, engaged in free-form gun-fights.

There was no way that Joe could judge the battle, let alone control it. The militia should still have a big advantage in sheer numbers, but with no massing of forces on either side that advantage was less effective. The fight was devolving into smaller battles and no one knew who was winning. What he did know was that their defenses had been penetrated, which meant that their plan had been ruined. If there was a fallback plan, it had been lost with Leo.

Joe gave up on controlling the battle. And as he stood there in the bank lobby, he became aware that he had only seen the one runner for some time. The other man had been gone for a long time, and the sergeant had not returned either.

He was not going to bet all he had on the outcome.

Joe turned on his heel and headed back through the building to the loading area in the rear. Earlier he had carried his unmarked boxes of gold and Hillsboro's best jewelry down to the bottom floor and had stacked them unobtrusively near the door.

He'd made sure a vehicle was left at the back of the building. The key was in his pocket. It was an old Chevy pickup truck, faded brown, four-wheel drive with a winch and a push-bar front bumper. It was packed with weapons, a drum of gasoline, and other supplies. It would take him a long way if the battle went to hell. He lifted each of the boxes into the back. Hopefully he wouldn't have to use the pickup, but he didn't have a victim's mentality.

Catherine's new shooting position on the second floor was much less effective than her higher position had been, but she kept at it. She wouldn't be able to do it for much longer. She was running low on ammunition for the M110, and she wasn't sure whether or not to continue sniping with her carbine when that was gone.

Suddenly she saw a rocket coming straight at her.

She dove under a heavy metal desk, cracking her head hard on the edge. Debris flew and immediately there was a deafening explosion and burst of light behind her. Hard objects pummeled her. She lay covered in dust and broken pieces of the room. Her ears rang. She was disoriented. She could hardly breathe.

She pushed back against broken pieces of furniture, drywall and concrete, struggling to crawl backwards to get out from under the desk. Her eyes, nose and mouth were filled with an acrid-tasting dust. Finally she could stand. She wiped her hands on her shirt and tried to clear her eyes. The air was so thick with dust that it darkened the room; she could make out no details. Coughing over and over, she fumbled with her clothing, trying to pull a piece loose to put over her nose and mouth.

She looked around in confusion. *Where's my rifle?* She remembered pulling it off the desk as she dove for cover, but she could not remember what had happened to it after that. Pulling back some of the debris piled around the desk, she saw the barrel sticking up. She began to tug at it and finally pulled the rifle loose after much effort.

Catherine stood fully upright and looked around. The dust had begun to settle. The small office she had entered had disappeared. There was a round hole in the wall just to the left of the window. Turning around, she saw that the back wall of the office, made of cinder block, had been blown out. A large irregular hole looked out into a shattered hallway. The space was a field of rubble.

The rocket must have passed through the wall before it exploded, she thought. *They know my position. Will they send another rocket to make sure of me?* The thought chilled her. She looked around desperately for her backpack and carbine. She could not leave without them. After pushing through the debris around the desk, she found the backpack with the carbine lying under it. Both had escaped the brunt of the explosion. She grabbed the pack and, with the two rifles in hand, stumbled out of the room before another rocket could be fired.

Struggling through the former hallway was like wandering in a nightmare. By dead reckoning, she found the door to the stairs. Pushing through it, she reached the relative safety of the concrete stairwell. She shuffled down the stairs to the ground floor and stopped to assess her situation.

She was almost out of ammunition for the M110. She was out of positions from which to shoot. The sniper rifle, with its powerful scope, was not good for close-quarters shooting. It was time to shift over to her Bushmaster .223.

She had four spare magazines plus one in the rifle, giving her a hundred rounds.

Leave the M110 here. I can pick it up later.

After propping the two rifles against the wall, she got her canteen out of her backpack. She splashed some of the water over her face and took a long drink. She put the canteen back, slipped on her pack, and grabbed the carbine. Her ears were still ringing, but she took a deep breath and exited the building. Billy was out there somewhere. She would try to link up with him.

Chapter 68

When Catherine had shown Billy the plan on the kitchen floor, he had said he would come in from the east, on the opposite side of the compound from where she was. She had to assume he had stuck to that. So she would head south and then east, steering wide of the compound, until she could come back to the barricades on the far side. She had seen the northwest corner breached by explosions, so she hoped the militia had been drawn away from the other sections to help counter the attack. The line of improvised obstructions was far from perfect. If Billy had been patient enough to wait for his chance, he had probably already gotten in.

She figured Billy would be going to the bank building. That was where Stansky would be.

She would skirt the battle and approach the bank building from the rear. Billy wasn't the only one looking for Stansky.

Cut off the head and the body dies.

After another volley of mortar rounds, Jason signaled his team to push forward. They scrambled from one point of cover to another. With Gibbs's help the attackers divided into two groups, led by Gibbs and Jason. When one team advanced the other laid down cover fire. Each group moved forward under cover fire. The return fire from the barricade was lighter now.

Gibbs came over to Jason. He was covered in sweat with a gash on his cheek that dripped blood off of his face. His eyes were blazing with energy.

"We should charge now. They're falling back," Gibbs shouted.

Jason nodded. "Have everyone open up, a short burst, then we charge," he yelled over the din of the battle.

Gibbs relayed the message. A moment later all the attackers let loose with a terrible hail of bullets. Then they charged. The woodsmen shouting some unintelligible battle cry flung themselves at the openings. The few defenders who hadn't fallen back were quickly overwhelmed and killed.

Jason ran through the gap in the barricade shouting, "Spread out in smaller groups and keep advancing," He began to sense victory. The woodsmen sensed it as well. With wild whoops they set off in their own smaller groups. Their blood was up. It was time to take revenge for their fallen kin.

Jason and Gibbs split the remaining military men into two groups as they moved forward. It was individual and small group rifle encounters now. The battle lines no longer held and mortars would do as much damage to their own as the enemy. The clansmen were rushing forward on a killing spree. The military went in two groups, staying together and overwhelming the scattered defenders.

"How can they get through?" Joe demanded.

The militia officer shook his head, afraid to speak. The few reports that were coming in indicated that, inexorably, they were losing the battle.

"Answer me! We got all the weapons we need. We know how to use them. There's more of us. What the hell do I have to do, blow up the whole town?"

"They got some good fighters...good shots. They don't panic."

"Who's leading them? Those valley farmers? They can't beat us."

"They got some of the army leading them. Plus they got some mortars."

"*What?*"

The officer reared back, blinking. "Soldiers," he said. "Army soldiers. With some of their heavy weapons."

"The army left! Days ago!" Joe shouted.

The officer looked fearful. "I saw them myself. Uniforms."

What the hell? Joe now knew he had a big problem.

He had expected to crush the attackers from the valley within an hour of their arrival. Then more had showed up, and the army was leading them. *But he had seen them depart. As arranged.* Had Roper double-crossed him? There was no advantage for Roper in doing that. It didn't make sense.

Somehow Joe had to concentrate his firepower to make it more effective. He made an effort to speak calmly. "You move all the heavier weapons, machine guns, mortars, rocket launchers. Bunch 'em together. Now. They're hitting us on one street to the north and one to the south. Pick one, aim your firepower there, obliterate anyone and anything, then go to the next block. The riflemen, they gotta hold each block until the heavy weapons get there."

"But the mortars—"

Joe got in the man's face. "What about them?"

"Half of 'em are gone," the officer said nervously. "And...if we move those weapons around, it'll expose them to incoming fire from the attackers that are already within the barricades—"

"It doesn't matter. You have to get this done. Your life depends on it. Now *go.*"

The officer stumbled out the lobby door, and Joe drew in a deep breath and let it out.

Soldiers. Plus mortars. He decided it was time to leave.

He was furious that all his work had come undone, but he was not going to wait around and let anyone catch him. He always had a backup plan. He'd strike out on his own and try again. He had the drive, and with his stash of gold, jewelry, and weapons he could gather some men to form a gang. The gold and jewels would only *really* be worth something again sometime off in the future, but the *hope* of that wealth would buy muscle, and that muscle would get him control of the things that people needed.

He'd lost Hillsboro. But he could do it again, and do it better. Joe headed for the loading dock and his pickup truck.

As he stepped out into the sunlight and went down the steps, he stopped and looked around carefully. He could hear the firefight along the street at the front of the building. Back here it was quieter; the loading area opened onto an alley, and the attackers had not yet come around this way. One of the reasons he had chosen the block for his gang's new base of operations was that the crisscross of alleys provided several different ways to leave. He'd have his pick. He would find a way out through the compound barricades and, if he hurried, he could be outside the town wall before anyone knew he was missing.

Joe unlocked the truck and climbed in. The engine started immediately. He drove down the alley and turned left onto another one, away from the sound of the gunfire. After he got out of the barricades he would leave by the eastern checkpoint.

Chapter 69

Billy heard the truck before he saw it. It was coming down the alley that crossed his own up ahead, from the right, from the direction of the bank. He brought his rifle up and started running towards the intersection. The pickup flashed into view. He opened up on full automatic. The truck accelerated hard and passed out of view, but his mind burned with recognition of the driver—Joe Stansky.

He reached the intersection in time to finish emptying his magazine at the back of the truck. Both rear tires blew out. The truck swerved, but it had reached the street. It turned right. He started to run after it. *It can't keep going with two flats.*

My shoulder!

Joe fought the wheel. The pain was so savage that he thought he might faint. *No.* He turned to the right out of the alley onto the narrow street behind the eastern barrier. No one was there. But the road was blocked.

Was he trapped? Joe snarled and wrenched the wheel to the left, almost going faint with the pain. The pickup didn't seem to be moving properly somehow; it wanted to crab sideways. He put the truck in four-wheel-drive mode and floored the accelerator. He aimed the truck at a little white Honda Accord in the line of obstructions. Smallest car he could see. He crashed into it. Kept the pedal down.

The car shifted. *Move! Why's it so hard? It's a teeny little car!* He heard weird sounds, screaming metal, a loud strange flapping. He stood on the accelerator, and the back of the white Accord began to move, began to rotate and then the whole car was moving, and he turned the wheel a fraction and pushed out between the Accord and the sedan next to it. Metal shrieked as he scraped through the gap and then he was out. He was free.

He powered straight across the road, up the little street he saw right across from the gap. *Just get out of sight, find my way from there.* But something was wrong.

He was not accelerating like he should. And the truck was shaking, and the steering wheel was doing strange things. The grinding continued, and there was a huge flapping that did not die down, and then the truck lurched and the flapping stopped. In his rearview mirror he saw one of his tires lying distorted in the road behind him. Now there was a deafening metallic racket.

That guy back there had shot out his tires. He'd torn them off trying to push through the barricade. Now he was riding on the rims.

I can't get anywhere in this.

In the mirror he could still see the barricade, the gap where he'd escaped. He saw a figure run out, past the white Accord, after him, a rifle in one hand.

Joe kept his foot on the accelerator and turned a corner, but the truck was not going much further. His shoulder was on fire, and the fuel gauge now read only two-thirds full. Maybe the fuel tank had been holed as well.

Catherine was approaching the eastern barricades at a full run, two blocks out, when she heard the sound of an engine. Then a flurry of shots. All the sounds of fighting were coming from other directions, from the north and the south, and further away. This was different, isolated, coming from the east. Something other than the main battle was going on.

Is it Joe? Billy?

She ran towards the sounds.

Her ears strained. The engine sound rose and screamed, then dipped to a more normal tone. It had definitely come from ahead of her, away from the main battle, but after a moment she was less sure. Was it moving? She guessed at the direction and kept up her sprint.

She was running across the street a block away from the barricades when she saw motion to her right. One block away, Billy was sprinting down the street away from her, his rifle in one hand. He turned a corner and vanished up the other street before she could call out. He was after someone or something. She turned and ran in that direction, trying to catch him.

After running four blocks, Billy saw the faded brown pickup sitting in the road. He stopped. It was at the far end of the block he had just reached. Had Joe abandoned it? It was perhaps two hundred yards from him. He couldn't see anyone on the driver's side.

He didn't want to be ambushed.

He began to walk slowly forward.

He had crossed perhaps a third of the distance to the truck when he heard rapid footsteps behind him.

Whipping around, he raised his rifle.

"Don't shoot!" It was Catherine's voice. He stared. She seemed to be coated with white dust from head to foot.

He turned back toward the truck as she caught up to him. "What's going on?" she asked.

"Joe's up there," he told her. "In the pickup, I think. I shot at it when it went by, I might have hit him. I know I got the rear tires. I'm goin' up there."

"It's pretty open from here to the truck," Catherine said. "Not much cover at all. We have to be careful."

"You don't have to go. This is my fight."

"It's all our fight."

They slowly walked towards the truck, rifles at the ready. Billy focused on the truck, with Catherine scanning the buildings around them. When they were about fifty yards away, the driver's door opened.

"Stop!" shouted Catherine. "Throw out your weapons."

"Don't shoot. I surrender," came the reply. Was that Joe's voice?

"Throw out your guns," Billy shouted.

A rifle fell out the door and clattered on the pavement.

"Now come out with your hands up," Catherine yelled.

"I'm shot." The voice sounded thick with pain. "Can't put my one arm up."

Joe Stansky climbed slowly out of the pickup and turned towards Catherine and Billy. He had a dark stain on his left shoulder. Billy saw that Joe still had a holstered pistol on his belt.

"Drop that pistol," he shouted.

Joe had begun to shuffle towards them. He stopped and slowly reached down and pulled the pistol out of its holster, then bent over to lay it on the ground.

"Kick it away from you," Billy said.

Joe awkwardly kicked at the pistol. It skittered fifteen feet toward them.

"Get down on your knees," Billy said.

Joe got down on his right knee, then he stopped. "I think I'm going to pass out...feeling light headed."

"I'll tie him up," Billy said to Catherine.

"Don't get near him. He may be tricking us. I'm not sure he's shot."

"Look at his shoulder. It looks like he's bleeding under his shirt."

Catherine's voice was cold. "I don't think we should get near him. Let him pass out for all I care."

"I'll tie his hands. Then he can't do anything. Right now he could do something the minute we take our eyes off him."

"Then we watch him."

"Shit, Catherine. There's a battle still going on. It might catch up with us. Then what do we do? I'll just tie him up."

With that, Billy started to walk towards Joe.

"Billy, don't!"

Billy turned. "Look if it helps, I'll leave my gun here. Then he can't grab it. You keep him covered."

He laid his rifle on the street.

He went on toward Joe. He passed Joe's pistol where it lay.

When Billy reached Joe, the man started to slump. As Joe went forward, he reached down to his left leg and pulled a small revolver out of an ankle holster.

"Look out!" Billy shouted.

Joe raised the weapon and fired, not at Billy but past him.

Billy lunged for Joe and grabbed the revolver before Joe could turn the pistol on him. He lost his footing and fell on top of him. The bigger man struggled to fling Billy off, but his free arm was weakened by the shoulder wound. The .38 was in Joe's right hand. He kept twisting his hand, trying to dislodge Billy's grip. Billy held on in desperation, pushing down on Joe, even shoving his head against him so he couldn't use all his size and strength. They twisted and squirmed in a deadly embrace on the pavement, puffing and heaving.

With an animal-like grunt of pain and effort, Joe brought his injured left arm up across his body, trying to find Billy's eyes to gouge them out. Billy pulled back instinctively. He twisted his head away from Joe's bloody fingers. He was losing control. Both his hands were needed to control the revolver, but that meant he was defenseless against Joe's left hand. He would either get his eyes gouged out or Joe would twist the gun into his chest.

"Catherine!" he shouted in desperation. Catherine didn't respond.

What had happened to Lori Sue flashed through his mind. He thrust his left hand down and pulled his hunting knife out of his belt. His grip on the gun with his right hand slipped away. He brought the knife up and jammed it into Joe's neck just as an explosion erupted in his right ear and everything went black.

Catherine struggled to her knees. The bullet had hit her in the left side and knocked her to the street. It felt as if she had been hit with a baseball bat. Her side was screaming in pain. She thought a rib was gone. With her right hand, she slipped her backpack off of her shoulders. It slid off her and hit the pavement with a thud. The release jolted her side, and she cried out.

She looked out through a haze, not yet focusing. She saw two bodies writhing and twisting on the ground. She turned to find her rifle. It was to her left. She lurched to her feet, crying out at the stab of pain, and stumbled to her gun. As she bent down to pick it up, she heard a shot. She dropped to her knees and clumsily brought the weapon around in her right hand. She couldn't make her left arm move against the pain.

The two men weren't moving anymore. Joe was on the bottom, the revolver lying loose in his right hand. Billy was sprawled on top of him. Even from this distance, she saw blood pouring from the right side of Billy's head.

"Oh God!"

She let the rifle fall. She got back to her feet and staggered towards the two men. Was Billy dead? First Bird, then Lori Sue, and now Billy? Catherine wept in anguish.

"No, no, no," she kept repeating as she approached the bodies.

She knelt down and rolled Billy over. He fell off Joe and lay on his back. She stared.

He was still breathing. Somehow he wasn't dead.

Tears blurred her already hazy vision. She grabbed the revolver out of Joe's hand and threw it toward the sidewalk. There was a knife handle sticking out of the side of Joe's neck. It had severed his carotid artery, and. his blood had sprayed out over Billy and the pavement around them. The flow was slowing to a trickle now. Joe was dead.

Choking back her sobs, Catherine turned back to Billy. How badly was he wounded? He was alive, but he could still die. She had seen that up close twice before. She examined his wound, gently wiping the blood away. It looked severe, but with a sigh of relief she saw that the bullet had grazed his head, traveling above his right ear in an upward path. There was a lot of blood, but the shot hadn't penetrated his skull. He might have a concussion, even a fractured skull, but there was no bullet in his brain.

She staggered over to the truck and looked in the bed. There was a folded blanket stuffed between two of the boxes. She pulled it out, brought it back and tucked it underneath Billy's head. She pulled Billy's knife out of Joe's neck and used it to cut a sleeve off of Billy's shirt for a bandage for his head.

When she was done, she tried to rouse him. His eyes fluttered as he slowly regained consciousness. She stood up, grunting with the pain, and slowly walked back to her backpack. She got out her canteen and brought it back. Her side was slick with blood under the coat and her shirt, but she tried to ignore it.

Billy didn't know where he was. There was a female bending over him, a girl in a baseball cap. She was trying to give him something to drink. She looked familiar. Even through the dirt he could tell she was attractive, but Billy couldn't place her. Had he been chasing someone or something? It was unclear in his mind.

There was a voice, the girl was speaking, but he couldn't hear her well enough to understand the words.

He watched her try again. This time he heard his name. There was a ringing in his right ear that was so loud it almost drowned out everything else. His left ear seemed better, so he turned his head to the right. A shooting, throbbing pain erupted along his right temple.

"Ahh," Billy groaned. "Hurt. It hurts," he mumbled. The girl, who was she? Where *was* he? And what he was doing lying in a street? The whole scene seemed so foreign. Then slowly his understanding began to come back to him, like a landscape emerging from the mist.

It took some time for Catherine to understand that Billy couldn't hear her. She raised her voice, and after a while he began to answer. Then she realized he was disoriented. Slowly, his memory of events returned. Catherine kept checking his head wound, making sure he didn't lose too much blood.

"Joe's dead?"

"Yeah," she yelled into his ear. "You killed him with your knife, just as he shot you. A second later and you'd have been killed. I would have been next. You saved us both."

"Shouldn't have gone up to him," he mumbled. "You were right."

"He would have pulled that surprise sometime."

"I didn't know about that kind of holster."

"Me either."

He seemed more alert. "What we do now?" he said.

The sound of the fighting seemed to have died down. Whatever its outcome had been. "We should get out of the middle of the street. If any militia come, we don't want to be out here. Can you move?"

Billy looked up at her. "I can crawl...I think."

Chapter 70

Frank Mason watched the battle for three hours from the third floor of the hotel, which was completely empty except for him. When he finally saw militia fighters starting to surrender, he knew it was time to leave. He had secured one of the City Hall cars, a long white Oldsmobile with a full tank of gas. It was packed for his escape. He had left the car in the unused parking garage beneath the hotel, and he was fairly confident that no one noticed when he pulled out and drove away. Now he headed for the gap in the city wall near the water mill, by the old canal that was going to be dug out. He figured it would be the least-watched route out of Hillsboro.

He didn't get that far.

When he was still over a mile from the gap, seven men jumped out into the street in front of him from behind a row of abandoned cars. Frank saw rifles pointed at him. He stopped and was about to back up when one of the men yelled to him that he would be fired upon if he tried to reverse.

He thought he recognized a couple of the men. Two were cops. But he didn't know the others.

"Get out of the car and approach with your hands raised."

Frank stepped out as directed. "I'm Frank Mason, head of the Safety Committee," he said. "I'm heading out to see what's going on at the checkpoints north of town."

"You're going in the wrong direction," one of them shouted back.

"I can't get through with the fighting downtown." He gestured toward the source of the faraway noise, which had now greatly diminished.

"Looks like you're trying to escape," another said.

"No. I'm going to try to get the men at the checkpoints to surrender and not come downtown to fight. I'm trying to help end this."

Just then Frank heard footsteps behind him. He turned. Charlie Cook had approached him from the other side.

Frank tried to keep his voice calm and professional. "Charlie, tell these men to let me through. I have to get to the checkpoints to make sure they don't get involved in the fight. It'll just cause more casualties."

"We've already neutralized them." Charlie's eyes were cold. "So I don't think you're going anywhere. I'm putting you under arrest."

"What for? I'm trying to help."

"So you say. But you didn't seem to be helping much that morning when the two civilians were tied to stakes and executed."

Frank tried to keep his expression neutral. The police chief just watched him. When Charlie spoke again, his voice sounded sad, but there was no trace of it in his eyes. "Do you even remember their names?"

Frank was aware that the other cops around him were listening intently. "Charlie, you saw the situation. There was no way to stop it. At least I could continue to work on the inside, trying to change things. You got left out after what you said."

Charlie's look changed to disgust. Frank glanced around at the others. They all had hard looks on their faces, and their weapons were all still leveled at Frank.

One of the officers was looking in through the back windows. "Looks like he was packed for a long trip."

"How about when you stood aside as Joe sent Leo after those farmers?" Charlie said. "You knew Leo was going to kill everyone in the valley. Seems like you didn't put up much of a fight to change that."

"But Charlie—"

"No buts, Frank. You're under arrest and no one is listening to your lies anymore. You picked your side. Just like you told me when I picked mine." Charlie turned to the officer standing next to him. "Put the handcuffs on him, Les. We're going to operate like a real police department from now on."

"You can't do this," Frank shouted as two men came forward and grabbed him. "This is what you just complained about."

"No, it's different. You're being arrested on the basis of actual evidence, for crimes committed against the civilians of Hillsboro. You'll get a trial, a real trial, and I'm going to read you your Miranda rights."

"To hell with Miranda. That doesn't have anything to do with us now. Let me go!"

"Yes, it does. It's about time we got back to normal procedures. You'll have your chance to defend yourself, but for now you're going to jail. Now listen carefully. You have the right to remain silent..."

Catherine and Billy huddled in the entrance of a Sprint storefront for perhaps a half hour. No one came by. The sound of gunfire had stopped.

"I'm getting pretty stiff," Catherine said. "I won't be able to move soon. Maybe we should get some help. Can you walk?"

"I don't think so. My head's still dizzy and I can't see right. You go."

Catherine struggled to her feet. The whole left side of her body was stiff and sore. She wasn't bleeding now, but her shirt was soaked with her blood. She wasn't sure she could use her carbine, but she worked it onto her back anyway.

"Keep your rifle close in case any militia come along. I'll be back as soon as I can."

He nodded. He looked bad, but he seemed to be stable.

She shuffled down the street. The only place there seemed to be to go was the compound itself. She knew she wouldn't be able to walk much further. *Hope I don't get shot.* She just hoped Kevin and Jason had won the day.

She was challenged as she approached the barricade. She managed to raise her voice to identify herself. She was not addressed again, and she didn't get shot. When she got to the barricade, she knew there was no question of her clambering through. She plodded along the perimeter, feeling like an old woman, until she came to the place where Joe had forced his way out.

Inside, off to both sides and in the street that led down the center of the compound, she could see small groups of people sitting. The looked to be under guard from a few people monitoring each cluster.

There was a larger group of people in front of the bank entrance. Dully, she headed toward them, passing torn bodies and weapons. A few people were walking back and forth between groups of prisoners.

One of them was Kevin. He was running towards her.

"Catherine!" he shouted. "I was so worried when I couldn't find you. I sent someone to check the building and all they found was your rifle."

"One of my rifles," she said, her voice almost a whisper.

He reached her and tried to embrace her, but she put up her right hand, wincing as the quick motion hurt her. "Don't. I got shot in the side and I think I've got some broken ribs."

"Oh, no. We got to get you over to the hospital. They've set up a triage station—"

Catherine shook her head. "Later. I'm not bleeding now. There's worse than me. I'll wait." She was lying, she could feel that her wound had begun to seep blood again from her walk. "Send somebody to get Billy. He got shot in the head, it grazed him, but he's not good. He's on Flanders Street, maybe five blocks up. He's in a phone store doorway."

Kevin waved over one of his men and told him where to go. He left at a trot.

A thought came to Catherine's sluggish mind. "Have you seen Jason? Is he all right?"

"He's working on securing the prisoners. Gibbs and I are collecting the weapons. When these people are locked up, we'll be able to spare a few people to try to connect with Charlie. I'm hoping his people have been busy. We need them to round up stray militia trying to leave town. Get the gates watched, if it's not too late."

"What happens with the civilians?"

"That's a headache." Kevin ran a hand over his face, and she could suddenly see how exhausted he was. "We're starting to see a few since the shooting stopped. They're coming out to see what's happened. We're telling them to stay inside until we've rounded up all the combatants."

Catherine started to sway. A blackness began to close in.

When she came to a moment later, she was sitting on the asphalt and the pain in her side was excruciating. She was only half aware that Kevin had caught her. The next thing she knew was that a van had pulled up beside her and Kevin was helping her into the passenger seat. She wondered where they had found the van, and then she took no more interest in anything until the hospital.

Chapter 71

Two days later the leaders of the battle gathered together in a conference room at City Hall. Kevin, Rodney Gibbs, Jason, and Charlie were there, along with Steve Warner and Bob Jackson, two of the technicians who had helped form the civilian resistance. Jason had persuaded Clayton to attend. Catherine had pulled herself out of her hospital bed for the meeting as well.

The gaps in the city wall had been re-manned by civilian associates of Warner and Jackson, to make sure that no one took advantage of the turmoil to infiltrate the town. A few of the militia had escaped in spite of Charlie's efforts, but no one wanted to pursue them. The new guards were instructed to keep a watchful eye out for them.

Almost all of the civilian members of the city government had survived the battle. They had not been inside the fortified compound. The ones who worked in the militia block and in Joe's offices in the bank tower had been ordered to stay home. Robert Goodman, an exception, had been found hiding on the third floor of the bank building. He was being held in the city jail until his level of criminal complicity could be determined, along with Frank Mason and the surviving members of Joe Stansky's core gang. For the moment, the rest of the city employees had been put back to work; the city still needed to function to provide what services it could to the citizens.

The relieved government workers had put up announcements at all the food centers that told the citizens what had happened and that a new government would be forming with the goal of ending martial law. Citizens involved with food collection and preparation had been told to report for their duties as usual.

"We've got to hold some elections soon. The people will expect that," Steve Warner said.

"First we need to figure out how to establish some candidates. We'll need interim leaders until that can take place," Charlie replied.

"Sounds like what we had before," the other technician said. "And what part do you think you'll play? You were on the wrong side of this for too long."

Jason leaned forward and cleared his throat. "Charlie got on the right side of things and has proved his worth as far as I'm concerned."

Steve Warner nodded and held up a palm to Jackson, but his face remained hard. "I agree. He stuck his neck way out linking up with us. I know it. Bob here knows it. But he's the police chief of the police state we just got rid of. It won't look right if he stays in. Not even to me."

The discussions went on for hours. To everyone's surprise, Warner did not want a top official position for himself. He argued that he and his fellow conspirators should not be the immediate leadership.

"Later, maybe," he said. "But right now we need popular leadership. We need some heroes. You," he looked at Jason, "came as rescuers. Everyone will see your group as the ones who saved Hillsboro. No one knows us, even though we were the resistance." He paused for a moment to reflect. "And, frankly, we could not have accomplished what you did."

Jackson frowned at this, but didn't disagree. Warner went on. "Before we can get to elections, it seems to me the best choice is someone they already think of as a hero."

It was finally decided that Jason would be the interim civic leader. Kevin would be in charge of defense and policing, using his men and the police who had remained loyal to Charlie. Charlie could have an advisory role, but the two technicians, representing the town's insurrection, insisted he have no official capacity or title. Charlie didn't object and Jason thought he looked relieved.

Catherine was surprised when Kevin nominated her to represent Hillsboro in a diplomatic outreach to the neighboring towns. They would soon hear about what had happened and would want to know what it meant, for Hillsboro and for them. The surrounding towns knew Hillsboro had been a threat under Joe's control so it was important to begin building bridges right away. They needed to know that there was new leadership and the time was right for cooperation. A regional association of towns needed to be presented, but as an association of equals. It would take an honest person to convince the other towns that Hillsboro was going to be a good neighbor. Catherine would be a non-threatening presence in her outreach to the other towns. The group unanimously approved her nomination.

After the planning discussion was done, Jason spoke with Clayton in the corridor outside. "How'd the survey go?" He asked.

Clayton looked sideways at him with a trace of a smile. He and a few of his people had been out touring the countryside the day before. He stroked his mustache with a fingertip. "Fine land round here," he answered. "Fertile. Least some of it. We be able to do well here."

"I figured as much," Jason said. "There might be a few surviving owners in Hillsboro. We'll check to see if anyone has claim to the properties, but I expect your people will pretty much have their pick."

Clayton's smile didn't change at all, but the mountain man's eyes were deep. "Got rid of that Joe Stansky for 'em. Seems to me they owe us."

"I'll help you work that out," Jason said, a little hurriedly. "I wanted to tell you, we can spare you as many trucks as you need to move your whole encampment. When do you want to go?"

"No sense waiting," Clayton said. He stuck out his hand. "I thank you."

Lori Sue was buried in a place of prominence in the city cemetery. She was part of a large funeral for all who had died in the fight—members of the United States Army, men from the clans, Hillsboro citizens who had joined in the attack. People from the valley came to celebrate and honor those who had helped liberate the town. Many of the citizens of Hillsboro attended the funeral. Some of them knew someone who had died; others just came to honor the fallen. The story of what had happened to Donna Bishop had begun to spread, and a surprising number of citizens wanted to honor Lori Sue, Donna's rescuer.

A stone carver had volunteered to carve a headstone for her grave. At the top it read, "LORI SUE MILLER", followed by the date of her death. There was no birth date, since no one knew it. Beneath the name and date, it read:

TWENTY-ONE YEARS OLD
LOVED BY BILLY TURNER
SHE DIED DEFENDING ANOTHER WOMAN
FROM AN EVIL MAN
"We girls got to stick together."

Billy spoke only briefly. He wasn't much for words. He sadly told the assemblage how she was the first girl to love and accept him, and how he missed her so badly. Donna Bishop spoke longer, eloquently telling the story of how Lori Sue had forced her way into her isolation, had brought her hope, and, at the end, had given her own life to save her.

Anne and her family stayed close to Billy at the funeral. In spite of their efforts, Billy remained devastated. He had fought loneliness ever since his daddy's death. When he had found Lori Sue, he had discovered a happiness greater than he had ever experienced. Now he was alone again. His valley friends were a small comfort in the face of his personal desolation.

A week later, there was a dual wedding in a Baptist church. The entire population of the valley had now arrived in Hillsboro, and they all joined in the celebration, but they were dwarfed by the rest of the crowd. The heroes of Hillsboro's liberation were marrying, and it seemed as if the whole town turned out for the reception, which was held at the site of the first trading day. With no restrictions this time, the crowd stretched away for blocks. Steve Warner had anticipated this and had persuaded Jason to have a full-blown banquet at the reception and have extra food distributed to all the food centers as well. Donna Bishop could be seen there with her son. They clung to each other with hardly a break for eating.

"You know you'll probably get elected mayor, Mr. Richards," said Anne to her husband with a smile as they ate. "You ready to give up farming?"

"I don't know. I'm not sure I like the idea of being a politician." Jason smiled back at her. "You ready to leave our beautiful valley?"

A hint of a frown slipped across her face. "I could do that...if it was for a short time. I like our life back in the valley. I hope you do too."

Jason put his arm around her and they kissed, ignoring the wave of hoots and hollers that rose from the rest of the banquet. "I do," he told her. "A short term of office is the only thing I could accept. I want to go back to where I met you. You saved me, by letting me into your life...into your family."

"And you saved us."

They looked into each other's eyes. The world closed in until it was just the two of them. They had come through so much. Anne's husband had abandoned her after the EMP attack and she almost hadn't survived. Jason's arrival had brought a new chapter to her life and to the lives of her two girls. And now she and Jason had a son, a new life. They both understood how lucky they were, and how fragile the peace was that they had attained.

Across the table, Catherine leaned over to Kevin. "You ready to become the chief of police?"

"I guess so, if my wife says it's okay to give up my commission."

She chuckled. "I think you did that when you sent Roper off by himself."

"Well, I can't do it officially until Stillman gets in contact. But I can tell him that I've been continuing my original mission in a manner required by the changing circumstances. Then again, there's the concept of *posse comitatus*..."

She punched him in the arm. "Are you trying to make me feel dumb? I never got to Latin lessons before the EMP attack."

"No, my dear," he said apologetically, rubbing his arm. "It means 'the sheriff's posse.' He can call one up in times of trouble and we have to respond. I hope Colonel Stillman sees it that way."

"He better not give you any trouble, or he'll have trouble with me," she replied with a fierce look in her eyes. "Anyway, you have my permission to be the police chief. If I'm going to be an ambassador, I want some security I can rely on."

The two of them smiled at one other. They had prevailed yet they both felt the burden of working to secure the gains that had been so painfully won.

"You're right," Kevin replied. "I guess I better take this job. Otherwise I'm unemployed. Not a good way to start out a marriage."

"Rodney," Kevin called out. "You going to help me run the police and defense department here?"

Rodney Gibbs looked up from his plate. With the exception of the mandatory toast as best man for Kevin, he had been quiet through most of the reception. There was no sadness in his face, but there was a distant look in his eyes; as if his mind was being called to another place.

The now ex-sergeant shook his head. "No, it's a good offer, but I finished what I said I wanted to do here. 'Do some good,' remember?"

Kevin nodded. The conversation around their table had stopped. Everyone was looking at Rodney.

"So," he continued, "I think it's time for me to head out to Missouri...to find my family, if I can."

Kevin looked at his sergeant; tough; solid; an Afghan and Iraq veteran; someone who had experienced discrimination as a black man, but who still hadn't begrudged Kevin his rank and inexperience. Rodney had taught him so much from his war experience; Rodney had patiently put up with his rookie mistakes and had helped him become a better officer. They had formed a strong bond. Kevin had thought, in the back of his mind, that they would always be working together. Now he would face this new job without Rodney working beside him. A sense of sadness swept over him.

"I guess I understand," he said to Rodney. "I'm going to miss you. Miss your council and your humor. You kept me from doing foolish things so many times."

"Yeah, I sure did." Rodney smiled. "But you'll do all right. You can handle yourself pretty well, and now you've been battle-tested."

Everyone was silent around them. Kevin got up off the bench, walked over to his sergeant, and embraced him.

"Even if I can handle the job, I'm going to miss working with you."

"We'll always be connected...by this." Rodney swept his arm around, indicating the tables of people, the crowd beyond, the whole city around them. "This is more good than we could ever expect to do in a lifetime."

"And now you've got a personal mission," Catherine said.

Rodney nodded gravely. "Who knows? Our paths may cross again."

"I hope so, but somehow I don't think so," Kevin replied.

"Don't stop hoping, you're too young to be cynical."

"And you're not? Keep being the realist, but don't *you* become a cynic."

They embraced again. Kevin looked at Catherine. She had risen too. He took the unspoken suggestion. He went to her, put his arm around her, and they walked away from the table.

"How do *you* feel about leaving the valley? Making our life here in town?" he asked her.

"I said I would go with you, wherever the army sent you," Catherine answered. "Events sent you here. You stayed for me, I know, but you also stayed for Hillsboro. So, yes, I can leave the valley to make our future here. I'm glad the valley's still close. But I feel that we should work with the town, to help rebuild it, as this country becomes whatever it will become. Ensuring Hillsboro's future will help ensure the valley's and Clayton's clans' futures as well."

She paused. "Donna asked me if this would be the end of the bad guys. I told her I didn't know...but I *do* know. I realize they don't go away. We need to build structures that don't allow them to take over our lives. I guess that's the part of the fight that will continue."

She turned to her husband. "I'm in...with you...for whatever the future brings."

They kissed long and hard, though Kevin was careful not to squeeze her too tightly.

When the crowd was starting to disperse and some of the guests were leaving, Billy went up to Rodney.

Billy had been sitting at the end of the long table. He was still recovering from his head wound. It had left a long scar down his right temple, and probably no hair would ever grow there again. He still mourned for Lori Sue. Since her burial he had just drifted between the apartment they had shared and City Hall. If someone asked him to help with something, he had helped, but he hadn't jumped into any of the re-organization efforts. He hadn't even gone out hunting. Both Catherine and Sarah had tried to cheer him up, but nothing seemed to work.

Rodney turned as Billy approached. "What is it, Billy?"

"I'd like to go with you...to Missouri. If you'll have me."

"Why would you want to do that?" Rodney replied. "You got your farm in the valley. You got kin here. Aren't the clans relatives of yours?"

"They ain't close kin and it's too sad here. I don't have anything here without Lori Sue. Everything reminds me of her."

"Well—"

"I can help. You know I can shoot. Hunt."

"Yeah, I know you're good with a rifle."

"And maybe, like you said to Lieutenant Cameron, maybe I can do some good...you know, help you."

Rodney smiled at Billy. He put his arm around Billy's shoulders. Billy stood about as tall as Rodney, but he wasn't nearly as solid as the powerfully built sergeant. Rodney gave him a squeeze.

"I'd be proud to have you go with me. It'll be quite an adventure, and I could use a partner."

For the first time since Lori Sue's death, Billy smiled.

The End

Afterword

"Uprising" is the rewrite of the two *Catherine's Tales* books and becomes Book 2 in the *After the Fall* series. The series continues in Book 3, *Rescue*. This story is about how Rodney and Billy set out for Missouri and get captured along the way. Jason and Clayton go to rescue them and challenge the power structure of a large town in Tennessee.

There are a rich cast of characters to write about and the evolving situation in the US after the EMP attack provides an interesting setting for subsequent stories.

If you enjoyed this story, please consider writing a review on Amazon. Reviews do not have to be lengthy and are extremely helpful for two reasons: first, they provide "social proof" of a book's value to the reader unfamiliar with the author, and second, they help readers filter through thousands of books in the same category to find ones that are worthy of their time investment. You provide an essential service to other Amazon readers with a solid review. I very much value your support.

Other novels published by David Nees:
Jason's Tale, Book 1 in the *After the Fall* series
Uprising, Book 2 in the *After the Fall* series
Rescue, Book 3 in the After the Fall series

Payback, Book 1 in the Dan Stone assassin series
The Shaman, Book 2 in the Dan Stone assassin series
The Captive Girl, Book 3 in the Dan Stone Assassin series

For information about upcoming novels, please visit my website at *https://www.davidnees.com* or go to my Facebook page; *fb.me/neesauthor*.

You can also sign up for my reader list to get new information. No spam; I never sell my list and you can opt out at any time. Scroll down from the landing page on my website to find the sign-up form.

Thank you for reading my book. Your reading pleasure is why I write my stories.

Made in the USA
Middletown, DE
14 June 2020